THE
DEATH
OF
COLONEL
MANN

A BEACON HILL
MYSTERY

CYNTHIA PEALE

A DELL BOOK

Published by
Dell Publishing
a division of
Random House, Inc.
1540 Broadway
New York, New York 10036

Library of Congress Catalog Card Number: 99-34766
ISBN: 978-0-440-61398-5

Reprinted by arrangement with Doubleday Books

Published simultaneously in Canada

Doubleday hardcover edition published April 2000
Dell mass market edition published January 2001

146614399

FOR
G.J.S.

THE
DEATH
OF
COLONEL
MANN

CHAPTER 1

COLONEL MANN WAS DEAD. OF THAT INCONVENIENT FACT there could be no doubt.

He lay sprawled, face up, on the garish Turkey carpet that covered the sitting room floor of his expensive hotel suite. A darkening crimson stain marred the bosom of his boiled white shirt. In his right hand he clutched a handsome silver-knobbed walking stick.

Addington Ames stood quite still, staring at the body. Although he knew the Colonel by reputation—who did not?—he had never met him. For years he had heard it lamented throughout Boston Society that the Colonel was in robust middle age, no more than forty-five or fifty. He will live on and on, people said, spreading his poison, bleeding us dry.

No more. Whatever harm the Colonel had done—and it was very great, Ames knew—he would do no more now.

In the harsh glare of the electric lights, the Colonel's face—fleshy, bearded—looked not robust but old. Already, Death had marked it for his own. Old, thought Ames, and vicious and corrupt, like the man himself.

He turned to glance at his companion, who stood behind him.

"Doctor?" he said. He moved a little to one side so that MacKenzie could step close to the body.

Dr. John Alexander MacKenzie, uncomfortable in the overheated room—in its advertisements, the hotel boasted of its central heating—crouched and felt the Colonel's forehead and then lifted his free hand. "Body's still warm," he said. "No rigor." The Colonel's skin was a sickly shade of blue-gray; his eyes, staring wide, were oddly flat. Dead eyes, thought MacKenzie: circles of black pupil, iris no longer visible. He'd seen eyes like these often enough during his service with the army on the western plains to know instantly when he was looking at a corpse.

Ames grunted. "This is the night when the Colonel held open house each week," he said. "I wonder, given his methods, that he did not keep a bodyguard with him."

Without touching the Colonel's bloodied shirtfront, Mac-Kenzie scrutinized the neat little hole in the fabric to the right of the third gold stud. Then, with difficulty and with the aid of his cane, he stood up. "There is his pistol on the desk," he said, gesturing. "But it looks to be a Smith and Wesson thirty-eight. Too large a caliber for a wound this size." He sniffed; he thought he could smell a faint odor of gunpowder, but he could not be sure because it was overlaid with a heavy, sweet scent that might have been the Colonel's hair pomade—or a woman's perfume.

Ames nodded. "So we may assume that he was not seized with a sudden fit of remorse and driven to kill himself."

"No," replied MacKenzie. "He did not do that. And yet, for the wound to be so accurately placed, the weapon must have been fired point-blank—just outside powder-burn range."

Ames thought about it. "A bold man, then. And someone the Colonel knew well."

"Yes. Perhaps he did have a bodyguard"—MacKenzie flexed his bad knee—"who turned on him—?"

"Possibly." Ames looked away, contemplating the middle

distance. He was a tall man, markedly taller than his companion, and whippet thin. His black hair was combed back straight from his high forehead; luxuriant dark brows arched over his brilliant black eyes. His nose was sharp and pronounced, his clean-shaven face as long and thin as he himself. He wore a gray Inverness cape over his dark coat and trousers; his neckcloth, of a good gray silk twill, was slightly frayed at the edges, as were the cuffs of his coat. He was two years younger than MacKenzie, who was forty-one.

Ames seemed to have come to some decision. Moving with care, he stepped around the Colonel's body to the ornately carved desk.

MacKenzie, as he always did when he was slightly unnerved, tugged at the end of his mustache. "Should we notify the staff?" he said. "Or the police—?"

Ames thought of Deputy Chief Inspector Crippen and his officious, offputting manner. No, he thought. Not Crippen; not yet. "I will speak to the manager when we leave," he said. "But before we do, I want to have a look around."

He tried the drawers on either side of the kneehole; all of them were locked. He paused, lifting his head to listen. He heard no sound. The noise of the city's streets, carriage wheels on cobblestones, the clop-clop of horses' hooves, the jingle of harness, all were muffled by the heavy plush draperies pulled shut against the night. Moreover, the Hotel Brunswick was an imposing structure, solidly built, its walls and doors heavy and thick enough to hide any sound from the other guests' rooms. Or, for that matter, from this lavishly furnished suite—heavily carved, serpentine-back sofa, overstuffed Turkish chairs—where the Colonel had lived.

And died.

There was a door on either side of the room. Ames went to one and opened it. It was a bedroom. The lights were turned on; he went in. He saw another door which, when opened, gave onto a gleaming white-tiled bathroom, a huge tub in a high mahogany surround, tall brass taps on the washbasin. He retreated and opened a door adjacent that revealed a large closet. He glanced at the Colonel's expensive clothing, neatly arranged; then he turned back to the bedroom. In contrast to the opulent sitting room, this was a sparsely furnished, oddly bare chamber, no personal possessions save a silver brush and comb atop the chiffonier. There was no exit, either into the corridor or into another suite.

He returned to the sitting room and tried the other door. It had a bolt that was unshot; nevertheless, it was locked.

He turned to face MacKenzie again. MacKenzie—and that revolting body sprawled on the carpet, seeming as menacing now in death as the man himself had been in life. Alive, Colonel Mann had known many secrets and had profited from them hugely. Now, in death, even though he would profit no more, he held those secrets still.

Ames had come here tonight on a specific errand—a very urgent errand concerning one of those same secrets. Perhaps he could still accomplish it. Pressing his lips together as if to keep himself from gagging, he stepped to the Colonel's body and felt in the pockets of the dead man's green velvet smoking jacket. Nothing. The trouser pockets, however, yielded a heavy gold watch with a finely chased case, half a dozen coins, a gold money clip that held three folded hundred-dollar bills, a silver toothpick—and a key ring with several large keys and one small one.

"Do you not think—?" MacKenzie began, but Ames silenced him with a look. They had not known each other long—for only six weeks or so—and the nature of their acquaintance made it difficult for the doctor to offer advice that was not asked for, let alone a reprimand.

The small key worked. Ames slid open the top right drawer. It was empty save for a check made out to Colonel William d'Arcy Mann in the amount of eight thousand dollars. It was dated with today's date—November 9, 1891—and signed by one Edwin W. Redpath.

Who was a man well known to Addington Ames, a fellow member of one of his clubs, a steady, solid, high-caste Boston citizen who led, to all appearances, a steady, solid, high-caste Boston life.

But somewhere, somehow, he or someone dear to him had slipped up, thus giving the Colonel the opportunity to extort from him this amazing sum of money.

Ames took the check, folded it, and tucked it into his pocket. He would return it to Redpath tomorrow: a secret favor from one club brother to another, no one—particularly Inspector Crippen—needing to be the wiser.

The second drawer held a small leather case that, when opened, proved to be filled with jewelry. Some of it looked very fine: a diamond necklace, a pair of emerald earbobs, a gold locket engraved with the initials E.M.C.

Ames closed the case, put it back, and went on to the next drawer. He was ordinarily the coolest of men, never allowing even the most disturbing circumstances to disturb him. But these were rather different from any circumstances he'd ever been in, so now he felt a little trickle of sweat run down his neck inside his starched collar, and he felt his heart, well tended through years of exercise at Crabbe's Boxing and Fencing Club, begin to pound a little too fast for comfort.

The bottom drawer was empty.

The top drawer on the left held a letter. For a moment he felt a little surge of triumph—at last!—until he remembered that he was looking for not one letter but a packet of six.

There was no envelope. He unfolded it and scanned it to the bottom of the page. It was written in a flowing, delicate, feminine hand; it begged the Colonel for mercy. It was signed with the initials G.K.

Ames knew a woman named Grace Kittredge; she was one of his sister Caroline's friends. She was a lovely woman of young middle age, a member of one of the best families in the city. Had it been she who had written this pathetic letter? What had she done to expose herself to the Colonel's cruelty? How had she put herself into his pudgy, greedy hands?

He refolded the letter and slipped it into his pocket alongside Redpath's check.

The bottom two drawers on the left were empty.

He straightened, conscious of MacKenzie's worried gaze. He understood: at any moment they were likely to be interrupted by another of the Colonel's supplicants—victims, rather. Such an interruption would be embarrassing at best, incriminating at worst.

Nevertheless, he had promised a young woman in difficulty that he would do what he could to help her, and he must keep that promise.

There was one more obvious place to look: a safe in the corner, its door slightly ajar. It was a large safe, four feet high; when he pulled open the door and peered inside, he saw that it contained a jumble of papers. They looked as though someone had riffled through them, leaving them in disarray. He lifted a handful, searching for the packet of letters.

He did not find it, but he did turn up a small ledger. He opened it, glancing through its pages. It seemed to consist entirely of lists of names written in a large, firm hand. With a little jolt, Ames realized that he knew most of them: they were the names of people prominent in Boston Society, pillars of the community, many of them noted for their good deeds, their upright moral character, their spotless reputation.

The Colonel, it seemed, had known differently.

Each name was preceded by a date—the first was some seven years before, 1884—and followed by a sum of money marked by a tall, elaborately drawn dollar sign. Beside each dollar amount, almost without exception, was a check mark.

Except at the last page, where the date was today's.

There he saw a list of names and sums—Mrs. Kittredge, $5,000; Benjamin Paddock, $15,000; Edwin Redpath, $8,000. Only Redpath's name and sum were followed by a check mark—presumably, evidence that the money had been paid.

And at the bottom of the page, the last name: Valentine Thorne, $6,000. Without a check mark.

He remembered how she'd wept, that unfortunate young cousin of his and Caroline's. *"He says he will put me into his dreadful scandal sheet, Cousin Addington! And you know that George will never marry me if I am involved in such a mess!"*

True enough, he'd thought. George Putnam was a sober, steady, very proper and even stuffy young man, and his family were a proper and stuffy lot, even for Boston. Even he himself, a member of one of the city's oldest families, admitted it: New York was flashy, Philadelphia was genteel, Boston was—well—proper. And often stuffy. And cold and unforgiving, he'd added to himself. Once ruined—as she would be if the Colonel printed his scandal about her—Val would have no hope of ever marrying a Boston man. She would have to go elsewhere, probably abroad, if she hoped to marry; and what would she find in one of those foreign places? Some foreigner, obviously.

No. Impossible. Val must stay here, free of scandal, and she must marry her very proper George Putnam. Ames had been appalled when, day before yesterday, she'd come to him and Caroline with the tearful story of her misadventure two summers before at Newport: an unfortunate escapade with a young man, indiscreet letters that she'd written to him.

Ames thought of him as a cad, but still, the fellow had had the decency to return them to her. It was, in the end, someone else who had betrayed her—stolen them, sold them to the Colonel, and thus put into his hands the means to blackmail her now, on the eve of her marriage to the very wealthy, very eligible, oh-so-proper (and stuffy) George Putnam.

"Six letters, Cousin Addington," she'd sobbed. "He wants a thousand dollars for each one. I told him I didn't have any money of my own, but he wouldn't listen. I'd find a way to get it, he said. Oh, what shall I do?"

It had been his sister, Caroline, who'd soothed the girl, cradling her head on her shoulder, gazing at Ames with a challenging look, promising Val that yes, Addington would go to see the Colonel, would somehow manage to put things right—and no, would never breathe a word to their Aunt Euphemia, the girl's elderly and famously intimidating guardian.

Take the ledger or put it back? He hesitated even as he was aware that he had no time to hesitate, no time to consider what must be done next.

He'd come for Val's letters. Apparently they were not here. He hadn't time for a more thorough search; he'd have to trust that the police wouldn't find them here either. Tomorrow—yes, tomorrow he'd go down to Newspaper Row in Washington Street, where the Colonel had an office. The proprietors of the city's reputable sheets—the *Globe,* the *Transcript,* the *Post,* the *Herald*—scorned the Colonel, of course, and would not accord his despicable rag, *Town Topics,* the dignity of the name of newspaper; nevertheless, the Colonel maintained the fiction, to himself if not to others, that he was one of their fraternity and kept his office alongside theirs.

There must be an assistant, Ames thought; and the assistant would have to be spoken to. He'd ask his friend Delahanty about it. Delahanty was the proprietor of a modest literary periodical; he knew even more people in Boston than Ames did, and more people of vastly differing social classes. Yes. Delahanty would know how to proceed.

He thrust the ledger back into the safe.

"All right," he said to MacKenzie. "Let us go."

But as he moved past the desk, something on the floor underneath it caught his eye. It was small, white, gleaming, with a bit of gold trim. He picked it up, holding it between finger and thumb as he examined it.

It was a pearl in the shape of a teardrop, with a gold filigree cap and tiny gold loop.

"What do you make of this, Doctor?" he asked, handing it to MacKenzie.

MacKenzie looked at it briefly before handing it back. "From a necklace, perhaps. Or an earbob?"

"Yes. Whose owner—or her husband—was in this room tonight on business with the Colonel."

Ames placed it on the desk and took from the breast pocket of his jacket a small morocco-bound notebook and a silver pencil. Rapidly he made a sketch of the pearl; then he replaced it on the floor beneath the desk. It was time to go.

He picked up his black, low-crowned trilby hat from the side table where he'd put it, crossed to the hall door, and cautiously cracked it open. The corridor was empty. With MacKenzie limping behind, he slipped out and closed the door softly behind them.

To their right, the elevator was just ascending. They turned left and, at the end of the corridor, ducked into a service landing that led to the back stairs. They heard the clank of the elevator's doors opening. Ames opened the door an inch or two and peered out. He saw a man emerge from the elevator, hesitate for a moment, and then turn toward them—and the Colonel's room.

He was of middling height with a fine full mustache and flashily dressed—brocade waistcoat, showy stickpin in his cravat, congress gaiters. He carried a bowler hat and yellow kid gloves, and on the third finger of his right hand he wore a large gold-and-diamond ring. He stopped at the Colonel's door, knocked, and went in.

"Come on," muttered Ames.

They went down the stairs to the ground level, out into an alley, and around to the front, where they entered the hotel once more. The lobby was as crowded as it had been earlier. The clientele was a prosperous one: fur-swathed women wearing silk and satin evening gowns and elaborate jewelry, and men in opera capes and carrying crush hats— collapsible top hats. In such a crowd, Ames's tall, lean, dark-clad figure did not attract attention unless one met his glance, in which case he was a compelling figure indeed. He made his way directly to the reception desk; MacKenzie limped behind at a little distance.

The clerk, a nervous young man who seemed out of his depth in such a position, hesitated when Ames asked for the manager.

"Who shall I say—?"

"At once, man!" Ames snapped.

In a moment more, the manager appeared.

"Yes, sir?" he said. Despite the fact that two men awaited him, there was no question about which of them had de-manded his presence; he spoke to Ames, hardly seeming to notice MacKenzie.

His name, lettered on his office door, was Harris. He spoke with a touch of hauteur, but Ames could sense his anxiety. All kinds of things could happen in a big, fashion-able place like the Hotel Brunswick, and many of them might spell disaster for the man in charge. And so the man-ager presented a smooth, bland face to the world, but his eyes were sharp, alert for catastrophe.

"Sorry to trouble you, Mr. Harris," said Ames. He did not sound sorry at all. "We need to step into your office for a moment."

The clerk was all ears; MacKenzie saw a cloud of disap-pointment settle over his face.

Safely inside, the door closed, Ames produced his card and introduced MacKenzie.

There was a slight pause.

"Yes?" said Harris. "Is something wrong, gentlemen?"

"I am afraid so," Ames replied.

"Well?" Harris was suddenly impatient.

"I did not want to inconvenience you," Ames went on smoothly, "but I thought you would want to know."

"Know—what?"

"There has been, apparently, some unpleasantness."

"Yes?" Harris barked it out.

"I am afraid that you will need to call the police." Already Ames was turning, preparing to leave.

"Police!" cried Harris, finally aware that something was very wrong indeed. "What do you mean? What is it?"

Ames turned back. "I have just paid a call on Colonel William d'Arcy Mann, up in Suite Four-twelve."

"And?" Harris was truly agitated now and beginning to perspire.

"And I regret to inform you, sir, that Colonel Mann is dead."

CHAPTER 2

"I THOUGHT HE TOOK IT RATHER WELL," SAID AMES. "Under the circumstances."

"Yes, well, I imagine he's paid to deal with all sorts of circumstances," MacKenzie replied. As they paused at the curb to allow a stream of carriages to pass, he flexed his knee.

"Bothering you?" said Ames, noticing.

"A bit, yes."

"Then let's take a herdic. It's a nasty night, and you don't want to slip and fall."

It was, in fact, just the sort of night he enjoyed. Fog had blown in with the dark, bringing with it the sharp, sour smell of the sea. Now the streetlamps bloomed with misty halos, and people walked with care over brick sidewalks and cobblestone streets made slippery by the thickening mist.

On such nights, MacKenzie knew, Ames often liked to prowl the city, walking, walking—no wonder the man was so thin! Through the narrow ways of the North End, inhabited almost entirely now by foreigners of one sort or another; along the broad new boulevards of the Back Bay, new-made land reclaimed from the smelly flats of the Charles; up and down the steep inclines of Beacon Hill, mansions on the south side, tenements on the north, communing perhaps with the ghosts of the souls who had lived there a century earlier, some of whom—the southsiders— were Ames's ancestors. These were always solitary forays. Ames liked to be alone, but even if he had invited MacKenzie to accompany him, the doctor would have had to refuse. In September, he had come to Boston from the West for an operation to save his knee, which, in April, had been badly damaged by a Sioux bullet. Only now, more than a month after his surgery, was he beginning to be somewhat ambulatory.

There was a herdic-phaeton stand at the corner. Beyond, to their left, lay the vast empty space that was Copley Square, anchored on two adjoining sides by the Romanesque bulk of Trinity Church and the Ruskinian Gothic Museum of Fine Arts. On the farthest side, which would house the Renaissance palace that would be the new Boston Public Library, there was only a huge hole in the swampy ground, where cedar pilings were being embedded in the muck to hold the massive weight of the building to come.

To their right lay the way home: to No. 16½ Louisburg Square, Beacon Hill. It was a long way, particularly since they had already walked it once just an hour before. MacKenzie would be glad of the comfort of a herdic-phaeton, such as it was; these were small, two- or four-seater cabs, unique to Boston, drawn by agile horses that made their way about the city at all hours.

Ames raised his arm; a herdic drew up from the waiting line and Ames gave the driver the address. They climbed in at the back and pulled the door shut.

"Caroline will take our news badly," Ames remarked as they settled themselves.

MacKenzie agreed. Caroline Ames, his companion's

sister, was by rights his landlady, just as Ames was his landlord; however, in his six-week stay in the city he had come to think of them as more than that, and they seemed to feel the same.

The cab rattled over the cobblestones as they hurtled down Boylston Street past the Public Garden and turned onto Charles Street. On their left lay the Garden, the bare, dark, skeletal branches of its specimen trees barely visible through the foggy lamplight. In summer, Caroline had told MacKenzie, swan boats plied the Garden's little lagoon; you could take an excursion around the miniature islands and under the miniature suspension bridge, with a boy pedaling the boat at the back, a beautiful curved white wooden swan attached to its front. MacKenzie hoped to take such an excursion with her himself, come the warm weather.

On their right lay the larger, darker Common. Dangerous at night, they had warned him, but during the day a splendid place to walk, when he could walk comfortably again. Down the Long Path under the tall elms, nursemaids pushing high-wheeled wicker perambulators, children playing tag and roll-the-hoop, and, in winter, skating on the Frog Pond.

They crossed Beacon Street and went on down Charles to where the steep slope of Mt. Vernon Street rose up Beacon Hill. The horse made the distance to Louisburg Square in moments, and then they were home: a tall, swell-front, red-brick town house, one of a row, with a bow window made of lavender-tinted glass, a shining black front door with a fanlight above and a gleaming brass door knocker in the shape of a hump-backed sea serpent. Through the shutters they could see the glow of the lamps in the parlor, and MacKenzie felt his heart lift; for him, Miss Caroline Ames was a perfect angel of the hearth, and he hoped that she had waited up for them.

SHE HAD. SHE SAT BY THE FIRE, A BOOK OPEN IN HER LAP; but enticing as it was, she had been too worried, her mind too unsettled, to read it—never mind to attend to the petit point that lay in the workbasket at her feet.

This dreadful mess! Poor Val! And poor Addington, needing to perform this distasteful errand, having to call on the notorious Colonel Mann and ask him to be merciful, to leave off hounding Val for money that neither Val nor Addington had.

Thank heaven Dr. MacKenzie had been well enough to go with Addington, she thought, and as the doctor's broad, honest visage floated up into her mind, she relaxed a little. It had been a fortunate day when Dr. Warren, who lived across the square, sent a note to Addington asking, in the most tactful way, if the Ameses might consider taking in a boarder. A man from the West, he'd said, a surgeon in the army who needed a place to recuperate after an operation that Dr. Warren was to perform on his knee.

At first the idea had rankled. She had worried that people would talk; they would gossip that the Ameses, brother and sister, did not know how to live within their means.

But their means, these days, were stretched perilously thin. Their father's will had left them, ten years before, provided with a small trust fund that had, with every passing year, been less adequate. They had hung bravely on until their mother died, more than a year ago now. Since then, they had thought about—and had even discussed, once or twice—various ways to increase their income.

The most obvious one was for Addington to find some kind of remunerative employment. But Addington—brilliant, talented in a dozen ways, with widespread "interests" in many things—had no vocation for any particular thing. Their father had been a lawyer, but Addington had not been attracted to the law. Their father's father had been in the China trade and had owned shares in various manufacturing companies here in New England; but the China trade had dwindled, and the shares, part of their trust fund, had diminished in value.

Their grandfather, one of the original proprietors of Louisburg Square, had put up this house in the eighteen forties and had died in it, secure in the knowledge that his descendants would live out their days in it as well. He could not have envisioned a time when his grandchildren might have to sell it.

Sell it! How could they do that? Sell this house, with its curving staircase, its carved white-painted wooden mantels, its serene high-ceilinged rooms filled with family treasures? The portraits of their ancestors gazing down upon them from the walls; the porcelains and ivories brought over long ago in the China trade; the slightly threadbare medallion-back sofa in the front parlor, the rosewood Duncan Phyfe sideboard and lyreback chairs in the dining room, the worn Turkey rugs, the grandmother clock in the hall— No. Even though its original elegance was somewhat tattered now, it was their lifelong home; they could never give it up. Somehow they would manage.

The thought that Addington might, after all, practice law, immuring himself in one of the great Boston law firms, had in fact been discussed between them, but Caroline knew that her many-talented brother would suffer in such dusty work. No: he needed to stay free, gifted amateur that he was, to follow where his interests led him. He had been one of the most brilliant students in his class at Harvard, she thought fondly, and now, years later, he was brilliant still. He must stay free, like so many of his wealthier acquaintances, to do as he wished.

But every year, prices went up while their income declined. After their mother's death, they had let three of their full-time servants go, retaining only the all-purpose girl, the faithful Margaret. Their cook was a daily who had Thursdays off; fortunately Margaret was handy in the kitchen and could fill in for her.

So the advent of Dr. MacKenzie had been a blessing in more ways than one, Caroline thought. His seven dollars and fifty cents a week in board money made an enormous difference in their household accounts. Now, each week, when Caroline sat at her little escritoire in her bedroom and totted up income and outgo, she had no need to worry at the end of it, wondering how they would manage. They could even afford little extras now: a roast every Sunday instead of every other, a new cloth for the dining room table, a new pair of high-button boots for herself instead of a visit to the cobbler once again to ask him to try to repair her old ones.

And Dr. MacKenzie had turned out to be a most agreeable gentleman, too—not intrusive, no trouble, not even in the days immediately after his operation, when they'd had to take his meals to him in his room (and grateful they'd been, then, for the elevator that they had installed for their mother's benefit). But he was so cordial, so congenial, they hadn't minded all the up-and-down—and now, as he recovered, he was proving to be a good companion for Addington.

Yes, she thought. They'd done well to take him in. And those few people who had made snide comments about the Ameses taking in boarders could very well keep their comments to themselves.

Outside in the square, the two men climbed down from the herdic-phaeton and Ames paid the driver. The herdic rattled off toward Pinckney Street as they climbed the short flight of granite steps and paused to clean their boots on the mud scraper by the door. Inside, they deposited their outer garments and hats on the hall tree in the vestibule; then they went into the parlor to greet Caroline.

She rose from her seat, her book sliding to the floor.

"How—how was it?" she asked. As fair as her brother was dark, she had soft brown eyes and curly light brown hair which she wore fashionably done up into a Psyche knot, with frizzy bangs over her forehead. Only two months out of mourning for her mother, she wore a gown of some soft stuff the color of bronze oak leaves. It was high-collared and long-sleeved, and, with its bustle, slightly out of fashion. Her only adornment was a mourning brooch pinned to her bodice. She was a trifle plump, but although she wished that she were more slender, Dr. MacKenzie did not.

Just now her eyes were wide with anxiety, and her sweet, pretty face, ordinarily pink-cheeked, was pale and drawn. MacKenzie hated to see her so; he hated knowing the bad news that her brother was about to give her.

"Not good," Ames said shortly. He strode across the room and took up his accustomed place, standing by the fire, one long, slim, booted foot resting on the brass fender. MacKenzie limped to the chair that had become his, a Morris rocker.

"Well, Addington?" Caroline said. "What happened?"

"Nothing," he replied.

"Nothing! You mean he—he wouldn't listen to reason? What did he say?"

Ames turned slightly to give her one of his looks. "Nothing," he repeated.

"But didn't you—"

"He was dead, Caro."

There was a moment of shocked and horrified silence. She went paler still, her hand flown to her bosom; then, faintly, she said, "How?"

"We found him on the floor of his suite," Ames said. His voice dragged a bit. "He had been shot," he added.

MacKenzie wondered at his brutal bluntness, but then he reminded himself that although Miss Caroline Ames was delicate in the way that all females were, ill equipped to deal with the harsher realities of life, she was nevertheless a

Boston female, and therefore blessed—or cursed—with a stronger, more steely character than that of females born and bred someplace else. Ames must have believed that his sister could deal with his news, MacKenzie thought, or he would not have divulged it. He pulled out his pipe (she'd given him permission to smoke when he first arrived, and very grateful to her he was) and lit up.

"I see," she said. For a moment—no more—she seemed to waver and weaken; then, with a visible effort, she pulled herself together and said calmly, "Well, then, you'd better tell me everything." She sank onto the worn brocade sofa opposite MacKenzie and folded her hands in her lap, prepared to hear her brother out.

And there was, after all, not so very much to tell; in less than five minutes he had said it all.

Then: "What are you going to do now, Addington?"

"Now?" He seemed puzzled. "What can I do now? Now it is in Inspector Crippen's hands."

"Oh, no!"

"I am afraid so. He will have some part in the investigation at least, and he may well be in charge. I heard last month that he has been promoted to the homicide division—if that can be thought of as a promotion."

"But, Addington—if Inspector Crippen has anything to do with it, they will never find who killed Colonel Mann! Remember last year at the Somerset—!"

He nodded; he shrugged. "Frankly, I do not give a picayune who killed the Colonel, and I would imagine that neither do you. We are well rid of him."

"Yes, but, Addington—what about Val's letters?"

He hesitated. "I don't know."

"But—we must get them for her! Are you sure they weren't there? Oh, I wish I'd been with you!"

A momentary spasm of outrage contorted his features as he envisioned that scene and at once dismissed it.

"No, Caroline, they were not there. I had little time, you

understand. I did not want to encounter another of the Colonel's supplicants."

"No. Of course not." She thought about it. "But that means—it means that we are no better off than before. And remember how the Colonel worked, Addington. If people did not pay him on Monday evening, he ran the item in *Town Topics* the next day. He always had the proof sheets— what are they called? galleys?—of his next issue with him in his hotel suite to show people exactly what he was going to say."

"How do you know so much about how the Colonel worked, Caroline?"

She waved a hand at him dismissively. "Oh, everyone knows that. And besides, Letitia Converse had a run-in with him last year. She told me all about it." She gave a little shiver of distaste. "Horrid man! Blackmailing people—spying on them! Oh, Addington! What are we going to do? Poor Val! You know the Putnams. They will never forgive her if her name shows up in that scandal sheet!"

"I believe the Colonel confined himself to initials."

"Still. It doesn't matter. He always put in enough detail so that people would know whom he meant. They will spot it—"

"Do such proper people read the Colonel's rag?"

"Everyone reads it, whether they admit it or not. You know that. And even if they don't see it for themselves, someone will be sure to tell them. People are always eager to pass along the latest scandal. Poor Valentine will be disgraced, and her future in-laws will hear of it soon enough, one way or another."

She thought for a moment, her wide, smooth forehead wrinkled in a frown. Then: "Addington, listen to me."

He threw her a wary glance. "What now, Caroline?"

"You must stop the publication of tomorrow's issue of the Colonel's paper."

"And how am I to do that, pray?"

"You can—well, you can talk to Mr. Delahanty, for a start."

A thought he'd had himself, but he did not think it necessary—or wise—to tell her so.

"And how can he help?"

"He will—oh, I don't know! Somehow he will know how to stop it! He is a kind of newspaper publisher himself, isn't he?"

"A literary magazine is not a newspaper, Caro."

"But it amounts to the same thing, for our purposes." A new thought struck her. "Addington! Surely, if the Colonel is dead, tomorrow's issue will not be published?"

"I have no idea."

"Well, you can find out, can't you? Mr. Delahanty can tell you! Say you will speak to him! And then—"

She hesitated, obviously given pause by the enormity of what she was about to ask him to do. "Then we will just see," she added somewhat lamely. "If the issue is held up—who knows, perhaps the police won't let it appear—then you have just that much longer to find those letters."

"Now wait a moment, Caroline. How do you propose that I do that? They were not in the Colonel's suite—"

"As far as you know."

"As far as I know, yes. But if they weren't there, how can we know where on earth they might be? I will simply tell Crippen to be on the lookout—"

"Oh, no! Who knows who will see them if Inspector Crippen gets his hands on them? If he bungles this case the way he did the theft at the Somerset—"

She turned to MacKenzie. "Last year, there was a theft of some silver at the Somerset Club." This, he knew, was one of Ames's clubs. "Inspector Crippen was in charge of the investigation, and Addington was very helpful to him. Inspector Crippen was all set to arrest the wrong man, when Addington pointed out that he *was* the wrong man. If it hadn't been for you, Addington—"

"Yes, well, that was an entirely different matter, wasn't it?" Ames had a slightly apprehensive look, as if he knew that he was in combat with her and was afraid she would win.

"So I think you ought to speak to him—"

"I will do no such thing. How can I possibly intrude myself into this case?"

She stared at him, implacable. "Why, because of Val, of course. Think what it will mean to her if she loses this marriage."

"She will not lose it."

"Yes, she will! You know the Putnams! They will cast her off and her heart will be broken! I am surprised at you, that you can be so unfeeling toward a member of your own family, a perfectly wonderful girl who has never harmed anyone—"

"Except herself," he interjected.

"All right—yes—except herself. She knows she did a foolish thing, and she is certainly paying for it now. I don't understand why you want her to suffer more!"

"I do not want her to suffer more, Caroline, but aside from everything else, you seem to forget that next week I leave for Egypt."

She stared at him. "Oh," she said softly after a moment. "I forgot all about that."

"Yes, well, I can assure you that I have not."

This was a long-anticipated event: a journey to the Valley of the Kings, an archaeological expedition under the leadership of Professor Bartley Harbinger, one of Ames's former professors at Harvard. Ames had been preparing for it for months; he would be gone until the spring.

He swung around and came to sit beside her. As if to soften what he was about to say, he took one of her hands in his. MacKenzie watched enviously.

"My dear, we must let events take their course. We are dealing now not with the theft of some silver, not even with blackmail, which is bad enough, but with murder. The police must become involved—and we must not," he added with heavy emphasis.

There was a brief silence. Then, to the consternation of both men, Caroline began to cry. She did it beautifully: a few soft sobs, a tear or two sliding down her cheeks. She removed her hand from her brother's; from the lace-edged cuff of her sleeve she produced a lace-edged handkerchief and proceeded, very delicately, to dab at her eyes.

"Now, Caroline—" Ames began. He wore that baffled look men had when they were dealing with a weeping female.

She shook her head. "No, Addington," she sobbed. "Say no more. I understand. You have your own affairs, which are more important to you than—than—" She emitted a little gasping wail. "Oh! I cannot bear it! Poor, poor Val!"

Ames patted her shoulder ineffectually. It did no good; she wept on. Then she darted a look at him.

"Addington?"

"Yes, Caro?"

"You have one week before you leave, do you not?"

"Yes, Caro."

"Well, then—" She dried her eyes one last time and turned to look at him. It was amazing, MacKenzie thought, how she could emerge from a bout of crying as pretty as when she began it.

"Then you have time to do something to help, after all," she said.

"Now, Caroline—"

"Yes!" She stiffened her already ramrod-straight posture. "You must! Because if you don't—"

He waited, knowing—dreading—what she would say.

"I will!" she finished triumphantly.

"Never."

"Yes! I will! Of course, people will talk. 'How dreadful that Addington Ames lets his sister go down to Newspaper

Row, where no proper lady should set foot,' they will say. 'How disgraceful that he does not exert himself to protect her, the way a lady should be protected, from all that is sordid and vile in the world.' Yes, Addington, that is what they will say."

He was not, ordinarily, a man who cared much about what people said. He had lived all his life secure in the knowledge that he was a Boston Ames, born into what Dr. Oliver Wendell Holmes had dubbed the "Boston Brahmin" caste. Such a place in the world gave a man a certain self-confidence, a certain imperviousness to idle gossip.

But now, confronted with his sister's accusations, he weakened. It was a sight that MacKenzie, for one, had never thought to see.

He reached into his inside jacket pocket, withdrew his notebook, and handed it to her open to the sketch.

"Oh!" She looked at it with great interest, all weeping done with. "What is this? A pearl? Where did you find it?"

"On the floor of the Colonel's suite, underneath his desk. The filigree is gold. Do you recognize it? Or do you have any idea what it might be?"

She studied the sketch intently. "It is from a necklace, I think," she said after a moment. "Or perhaps—it is hard to tell—perhaps it is an earbob drop."

"Yes."

She looked up at him. "And you think someone lost it—?"

"I do not know, but I believe it must have been dropped there tonight, or the daily chambermaid would have found it when she went in to clean this morning."

"Yes. Of course."

"You have never seen such a pearl before? As part of a necklace belonging to someone you know, perhaps?"

"Well, I—I don't know." She thought about it for a moment. "I mean, everyone has pearls. Mine are from my mama, as I suppose most people's are." She smiled at Mac-Kenzie. "We don't *buy* our pearls, Doctor, we simply *have* them."

"Yes." He nodded and smiled at her in return.

"But this—" She turned back to her brother. "This is a very unusual pearl and obviously part of a very handsome set, whether it is necklace or earbob."

"But you cannot recall seeing such a piece worn by anyone of your acquaintance?"

"No." She shook her head slowly, thinking about it. "And I am sure I would, since it is so very distinctive." Rather reluctantly she gave the notebook back to Ames.

"But at the Cotillion tomorrow night—" he ventured.

"Yes, of course," she said, brightening. "Everyone wears their best to the Cotillion. I will keep a sharp eye—and you must, too, Addington."

The Autumn Cotillion was not an event he ordinarily attended, and not an event he looked forward to attending now. But tomorrow night, he must escort Valentine to it, since she had no other male relative to do so. It was the post-debutante ball held every November for the previous year's "buds," their last formal appearance together before the new season's debutantes came out at the Christmas ball. Caroline was on the committee; she had been frantic for weeks, arranging things.

"What is more," she went on briskly, giving him a challenging look, "you have a week, as you say, until you leave with your expedition. You can do much in a week. And then, after you go—"

He shook his head emphatically. "No, Caroline. You must not become involved. I forbid it."

She smiled sweetly. "Perhaps I will not need to. Perhaps by that time it will all be settled, and Val will have her letters back, and no one need be the wiser."

"Don't count on it. The police will be very busy in this

case, and the newspapers—" He shook his head, thinking of what the city's journalists would make of such a scandalous affair. And for Caroline to be mixed up in it!

He stood up. "We will discuss it in the morning, Caroline. I make no promises."

He left them then, and went upstairs to bed.

MacKenzie thought that he, too, should retire, but he was so enchanted by the thought of having a brief moment alone with her that he stayed where he was.

They did not speak for a time, but it was not an uncomfortable silence. Already, in their brief acquaintance, they had become—within the bounds of etiquette—easy and friendly with each other.

At last, with a rueful smile that caught at his heart, Caroline turned to him and said, "Do you have any idea why this is so important, Doctor? Finding Val's letters, I mean."

His pipe was nearly finished; he took a last couple of puffs. "Why, yes," he said, "I imagine I do."

"I wonder," she said. "It is so different for men, isn't it? I mean, a man can withstand scandal and go on to make a perfectly respectable marriage. Even a quite advantageous one. But for a woman— Well, we are more vulnerable to scandal. If this business comes out, Val will be so disgraced that she will never be able to marry someone here in Boston." Her tone made it clear that such a fate would be dreadful indeed. "She would have to go to—oh, I don't know. New York, Philadelphia. Perhaps even abroad. Imagine it—to marry a foreigner!"

"People do that," he said. "I read in the papers only last week about some young American miss who married a duke in London."

She waved her hand dismissively. "Yes—and she will be separated from her family forever—marooned over there! How awful! Poor thing!"

He thought that many young women would not think it

awful at all to marry a duke, but in the face of her vehemence, he kept his opinion to himself.

"No—Val must stay here," she went on, "and she must
marry George Putnam. She really is in love with him, you
know."

He didn't, but he nodded to show that he did, and, more,
to encourage her to continue talking to him. He loved to
have her talk to him; she was the only woman, aside from his
long-dead mother, who ever had.

"It is not that George is so terribly wealthy," she said
thoughtfully. "I mean, he is, but it really is a love match. It is
so sweet, isn't it, when young people are in love." She herself was thirty-five. "I will give Aunt Euphemia this much:
she has never been ambitious for Val in that pushy way. Not
like Isabel Dane. Her daughter Alice is Val's best friend,"
she added, aware that MacKenzie was still unfamiliar with
the city's interlocking relationships. "Isabel says that she has
quite a good catch for Alice nearly on the hook. 'A very
warm young man,' she said. Rich he may be, but it is so very
vulgar to speak of it like that."

She stood up and began to pace the room; as she did so,
she rerouted her meandering thoughts and came back to the
point.

"I will speak to Addington again first thing tomorrow
morning," she said with some little asperity. "He must find
those letters—he must! Val's entire future depends upon it."

"Then we may hope that he will," MacKenzie said softly.

She stopped and fixed him in her gaze. "And if he does
not—why, I shall! Cousin Miranda never even need know
about it." Cousin Miranda was a cousin several times removed, a resident of the town of Magnolia on the North
Shore, who had been promised the treat of a winter in the
city if she came to stay at Louisburg Square during Ames's
absence, thus preserving the proprieties.

Caroline took her seat by the fire once more. "You must

be tired, Doctor. Even though you are recuperating so well, you mustn't think that you have recovered entirely."

She was right, of course. He would be glad to go to his room, which was a comfortably furnished chamber at the back of the third floor. It faced the river and Cambridge beyond. On clear days he had a fine view of the sunset, and even in the rain he could see a far way down across the clustered rooftops of the houses that clung to the hill as it descended toward the water.

So he heaved himself up, knocked out his pipe into the fireplace, reached for his cane, and bade her good night. His last sight of her was as she sat by the fire, already lost in thought, the flickering, ruddy light gently playing over her gown, her lovely face.

As he made his way back along the hall to the elevator, it occurred to him, not for the first time, to wonder how a perfectly delightful woman like Caroline Ames, so worried about her young cousin's marriage, had never herself been spoken for.

CHAPTER 3

Despite the previous night's fog, the morning dawned bright, and by eight o'clock they were in the dining room. Ames had opened the morning *Globe* that lay folded by his place and had begun to read the account of the Colonel's death. After a moment they heard the creak and thump of the dumbwaiter in the back passage, and then the maid came in with the breakfast tray and deposited it on the sideboard.

"Thank you, Margaret," said Caroline. The servant bobbed down and up in a quick curtsy and went out, softly closing the door behind her.

"Tea, Doctor?" asked Caroline. "Or coffee? And do take your breakfast before—"

She was interrupted by the sound of the door knocker, followed immediately by a loud pounding.

"What on earth—?" Caroline exclaimed.

At once, Ames threw down the newspaper, rose, and left the room, muttering an oath as he went. Overcome by curiosity, Caroline and the doctor followed.

Ames had opened the front door.

"Yes?" he barked.

"Mr. Ames?" The man who spoke was so small that they could hardly see him over Ames's shoulder.

"Who are you?" Ames demanded.

"My name is Miller. I'm from the *Post*. We would like to have your story, sir—in the matter of Colonel Mann, I mean—and we are prepared to pay for it."

Caroline caught her breath. The nerve of the man! She couldn't see her brother's face, but she saw him visibly stiffen and she could imagine his expression, rigid with anger.

"Get out," Ames said curtly.

"But, Mr. Ames, if you would just give me a moment—"

"Get *out!*" Ames thundered. He seized a walking stick from the hall tree—it had been their father's, never used since that good man's death—and brandished it as if he would strike the interloper.

The little man retreated down the front steps. "Now, there's no need to take on so, Mr. Ames. I'm making you an honest offer. It will take only a few moments of your time, and you can profit—"

"*Out!*" thundered Ames, and now he struck at the reporter and missed him only because the man scurried back across the sidewalk to the curb. "And stay out! If you show your face here again, I'll have you arrested for trespassing!"

Caroline, on tiptoe, saw the reporter dart away along the square toward Mt. Vernon Street. Ames stayed where he was, standing in the open doorway, watching him go. Then, shaking his head, he slammed the door shut, returned the walking stick to the hall tree, and turned to see Caroline and MacKenzie.

"Damned scoundrel," he muttered.

"How dreadful," Caroline breathed. "Why did he come to you?"

"Because I gave the hotel manager my card."

She looked a little ill. "You did? You didn't tell me that last night. Why did you do that? That means that you will be—you already are—connected to the case."

"So it says in this morning's *Globe.*"

"But that is absurd! The police cannot believe that you of all people would commit murder!"

"Of course they can. And they probably will for an hour or two, until they come to their senses."

"And the newspapers will hound you—"

"Not if they know what's good for them," he glowered. She had seldom seen him so angry. "I brought it on myself, of course, by identifying myself to the hotel manager, but still. I don't intend to allow myself—or you—to be harassed by that pack of jackals."

"They need sensation stories to build their circulation," MacKenzie said as the three of them made their way back along the hall.

"Well, they can get them from someone else," Ames fumed. "They'll get nothing from me. Damned prying journalists—offering to pay me, no less!"

At breakfast once more, trying to pretend that the unpleasant incident had not happened, Caroline poured coffee for MacKenzie. Then, wincing a little—his knee always ached in the morning—he went to the sideboard and lifted the lid of the silver porridge tureen and contemplated its steaming, glutinous contents. Oatmeal. Again. In the army, he'd been used to bacon and eggs and hash brown potatoes for breakfast, which here—minus the potatoes—were served only on Saturdays. Suppressing a sigh, he helped himself and returned to the table.

"Addington?" Caroline said, still holding the coffeepot.

No answer. Ames was buried in the newspaper. She longed to see it for herself, but she would not have dreamed of asking for it before he had done with it.

"Coffee, Addington?" she asked a little louder.

"What?" He lowered the newspaper to peer at her. "Oh—no, no thank you, Caro. Tea, please."

She poured, and as she handed him his cup, pounced on her opportunity. "What do they say about the Colonel?"

"Quite enough," he replied. "They have some of the

details wrong, but on the whole, they have the story. And yes, Caro, your friend Crippen is in charge of the case."

Why her friend, in particular? MacKenzie wondered; but of course he could not ask.

Caroline rolled her eyes. "Can you imagine how many happy people are reading this news this morning?" she said. "Not that anyone's death is a cause for happiness," she added quickly.

As she rose to get her porridge, Ames cocked his head as if he were listening for some sound that only he could hear. "Yes—I can hear the shouts of celebration now, all over the city."

"Don't joke, Addington."

"I am not joking. Merely—ah—using a little poetic license." He studied the newspaper for a few moments more and then passed it to her. She devoured it avidly, ignoring her plate of porridge growing cold before her. Yes, there was Addington's name. It gave her a nasty little shock to see it.

Ames rose to get his breakfast, and for a time he and MacKenzie ate in silence. Then, from the front of the house, they heard the door knocker once more and, after a moment, Margaret hurrying to answer. The three of them waited tensely for the worst: another prying journalist. But in the next moment, Margaret knocked and entered the dining room, followed closely by a strikingly beautiful young woman.

"Miss Valentine, ma'am," said Margaret unnecessarily. She looked a little put out, as if the young woman, by not waiting to be announced, had not followed proper etiquette—as, indeed, she had not. As Margaret left them, she closed the door unnecessarily hard.

"Why—Valentine—" Caroline had half risen at her cousin's entrance; now she sank back into her chair, while the men stood to greet the visitor.

She was small and dark-haired, dressed in a fashionable

dark blue "tailor-made" walking suit. Her violet eyes, lovely as they were, were shadowed by worry, and her face, under the brim of her flat, tip-tilted little hat, was pale and drawn, as if she had not slept well. Ames held a chair for her and she sat, waving away Caroline's offer of a cup of tea.

"Well, Cousin?" she said to Ames. "Did you—what happened?"

Ames had resumed his seat, but MacKenzie had not. Although Valentine had not seemed to notice that he was in the room, he must, he thought, take his leave, breakfast forfeited, since this was obviously to be a private family discussion. However, as he started to turn from the table, Caroline shook her head. "No, Doctor," she said, "please stay. I am sure that Val does not object, do you, Valentine?"

"What? Oh—no, not at all." The young woman hardly glanced at him as he resumed his seat; all her attention was on Ames. He sat at the head of the table, his chair pushed back a little, his elbows resting on its arms and his hands pressed together under his chin as if he were praying. He said nothing for a moment, merely watching Valentine as if he were trying to judge her state of mind, her ability to deal with bad news.

MacKenzie's porridge was growing cold; tentatively, hoping no one would mind, he began to spoon it up.

"Valentine—" Ames began.

"You didn't get them." It was not a question; they heard her voice break as she spoke the words that, in her mind at least, foretold the ruin of her life.

"No. We did not."

"We? Did you go with him, Caroline?"

"Ah—no," he said before his sister could answer. "Dr. MacKenzie was with me."

She threw the doctor a quick glance and returned to Ames.

"Well? What did Colonel Mann say? Did he listen to you?"

"Val, dear—" Caroline began. She had folded the newspaper onto her lap.

"He did not say anything, I am afraid," Ames interrupted.

"But—"

"He was dead," Ames said, very gently.

Valentine sat stunned, her mouth open, her eyes darkening with shock. At once Caroline got up and put her arms around her, but she did not respond. She continued to stare, speechless, at Ames.

"And in fact it was worse than that, I am afraid," Ames went on. "Someone had shot him."

"*Oh!*" For a moment they thought she might faint, but she did not.

"Addington—go easy—" warned Caroline. "Doctor, could you pour her a cup of tea—no, coffee—"

He did as she asked, even as he wondered if smelling salts might not be more appropriate.

"But—how—" Valentine was struggling with Ames's news; what she said next astonished them. "He was certainly alive when I saw him at four o'clock," she blurted.

"When *you* saw him!" exclaimed Caroline. "You mean you went to him again?"

Valentine had had an initial interview with the Colonel, they knew, during which he'd made his demand for money in return for her letters.

"Yes. I thought—I thought— Oh, I don't know what I thought! I was so ashamed of having to ask Addington for help, and I thought perhaps, after all, I could get the letters back on my own. I knew you were going to see him later, but I thought—I wanted to be able to come around and tell you it wasn't necessary, you didn't have to go to him because I had gotten them back myself. Of course, I was mistaken," she added with some bitterness.

"He was not—agreeable to your request," Ames said flatly.

"No. He— Oh, he was horrid! He laughed at me. I thought I would die of shame, standing there and begging him for mercy—"

"Don't say such things, Val," Caroline said. "Drink some coffee—have you had breakfast? Give me your gloves—that's right. You mustn't upset yourself."

As Valentine allowed Caroline to take her gloves, MacKenzie caught a glimpse of a large sapphire-and-diamond ring on the third finger of her left hand. A good marriage indeed, he thought.

Caroline was still trying to comfort her young cousin. "Remember that the Cotillion is tonight, dearest," she said, "and you want to be fresh and rested for it. Addington has his evening suit all laid out," she added. "And I must say, he will look very handsome, escorting you down the stairs."

Valentine seemed not to hear.

"What happened?" she said to Ames, her voice hardly more than a whisper. "Tell me—please."

Briefly, he did. "And I assure you that I searched thoroughly," he added. "The letters were not there—or if they were, they were well hidden."

She was silent for a moment, absorbing it. Then: "But I *saw* them."

Ames made a small exclamation of surprise, but she did not seem to notice.

"They were right there on top of his desk," she went on. "He took them out of a drawer and put them there, as if to taunt me. I wanted to reach over and snatch them up—I would have, if I'd thought I could escape before he caught me. He was somewhat overweight, after all. I don't suppose he could have run very fast, do you?" She made a sound that was half sob, half laughter.

"Did you see him put them away again?" Ames asked after a moment.

"No." Valentine shook her head, and in that one word they heard her despair.

"So if he had the letters at—what time? Four o'clock? If he had them then, he probably still had them when—"

"He was killed," said Caroline. She met her brother's eyes; for the moment, she forgot the need to console their young cousin.

"Exactly," said Ames. He lifted an eyebrow at his sister, pushed back his chair, and stepped to the back window that gave onto their small walled garden. It was November-brown now, only a few evergreen shrubs showing any color; he stared out at it, unseeing. Then he turned to them once more.

"How do you think the Colonel got those letters in the first place?" he asked Valentine.

She had taken out a handkerchief to dab at her eyes. Now, very delicately, she blew her nose; then she thought for a moment.

"I don't know," she said. "I had them hidden in my room."

"Where?"

"In a locked box at the back of my closet. Oh, *why* was I so stupid as to keep them?" she burst out. "I should have burned them!"

To this, they all silently agreed.

"Who knew about them?" Ames asked.

"Why—no one. Except *him,*" Val added bitterly.

They understood: she meant the man to whom she had written them. And who had, in the end, been gentleman enough to give them back to her.

"And no one has access to your room except—?"

"Well—Aunt Euphemia, of course. And the servants."

"Have you asked your maid about them?"

"No. I was afraid to—afraid that if I began to question her, Aunt Euphemia would find out about the whole affair, and she would—" Valentine took a deep breath. "I couldn't risk that."

Aunt Euphemia Ames—their late father's eldest sister—

was a fierce, proud old woman whose ideas of proper conduct for young ladies like Valentine had been formed in an
earlier, stricter age. And while she herself had behaved
boldly, and sometimes even recklessly, in her own youth, it
had been in the service of the Abolitionists and therefore
permissible. An affair of the heart, such as Valentine's ill-
fated adventure with the young man of the letters, was beyond Aunt Euphemia's ken. She had never married; as far as
Caroline knew—and it was fairly far—she had never even
had a suitor.

"Friends?" Ames persisted. "Do your friends not sometimes visit with you, in your—ah—boudoir?"

"Well—yes, of course, but how—no one knew—"

"Someone did," said Ames, his face grim. "And now, I
am afraid, someone else does, as well."

It did not seem possible that she could grow any more
pale, but she did, very visibly, as she said, "You mean, Colonel Mann gave them to someone? But why would he—"

"No. That is not what I mean." Ames resumed his seat.
"What I mean is that the person who killed him may well
have taken them."

There was a long moment of silence as she absorbed it.
Then: "Oh, dear heaven."

"Addington! For pity's sake!" Caroline said sharply. "Do
you need to speak so?"

He gave her a look. "If it is so important that those letters
be retrieved, then we must look the facts in the face. We
now have a murder investigation under way. At any moment, I myself may be arrested for the crime."

"You!" exclaimed Valentine. "But that is ridiculous!"

"Of course it is ridiculous, but I discovered the body"—
he threw a half-smile at the doctor—"with Dr. MacKenzie,
it is true, but Crippen will see that he lacks a motive. I,
however, had some delicate business with the Colonel, a fact
that probably makes me a very good suspect indeed. Of
course, Crippen will soon realize that he is mistaken, but in

the interim— Well. Perhaps I can get to him before he gets to me, and that may work in my favor. Meanwhile, I think it is important, Valentine, that you try to behave as if you haven't a care in the world beyond seeing that your gown is ready for tonight. Is it, by the way?"

With a visible effort, she wrenched her thoughts away from Colonel Mann and his threats and his blackmail.

"Yes."

"And do you have something to occupy your time to-day?"

"Yes. I am to spend the day with Alice—if she is well enough."

"Good," said Ames. "Then I suggest that is what you should do. Go to Alice, try to pretend that you haven't a worry in the world."

"Is Alice not well?" Caroline asked.

"She hasn't been. Not for weeks." This was news to Caroline, but she let it pass. "Mrs. Dane has been worried about her, I know. Alice said she wanted to take her to Baden-Baden for the cure, but I think that Mr. Dane would never allow it."

"Why not? Surely he could bear to be parted from her for a month or two."

"Oh, I don't think it's that. It's the expense. He is very . . . close."

"Close!" Caroline exclaimed. "He could buy and sell us all! The only reason Alice had such a nice coming-out last year is that he shares Isabel's ambitions for her, and he wanted to make a good show."

MacKenzie was surprised at that; ordinarily Caroline Ames was the kindest of women, never speaking ill of anyone. Except, apparently, Mr. and Mrs. Dane.

Momentarily, Valentine had been diverted by talk of her friend; now her worry and fear seemed to settle over her again. She sat immobile in her chair as if she did not have the strength to rise, her eyes fastened onto Ames as if he were her only hope. As, indeed, he was.

"What do you think will happen, Cousin Addington?" she asked softly.

"I don't know. The police will do their usual work—with some delicacy, one hopes, given the circumstances—and sooner or later we may expect someone to be arrested and charged with the crime."

"But my letters—"

He shook his head. Although he was a proud, reserved man, he was not an unkind one; he did not want to hurt her, or alarm her, any more than necessary. On the other hand, he was not a man to deny unpleasant realities. "I am afraid that since it is now in the hands of the authorities, we can do nothing—"

"Oh, please!" Her voice broke, and for a moment she pressed her hands to her face as if to forcibly hold back her sobs. "You must get them back! George would never want to marry me if those letters are found, and I couldn't bear it if he threw me over! I would be disgraced for life!"

Casting a reproachful look at her brother, Caroline bent over the weeping girl and gently urged her to rise. "Come upstairs with me, Val. You can freshen up and calm yourself a bit. You don't want to go to Alice's like this."

As if Valentine were a little child instead of a grown young woman about to be married, Caroline urged her up and out of the room, leaving the men to their belated breakfast. They heard the whine and moan of the little elevator as it ascended to the second floor, where Caroline's room was.

Ames said nothing, merely finished his meal and the newspaper both, by which time Caroline had rejoined them. She poured herself a fresh cup of coffee and sat at her place, pushing aside her uneaten porridge. "I don't suppose I dare hope that Euphemia will never learn about all this," she said.

"Undoubtedly she will, sooner or later," remarked Ames. He offered the newspaper to her, but she refused it so he passed it to MacKenzie.

"Is the young lady all right?" the doctor asked before he scanned it.

"Yes. She's going to rest a bit before she goes to Alice's. Poor Val! The arrangements for the wedding are well under way"—it was to be in May, when Ames would be home from Egypt—"and she will look so exquisite in her wedding gown. What a shame to spoil it all because of some foolishness she was involved in summer before last." At Newport, where ambitious women like Isabel Dane summered as they fought for social position. Val, because of her friendship with Alice, usually accompanied the Danes, but this past summer she'd chosen to go to Maine with the Wingates instead. Caroline hadn't known why until three days before, when she'd poured out her story of Colonel Mann's blackmail. "I just can't believe that people can behave so—so—" She searched for the right word.

"Viciously," MacKenzie offered.

"Exactly," she said. "Thank you, Doctor. Yes—so viciously."

She sipped her coffee; then: "Addington."

"Yes, Caro?"

"You must find those letters."

He hesitated before he replied. "So you keep saying. But how?"

"Oh, how should I know? But you must—you absolutely must! Think of it! Hasn't Val had enough trouble in her life, losing her parents like that—poor Aunt Rachel, I shall miss her till I die—and now this!"

"Yes, but—"

"Addington! Val is family!"

"I know that, Caro, but—"

"How can you refuse to help her? You cannot just let this scandal come out and ruin her life!"

She was like a small, plump, fierce bird pecking away at his resistance. MacKenzie admired her tremendously.

Ames took a deep breath. He looked, for a moment, like a man condemned.

"Caroline, listen to me. No—do not interrupt. There has been a murder. The man who was killed had many enemies. One of those enemies may be, and probably is, the man who did the deed. And that man may—I repeat, *may*—have taken Val's letters. Now, how am I—how are we, if you will—to discover who that man is? The police—"

"Oh, do not tell me again about the police!" She was really angry now; MacKenzie had never imagined she could be so passionate. He felt a little thrill even as he wondered at her temerity in speaking so to her brother.

"You know what the police are!" she added.

"Yes. I do. Our cousin, Standish Wainwright, sits on the Board of Police Commissioners, if you recall."

She brightened at that. "Of course! And he may be of help, do you not think?"

"No. I do not think. He will be extremely put out if he discovers that I am meddling in what is none of my affair—"

"But that is the point! This *is* your affair! It is *our* affair! Oh, how can you be so cruel? I thought better of you, Addington! Truly I did."

For a long moment he contemplated her. MacKenzie understood that a kind of silent battle, no less intense for its silence, was being waged between them, and he could sense Ames beginning to wither under the force of her will. Like many women, he thought, despite the fact that men spent their lives protecting them, sheltering them from the harsh realities of the world, keeping them safe in their domestic sphere, she was the stronger—and by far the more hard-headed.

"All right, Caro," Ames said at last.

Instantly she brightened. "What are you going to do, Addington?"

"I will go to see Inspector Crippen."

Just then the grandmother clock in the hall began to strike the hour: nine o'clock.

"This morning?"

"I imagine he will be rather busy this morning."

"But you could at least inquire? You could at least see if he is there, if he could give you a few minutes of his time—"

"I was going to go around to Crabbe's—"

"Oh, Crabbe's! How can you think of boxing and fencing at a time like this? No—please go to see Inspector Crippen. And tell him—"

"Yes?" He withered no more; he arched a skeptical eyebrow at her, as if he dared her to continue to order him about.

Suddenly she smiled at him—a charming, almost coquettish smile, delightfully feminine. Even though it was not directed at MacKenzie, he was charmed by it; her next words, however, ruined the effect.

"Tell him that I send him my best. Ask him to tea if you like—any afternoon. He especially liked Cook's Sally Lunn cake, if I recall correctly."

Chapter 4

HALF AN HOUR LATER, AMES AND THE DOCTOR MADE THEIR way up along the steep brick sidewalk of Mt. Vernon Street to the top of Beacon Hill, where they turned down Joy Street toward Boston Common. A sharp west wind had blown away the previous evening's fog, and now the sun glowed on the redbrick town houses lining the way, each with its shining black shutters and gleaming brass door knocker. The sky was a deep blue that MacKenzie had never seen on the western plains, and carried on the sparkling air was an invigorating sea tang that he had never smelled before he came to Boston.

He watched his footing carefully, aided by his cane. He wore a stout overcoat, a bowler, and a worn muffler that he'd had for years. He'd been a little embarrassed about that muffler at first, until he'd seen that the Ameses, Boston Brahmins though they were, sported articles of clothing that were even older and shabbier than it. This morning, however, Ames looked smart in his gray tweed Inverness cape and black trilby. He tipped his hat now to a woman passing, and paused at the corner of Beacon and Joy to allow a delivery wagon to turn up the hill.

The Common lay before them, bare trees whipping in the

chilly wind, a few hardy nursemaids pushing perambulators. Beyond, across the Common, they could see the white spire of the Park Street Church; nearer, up the hill to the left, stood the redbrick, white-columned State House with its glittering golden dome. A line of handsome brick and brownstone town houses stretched on one side down Beacon Street, and on the other, down the steeper slope of Park Street.

"I need a moment at the Athenaeum, Doctor," said Ames as they started up Beacon Street. "It is on our way in any case, and I promised Professor Harbinger that I would pick up a particular volume for him before the expedition. Amazingly enough, the Harvard library did not have it."

"You will have a fascinating adventure over there," MacKenzie commented. He himself, before coming to Boston, had never been east of Pittsburgh.

"Yes," said Ames with some enthusiasm.

At the Athenaeum, a large, rather gloomy brownstone affair with, coincidentally, Egyptian detailing in its architecture, MacKenzie waited at the desk while Ames signed for his book. This place was, he knew, the haunt of many a Boston Brahmin; he could see a few of them now, early though it was, nodding over newspapers and periodicals in the high-ceilinged reading room that overlooked the slate and granite tombstones of the Old Granary Burying Ground.

Outside on the street once more, Ames gestured to their right. "Not far to go now. Inspector Crippen's lair is just down there, across Tremont Street beyond King's Chapel."

"Do you think he will—ah—object to your involving yourself in the case?" MacKenzie asked.

"Yes, I suppose he will. On the other hand, he is not a fool. So if he believes I can be helpful, why, then, he may listen to reason after all. He could do very little in any case to prevent my making my own inquiries, but I do not want to alienate the man."

They came to the corner of Tremont Street and waited to cross through the clogged traffic. A horse had gone down; its driver was whipping it ferociously. A little crowd had gathered, and a woman was berating him, ordering him to stop, but he ignored her.

They passed King's Chapel, a granite building with an oddly truncated tower, and came to the baroque, Second Empire pile that was Boston's City Hall—and its police headquarters.

Inside the massive oak doors, the atmosphere was hushed yet oddly busy. Coatless clerks hurried back and forth; once or twice a more senior official in dark coat and celluloid collar walked by. Once, MacKenzie saw a female, dressed in a dark skirt and white shirtwaist, sleeve protectors neatly fastened over her cuffs. She was, he thought, one of the new breed of women making their way in a man's world, and he felt sorry for her.

Crippen's department was on the second floor at the end of a long corridor. The office was busy, with several desks occupied by young men in mufti; one of them pounded away at a typewriting machine, making a distracting clatter.

On the opposite wall was a closed door, half glassed with opaque pebbled glass lettered with "Deputy Chief Inspector" in black. When Ames approached one of the secretaries and inquired for Crippen, the fellow nodded his head toward the door with a little grimace.

"Pretty busy right now, sir. Can I take a message?"

"No. I think, if you announce me, that he will see me," said Ames; he spoke smoothly but with a certain air of authority. He had that way about him, MacKenzie thought—of a man born to the highest class in this crowded little city, a man accustomed to not tolerating any nonsense from those whom he deemed his inferiors.

As the secretary hesitated, Crippen's door burst open and a harried-looking uniformed officer sped out, neglecting to close the door behind him.

Ames took his opportunity and went right in.

"Inspector! How are you this morning?"

The man whom he addressed stood behind an enormous desk piled high with papers; he was short, gray-haired, and softly rotund. He had a shrewd, ugly face unadorned by mustache or beard or sideburns; between his teeth he clenched a smoldering cigar that gave off a nearly overpowering stench. He wore a hideous brown checked jacket, a mustard-yellow waistcoat, and a green cravat, all a trifle too tight, so that he gave the effect of bursting out of them.

For a moment he stared blankly at Ames, not recognizing him. Then, removing his cigar from his mouth and depositing it in a battered metal ashtray, he broke into a welcoming smile, exposing a gap where his right eyetooth should have been. MacKenzie thought that the smile had something about it of a cat who had swallowed a canary.

"Mr. Ames! Well, I never! Just the man I wanted to see!" He came around his overflowing desk, hand outstretched, grasped Ames's, and pumped it heartily.

"I thought I would save you the trouble of calling on me at home," Ames said, smiling in return. "Although I should tell you that my sister would be happy to see you again. She wants you to come to tea any afternoon that you have a free hour."

"Does she, now?" Crippen smiled even more broadly. "Lovely lady, your sister. You going to allow me to court her, one of these days?"

MacKenzie found this remark tremendously offensive; it was all he could do to put on a polite face as Ames introduced him.

"Well, gentlemen, sit down, sit down," Crippen said, seemingly oblivious to the fact that Ames had not answered his question. He swept a pile of papers from one of the two wooden chairs facing his desk.

"Now, Mr. Ames, about this business last night," Crippen went on, taking up his position behind his desk but not sitting down, an action that might have removed him from sight.

"Yes, indeed, Inspector. It certainly is a business, isn't it?"

Crippen sighed. "And it was you who discovered him. I must say, Mr. Ames, you left his rooms in a state. Looked like a tornado hit in there. Why'd you do that, eh?"

The man in the corridor, Ames thought.

"I didn't," he replied. "The Colonel's rooms were in perfect order—more or less—when I left."

"Oh?" Crippen peered at him. "Then who tore 'em up like that?"

Ames shrugged. "I have no idea."

"I wish you had come to me directly," Crippen said. "As it is—"

"Don't tell me you are going to put me at the head of your list of suspects, Inspector." Ames was not quite smiling.

"Tell me why I shouldn't."

"Because—obviously—I didn't commit the crime." He was smiling a little now.

"Didn't you?" Crippen hooked his thumbs into his vest pockets and rocked back and forth on his heels.

Ames's smile faded. "Of course not, Inspector. If I had, I can assure you that I wouldn't be here."

"Do you happen to own a gun, Mr. Ames?"

"No."

MacKenzie did, but he had no intention of volunteering that information.

"The gun we saw on the Colonel's desk—" Ames began.

"Was not fired." Crippen contemplated him thoughtfully. "In my experience, Mr. Ames, the person who discovers the body is more often than not the person who done the deed. What do you say to that, eh?"

"To that—why, I say that it may very well be so. But not in this case."

Crippen contemplated him for a moment more. "All right. I'm going to believe you. For the moment, at least," he added. "But if you didn't go to see the Colonel last evening in order to put him out of his misery, so to speak, why were you there?"

"It was—a private matter."

"Come now, Mr. Ames. You can do better than that." Crippen spoke softly, but suddenly he seemed vaguely menacing.

"All right, then, a delicate matter. As you can imagine," Ames said. "But—in confidence—"

"You'll have to give a statement," Crippen broke in.

"Very well. I am perfectly willing to do that. But what I am about to tell you will not be in it. I went to retrieve—or try to retrieve—a certain packet of letters."

"Aha," said Crippen. "Did you get 'em?"

"Unfortunately, no."

"Letters belonging to—?" Crippen asked, squinting a little.

"A young lady of my acquaintance. A somewhat foolish young lady, I might add, and the letters were apparently just as foolish as she was when she wrote them."

"And the Colonel got hold of 'em," Crippen said.

"Yes."

"And wanted money for 'em."

"You seem well acquainted with his methods, Inspector. Have you had run-ins with him before?"

"No. But it's my business to know about men like him," Crippen said grimly, "and I do. So you searched for these letters?"

"I—looked for them, yes. I disturbed nothing, I assure you."

Crippen looked at him skeptically. "Nothing?"

"Nothing." How easily the lie came to his lips, Ames thought.

"You know for sure the fellow had 'em?"

"Yes. He had them yesterday afternoon, at any rate, as late as four o'clock. And so I assumed—"

"Yes, Mr. Ames? You assumed what?"

"That whoever killed him took them."

Crippen thought about it. "Possible," he said.

"And so if you should happen to discover them, I can assure you that the young lady would be most grateful to have them safely back."

"Evidence in a murder investigation—"

"I understand. But since my sister and I stand ready to help you in any way we can—"

"Now, how would that be, Mr. Ames?"

"Well—for instance—there is the matter of the galleys."

"The what?"

"The early proof sheets of what the Colonel was prepared to print in his paper. As I understand it, he showed them to the people whom he had—ah—marked for extortion, so that they could see exactly how they would be publicly exposed if they did not pay him what he demanded."

"Oh. Those." Crippen nodded confidently. "We have 'em."

"Do you, indeed? I did not see them in the Colonel's suite—"

"No."

"May I ask where you found them?"

"You may. But I can't tell you."

"Could I see them?"

"Oh, well, now, I don't know about that, Mr. Ames. That might be against regulations." Suddenly, Crippen grinned. "But if your sister were to come in, now, and ask—"

Ames shook his head. "Out of the question. This is no place for a lady."

Crippen shrugged. "Suit yourself. And now, if you will excuse me—"

Ames put out a hand. "Yes, Inspector. I'm going—and I will give a statement to your stenographer. One or two questions before I do, if you please."

"Well?"

"There was a door in the Colonel's room that led—I think—to a connecting suite. I tried it, but it was locked."

"Nothing unusual about that, is there?"

"No. Except that while it was locked, it was also unbolted on the Colonel's side."

Crippen shook his head. "We checked that out last night. No connection to the Colonel's death."

"You checked it out? But who rents that suite?"

"No one—I mean, no one pertinent."

"But who?"

"I can't give you that information."

A look passed between them.

"You must give me this much, Inspector," Ames said then. "I did perform my citizen's duty by reporting the Colonel's death. I could simply have left the hotel without notifying the manager, and consequently the Colonel's body might not have been found until hours later—possibly not until sometime today. That would have hampered your investigation, wouldn't you agree?"

Don't put his back up, MacKenzie thought. The inspector struck him as the type of man who was jealous of his authority and would not relish being forced to assent to obvious points made against him.

"Look here, Mr. Ames," Crippen said. "It's like this. If you—or your sister—know of anything that might help us in our investigations, you have an obligation to come forward."

"As I did last night, and as I have done again this morning."

"Correct. And just between the two of us—" He flicked a glance at MacKenzie.

"You may speak freely before the doctor," Ames said quickly.

"Just between the three of us, then," Crippen resumed. "You can be charged with withholding evidence—"

"Oh, nothing so serious, surely, Inspector. I am entirely ready to cooperate with you. Take the galleys, for instance. They will be filled with hints, and suppositions, and initials—never a complete name, I am certain. And how are the police—who, if I may say so, do not mingle in the circles the Colonel targeted—how are the police to decipher them? Because you may be sure that it was someone who was about to be exposed in the Colonel's newspaper who killed him. Someone who knew that public disgrace was imminent. And someone, therefore, who was desperate enough to visit him during his weekly open house, and—"

Crippen held up his hand. "Enough, Mr. Ames. I take your point."

"So you will let me have a copy?"

"I can't do that."

"Then let me see them, at least," Ames persisted.

Crippen pursed his lips. "I'll consider it. I make no promises."

"And if you should happen to turn up the letters—"

Crippen gave him a look.

"I would be in your debt," Ames finished.

Crippen blinked; he almost smiled. Apparently, MacKenzie thought, to have Addington Ames in his debt was an appealing prospect.

"We'll see, Mr. Ames. All in good time. And now—"

Someone rapped on the door.

"If you'll just speak to my sergeant," Crippen said, "the stenographer will be with you directly. Oh—and one more thing."

"Yes?"

"There will be an inquest."

Of course, Ames thought. He'd forgotten about that. "When?" he asked.

"Don't know yet. It's not up to us, it's the District Attorney who calls it. But you'll have to testify."

Ames thought of his expedition to the Valley of the Kings. A week from tomorrow.

"Certainly, Inspector."

They took their leave. In the outer office, Ames was handed over to a young man with a pad and pencil and escorted to a room down the hall. In less than half an hour he was back, and he and MacKenzie made their way out to the street once more.

"Not bad," said Ames. "It could have been worse. How is your knee?"

"Better than I expected," MacKenzie replied. He thought of Dr. Warren's instructions: plenty of rest, no strenuous activity. But he was bored with his convalescence, and this little adventure had piqued his interest.

"Good. Then we can call on someone who may well be of more help than Inspector Crippen—for now, at least."

CHAPTER
5

CAROLINE HAD STOOD FOR A MOMENT AT THE LAVENDER-glass bow window, watching her brother and Dr. MacKenzie make their way along the square toward Mt. Vernon Street. Dr. MacKenzie seemed to be mending rapidly, she thought. In her mind's eye appeared the portion of his anatomy that had been injured and on which Dr. Warren had operated; quickly she banished it. She knew what men's knees looked like, of course; but to think of Dr. MacKenzie's knee in particular unnerved her a bit. Such a nice man, she thought—and, unexpectedly, a good companion for Addington, who lived too solitary a life.

With a little sigh, she turned from the window. She had a busy day—and night—ahead, with no time to stand here, woolgathering about John MacKenzie. She liked him—yes. And beyond that— Well, she'd given up hope of any romantic entanglement years ago.

Dr. MacKenzie was a most delightful boarder—or guest, as she preferred to think of him. No more.

She'd started upstairs to her room when she heard the door knocker. She paused halfway up the curving staircase, her hand gripping the shining mahogany banister. No one called at this hour—except in some emergency like Val's, an hour earlier. Or perhaps it was another one of those dreadful men from the newspapers. Well, she wouldn't have to see him, and thank goodness Addington wasn't at home.

It was Val. She'd been all right when she'd left to go to Alice's, but now she walked in slowly past Margaret, almost as if she were in pain.

"Why—Val!" Caroline exclaimed, hurrying down. "What is it?"

Val stood immobile in the front hall.

"I—may I sit down?" she asked faintly.

"Yes, dear—of course—in the parlor—Margaret, please bring tea."

"Oh, Caroline, I am so embarrassed—"

"What's wrong, dear? What happened?" In the parlor, Caroline sat down beside her, took her hands, and began to peel off her gloves. Val's hands were very cold, and she chafed them a little.

"I—they wouldn't let me in," Val gasped.

"Who wouldn't? What are you talking about?"

"The butler at Alice's. He—he said Alice was not well, and she couldn't receive visitors today. It was her mother's orders, he said."

"Not well? But she is to go to the Cotillion this evening! And from what I gathered from her mother on Sunday, a very important young man will be there as well. Alice really shouldn't miss it."

"No. No, she shouldn't. But, Caro, you see—as I told you, Alice hasn't been well. When she came back from Newport in September, she looked terribly peaked. Mrs. Dane said that she and Alice had been to a funeral in New York, and Alice had taken it hard."

"Who died?" Caroline asked, momentarily distracted. Births and deaths were always of interest even if she didn't know the people involved.

Margaret knocked and entered with a tray. She looked

distinctly disapproving, Caroline thought, at this interruption of her morning routine.

"I'm not sure," Val replied when Margaret had left. "Some great-aunt or something."

She accepted a cup of steaming Darjeeling and wrapped her hands around it to warm them, lost for a moment in thought.

Then she said, "I don't think that Alice is ill at all, Caroline."

"What do you mean? If the butler said—"

Val shook her head. "I didn't believe him. I think he was lying."

"Lying! But why would he do that?"

Val took a sip or two. Then: "I think Mrs. Dane saw the morning papers."

Caroline understood at once: Addington, by discovering Colonel Mann's body, had become instantly notorious. And because Val was his cousin, so had she, even if people knew nothing about her own involvement with the Colonel.

"Mrs. Dane has always been so very careful with Alice," Val added.

Yes. Isabel Dane had been a most tyrannical parent to her only child. Overprotective, Caroline had thought, even beyond the normal bounds of strict protection under which all girls of good family were brought up. And yet, she was pushy—never bothering to hide the intensity of her search for the right young man for Alice to marry.

"And if she saw the news about Cousin Addington finding Colonel Mann's body—and I believe she did, she always reads the morning papers—she probably feels that we have scandal attached to us, and she doesn't want Alice to associate with me any longer. Or not, at least, until it blows over."

"But, Val, you and Alice have been best friends since you were barely out of walking strings!"

"I know."

"I think it's just outrageous!" snapped Caroline. "Don't they have any loyalty? If anything, they should rally round in time of trouble. That's when you know who your real friends are, when trouble comes."

"Oh, Caro, you mustn't blame Alice! It isn't her fault!"

Caroline heaved a sigh. What a mess! "I don't blame Alice, poor, weak little thing that she is," she said. "I know she's your dear friend, Val, and I mean no offense. But I do blame her mother. Isabel is from New Hampshire, and because of that I've always tried to make allowances for her. But this is too cruel! I imagine Alice isn't any happier about it than you are."

"No. But there is nothing she can do. Mrs. Dane is determined to make that marriage for her—"

"The warm young man she was so eager to tell me about," Caroline interjected.

"Yes. And if she believes that Alice's reputation will be harmed by associating with me, why, then, she will not allow Alice to see me. It is as simple as that."

"And as complicated," murmured Caroline. "Because to tell you the truth, Val, even a woman as ambitious for her daughter as Isabel Dane cannot insult people too much. People will learn of this, and they will not approve of it."

"Of course they will approve of it," Val said despairingly. "No one will want to be associated with me now! And the Putnams—"

She set down her cup, and Caroline put her arms around her and held her for a long moment. Then she gave Val a little shake and released her.

"Listen to me, Val! We cannot let someone like Isabel Dane upset you like this. I am going to take you upstairs now, and you will wash your face and perhaps even dust on a little of my rice powder—yes, just a touch—and then I will take you to Sewing Circle."

This was one of the many organizations that Caroline belonged to, and perhaps the most important: the Sewing Circle formed in her coming-out year, seventeen years before. Each year's crop of debutantes had one. They met once a week, and they would go on doing so until they died. The ostensible purpose of a Sewing Circle was to sew clothing for the poor, but its real purpose was to perpetuate those close bonds of family and friendship that united the Brahmin class. Two hours of sewing, followed by lunch, followed by another hour of sewing, all of it enlivened by genteel laughter and conversation, much of it gossip.

Caroline would have gone to this day's Sewing Circle if she'd had to be carried there on a stretcher; she could imagine the talk, this morning, about Addington's adventure with the Colonel. She must go, today of all days, to face her friends—and they were friends, for the most part—and let them see that although scandal had brushed the Ameses, it had not scarred them. Or not yet, at any rate.

And she would take Val with her—one guest per member per month was allowed. As yet, Val's only fault was that she was Addington's cousin; if worse came to worst, Caroline told herself, if Val's real connection to the Colonel came out, why, then, she would take Val again, as often as necessary to show that Val's family support was as strong as any. Val had her own Sewing Circle, of course, but it met on Thursdays. By then, who knew what she might have to face? Taking her along today would provide her with a kind of insurance.

A short time later, they marched down the steep slope of Pinckney Street, across Charles, and down to Brimmer Street, where today's gathering was to be held. The stiff wind off the river cut through Caroline's woolen jacket, and her stomach felt queasy, but she ignored it. Head high, bonnet ribbons fluttering, she walked briskly, as was her wont; straggling pedestrians, truant children, hustling delivery persons, did not deter her, for she swept past them, her skirts barely skimming the pavement, striding along in her stout new walking boots, a determined look on her face. She was, as MacKenzie had seen, the sweetest of women, the kindest and most generous; but she was a Boston woman, after all, and so when she had an urgent errand to perform, she strode swiftly and purposefully, and woe betide the man or beast who stood in her way. Val, trotting along beside her, struggled to keep up.

Caroline felt as though she were about to go into battle—as, in a way, she was. These friends whom she was about to confront were only human, after all, and so she knew they would delight in this small sensation in their rather constricted lives. She would have felt the same herself, she admitted, had scandal touched anyone else.

Mrs. Everett Crowninshield welcomed them, and a little silence fell as they appeared; then a genteel murmur of welcome flowed around the room. Caroline introduced Val to those two or three women who had not met her—there were fifteen women altogether—and settled herself with Val at her side. From her plush bag she took the shirt she was making for some unknown poor boy.

Val, having nothing to sew, sat with her hands clenched in her lap and responded politely to the few remarks addressed to her. Caroline, alert, knew that many surreptitious glances were being thrown their way; she knew that every woman in the room, although hesitant to bring up the subject directly, was acutely aware of Addington's adventure last night.

But then at last, Mrs. Eleazer Lodge—Emmie to her intimates—took advantage of a momentary lull in the conversation and said, "Caroline, dear, I saw your brother's name in the newspaper this morning."

They all understood that this was the equivalent of throwing down the gauntlet—a challenge to a duel. For people like themselves—proper people, the very best people—it was not proper at all to have one's name in the newspaper save for three occasions: one's birth, one's marriage (should that happy event take place), and one's death. Otherwise, people like themselves kept their names out of the newspapers, away from the vulgar eyes of the increasingly vulgar populace.

Caroline tensed; she paused for a moment in her sewing. "Did you?" she said, smiling thinly.

"Indeed I did. So very tiresome, to be involved in a—"

"Emmie, will you have more tea?" Mrs. Crowninshield broke in. It was rude to interrupt, she knew, but far more so to allow Mrs. Lodge to continue.

A faint rustling traveled around the room as the tension broke and the ladies rearranged themselves. Although they were all eager to know the details of Addington's connection to Colonel Mann, they were none of them—except for the intrepid Mrs. Lodge—bold enough to put the question to Caroline directly.

Mrs. Lodge declined the tea, but she persevered with her questions.

"Caroline, why did Addington go to see the Colonel?"

Caroline met Mrs. Lodge's glance steadily. She had known Emmie Lodge since childhood; she had never particularly liked her.

"It was private business," she replied, still with that thin smile.

Val clenched her hands in her lap. Dear Caroline—how brave she was, how splendid!

"Indeed?" Mrs. Lodge pursued. She was hot on the scent now and would not be put off. "I don't suppose you could tell us—"

"Emmie!" said Mrs. Crowninshield sharply. As hostess, she felt an obligation—a moral duty—to keep matters on a civilized plane. Here it was, not yet eleven o'clock, and the day was threatening to dissolve into the thrust and parry of a verbal duel, no less deadly for the lack of tangible weapons. Words alone, Mrs. Crowninshield knew, could be lethal enough. However would they get through lunch?

Mrs. Lodge turned her stern gaze upon her hostess. "I am merely asking a question, Amalia," she said.

"Perhaps your question is—"

"Too direct," Julia Norton interjected. She threw a warning glance around the room. "Or too personal," she added. "Really, Emmie, how can you—"

"Thank you, Julia," Caroline said. "It is all right. I understand that many people have an interest in—the events of last night. Perhaps," she added with gentle emphasis, "even many people in this room."

Several women flushed, and one of them turned bright red. Mrs. Lodge, temporarily defeated, fell silent. Then Ida Curtis, who as everyone knew had no more sense than a flea, piped up: "I think we can all be glad that we are rid of him." She meant, of course, not Addington Ames but Colonel Mann.

Several of the women glared at her, but that only prompted her to add: "Well, *I* am, at least! He was a dreadful man—dreadful! Blackmailing people—!"

"And how do you know about his blackmailing, Ida?" snapped Mrs. Lodge.

"I—I've heard tales."

"Indeed?"

"Yes!" Mrs. Curtis had been whipped up to a high pitch of defiance now, and she would not be deterred. "That awful Bradshaw case—do you remember? I always thought Colonel Mann was behind that. Pansy Bradshaw was the niece of my dearest friend, and to see her disgraced in that way—"

There was a moment of silence as they thought about the unfortunate Miss Bradshaw, who had departed Boston three years before and was rumored now to be living in Monte Carlo.

"I never knew exactly what happened," Mrs. Curtis went on, "but I am sure the Colonel had his hand in it. And if I ever find out who told him—" She looked defiantly around the room, a small, vengeful spirit in the midst of all that female propriety.

"There, there, Ida. Calm yourself," said Mrs. Crowninshield. She cleared her throat and spoke to the woman sitting next to her. "I wanted to ask you, Mary, if you would be kind enough to assist with the Thanksgiving baskets."

Her neighbor, who had been reflecting on the Colonel and his nefarious deeds, started. "The baskets? Oh, dear, I'm afraid I can't. I committed only last week to the Christmas Revels. And you know how much time that takes— Isabel demands rehearsals nearly every day, right up till the performance."

The Christmas Revels were a perfectly worthy cause, as they all understood: a charity performance, the proceeds of which went to a settlement house in the North End. Isabel Dane was in charge of them.

Mrs. Crowninshield did not mind being turned down; she had achieved her purpose, which was to turn the conversation away from the terrible Colonel and his misdeeds.

And that little success allowed her to keep on turning it, to the Cotillion tonight, and to the latest fashions—bustles were going out, sleeves were expanding at the shoulder— even, in the end, to that familiar and never-boring New England topic, the weather.

Caroline looked down at the shirt in her lap. The side seam was crooked; she'd have to rip it out and start over.

Three hours later, after a luncheon of *oeufs en gelée* and some kind of gussied-up scrod (Mrs. Crowninshield had recently acquired a French chef, much overrated, people agreed), Caroline and Val walked back up Beacon Hill to Louisburg Square. If Val was not entirely recovered from the pain of the affront she'd suffered that morning at Isabel Dane's, Caroline thought, she was at least well on the way.

They parted at the door of No. 16½; Val and Aunt Euphemia lived over toward the Common, on Chestnut Street.

"Get a little rest if you can," Caroline said, embracing her young cousin.

"Yes," Val replied.

"And we will all have a wonderful time tonight! Did Addington tell you what time we'd be picking you up?"

"Around nine, I think he said."

"Good. That will give you a chance to straighten your gown and make any little adjustments you need to make before the Grand March at ten."

"Yes."

"And you should eat a little something extra at tea. Supper won't be served until after midnight."

"I will."

Val turned away then and walked along the square to Mt. Vernon Street. Caroline gazed fondly after her. Never having had children of her own, she had always lavished affection on this orphaned cousin; she loved the girl as if Val were her own daughter, and she was determined not to let her be hurt any further by this dreadful business of the letters. Those Putnams *would* accept Val, she thought, scandal or no scandal.

With her face set in hard lines of determination that would have alarmed her brother, she mounted the little flight of granite steps to her door and went in.

CHAPTER
6

ON NEWSPAPER ROW, ON WASHINGTON STREET AROUND
the corner from City Hall, Ames led the way along the
crowded sidewalk, searching, until he stopped before a
doorway cluttered with a dozen small signs. "Here we are,"
he said, starting up the narrow stairway. "Let's hope he's
in."

MacKenzie lumbered behind; fortunately they had to go
up only one flight. Down a hallway they came to a door
labeled "Boston Literary Journal." Ames knocked, and
without waiting for an answer, opened it. They entered a
small office containing a desk and two tables, all piled high
with stacks of paper that looked like manuscripts. Seated
behind the desk was a man in his mid-thirties; he had the
reddest hair MacKenzie had ever seen, worn long over his
collar, and bright blue eyes in a thin, almost ascetic-looking
face decorated with extravagant mustaches that reached
down to his jawline. At once, he leaped to his feet.

"Ames!"

"Good morning, Desmond. Hard at work as usual, I
see."

They shook hands, and Ames said, "Doctor, this is my
good friend Desmond Delahanty. He is the proprietor of

this dubious enterprise, but you must not hold that against him."

"Delighted to see you, Doctor," said Delahanty. He spoke with a pronounced Irish accent. "I've heard all about you—oh, yes. Word gets around in a small place like Boston."

"You had a good trip?" Ames asked him. And to MacKenzie: "Desmond has just returned from his annual visit to Dublin to see his mother."

"Very good, yes. A calm crossing, for once. And of course I came back to this—" He indicated the blizzard of paper that inundated his office.

"So many hopeful scribblers," murmured Ames with a smile.

"Yes, but every now and again I find a gem. And what are you doing downtown at this hour, Addington? Consulting with the police?"

"You have seen the morning papers," Ames replied.

"Of course." Delahanty grinned. "Did you do the deed? If you did, I shall arrange a ceremony of appreciation for you."

Ames shook his head. "Don't let your imagination run away with you, Desmond. I had personal business to discuss with the Colonel, and I was most grievously disappointed to discover that he was in no condition to talk to me."

"Personal business? Surely not."

They settled themselves into rather rickety chairs, and Ames gave a brief explanation. "I cannot tell you the young lady's name, you understand. But I would like to see the galley sheets."

"To discover who visited him."

"Yes. And then to discover which of those visitors took the letters."

"You searched his rooms?" Delahanty asked, his eyes sparkling with mischievous interest.

"Briefly—and unsuccessfully."

Delahanty tipped his chair back precariously. "But why would someone take your young lady's letters?"

"If I knew that, I might know who the person is. I doubt it was a random choice. I suspect that the person who took them knew how to make good use of them. As I understand it, the Colonel always had a number of visitors on Monday evenings. I doubt the letters were taken while he was still alive; therefore, I must assume that the person who took them was either the person who killed him, or someone who came in afterward. For the moment, I thought that you might take us around to the Colonel's office to see what we can see."

"You will see the Colonel's assistant, I suppose, but he is little more than an office boy. I doubt he would know much."

"Still. He might be useful. But that brings me to another question, Desmond. The Colonel must have had a large network of—what shall we call them? Spies? And of course he constantly ran the risk of being sued for libel. How did he stay clear of the law?"

Delahanty nodded and smiled knowingly. "About the spies, I cannot tell you, but surely he must have had informants well placed everywhere. The man's knowledge was amazing! And as for the law—now, you won't find this documented anywhere, but it is known that the Colonel had a partner."

"How do you mean? A fellow blackmailer?"

"No. Not quite. But there is a man who advised him. Vetted his information before it was published. And for that very reason—to avoid a libel suit."

"A lawyer."

"Yes. I don't know his name. But whoever he is, he has done his job well. There has never been, as far as I know, any attempt to stop the Colonel."

"Until now," said Ames dryly. "Now he is stopped for good and all."

"We hope," amended Delahanty.

In a moment more they were descending the stairs to the street where, fifty feet along, a man pulled up short when he saw them.

"Delahanty!" he exclaimed. "As I live and breathe."

Delahanty, not offering his hand, gave him a wary look. "Babcock."

"Right the first time." Babcock grinned. He had a slovenly, disreputable look to him, hair mussed, overcoat unbuttoned, pockets bulging with bits of paper, cravat carelessly tied. "And your friends are—?" He gave Ames and MacKenzie a careful look, as if sizing up their worth to him.

With obvious reluctance, Delahanty introduced them. Babcock brightened when he heard Ames's name, and then a calculating look came over his face. "You could stand to make a nice sum of money, Mr. Ames, if you would speak to me."

"Watch out, Ames," Delahanty put in. "Babcock here is associated with the *Globe.*"

Ames lifted his chin and stared down his nose at the journalist. "No," he said.

"You're sure? We'll spell your name right, give you a front-page headline."

"Get away," Ames said. His gloved hand had curled into a fist, but he reminded himself that he was not on his own doorstep here. Still, the fellow was a perfect bounder. He deserved to have his ears thoroughly boxed.

Babcock held up his hands in a gesture of mock surrender. "All right. No need to get hot under the collar." He fished in the pocket of his voluminous overcoat and withdrew a grubby card. "Here I am, if you change your mind. Don't talk to the *Post,* they haven't a decent writer on their staff. 'Morning, Desmond."

Ames did not take the card, and so Babcock thrust it back into his pocket, offered a mocking half-salute to them, and loped on down the sidewalk.

Delahanty shook his head. "Damned offensive, those fellows. Whatever they're paid, it isn't enough to do such work. Come on, let's see what we find at the Colonel's bailiwick."

What they found was nothing: a surly youth who professed never to have seen a packet of six letters, and who whined that he didn't have the Colonel's galleys, either, because the police had taken them. He seemed to think of that action as a personal affront.

In ten minutes they were outside once more. Delahanty touched Ames's arm. "I can get you a copy of those galleys," he said.

"You can? How?"

"I use the same printer as Colonel Mann does—did, I mean. He's cheap—and fast. He'll run off a copy for me, see if he doesn't."

"That would be most helpful, Desmond. And now"—Ames glanced at the tall round clock on a post that stood at the edge of the curb—"it is nearly noon. What do you say we lunch at the St. Botolph? Perhaps we will hear something of interest."

AT THE LARGE COMMUNAL TABLE AT THE ST. BOTOLPH Club on lower Newbury Street, Ames leaned back in his chair to allow the waiter to put before him a plate of soup. It seemed to be cream of pumpkin. At the St. Botolph, you ate the menu for the day, whatever it was: boiled cod or baked beans or hash and eggs, plain Yankee food for plain-living Yankees, no matter how wealthy they were. Delahanty—an Irishman of modest means—had been admitted to membership (thanks to Ames's sponsorship, and over the objections of some of the older members) because he edited a literary magazine, for the members of the St. Botolph fancied themselves to be "artistic" as well as what, for the most part, they were in fact: highborn, plain-living Boston Brahmins.

The atmosphere of the place this day was rather different from the usual low-key male give-and-take and sotto voce trading of financial information. When Ames entered, there had been a moment of surprised silence, followed immediately by a volley of congratulations.

"Well done, Ames!" someone cried.

"Got the fellow at last!" cried someone else.

"Death to the Colonel!"

"Damned scoundrel! Hope he roasts in hell!"

Ames had paused in the doorway, scanning the larger than usual crowd; a small, almost complicit smile crossed his face as he nodded his greetings to them. Before he took his seat, a few of the members rose to shake his hand; clearly, MacKenzie thought, Ames was generally assumed to be the Colonel's killer and was, therefore, in this place at least, the hero of the hour. The St. Botolph Club had undoubtedly been rich hunting grounds for the Colonel; MacKenzie wondered how many men in this room had been forced to pay up to him.

Or, for that matter, whether one of them was the man Ames was looking for.

The newcomers sat down; the hum of general conversation resumed. Ames noted several bottles of champagne on the table—not a usual thing. He tasted his soup: not bad.

"Did you do the deed, Ames?" asked a red-faced, white-haired man sitting across the table. "Don't worry, we won't tell. We'll get up a purse for you—give you a medal!"

"Ames didn't do it," said another man. "No motive. No scandal in your family, right, Ames?"

"Acting for a friend, were you?" said someone else. "Decent of you. But who do you think might have done it?"

"The police will have enough suspects to keep them busy for some time, I should think," Ames replied easily, falling in with their jovial bantering. "And since I was—fortunately—accompanied by my friend, here"—their eyes turned briefly to MacKenzie—"I can say with some assurance that he will vouch for me. The Colonel had gone to his reward, whatever it will be, well before we arrived."

"But, seriously, Ames," the white-haired man said, "what do you think? Any ideas?"

A dark-haired man wearing a pince-nez and a waxed, "dandy" mustache spoke up. "Remember that case last spring? The man whose mistress betrayed him? What was his name? Winchester?"

A few of them nodded. "Yes—it was Winchester," someone said. "He's just filed for bankruptcy. But how about Garwood Royce? That was a messy affair, as I recall."

More murmurs of assent. Then other offerings came forth: the case of Esther Goodrich, and poor Mrs. Fielding, and the Morison girl, what was her name?

The conversation died down while the soup plates were removed and servings of wet, steaming cod and overdone vegetables were put in their place.

"And don't forget David Wilcox," someone said when the waiters had gone. "Where is he now? California?"

No one seemed to know.

"And what about the Bradshaw case?" offered the red-faced man who had first spoken. "I could never understand how Colonel Mann got that information. The Bradshaws were always so discreet."

"But not discreet enough," said Pince-nez. "Mark my words, gentlemen." He cast a warning look around the table, smiling in an unpleasant way. "Someone always knows. A disaffected servant, or an impecunious relative, or even a fellow club member. It's human nature! Someone will always be on hand to sell you out."

It was a dispiriting thought, and for a moment they ate in silence, digesting it along with their food.

Then Ames addressed a man who had not yet spoken; during the entire discussion, he had remained aloof. And yet, MacKenzie realized, he had been watching all of them, rather like someone closely observing a tribe of natives engaging in their primitive rituals.

"Professor?" asked Ames. "Can you enlighten us at all?"

The man whom he addressed was a slight, gray-haired individual with a high, domed forehead and a neatly trimmed beard. He had a look about him of ferocious intelligence, but more than that, of an avid curiosity, as if he burned to know everything about them—perhaps even more than they knew about themselves.

Delahanty whispered to MacKenzie: "William James."

It was a name MacKenzie knew, and he looked at the professor with more interest. James's monumental work on the principles of human psychology had come out the previous year, and its fame had penetrated even into the wilderness of the western plains.

Professor James smiled a little and dabbed his mouth with his napkin, which he placed neatly on the table beside his empty plate.

"*Schadenfreude,*" he said.

Ames tilted his head slightly. "Of course. But beyond that—?"

James glanced around the table; like the good professor he was, he wanted to make sure that everyone understood him. "*Schadenfreude*—German is the language of science, so beautifully precise—means taking delight in someone else's sorrows. That is what gave the Colonel his power, of course. Pride, shame, fear—the opinion of those whom we allow to judge us—those were what he traded on."

"Yes, well, that's true enough," said Pince-nez impatiently. "But what about who killed him? What do you think about that?"

James shrugged slightly, as if the matter were of no importance to him. "There is a criminal type—the Italian, Lombroso, has described him very well. If I could examine each one of you, take a look at your skulls, the shape of your heads—that might tell me something. Or, at least, Signor Lombroso thinks it might. I imagine the late Colonel's skull would be an interesting thing, filled with telltale bumps and hollows." He was smiling broadly as he spoke; he held up his hands and wiggled his fingers suggestively. They were broad, strong-looking hands, not what one would expect the hands of a world-famous scholar to be.

"But seriously," said Pince-nez, "who do you think—"

"Motive," said James succinctly. "But then again, as you have said, obviously half of Boston had a motive for the crime. So the police will have to narrow it down to whoever had not only the motive but also the opportunity—and the means."

There was a slight shift in the atmosphere of the room, an uneasiness, as the members glanced at one another. Which of us does he mean?

"And that man will prove to be, I think—"

They hung on his words, every eye trained on him.

"—the man most threatened by the Colonel, and therefore the man with the most to lose. I must return to Cambridge. Good-day to you, gentlemen."

With a final nod around the table, he left them. There was a little silence after he went, as if his calm, dispassionate words had somehow deflated the balloon of everyone's fancies.

The luncheon broke up not long afterward. People shook hands, made appointments, wandered off to the afternoon's business. In the lobby, while Ames and Delahanty made their arrangements, MacKenzie studied the posted announcements of upcoming events. The club's annual Art Show, he noted, was to have its opening reception on Saturday afternoon. And next week, on Tuesday evening, the noted journalist and world traveler, Godfrey Orcutt, was to give a talk. Both, he thought, might be interesting; he had lived for so long in the western wilderness, cut off from the amenities of civilization, that he felt starved for events like these.

"You'll have those galleys—when?" Ames asked Delahanty.

"I'll stop at the printer's on my way back to the office," Delahanty replied. He noticed MacKenzie studying the announcement board. "Orcutt's talk should be interesting, Doctor, if you're free. He's a real adventurer—as much as Henry Morton Stanley ever was. His dispatches about his journey up the Amazon were fascinating."

He glanced at the wall clock—it was five minutes till two—and turned back to Ames. "I've an appointment at three with a lady scribbler, heaven help me. But I've time for the printer before I see her, and if he's not too busy, perhaps I'll have them by tonight. I'll bring them around."

Y OU—YOU TOOK THIS FROM HIM?" EDWIN REDPATH'S face was long-chinned and sallow, framed by heavy Dundreary whiskers—and, just now, blank with shock. His eyes, however, betrayed a glimmer of relief as he fingered the check—his own check, made out to Colonel Mann—that Ames had just handed to him.

"Yes," Ames replied.

They were in the dim, high-ceilinged library of Redpath's mansarded town house on Commonwealth Avenue.

"But—how did you—" Redpath was known as a hard man of business; it was odd to see him so disconcerted.

"I was looking for something," Ames replied shortly. "In the course of doing so, I came across your check."

Redpath's face sagged a little, and his eyes became watery. "I am rather pressed for cash at the moment, but the fellow was going to print his filth—"

"You saw what he was going to publish?" Ames interrupted. "He showed you the galley proofs?"

"Yes." Redpath took out his handkerchief and loudly blew his nose.

Ames wondered if he should tell him that the Colonel's rag might come out after all—unedited—albeit a bit late.

"So you went to him about what time?" Ames asked.

"About five-thirty."

"You're sure?"

"Yes. I had another appointment at six."

"And the Colonel was in good health when you saw him?"

"Damn his soul—yes, he was in fine fettle."

"Happy to have your money, of course," Ames murmured. "And you say he had the galley."

"Yes."

"Did you see anyone else while you were there? Anyone going in or out?"

Redpath nodded. "I did, as a matter of fact."

"Can you describe him?"

"It was a woman. She was coming toward the Colonel's rooms as I left."

"Did you see her go in?"

"Yes."

"And her appearance—?"

"Sable cloak," Redpath said, remembering. "Must have cost someone a pretty penny."

"Was she tall? Short?"

"Oh, quite tall. And very handsome."

"Age?"

"Not more than thirty."

"Did she seem upset? Fearful?"

Redpath shook his head. "No. She seemed—angry. And she had an imperious air, as if she were used to being noticed and didn't seem to mind it," he added disapprovingly.

Ames nodded, but before he could reply, Redpath spoke again. "And I can tell you this, although I don't know how helpful it will be. Before I myself went in to see the Colonel, as I stood at his door—I had already lifted my hand to knock—I heard him speaking to someone."

"Ah." Ames leaned forward in his chair, his fine dark eyes alight with interest. "Man? Woman?"

"Man. I couldn't make out exactly what was being said, but both voices were angry."

"You saw him as he came out?"

"No." Redpath blinked a few times, as if only now he realized the implication of what he said. "No, I did not, come to think of it. The argument stopped. I waited a moment, and then I knocked. Colonel Mann—damn him!—called 'Come!' and I went in."

"And—"

"He was alone."

Ames sat back with a small nod of satisfaction, but he said nothing.

"Now, that is odd, isn't it?" said Redpath. "It only just now strikes me. What do you make of it?"

"Nothing, for the moment."

"Do you—*did* you have business of your own with that damned rascal? But obviously you did, or you wouldn't have been there."

"I was there on behalf of a young friend," Ames said. "A packet of her letters had fallen into the Colonel's hands, and I had agreed to try to get them back. You didn't see them, by any chance?"

"No."

Ames shrugged. "I didn't suppose so."

"I am eternally grateful to you, Ames," Redpath said fervently. "You have saved me a good deal of embarrassment."

"I should warn you that you may see the police," Ames said, and he told Redpath about the Colonel's ledger. "I am reasonably sure that the check mark indicated you paid. So if the police manage to figure that out—"

Redpath shrugged. "I'll deny everything. They can't

prove I paid—can't prove I was there, for that matter." He held up the check and with great deliberation tore it in half and tore the halves again.

"True." Ames nodded. "And this meeting between us today did not happen."

"Of course it didn't."

"You can instruct your butler?"

"Certainly. He's been with me for years."

They took their leave. The westering sun sinking behind the buildings in the distance made long shadows of the spindly trees along the mall, and people hurried along in the freshening wind as twilight came on. It would be a chilly night for the young ladies dressed in their finery for the Cotillion, Ames thought, and he sighed to himself, thinking of a lost evening when he might have been reading by the fire in his study. He loathed big "do's" like this; only for Val would he subject himself to the discomfort of his patent-leather dress shoes and long-tailed evening coat.

"You're sure you want to go through with this affair to-night?" Ames said, casting a wary glance at his companion. His sister had invited the doctor to attend.

"Oh, absolutely," MacKenzie replied. "Most kind—most kind—"

Ames grimaced; it might have been a smile. "You'll have a headache from the noise and a bad digestion from the supper—if you can get any in the crush. And sore feet— No. You won't be dancing, that's one advantage you'll have over the rest of us."

But I might try, thought MacKenzie.

They took a herdic back to Louisburg Square, and by the time they arrived it was nearly dark. Lights gleamed from the windows of the tall brick town houses that surrounded the little oval of greenery in the center, and as they alighted they caught the delicious odor of roasting lamb from someone's areaway. Not from the Ameses', however; an extra-large tea would suffice this day, Caroline had said: "They put on a splendid supper at the Cotillion, and we don't want to spoil our appetites."

She was a frugal woman, MacKenzie thought approvingly. Not stingy, but frugal. His spirits lifted as he saw her now, glancing out at them through the lavender-glass bow window.

Ignoring the warning throb in his knee, he followed his landlord into the house.

CHAPTER 7

As the two men entered the parlor, they were followed almost immediately by Margaret with their tea.

"Well, Addington?" Caroline asked. "What happened? Hello, Doctor."

She looked a little disheveled and she put her hands to her hair, trying to smooth it.

"I misplaced my ivory fan," she said, laughing. "And I only just found it—in a box on the top shelf of the closet in the guest room. I can't imagine how it got there."

She looked younger than usual, MacKenzie thought, and prettier, too, with her face slightly flushed, her hair slightly disarranged. In the hissing light of the gas jets, her eyes seemed to have a special glow. He eyed the tea tray, which was unusually full: scones and Sally Lunn, of course, but small watercress sandwiches, too, and a plate of cold sliced ham, and a heavy-looking concoction, brandied fruit cake.

Caroline sat down to pour, but she couldn't refrain from looking up at her brother and asking, "Did you see Inspector Crippen?"

"Yes," he replied, helping himself to a plate of food. Despite his lunch at the St. Botolph, he was hungry; he put it down to nervous tension.

She gave him his tea. "Well? What did he say? Was he—receptive?"

"To any mention of you, Caro, yes, indeed." Ames smiled at her. "You have made a conquest, you know."

She shook her head at him dismissively. "Don't say that. He is—well, you know what he is. Did he give you any information? Oh—Doctor—I am so sorry. Here is yours," she added, handing him his cup.

Just one of those scones, he thought, mindful of his spreading girth. He took one and spooned on it a dollop of shimmering ruby-red currant jelly from a cut-crystal bowl.

"Not in particular," Ames said. Briefly, he told her about their day—omitting the visit to Edwin Redpath—and as he finished, they heard the front door knocker.

"That will be Delahanty," said Ames; they heard Margaret's delighted voice, and then laughter. Delahanty, indeed, MacKenzie thought.

He came in carrying a folded sheet of paper. "Miss Ames—Addington—Doctor—here it is." He handed it to Ames, who unfolded it and began at once to study it.

Meanwhile Delahanty settled himself and accepted tea. He was ruddy-faced, as if he had walked briskly in the evening chill; he wore a long, knitted blue muffler which he had not bothered to remove when he came in.

Caroline made polite conversation with him for a moment, but she was longing to examine the Colonel's galley sheet for herself. After a few moments, Ames made an exasperated sound and handed it to her.

"Here, see what you can make of it. Fourth line from the end seems to be the reference to—what we were looking for," he amended, remembering that Delahanty, good friend that he was, was nevertheless not privy to their young cousin's troubles.

It was, she saw, a venomous list of initials, hints, innuendos. And, yes, there was Val—"V.T."—near the bottom.

"The amorous correspondent," Colonel Mann had dubbed her. And if the Putnams ever saw that—!

"Yes," she said, "I think you are right, Addington. Oh, that terrible man!"

She looked up at them, her soft brown eyes startlingly alive with anger. "Dare I say that I am glad he is dead? I do say it. Look at the harm he does—"

"No more," said Delahanty with a smile.

As if she had not heard him, she said, "And look at this, Addington! 'Mrs. T.C. is known for her impetuous behavior—too much tripping the light fantastic.' " She glanced up at them. "Do you know what that means?"

"No," said Ames.

"It refers to that silly woman, India Choate. She has been married these ten years, and still she flirts with every man in shoe leather. I cannot imagine why her husband does not curb her."

"If her indiscretion is so well known, how could the Colonel hope to embarrass her?" Delahanty asked.

"This is a somewhat more serious matter, I believe," Caroline replied. "I heard only the other day that her husband was threatening to divorce her—*divorce* her, can you imagine? Apparently she made an absolute spectacle of herself at the Homans' ball two weeks ago. And here, Addington! Look at this! 'Mrs. B.K. has a very clever son—too clever, perhaps, even for the authorities at his college.' Now, what can that mean?"

Ames thought of the letter that he had found in the Colonel's desk—a letter from a "G.K." pleading with the Colonel for mercy. He shook his head. Who knew the heart of another? Every man—and woman—had a dark side, hidden for the most part, exposing itself from time to time to put its owner in danger.

Caroline had returned to the galley, shaking her head, uttering little *tsks* of outrage at each new item whose subject she could identify.

"Mr. B.P.," she read, and then looked up. "The Paddocks left last week for South Carolina. I wonder if— And here, Addington! Look at this— 'A noted—or should we say notorious—lady thespian should leave that racing fellow and his cronies.' " She looked up at them. "Do you know who *that* is?"

"Mrs. Vincent, I imagine," Delahanty said.

"Of course. Who else could it be? Colonel Mann ruined her once, so why can he not let her alone now?"

Ames thought of Redpath's description of the woman in a sable cloak.

At MacKenzie's curious look, Delahanty explained: "Do you like the theater, Doctor? Yes. So do I. One of the ornaments of the stage here in Boston is a most beautiful lady— ah, well, Miss Ames, I don't suppose she *is* a lady anymore, is she? Howsoever. She is, or was, a member of a Boston family as fine as the Ameses, here. And then about five years ago, the Colonel discovered something scandalous about her—an adulterous affair—and printed it in his paper. Her husband divorced her, she was thrown out without a penny, and everyone expected her to starve in some dreary room in the South End. Instead"—and here he laughed—"she went on the stage and made a great success of it. She's the resident star at the Park Theater. Of course, that's not something a proper lady should be, but I suppose she thought that under the circumstances, no more harm could be done to her reputation than the Colonel had done already. She's very popular. Have you seen her new thing, Addington? *Lady Musgrove's Secret,* it's called. I saw it the other night. She's a fine figure of a woman, I'll say that for her."

Caroline might have taken offense at this, but she did not. "Serena Vincent was always beautiful," she said mildly. "Serena Sohier, she was, before she married. I remember when she came out, she was the 'bud' of the year. Everyone predicted a glorious marriage for her. And then she surprised us all by marrying Samuel Vincent—"

"And lived to regret it," Delahanty interjected.

"Oh, yes. It was a mistake from the first. We all understood that; we wondered why she didn't. And now, of course, no one receives her, no one even admits to knowing her. Poor woman!"

She shuddered. She herself could never have withstood disgrace as bravely as Serena Vincent had done, but Mrs. Vincent had come out of it seemingly unscathed. What scars remained on her heart, her soul, were not for the world to see.

"She travels in fast circles now, from what I hear," Delahanty said.

At last Caroline let the galley fall to her lap, and with a murmured word, Delahanty took it and began to read. She looked up at Ames. "Tonight at the Cotillion, Addington—"

"Yes."

"That pearl." She shook her head. "I *know* I've never seen it before. But tonight, perhaps—" She broke off with a bitter little laugh.

"I had intended to enjoy myself this evening," she went on. "I always do at these affairs. The girls are so lovely in their dresses—thank goodness, post-debutantes don't have to wear white, the way the 'buds' do—but now, if I must look for that pearl . . ."

She turned to their visitor. "You have been most kind, Mr. Delahanty. We are very grateful to you."

"Not at all, ma'am." Tactfully, like the good friend that he was, he made no embarrassing inquiries—about the pearl or anything else.

She fell silent for a moment, thinking. MacKenzie was distressed to see a sharp little vertical line appear between her brows; he wished he could say something to erase it.

"Addington!" she said suddenly.

"Yes?"

"How do you suppose the Colonel got all his information?"

Ames thought of the bleak words the member at the St. Botolph had uttered: *"Someone will always be on hand to sell you out."*

"He had his informants," he said simply.

"But who? Who would be vile enough to go to him with private information, things no one should ever know—"

"Servants," said Delahanty. "Impoverished relations. There are many people who—"

"No," she said. She looked away, thinking about it. "Some of that material"—she waved her hand at the galleys, which Delahanty still held—"is not so very private, I grant you. But other things—like the Bradshaw case, Addington. How did the Colonel get his hands on that? It is impossible to understand how he—" She wrestled with it for a moment. "Addington," she said then, and her voice was choked a little. "Think what it means!"

"Yes, Caro. I have done so."

"It means—" She looked around at the little circle of faces, three good and decent men, any one of whom she would have trusted with her life—or with her darkest secrets, had she had any.

"It means that no one is to be trusted, Addington! It means that we are betrayed on all sides—by our friends, by the servants who live with us, even by our families! I cannot believe it. I refuse to believe it!"

He contemplated her from beneath his dark brows; on his long, lean face was an expression very much like pity. "Apparently you must believe it, my dear."

She closed her eyes for a moment, as if she were in pain. Then she looked around at them again, and it seemed to Ames—to all of them—that iron had suddenly entered into her soul.

"Someone in Boston Society," she said, "someone whom we see all the time, perhaps even someone who is well known to us—is a spy."

CHAPTER 8

CAROLINE KNEW FROM THE MOMENT SHE ENTERED THE ballroom that this evening would be a difficult one. Her corset, for one thing: she'd had to lace it tight—too tight— in order to fit into her only ball gown, a gray silk affair, trimmed in Valenciennes lace, that she hadn't worn since before her mother died. She was going to grow even more plump in her old age, she just knew it; she doubted she would have the strength of character to lace tightly enough, as the years passed, to fit into all her clothing. Styles would change, of course, but she would happily wear her old clothes as long as they lasted, if only she didn't have to lace more tightly to fit into them.

Even more troublesome than tight lacing, however, was the reception she was getting here tonight. Ordinarily, on these occasions, she was effusively greeted by dozens of friends and acquaintances and near and distant relations— people she'd grown up with, people she'd known all her life. With no sense of self-importance, she knew they liked her; for the most part, she liked them back.

Tonight, however, was going to be different. People greeted her, yes, but she saw the suspicion in their eyes, she sensed their lack of enthusiasm as they spoke to her.

She fixed a brilliant smile on her face and proceeded through the crowd. She was looking at the women's jewelry. So far, she'd not seen anyone wearing pearls that matched Addington's sketch.

The hall was warm and noisy; MacKenzie, under his gray wool sack suit, was perspiring as he followed her. Surreptitiously, he removed his handkerchief from his breast pocket and mopped his brow. As happy as he was to have this time with her, he was nevertheless uncomfortable in this setting and not just because of the heat. He hadn't been to a dance in years; he wasn't sure of the proper etiquette. His knee felt all right, though; he'd ask her to dance, he thought, before the evening was done.

The girls and their escorts were taking their places for the Grand March that was to open the ball.

"There is Alice Dane," Caroline said, as much to herself as to MacKenzie. "And her father," she added.

MacKenzie looked, but he was unable to make out which couple she referred to. They all looked alike to him. He murmured something in reply, but in her mind she had moved on, and she didn't hear. She had started toward the stairs to the balcony, where she and MacKenzie would watch the procession, when an imposing figure of a woman caught her eye.

"There!" she said. "There is Alice's mother. I am going to speak to her."

Over near the chaperones' row, Isabel Dane was deep in conversation with two women who, like Caroline, served on the dance committee; undoubtedly, Caroline thought, Isabel was finding fault with something.

"Hello," she said, smiling brightly at the three of them. She noted that the other two looked relieved as she approached; in the next moment, they melted away and Caroline was left alone with Isabel Dane.

That lady was an impressive personage, tall and solid, wearing an excessive amount of jewelry—no pearls—to ac-

cent her mauve shot-silk evening gown. Her heavy jaw tightened as she greeted Caroline, and she seemed to tilt a bit, as
if she hovered, waiting to make a hasty exit.

"I was sorry to hear that Alice was not well this morning,
Isabel," Caroline began. "Is that warm young man going to
be here tonight?"

Mrs. Dane's eyes were chilly. "Yes," she said. "Now, if
you will excuse me, Caroline—"

"Wait." Caroline put her white-gloved hand on Mrs.
Dane's arm, which was similarly covered, up to beyond the
elbow, with white kid. This gesture, they both understood,
was somewhat too familiar under the circumstances. "I need
to speak to you, Isabel. Did you send Val away this morning
because of what you read in the newspaper about Addington?"

At this direct assault, Mrs. Dane's jaw tightened more
and her mouth twitched. "I have always liked Valentine—
you know I have—but at the moment we must be very careful of Alice's reputation." Her hefty shoulders lifted in a
slight shrug. "I don't make the rules, Caroline. I simply try
to follow them. This young man is a superb match for Alice.
I don't want anything to endanger it."

"But it wasn't Val's fault that Addington's name was in
the newspaper!" exclaimed Caroline. Mentally she crossed
her fingers.

"I don't say that it was. But that is beside the point. He is
her closest male relation—he has escorted her here this evening. The connection cannot be denied."

"Of course it can't. But still—"

For a moment, Caroline thought she detected the faintest
hint of pity in Mrs. Dane's eyes.

"Give it a few weeks, Caroline. By that time, if all goes
well, Alice will be formally engaged. He means to ask her
father for her hand any day now, I am sure of it." Now Mrs.
Dane's eyes gleamed with the anticipation of her triumph.

"I congratulate you," murmured Caroline. "And if I

understand you, Val will be welcome again when Alice has safely made her catch."

"He is a splendid catch," Mrs. Dane replied. "Worth anything necessary to get him."

"Even hurting Val's feelings?"

"Nonsense! Val's feelings don't need to be hurt. Wait a bit, Caroline. For the engagement to be confirmed, for this business—whatever it is—of Addington's with the Colonel to blow over. And then all will be as it was."

No, thought Caroline; it won't. Friendship was not something that could be put aside, even temporarily.

"Excuse me," said Mrs. Dane, her gaze darting beyond Caroline. "There is Elizabeth Dwight. I must ask her about her musicale next week." And with no more of an adieu than that, she moved majestically away, leaving Caroline to seethe with righteous anger.

The nerve of the woman! To cast Val aside like that, when the girls had been friends for life! She scanned the room. Yes, there was Alice now—and a pale, washed-out little thing she was, compared to Val's dark, vivid beauty. How much was this warm young man worth, Caroline wondered, that Isabel was willing to behave so badly to get him?

"Come, Doctor," she said grimly. "They are about to start the Grand March."

They made their way up the stairs to the balcony and sat on spindly chairs close to the railing, where they had a good view of the proceedings. The marchers were in place; the orchestra leader tapped for silence, brought down his baton, and the music began.

For a time, Caroline forgot her anger with Isabel Dane as she gazed at the spectacle below. There—there were Addington and Val, the handsomest couple by far. Val looked outrageously beautiful in a violet-blue gown trimmed in black velvet, and, at her neck and ears, her mother's pearls (smooth and round, no gold filigree cap). She seemed to have banished her fears, and now she held her head high as she moved along in the stately procession, looking as though she hadn't a care in the world. There were perhaps twenty young women and their escorts in the march; they made their way down the staircase and took their places on the dance floor. When the music ended with a flourish, the men bowed and the girls curtsied, first to the men and then to the onlookers, who applauded vigorously.

And then, at last, the dancing began. The young women danced first with their partners of the march, and then with the partners named on each girl's dance card. Caroline studied the dancers swirling around the floor, her kid-gloved fingers tapping the rhythm of the music. Briefly, her thoughts swept back to the time, many years before, when she had made that procession on her father's arm and afterward had danced the night away. And the last dance, the dance just before they'd gone in to supper, had been with a tall, fair young man with a wistful smile and a way of looking at her that made her heart long for him. . . .

Stop it. She met Dr. MacKenzie's eye and felt herself flush. Then one of the women on the committee came to speak to her and she was saved from her reminiscences.

Half an hour later, the evening proceeding well, she stood up. "Shall we venture down, Doctor?" she said. "I must circulate for a time, I fear."

"You go ahead." He hated what she called circulating; he'd never been fluent at small talk.

Downstairs, she moved for a time around the edges of the dance floor, and then she saw Addington's tall figure making his way toward her. He was carrying two cups of punch; he gave one to her.

"How goes it?" he asked.

"Badly," she gloomed. "Isabel Dane is a perfect—oh, I can't think of a name to call her!"

"Bully," he supplied. "That's what she is—a bully. Her daughter will do well to marry and get free of her."

"Yes." Caroline sipped her punch. "How is Val?"

"Very well. No one has cut her, and that's something."

They gazed for a moment at the dancers. Val was doing her best with a short, plump young man who was known among the younger set as a "card."

"Where is George?" Ames asked.

"Over there, with his mother."

Caroline caught Mrs. Putnam's eye, nodded, and looked away.

"Are you going to speak to her?" Ames asked.

"I must, sooner or later. But not just yet." She smiled up at him. "I saw you in the Grand March, Addington. And dancing afterward—you and Val were the handsomest couple on the floor."

He made a small moue of distaste. At Crabbe's he fenced regularly with grace and skill; he knew it, and he enjoyed it. Dancing was something else.

"Look at them all," he said. "Dancing as if they hadn't a care in the world. And all the while—"

All the while, underneath this glittering facade, lay scandal and ruin. Every week, these people, or people just like them, were—had been, he corrected himself—exposed to the Colonel's blackmail; every week, these people, orpeople just like them, had committed some indiscretion—or worse —that made them vulnerable to the Colonel's rapacious greed.

She knew his thoughts; she always did. "Yes," she said. "Hard to believe, isn't it?"

A petite, brightly smiling woman approached; she wore a black silk gown and many diamonds.

"Hello, Caroline. Mr. Ames."

It was Marian Trask, a little blackbird of a woman with shining black hair, bright black eyes, and a perky manner; some few years older than Caroline, she was one of the women known in Boston Society as "smart." This meant that she'd kept her figure, kept her sense of style, and refused to allow herself to age, gracefully or not, as so many

Boston dowagers did. It would be years before she was considered a dowager, but it was obvious that she intended to avoid the appellation as long as she could.

Anticipating female chatter, Ames greeted her and excused himself.

"This is a splendid turnout, isn't it?" Mrs. Trask chirped to Caroline. "I see your pretty young cousin—such a lovely girl, isn't she?"

"We think so," Caroline replied.

"The wedding is when?"

"May."

"Ah. Well, she'll make a lovely bride." Mrs. Trask's busy brain hopped to its next thought. "Agatha needs clothing," she said. "Might your church have anything extra?"

She referred to Agatha Montgomery, proprietress of a home for fallen women over in the South End.

"Really?" Caroline replied. "She didn't tell me that when I saw her last week. We might have some," she added.

"Thursday is my afternoon there," Mrs. Trask said. She and Caroline and others in their circle tutored Miss Montgomery's charges. "If you could let me know before then, so that I can tell her?"

Caroline scanned the room as Mrs. Trask moved away. She thought of Agatha's girls—so worn, so dejected—and compared them to these lively young women before her. Life, she thought: it's all luck.

Then she came back to the important business of the evening. Pearls: who is wearing pearls?

Nearly every one of the post-debs, it seemed; modest and not too showy, pearls were the thing for unmarried young women. Among the older women, relatives and chaperones, the display was more varied: diamonds, emeralds, a few rubies worn by the more daring. Nothing was new; as Caroline had said, Boston ladies did not buy their jewelry, they simply had it, passed down through the generations, occasionally reset, hardly ever purchased.

No. She couldn't see anything that looked remotely like the single pearl Addington had shown her.

A young man was coming her way. Their eyes had met; it was too late for him to pretend he hadn't seen her.

"Miss Ames."

"Hello, George."

George Putnam was tall and heavyset with a pale complexion and a wary air—a Putnam family trait. Caroline often had to remind herself, for Val's sake, that wariness was not the worst quality in a prospective husband; at the very least, George would never lose his money in some rash speculation.

He took her small hand in his large one and released it immediately.

"Val is pretty tonight, isn't she?" Caroline said.

"Oh—yes, she is," George replied, as if that observation hadn't occurred to him.

"I haven't had the chance to speak to your mother," she said. "Will you come with me while I do so?"

He hesitated, and then he realized she'd seen his hesitation, and he blushed.

"Thank you, George," she said swiftly. She put her hand on his arm and moved toward the place along the wall where his mother sat.

As she approached, she felt Josephine Putnam's gaze boring into her. Go ahead, she thought, look me over. And I will do the same to you.

"Hello," she said, planting herself in front of the unsmiling woman who was Val's prospective mother-in-law. "What a good turnout tonight, isn't it?"

Mrs. Putnam looked Caroline up and down before she replied. "Yes, it is," she said; she did not smile, did not invite Caroline—as she should have done—to sit with her.

"And Val looks perfectly lovely, doesn't she?" said Caroline. She lifted her chin and stared down her nose at Mrs. Putnam, who, after a moment, looked away.

"I hadn't noticed," Mrs. Putnam said.

Caroline felt as though she'd been slapped. *Hadn't noticed!*

"There she is now," she said, trying without success to keep the anger from her voice. "Just there, by the orchestra."

Mrs. Putnam ostentatiously looked in the other direction. Caroline, for the first time in her life, understood what people meant when they said their blood boiled.

"Good evening," she said abruptly, and turned away. She was so angry that she was trembling. Oh, that terrible woman! She would regret this—Caroline would see to it that she did! Insulting Val, insulting all of them—!

Halfway back to Dr. MacKenzie, she allowed a heretical thought to come into her mind. If the Putnams were to shun Val in the wake of Addington's unfortunate encounter with Colonel Mann, would that be the worst thing in the world to happen? Only that morning she had begged Addington to try to find Val's letters, and all because she hadn't wanted Val's marriage to George to be endangered. Had she been right to do that?

She sighed and shook her head as she climbed the stairs to the balcony to rejoin the doctor. It was all so complicated!

MacKenzie screwed up his courage. "What do they call this one?" he asked, meaning the name of the dance. People were galloping about energetically in time to the music—not a waltz; he wouldn't dare try it.

"The Boston," she said, and laughed at his expression. "It's very athletic, isn't it? I used to do it, but I wouldn't try it now."

"Perhaps—if we get something more—ah—sedate—you would favor me?" he asked. He heard himself stammer a bit, and he berated himself. She'd never accept if he sounded like such a dolt! Had she even understood what he'd meant?

But to his relief, she did understand, she did accept. She snapped open her fan, fluttered it a few times, and said, "That would be lovely, Doctor. Thank you."

A few moments later, they made their way down to the dance floor. While the hippity-hop thing continued to its end, he waited while she spoke to this person and that. She knew everyone, it seemed.

Across the floor, he saw Ames. With a little shock, he realized that Ames had just been snubbed: he'd spoken to a fellow, and the fellow had turned away without a reply. Amazing! MacKenzie peered through the weaving, bobbing crowd; for a moment he lost sight of Ames, and then he saw him again, making his way toward them around the perimeter.

". . . call on me and we'll see what we can do," Caroline was saying to someone. Suddenly the music stopped and a hum of conversation rose to fill the void.

"Hello, Addington," she said. "Any luck?"

He knew what she meant. "No," he said shortly. He glanced at MacKenzie. "Rather a different reception here than at the St. Botolph," he said.

"What do you mean?" Caroline asked.

He gave her a little smile. "At the club I was a hero. Not so here."

He thought longingly of where he would be one week from tomorrow: safely on board ship, voyaging to Egypt. The vision glowed in his mind: the blazing sun, the vast desert. Who knew what treasure they would find? And—at the moment even more alluring—he would be far from Boston, far from this nasty mess, from people's prying eyes and malicious gossip. He couldn't wait to go.

His conscience chafed at him then: poor Val! To leave her to this morass of scandal and possible ruin . . . But he'd anticipated this trip far too long to give it up now. Not even for Val would he do that.

As if to prick his conscience further—and his was a New England conscience, after all, sharp and relentless; a Puritan conscience, in fact—Val came up to them just then. She was laughing—thank goodness—and putting her hands to her hair in mock dismay. "Look at me, Caroline!" she exclaimed. "Has my back hair come undone?"

She turned slightly; Caroline inspected. "No, dear. It's fine. Why?"

"Bridget was clumsy tonight. She had to try three times before she got it right." Bridget was Val's maid: a sharply intelligent Irish girl whom Val had selected over Euphemia's objections about having an Irish person in the household.

The music began again: a two-step, a slow, sentimental, popular song, "Lily of the Valley." A young man approached, one of the Wigglesworth clan. "Miss Thorne?" he said brightly. "I believe I have this dance."

She made a pretense of looking at the little dance card dangling from her kid-gloved wrist. "Yes," she said. "You do."

MacKenzie turned to Caroline.

"Of course," she murmured. They stepped to the dance floor.

He was not the best dance partner she'd ever had, but no matter. She adjusted her steps to his, being careful not to step on his boot toes; carefully, she maintained the proper six inches of distance between them. Not that he tried to hold her more closely; he was, she thought, the soul of propriety, as much as any Boston man. He was just slightly taller than she was, and she found that much more comfortable than tilting back her head to look up at someone tall—like Addington, for instance.

One-two, one-two. She hummed the tune; she felt—amazingly!—quite young. As she passed Val and the Wigglesworth boy, she lifted her left hand from MacKenzie's shoulder to wave at them. Val waved back.

Oh, it was delightful to be on the dance floor again! When she was young—Val's age—she'd loved dancing more than anything, particularly the waltz. When Dr. MacKenzie's knee healed more, perhaps she'd waltz with him sometime; and then, at that daring thought, she felt herself flush and hoped he wouldn't notice. Her breath came a little fast, and she felt the pressure of her corset against her ribs. She longed to take a truly deep breath, but she could not; through long years of habit, she forced a succession of rapid little shallow breaths instead.

The music ended. They made their way to the edge of the dance floor. Caroline glanced around. Addington was talking to a tall, white-haired man who had been, she knew, a partner in their late father's law office. And where was Val—?

There she was.

Val—and Alice Dane. They were talking rapidly, as if they hadn't a moment to spare. And indeed they did not, for now Caroline saw Isabel Dane bearing down on them, her face dark with disapproval.

Yes, she thought, you are a bully, Isabel Dane, and you will bully that daughter of yours into a nervous collapse if you don't take care. She edged nearer, Dr. MacKenzie forgotten for the moment. It would be rude to intervene, but then, it was rude of Isabel in the first place, to behave so.

". . . must insist," Isabel was saying to Val.

Val's eyes flashed with anger. "I don't care, Mrs. Dane!" she blurted. "I think you are very unkind!" Abruptly, she turned away.

"Val—" Caroline put out her hand to stop her, but Val pulled away and plunged into the crowd.

Caroline felt a surge of righteous anger well up inside her. How unfair of Isabel! She must say something to the woman; she couldn't let this snub pass unremarked.

She halted perhaps six feet away. Alice looked distraught, her face deathly white. Her thin little bosom heaved beneath the modest pale blue bodice of her very expensive but not terribly flattering gown.

Caroline froze. She hadn't intended to eavesdrop, but now she did.

"How many times do I have to tell you, Alice," Isabel said. She didn't seem to notice Caroline. "You are not to see that girl again!"

"But, Mama—"

"Don't argue with me!" Menacingly, Isabel seemed to swell; the cords in her neck stood out, and her mouth barely opened to emit her words. "You are not to associate with her! Do you understand?"

Alice visibly wilted. "Yes, Mama."

"Good. Now try to seem as though you are enjoying yourself. There he is, over there, and he is coming toward us. Look as if you are happy to see him. Quick, or else—"

"Hello, Alice." Marian Trask stepped up beside them. Caroline stared, fascinated, at the expression on Alice's face: a flash of horrified recognition.

"How pretty you look this evening, dear," Mrs. Trask went on. "I haven't seen you since Newport. Your summer there was most enjoyable, wasn't it? Such an interesting place, Newport."

Bright little blackbird that she was, Mrs. Trask gleamed merrily at Alice. Her little white teeth glistened as she smiled at the girl; her still-pretty little face crinkled up in delight, her little pink tongue darted in and out once, twice, moistening her little red lips.

Alice stared at her for a moment, seemingly spellbound.

Then Mrs. Trask turned away, and as the music started up again, Isabel began to berate her daughter once more. But because of the music, Caroline couldn't hear; she could only see Isabel's angry expression, Alice's trembling form, her contorted face as she listened to her mother's chastisements.

And then, suddenly, Alice fainted.

No one noticed at first; the dancers thronged the dance floor, the music drowned out every voice, the crowd pressed in on all sides.

With a startled exclamation, Caroline hurried forward and crouched at the girl's side and began, very gently, to slap Alice's face to try to revive her.

And now it was Isabel Dane who seemed frozen. She stared down at her daughter; several people noted at the time, and commented later, that her expression was not one of concern, but of—yes—fury.

"Alice!" said Caroline. She was nearly breathless, kneeling in her awkward encasement of corset and layers of fabric, but she ignored her own discomfort in the face of this crisis. "Alice! Can you hear me?"

At once, MacKenzie was at her side; he kneeled also, despite the danger to his knee. He stripped off one of Alice's gloves and felt the pulse at her wrist and then at her throat; he opened an eyelid. People were beginning to notice now, and someone offered smelling salts. MacKenzie lifted Alice to a sitting position and held the bottle under her nose. After a moment her eyelids fluttered; after a moment more she opened them.

Instantly, she realized what had happened. With a startled little cry she tried to stand, but MacKenzie put a restraining hand on her arm.

"Wait a moment, child," he said (for she did look like a child—so thin, so peaked). "Let yourself come fully around before you try to stand."

Alice began to cry. By that time, Ames had seen and had made his way to them; he helped Caroline to her feet, and then MacKenzie. "What's wrong?" he muttered to Caroline.

"I don't know," she whispered back. "She fainted. Isabel was scolding her. Perhaps Isabel's butler told the truth this morning when he said Alice wasn't well."

"In which case," Ames murmured, "her mother should have treated her more gently."

Isabel Dane, at last, bent to her daughter, and with what seemed unnecessary force pulled her to her feet. If she was aware that Alice's brilliant prospect was among those who observed this little drama, she gave no sign. Without a word, without meeting anyone's glance, she gripped Alice's arm tightly—too tightly—and marched her off the floor.

The music, all this time, had continued, but the dance floor was only half full. Now, abashed at having been so unmannerly as to stare, people drifted back to dancing.

Caroline felt a touch on her arm. "What happened?" Val asked.

"Alice fainted."

"Perhaps she really is ill," Val said. "And I thought—"

"Never mind, dearest," Caroline said quickly. "If she is, her mother will surely have the doctor to see her." She looked around; no sign of George. "Now come along. I'd like to freshen up in the ladies', wouldn't you?"

Ames and MacKenzie watched the two women go. Mac-Kenzie was aware that he felt what he always felt, now, when Caroline went away from him or he from her: a small sense of desolation.

Ames was thinking of something very different: that time was rapidly going by, and he was no further along in his search for Valentine's letters.

CHAPTER
9

IN THE SMALL HOURS, DR. MACKENZIE, UNABLE TO SLEEP after the excitement of the evening, lifted his head from his pillow. He was sure he had heard—yes. There. The creak of a floorboard in the hall; the sound of someone treading carefully, stealthily, past his door.

He listened, straining to hear. He heard the clock in the nearby Church of the Advent strike three. Then he heard footsteps on the stairs that went up to the top of the house, the fourth floor.

Alarmed, he sat up. His pistol lay in the drawer of the night table beside him. He swung his feet onto the freezing floor and shrugged on his bathrobe, slipped his feet into his felt slippers, and silently slid open the drawer to take out his weapon. He dropped in three bullets; then he went to the door, opened it, and peered out.

Nothing: no sound, no light.

He stepped into the hall, and now he felt a draft of cold air. A thief in the night, he thought, escaping over the rooftops. This neighborhood had always seemed safe enough, but if a burglar had made his way into the house and was now trying to flee, he, John MacKenzie, could do no less than try to apprehend him.

As he made his way up to the fourth floor, he felt the cold air pouring in. At the end of the hall was a half-flight of steps; as he began to climb them, he saw that the door at the top was ajar.

In another moment, he had stepped out onto the roof. There was no moon, but the sky was clear, the wind bitter cold.

He saw a movement—a figure emerging from a little shedlike structure on one side.

"Halt!" he cried as he raised his pistol to fire.

"Don't shoot, Doctor," came Ames's voice. He carried a bright brass telescope that shone even in the dim starlight.

"I thought—" MacKenzie began; he broke off as he heard Ames's low chuckle.

"That I was a burglar? I should have warned you that I sometimes come up here at night to stargaze."

He was setting up the instrument on a tripod, tilting it to exactly the right angle, focusing it.

"It's cold tonight, Doctor," he said as he worked. "Don't catch your death. And mind your step near the edge—it's a long drop. *Sic quoque itur ad astra,* as Virgil more or less said—'This way, too, is a passage to the stars.' "

"I had no idea that you were an astronomer."

"Only an amateur. And I have been too busy recently to be even that. But tonight, when I saw that the weather was still clear, I thought this might be my last chance before going away."

Ames stood with his eye pressed to the glass. His tall, thin-legged figure looked as storklike as the tall, thin-legged tripod. In rapt silence he gazed up at the stars. Even to the naked eye on this brilliantly clear night, they were quite distinct; MacKenzie saw the Dippers big and small, and Cassiopeia, and the brightest star in the skies this night, the brilliant, blue-white Vega.

Ames moved the telescope slowly so as to be able to see

one bit of sky and then another. At last he turned to Mac-
Kenzie.

"Have a look?" he said.

MacKenzie stepped forward. When he had looked at the
night sky out on the wide open plains of the West, it had
seemed, paradoxically, both more vast and yet closer—
sometimes almost close enough to touch. Here it looked
properly distant—until he put his eye to the lens, when suddenly it sprang into huge proximity. The telescope was directed to Vega, and now, so much closer, it startled him—
humbled him—with a brilliance greater than he could have
imagined.

After a moment he stepped back. Ames reset the telescope, looked through the lens, and then again he stood
aside to allow the doctor a turn. "The Andromeda nebula,"
Ames said. "My friend Mr. Percival Lowell, who is not an
amateur but a professional, tells me it is the most distant
object that the human eye can see. It lies beyond our uni-
verse, if you can conceive of such a thing."

MacKenzie looked. He saw a cloud of luminosity dotted
with bright pinpoints. He gazed for a few seconds more;
then, nearly overwhelmed, he said, "Thank you." He sin-
cerely meant it. He was grateful to Ames for that brief
glimpse of the heavens; more, he was intrigued. Astronomy
was, he thought, an essentially romantic field of study, an
expression of yearning to know what lay beyond the lonely
little planet Earth. Until now, he would not have suspected
that Addington Ames had a shred of the romantic in his
temperament.

Ames cast a critical eye over his lodger. "You are shivering," he said curtly. "You'd best go in. I don't want Dr.
Warren to accuse me of causing the death of one of his
patients."

He was right, of course. And so MacKenzie went indoors, back to his room, where he got into his bed and lay
warm and comfortable, drifting off to sleep while he

thought of the little drama taking place on the roof—Addington Ames, stargazing.

THE NEXT MORNING, CAROLINE WAS LETTING HER PORridge cool while she hurriedly read the morning *Globe* before she gave it up to her brother.

"They have your name here again," she said to him.

"Why not?" he replied. "It adds a little something to the story, I would think."

He said this, MacKenzie knew, not from any sense of self-importance but simply as a statement of fact.

Caroline, remembering Josephine Putnam's coolness the evening before, made a wry face. "Since you had nothing to do with the Colonel's death, Addington, I would think they'd let you alone."

"Why should they? If adding my name to the story helps them to sell papers, then they will add it. They are hardly concerned about my sensibilities—or yours."

Shaking her head, she handed the paper to him. "Good morning, Doctor," she said to MacKenzie.

He took his porridge and settled himself at the table. The morning sun did not reach this room, but he could see the bright day outside, and he remembered the brilliant night sky he'd briefly seen with Ames, up on the roof. That man—that eager, yearning soul—had been very different from the composed, reticent figure sitting here now. Still waters, thought MacKenzie. The much-anticipated trip to Egypt should have revealed to him Ames's true nature, which ordinarily the man kept so well hidden under his dry, reserved exterior.

"Such a lovely evening, wasn't it?" Caroline said as he began to eat.

"Very."

"I've never seen such a handsome crop of post-buds. Some of them individually, of course, are always beautiful.

The Codman girl, back in 'eighty-five, was quite exquisite. And Aimee Parker's niece, I remember, even though she did have red hair, poor thing. And—"

She broke off. "Addington," she said, turning to her brother.

"Yes?" He did not stop reading, and so she tried again. "I have just remembered something."

"Yes?"

"Addington, listen to me."

The paper came down; he met her glance. "Yes, Caro. I'm listening."

"Do you remember Mr. Hemenway's daughter?"

He blinked. "No."

"Yes, you do. The last time I saw her was at Symphony, four years ago." Her voice wavered, then strengthened once more. "She was engaged to be married to the Motley boy. And then— Oh, it was too horrible! They said it was an accident, but Ethel Loring told me—and I remember I told you—that it wasn't. Eleanor Hemenway drank chloroform. It could not possibly have been an accident. It happened right after—right after her initials appeared in the Colonel's paper. Her father nearly went mad with grief. He saw Colonel Mann in the street one day not long after and attacked him. Surely you remember that, at least."

He nodded slowly as it came back to him. Wisely, the Colonel had not pressed charges.

Caroline turned to MacKenzie. "Old Mr. Hemenway never recovered from it—from losing his daughter like that, and all for nothing."

"You mean the Colonel printed something about her that wasn't true?" MacKenzie said.

"Oh, who knows if it was true or not! That isn't the point, is it? The point is, is anything the Colonel prints worth a life? She was such a lovely girl. And to die like that—"

She pressed her lips together as if to contain her outrage.

Then: "The point I am trying to make, Addington, is that if you are looking for someone with a reason to kill Colonel Mann, Henry Hemenway is as good a prospect as anyone I can think of. I can't imagine why I didn't think of it sooner. He told Ethel—who is his sister's sister-in-law—that the next time he saw the Colonel he would finish the job. Last summer at Nahant, Ethel told me he is becoming more and more reclusive. He never goes out, just sits at home, brooding. Eleanor was his only child, and apparently he cannot recover from her death."

Ames drank his coffee. Then he met his sister's insistent gaze. He nodded. "You are right, Caro. I had forgotten the Hemenway case."

"Well, then," she replied with an air of having settled the matter. "I think you should go to see him."

"What, and tear the scabs from a sorrowing old man's wounds?"

"And ask him—"

"If he finally managed to murder the man he held responsible for his daughter's death? Really, Caroline, it would be beyond the bounds of good manners—"

"It is beyond the bounds of good manners to allow Val to suffer the same fate!" she snapped.

MacKenzie was amazed at her vehemence, and apparently Ames was as well, for now he stretched out a hand to her, patted her arm gently, and said, "You mustn't allow yourself to become too caught up in this affair."

"Of course I am caught up in it. How can I not be? You didn't see the way Josephine Putnam behaved last evening. She was just barely civil to me, and she hardly even looked at poor Val. If we do not get those letters back—if this horrible business does not come to an end, and quickly—Val may be driven to—to—"

"No," he said softly. "To do what the Hemenway girl did? No. Not Val."

"How can you be so sure?" she challenged him.

MacKenzie saw that her soft brown eyes were brimming with tears; he longed to comfort her, but he didn't know how.

"Because Val is like us," Ames replied. "She may appear to be delicate, but underneath she is one of us, and that means she is strong enough to weather any scandal, no matter how bad it may seem at first."

Caroline was not reassured, but she nodded and began to pick at her breakfast. He was trying his best, she thought. Pray he succeeded in the few days remaining before he left the city.

CHAPTER
10

A SHORT WHILE LATER, AMES AND THE DOCTOR BOARDED
the Green Trolley on Charles Street and settled themselves
for the ride down Beacon Street along the Public Garden,
and around on Arlington to Marlborough. Here, the mansions were not quite so grand as those on Commonwealth,
one block over, but they were handsome enough, MacKenzie thought as he gazed at the parallel rows of brick and
brownstone town houses.

They alighted at Fairfield Street; the trolley bell clanged
as the horses started up again, heading toward Massachusetts Avenue. A few steps along, and they came to Henry
Hemenway's home. Ames had heard that Hemenway had
spared no expense when he'd built the house not long after
his daughter's birth, but now the place looked poorly kept.
A ragged vine climbed the front, the brownstone was chip-
ping, and the brass door knocker was badly in need of a
polish.

He lifted it and brought it down sharply. No answer. He
tried again. MacKenzie, waiting beside him on the doorstep,
grimaced in the raw east wind; despite the fine day, that
wind, coming in off the sea, foretold a change.

The door cracked open and a maid peered out at them suspiciously. "Yes?"

"Mr. Hemenway, please," said Ames, proffering his card.

The maid ignored it. "I'm sorry, sir. Mr. Hemenway is not at home."

She started to shut the door, but Ames put a hand against the panel. "It is important. Is he in?"

She hesitated. Then, grudgingly, "I'll see."

Ames thrust his card at her again. "Take this to him. We need only a moment of his time."

Glancing up, MacKenzie thought he saw a blind move at a window on the second floor. After a few moments, the maid returned and they were admitted.

The house had an air about it of not being lived in. Ames looked around, but there was not much to see. All the doors leading off the foyer were closed; only one dim gas jet lightened the gloom.

The maid led them upstairs to an equally gloomy hall, where she knocked and showed them into a room with book-lined walls and a massive desk. Over the mantel was a portrait of a beautiful young woman. From a chair by the unlit fire, an old man was getting up to greet them. In the light of the gas jets on the wall, MacKenzie could see that he was rather stooped, with long white hair and a beard that needed trimming.

Ames held out his hand, and after a moment the old man took it.

"Mr. Hemenway," Ames said. "It is very good of you to see us." He introduced MacKenzie, who was surprised at the strength of Hemenway's handshake.

"Well, what is it, Mr. Ames?" Hemenway said gruffly. He did not ask them to sit.

"It is about a most painful matter," Ames began.

Hemenway stared at him, unflinching, but his mouth worked.

"About—the death of Colonel Mann," Ames said.

"It said in the newspaper that you found him."

"Yes."

"Did you do it?"

"No. But I did have business with him that I was unable to transact." Briefly, Ames told his story while Hemenway listened impassively.

"And how do you think I can help you?" Hemenway asked when Ames had finished.

"I don't know. But I thought perhaps you might have visited him—"

"You mean you thought I might have killed him at last, as I have publicly threatened to do?"

Ames shrugged.

"Well, sir," Hemenway said, "I did not."

"Did you see him on Monday evening?"

"No."

Ames waited until Hemenway burst out, "All right! Yes, I did go to him then."

"At what time?"

"Not long after eight."

"And—?"

"He was dead. Someone had done my work for me."

"May I ask—did you have a reason for going to see the Colonel on that particular night?"

Hemenway hesitated, blinking his rheumy old eyes. "Monday was the fourth anniversary of my daughter's death."

"I see."

"I wonder if you do."

"Well, then, quite possibly I do not. But if you will allow me—did you see anyone while you were there?"

"No. Just a couple of guests in the hall going to their rooms." Hemenway shook his head. "I didn't kill him, Mr. Ames. I wish I had."

And now at last his grief overcame him. His face crumpled and his shoulders shook as a sob wrenched from his throat. He put his hands over his eyes; after a long moment he took them away again.

Ames felt acutely uncomfortable. In his world—his small, proper, neatly ordered world—men did not weep, and if they did, they did so in private.

Hemenway took a deep breath. "I apologize, gentlemen. You understand—Colonel Mann robbed me of all that was precious to me. He dirtied the name of my daughter and drove her to her death." He glanced up at the portrait, then quickly looked away. "You can see for yourselves what she was. And that man— Well. He has been a cancer on the body—and the soul—of this city for years. I am not going to pretend to be shocked—or even saddened—that at last someone has done what I should have done long ago. I tell you again, I did not kill him. But now that I have told you I visited him on the evening when someone did, I must assume the police will learn that fact also."

"Not from me," Ames said.

"But from someone, yes? And so now I will set about getting myself a believable account of where I might have been at that time. It would be ironic, would it not, if in his death the Colonel managed to injure me yet again?"

Ames was disposed to believe Hemenway when he said that he had not killed Colonel Mann. Still, Hemenway's guilt or innocence was not the issue, or not for him, at any rate. The issue, he reminded himself, was Val's letters.

"When you were in the Colonel's suite, Mr. Hemenway, did you by any chance see the packet of letters I need to recover?"

"No."

"I know he had them at four o'clock. When I went to see him at a quarter to nine, he was lying dead on the floor and the letters were missing. For lack of any more plausible theory, I believe that the person who killed him took them."

"To continue the Colonel's blackmail?"

"Possibly. Probably, in fact."

Hemenway shook his head. "I can't help you, Mr. Ames. I wish I could—to strike one last blow against that—that—devil!"

"You are positive you didn't see such a packet?"

"Yes. But then again, I wasn't looking for 'em, was I?"

Ames thought of the missing galley. "Did you take anything away with you?"

Hemenway hesitated. Then: "I saw his proof sheets lying on his desk. I thought of all the grief they held—and would cause if the wrong person got hold of them."

"So you took them?"

"Yes. I burned them"—he gestured at the fireplace—"there. Will his paper come out this week?"

"I don't know."

"The world has one less scoundrel in it now, Mr. Ames, and I hope one day to shake the hand of the man who removed him from our midst. Do I shock you?"

Ames shook his head. "No, sir, I cannot say that you do." He held out his hand again. "I thank you for your time, sir. It was not my intention to open old wounds."

"They've never been closed, Mr. Ames."

SHE WAS THERE WHEN YOU CAME HOME FROM THE COTILlion?" Caroline asked.

"Yes. She saw me to bed." Val was pale, on edge.

"So sometime between then and the morning—"

"Yes."

Val's maid had vanished.

"But *why?*" Caroline asked. "It is not as if she was unhappy with you."

"No. She seemed happy enough."

"*Oh!*" Caroline clapped her hand to her mouth. But it was no use; the thought had come to her, and she had to voice it. "Do you think it was she who took your letters?"

"I suppose so." Val's eyes were bleak as she struggled with this betrayal.

"And gave—or sold—them to the Colonel? Or"—and this was the most difficult proposition of all—"did someone else know about them and bribe her to take them?"

Val stared at her. "How could anyone have known? I never told a soul."

They heard the thump of the dumbwaiter in the back passage, and Caroline went to fetch the tray. Cook had given them not only tea, but a few slices of bread and a dish of butter. Good. Val had probably had no breakfast; she needed this little nourishment.

She poured. When Val did not take any food, she buttered a slice of bread and handed it to her. Val looked at it for a moment as if she didn't know what to do with it; then she accepted it and began to eat.

After a moment, her eye fell on the book lying on the table beside Caroline's chair.

"Is that the new Diana Strangeways?"

"Yes." It was one of the few little luxuries Caroline allowed herself: the purchase, each October, of the annual offering by England's premier lady novelist, whose sensational tales of love and adventure enthralled readers on both sides of the Atlantic. "I'll give it to you when I've finished," Caroline added, knowing that Val understood "give" to mean only "lend." Ordinarily she did not lend books, having discovered long ago that many people did not feel constrained to return them; but Val was different. She always brought them back promptly, and always in good condition.

Then, hesitantly, with great delicacy, Caroline said, "Val, you know I don't want to pry, but—"

Val waited, eyes downcast.

"But—where did you meet him?"

Val looked up. She knew who "him" was: not George Putnam but that other. The one who had so briefly enchanted her and who had, in the end, caused her such grief. "At the Christmas Revels, two years ago."

This enormous production was held annually in Sanders Theater over at Harvard, a gala celebration of the season, the profits donated to charity. The participants were amateurs drawn from Boston and Cambridge Society; for weeks they rehearsed diligently, learned songs and dance steps, learned lines. Caroline had participated once, some years earlier before Isabel Dane took it over, but she hadn't enjoyed it—too raucous, too exhausting—and she had never done so again. But she knew that because of the great number of people involved—two or three hundred—the Christmas Revels were known as a place where more than one match had been made.

"And . . . you became . . . friends?"

"More than that. We met secretly all through the spring. He—said he loved me. I wrote those letters to him—those awful letters. He was at Newport that summer—"

"Summer before last."

"Yes. I was staying with the Danes, as I always did. And over the course of the summer, he—found that he didn't love me, after all. So he gave the letters back."

"And you are sure that he never told anyone about them?"

"I can't be sure, of course. But I doubt he did." Val's face suddenly twisted with pain.

"I'm just trying to think about who—"

"Yes, Caro. All I can tell you is I don't think he told anyone. And after all, he was decent enough to return them. After . . . it was over."

But it wasn't over, thought Caroline. It went on and on, shadowing their lives, threatening disaster.

She wanted very badly to ask the young man's name, but she didn't quite dare.

CHAPTER
11

THE HOTEL BRUNSWICK, AT MIDMORNING, SEEMED A BUSY place, well run. No one, this morning, would have guessed that only two days before, a scandalous crime had been committed on its premises.

"No need to disturb the manager," Ames murmured as he and MacKenzie crossed the lobby. "We'll just have a look upstairs on our own."

They avoided the elevator and went up the stairs. MacKenzie's knee began to throb before they reached the third floor, and Ames waited with him while he rested; then they went on. The fourth-floor corridor was quiet and empty, the door to Colonel Mann's suite closed. But the next door was slightly ajar. Ames pushed it open.

Inside was a chambermaid making the bed. When she saw Ames, she gave a frightened little cry.

"Excuse me," Ames said pleasantly. He stepped into the room, motioning MacKenzie to follow. "Do not alarm yourself. Could you tell me whose room this is?"

The maid stood stock-still, staring at him. No doubt, he thought, the police had given her a rough going-over.

"Yes?" he said, smiling at her. He took out his worn

leather coin purse. "Could you?" He fished out a one-dollar coin.

The maid's eyes fastened on it. Then she looked up to meet his dark, intent gaze.

"No harm will come to you," he said. He stepped toward her, holding out the coin. "And you may have this in return."

The maid had a little struggle with herself; then she held out her small, chapped hand and Ames put the coin into it.

"Mr. Longworth, sir," she said softly. She was looking at the coin.

"Ah. Would that be Richard Longworth?"

The maid nodded.

Ames pressed his lips together, his mind racing. It was a name he knew—a name that bore out Delahanty's statement that the Colonel had had legal advice.

Richard Longworth—a fellow member of the St. Botolph, although Ames did not know him well—was the scion of one of the city's first families. He was also a man with a shadowed reputation—for gambling, for loose living, for running through his wife's fortune. And, Ames thought, he was a member of the Bar.

He fished another dollar coin from his purse. The maid watched him, seemingly fascinated.

"I am going to ask something else of you," he said. "Could you leave us for five minutes? Here is another dollar. You need not worry. We are not the police, nor will we tell the police that we have been here. Can you do that? Leave us for five minutes?"

The maid looked very frightened—to be caught out in this would certainly mean her job, MacKenzie thought—but she held out her hand and Ames put the second coin into it. Then, quickly, she darted out, closing the door behind her.

Ames looked around. In contrast to the Colonel's suite adjoining, this was an untidy place. He saw clothing draped over furniture, books piled on the floor, papers scattered over the small desk by the window. On a table were two empty wine bottles and a half-empty bottle of brandy. A breakfast tray lay on another—half-empty coffee cup, half-eaten pieces of toast. He crossed to the door that led to the Colonel's suite and tried it. Locked. No bolt on this side.

He turned to the high chiffonier, on which stood a photograph in a silver frame. It was of a man in his late thirties or early forties, formally dressed. His high-browed face had a clever look to it, and he was smiling a small, wry smile. He had a neatly trimmed mustache; his top hair was slightly thinning. Below the photograph were two dates: 1843–1890.

After studying it for a moment, Ames turned away. On the night table was a single withered rose that had once been pink; beside it lay a program from the Park Theater for its current production, *Lady Musgrove's Secret.*

He went to the desk. It held a jumble of papers—bills, invitations, racing forms. He slid open the wide top drawer. It held a single sheet of paper, an unfinished letter written in a large, bold hand:

My Darling:
I write this with a heavy heart. I cannot believe that you would abandon me. Say you will not, and I will do anything you desire. But I cannot live without you—I cannot! I beg you, do not condemn me to that hell. Please, please *tell me that you*

Ames left the letter where it was and slid shut the drawer. He had only a moment more. What was here to help him?

He stepped to the half-made bed and slipped his hand under the mattress. He felt something hard; he pulled it out. It was a morocco jewelry case. He opened it.

"Look at this," he said softly to MacKenzie, who stepped near to see.

On a bed of pale velvet lay a diamond bracelet. MacKenzie gave a low whistle.

"He trusts the help," he said.

"Either that, or he drinks to the point where he cannot remember where he's put his valuables."

The bracelet, Ames thought, was undoubtedly intended for the recipient of the half-finished letter. He doubted that Longworth's wife was that woman.

He closed the case and slipped it back under the mattress. The chambermaid could live for the rest of her life on what that bracelet would bring, but she seemed too timid to take it, even if she knew of its existence.

He straightened and looked around. This room held a sense of the man who occupied it, far more so than had the Colonel's. The man who lived here—when he did not live with his wife—was a man of impulsive acts, a careless man, a man who apparently lived two lives, at least.

But the room told Ames nothing about his own urgent business.

Just then they heard voices in the corridor. They tensed; the voices faded.

"All right, Doctor," Ames said. "We must go. Richard Longworth is the scapegrace son of a man my father held in high esteem. And now, knowing his connection to Colonel Mann, I would very much like to talk to him."

He went to the door and cautiously opened it. The corridor was deserted. They let themselves out, closing the door softly behind them. As they walked toward the stairs, they passed an open door. Ames looked in and saw the maid at work. "Thank you," he said softly. She had no reaction; she simply stared at him as if she'd never seen him before.

When they stood outside on Boylston Street once more, Ames looked unseeing at the busy thoroughfare.

Richard Longworth! A man who lived high—higher than his income. A man who had something about him that was not quite—in the Boston phrase—"steady." The exact type of man who would have been an adviser to the Colonel.

It was not quite noon. "Come on, Doctor," he said. "I am reluctant to give you lunch at the St. Botolph twice in one week, but if Longworth is there, I would very much like to talk to him."

But at the club they were told that Longworth was not in. So they went home to take their lunch at Louisburg Square.

CHAPTER 12

"DISAPPEARED?" AMES EXCLAIMED. HE HAD JUST BEGUN to spoon up his soup, which was split pea, thick and spicy, far better than the fare at the St. Botolph Club. Now he paused, his dark eyes intent on his sister. "And Val has no idea where she might have gone?"

"No. But she does know—in hindsight—that the girl was upset about something. She was all thumbs last night, Val said, doing Val's hair for the Cotillion."

"Was she there when Val got home afterward?"

"Yes."

"But not this morning?"

"No. Addington—think about it—it may have been she who took Val's letters."

Ames stared at her, but she could tell he did not see her. Then: "Could she have done this on her own? Or did someone put her up to it?"

"Oh, the latter, I'm sure."

"And that same someone gave—or sold—the letters to the Colonel."

"It would seem so." How horribly depressing, Caroline thought. The servants with whom we live, betraying us, selling our secrets.

"And when the maid learned that the Colonel had been murdered—" MacKenzie began.

Ames nodded. "She panicked and fled."

"So either she feared for her own life . . ." Caroline hesitated.

"Or someone killed her, as well," Ames supplied.

Caroline put down her spoon. Suddenly she was no longer hungry. "Did you see Mr. Hemenway, Addington?"

"Yes." And he told her about that sad interview, and then about his visit to the Hotel Brunswick.

"Richard Longworth?" said Caroline. "But—how could he possibly have been the Colonel's lawyer? His wife is the dearest person in the world!"

"I don't follow you. What does the character of Longworth's wife have to do with anything?"

"Why—because—" She turned to MacKenzie. "Lydia Longworth—she was a Saltonstall, and a Cabot on her mother's side—came out just a year ahead of me. Even then we all knew that she had a penchant for him. It took him long enough, but in the end they did marry. No children, I believe. I haven't seen her in ages. They say she's not been well. And if her husband is—was—connected to the Colonel, I can understand why. Such a connection would make even the strongest woman ill, and Lydia was always rather delicate."

She spoke freely because she believed that the doctor was as interested in the minutiae of Boston lore as she was. And, indeed, he seemed to be: he listened intently, gazing at her from across the table, a slight smile visible under his mustache.

"Did you know her well?" he asked. He did not care a whit about Richard Longworth's wife, of course, but he did want Caroline to keep talking to him.

"Not very. She was not easy to know. But a lovely girl—a

lovely woman now. They have had their troubles, I must say. I heard that Longworth was seriously in debt, and that Lydia's father refused to help him."

"And what about his own father?" MacKenzie asked.

"I never knew him, but I believe—" She turned to Ames. "Was he not a friend of Papa's, Addington?"

"Yes." Ames had finished his soup and was wiping his mouth with his napkin.

"Where are you going?" Caroline asked as he rose.

"To see Longworth Senior," he replied. "I have no idea if he even knows that his son had such an unsavory connection. It may be my unpleasant task to enlighten him. Doctor? Will you come?"

MacKenzie, who was only halfway through his meal, was torn. He would have preferred a quiet afternoon by the fire with Caroline; on the other hand, busy as she was, he doubted she would stay at home in any case. So he put down his spoon and, with a smile and a nod to her, accompanied his landlord through the door.

THE ELDER LONGWORTH WAS A MAN OF SOME SEVENTY years, tall and spare, gray-haired, gimlet-eyed, with an abrupt manner that bordered on arrogance.

"Yes, Mr. Ames?" he said. He held out his hand; Ames took it and then introduced MacKenzie.

They were in the front parlor of Longworth's house on Beacon Street just beyond Clarendon. Although Longworth Senior had been acquainted with his own father, Ames had never met him. Now he contemplated this intimidating old man—intimidating even to him—and wondered how to begin.

"This is a most delicate matter, sir," he said. "And I can assure you that Dr. MacKenzie here will keep whatever we say in the strictest confidence."

Longworth's eyes flicked over MacKenzie's solid form and came back to Ames. "Well?" he said. "And what is it that will need such strict confidence?"

Does he really not know? Ames thought. Perhaps not.

"It is about—your son, sir," he said.

Longworth's face settled into even harsher lines; his mouth drew down, and his left eye twitched a little. "Yes?"

"And about his connection to Colonel Mann."

"You found the Colonel's body," Longworth said.

"Yes."

"Had you business with him?"

"Yes."

"What has my son to do with it?"

"I am given to understand that he was an associate of the Colonel's." Ames was bluffing, but only a little.

"I have no idea with whom my son associates."

"Sir, in all honesty, I do not care about your son's associates. I am merely trying to put my hands on a certain packet of letters that were in the Colonel's possession shortly before he was killed. That is why I went to his suite on Monday evening—to get them—but I arrived too late. Someone—I believe it may have been the man who killed the Colonel—had already made off with what I was looking for."

"You accuse my son of murder?"

"Not at all. But since he was an associate of the Colonel's, I thought perhaps he could tell me who might have gone to the Colonel that evening. Or, failing that, perhaps he could tell me who supplied the letters to the Colonel in the first place. My only interest is in retrieving them. A young lady's future depends upon it."

Most men, at that, might have softened a bit, but not Longworth. Although MacKenzie had never met his son, he began to feel a twinge of sympathy for him.

"I can tell you nothing," Longworth said.

"Not even—"

"Nothing. It may not surprise you to learn that my son and I are—estranged. We have not spoken in more than a year."

"I see."

"And if we were to speak," Longworth went on as if he had not heard, "it would be only to indulge in mutual recrimination."

Despite his forbidding demeanor, MacKenzie thought, he apparently wants to unburden himself.

"I beg your pardon," Ames said softly. "I wanted only to—"

"You are not married, Mr. Ames," Longworth said. It was not a question.

"No."

"A pity. Your father was an excellent man. Excellent. If you were to marry and have a son, you would pass along your heredity. We need heredity like yours these days. Instead of—"

MacKenzie could not be sure, but he thought he heard the old man's voice crack a little. Amazing.

"My wife's family—my late wife—had weakness in it. I blame that weakness for my son's behavior. Her older brother failed in business, after which he drank himself to death, and her younger brother succumbed to gambling. Not here, thank heaven. In Europe. But there was bad character there, you see—not that I knew of it when I married her, or I never would have done so."

Cold and colder, thought MacKenzie. He could not repress a shiver, although he had not taken off his coat.

"My son," said Longworth, his voice dripping scorn, "took after his mother's side of the family. By the time he managed to finish law school, I had nearly despaired of him. I sent him away—to Argentina—to see if there, he could make his fortune."

"And did he?" Ames asked. He had given up any hope that this implacable man would be of help to him in his quest for Val's letters, but in spite of himself he felt a morbid interest in what Longworth had to say.

"No."

"He came back—?"

"Yes. After five years of failure, he came back. And here in Boston, he did the next best thing to making a fortune on his own. He married one. A small one, to be sure, but a fortune all the same. From what I understand, he has managed to run through all his wife's money and alienate his father-in-law into the bargain. They have bailed him out more than once, but I doubt they'll do so again."

He broke off abruptly and turned away. They heard him clear his throat as if his unshed, bitter tears threatened to choke him. Not so cold, after all, thought MacKenzie; brokenhearted, in fact.

For a moment, Ames hardly knew what to say. Then, feeling that he had to say something: "I am very sorry, sir. I did not intend to call up unhappy memories."

Longworth shook his head. "You did not call them up, Mr. Ames. They are with me every day. So you see, I confess to you that my son is a wastrel, he is a gambler—certainly he is a failure at the law, and why the Bar admitted him I could never understand—but I do not think even he would stoop so low as to work for Colonel Mann. And certainly he is no murderer."

"Does he have any practice at all in his law office?"

"He did. But after his partner left him, it fell off."

"I see. Is his partner still in Boston?"

"His partner is dead, Mr. Ames."

"Of—?"

"I have no idea."

The interview was over. Outside, starting down Beacon Street, Ames was silent for a time, and then he said, "A sad case, wouldn't you say, Doctor?"

"Yes, indeed. It is always sad when parents and children are estranged."

"And when children so singularly fail to live up to their parents' expectations."

Ames thought of his own father. They had not been close, but at least his father had never evinced any disappointment in him. When Ames declined to join his father's law practice, the decision had been accepted with a mere lift of an eyebrow; nothing more. And if the older man had been puzzled by his son's failure to settle on a profession, he had never indicated it by so much as a single remonstrance.

Which had been, in itself, a kind of abandonment, Ames thought now. Surely most fathers—like old Longworth, for instance—tried to influence their sons' chosen life paths? He realized now, really for the first time, that perhaps his own father had been remiss. Not that he himself would have wanted pressure of any kind; he would have resisted it, thus perhaps creating a breach such as existed between the Longworths, father and son.

No. It had been better the way his own father handled the matter. Or failed to handle it.

They reached the corner of Berkeley Street. To their left lay the Charles, gray and ruffled in the autumn wind. Straight ahead, on down Beacon Street past the Garden, lay Charles Street and Beacon Hill: home.

But Ames did not want to go home, not yet. Val might be there, seeking solace, seeking help that so far he had been unable to give.

He paused at the curb. A handsome equipage was just passing, a shiny maroon brougham drawn by a spirited pair of matching bays. The passenger—an attractive woman— seemed to be nodding to him, and so although he did not recognize her, he lifted his hat.

Then, energized by the incident, he turned to MacKenzie and said, "Let us pay a call, Doctor, on someone very different from Mr. Longworth."

CHAPTER 13

AT THE BERKELEY ARMS, AN ELEGANT APARTMENT HOTEL on Berkeley Street between Commonwealth and Newbury, the uniformed doorman scrutinized Ames and MacKenzie briefly; then he opened the door to admit them to the marble and brass and darkwood lobby. A concierge sat at a desk; he was small and dark and foreign-looking, very haughty.

He examined Ames's card and nodded once, abruptly, waving his hand toward the elevator. "Numbair seexseventeen," he said.

They went up. On the sixth floor, they turned down a thickly carpeted corridor. The place was hushed, redolent of money.

Six-seventeen was a door like all the others: gleaming wood with a bright brass number, a push-button bell to one side. Ames had just positioned his gloved finger to press it, when the door burst open and a young man came rushing out, nearly colliding with them. He was tall, and handsome in a pretty way; his brown hair was tousled, his flushed face bright with laughter.

"Oh—I say! Sorry!" he exclaimed. He recovered himself and went jauntily down the corridor.

Ames glanced after him and then turned to the open door. A woman stood just inside, a smile still lingering on her face. Ames realized with a little shock that it was a beautiful face. Astonishingly beautiful—the kind of beauty that one seldom encountered. A perfect oval, creamy white skin, crowned by a mass of auburn hair; wide greenish eyes under dark brows, a lovely line of cheek from forehead to chin, a full red mouth revealing twin rows of perfect teeth.

"I beg your pardon," Ames began. MacKenzie noted with amusement that he seemed a trifle flustered.

"Certainly," the woman said. She drew herself up; under the fabric of her green silk gown, they could see the outlines of a magnificent body. She seemed not to be wearing a corset—or, indeed, undergarments of any kind.

"I—ah—Mrs. Vincent?" Ames said. He was fumbling for his card case.

"Yes." She was perfectly composed now, surveying him—surveying them both—with those wide eyes, heavy dark eyelashes sweeping up and down as she took them in. Behind her hovered a maid.

"I wonder if you—" Ames had finally found his card; he held it out to her.

She took it and glanced at it. The expression in her eyes cooled, became suddenly wary; her smile had vanished entirely.

"Yes, Mr. Ames?"

"I—we—wondered if you would be so good as to give us a few moments of your time," Ames said. He had recovered his composure, and he spoke with his usual courteous, confident air.

Mrs. Vincent hesitated for a moment. Then without a word she stood back to allow them to enter. MacKenzie could see the maid's look of disapproval; then he was surprised to hear her say, "No time for it, Missus."

"It's all right, Hilda," said Mrs. Vincent. "They won't be long—will you, gentlemen?"

She had turned to lead them inside. As they passed through the foyer, Ames saw a handsome fur draped across a carved wooden chest. A handsome fur: a sable cloak, in fact.

"Will you sit down?" Mrs. Vincent said with a graceful movement of her hand. "It is too late for me to offer you tea, I am afraid—I must be at the theater in less than an hour—but I can give you a little time."

Her parlor was tastefully furnished with sofas and chairs covered in silk and brocade in soft shades of green; a fire crackled on the hearth beneath a white marble mantel, and a small Yorkshire terrier lifted his head from the large silk pillow where he lay to briefly examine the newcomers. He growled once, but at a word from his mistress he subsided.

Mrs. Vincent positioned herself on a pale green love seat fringed in darker green; Ames introduced MacKenzie, and both men took chairs opposite.

"I apologize for the little contretemps at the door just now," Mrs. Vincent said.

The maid had not offered to take their things, and so now Ames sat perched on his seat, twisting the brim of his hat in his hands. His gloves, MacKenzie noted, had fallen to the flowered carpet, which, like everything else in the room, including its mistress, looked to be of high quality, very expensive.

"We did not mean to interrupt—" Ames began.

"Not at all. He was just leaving. Young men can be so careless and impetuous, can they not?" She was smiling again; it was a devastating smile, one that MacKenzie imagined must have devastated many men, young and old alike.

"They can be, yes," Ames replied.

"He was careless and impetuous last summer at Newport, as well. I had to rescue him."

Newport again, Ames thought. Where Val had had her own troubles two summers before. Well, whoever this young man had been involved with there, thank heaven it wasn't his young cousin, who had been safely in Bar Harbor.

He tilted his head, inviting her to elaborate. Which, Mac-
Kenzie realized, she was only too happy to do. It was her
way of establishing herself with them—establishing a kind of
authority over them. Her voice was enchanting, vibrant and
low, but he had the sense that onstage, she could project it
to the farthest seat in the second balcony.

"He was discovered in—well, in an embarrassing situation. In flagrante, in fact. He had to make a hasty exit, and
so he came to me. Fortunately, I was a guest on Commodore
Vandergrift's yacht—do you know him? He is from New
York—and I was able to give him, literally, a berth."

"How fortunate for him."

"Yes, wasn't it? Unfortunately for me, now he thinks he's
in love with me."

"I imagine that many men do."

Mrs. Vincent included MacKenzie in her glance. "One of
the hazards of my profession, Mr. Ames."

"Indeed."

Ames was remembering that he had met this woman once
or twice, years earlier, when she was still a member of his
small, chilly circle. But beyond the fact that he had met her,
he had no memory of her, and how could that be? Surely a
woman so exquisitely beautiful would have made some impression on him.

And now she sat before him, perfectly composed, speaking of her profession—her profession!—as easily as she
might have spoken of the weather.

As he well knew—and certainly she did, also—her profession was considered to be no better than that of a scarlet
woman. Her profession was one that no decent female
would adopt. Her profession was one that she herself had
adopted only in the extremity of her disgrace, having been
divorced by her husband in the aftermath of a scandal fo-
mented by Colonel William d'Arcy Mann.

"You are having a success in your current production,"
he said.

She smiled. Ames felt an unfamiliar sensation in the region of his heart. "Yes," she said; she was not embarrassed at all to say it.

"It must be a tiring schedule—"

"Mr. Ames, I am somewhat pressed for time. What do you want of me?"

Her bluntness—her near rudeness—startled both men. Perhaps, thought Ames, she has been coarsened by her years in the rough and tumble world of the theater.

Then again, he had no doubt that she knew, at least in a general way, why he wanted to speak to her. Surely she read the newspapers; surely she knew that he had discovered the Colonel's body.

And since she had been mentioned in the Colonel's galleys, and since he'd seen her sable cloak just now in the foyer, surely she was the woman whom Redpath had encountered at the Hotel Brunswick on Monday evening. She could, therefore, just possibly be of help to him.

"I am looking for a certain packet of letters that belong to a young friend," he began. "Somehow, I do not know how, they fell into Colonel Mann's hands."

He thought he saw her tense.

He continued: "And the Colonel—"

"Was blackmailing your friend, and so you went to his suite to try to get them back."

"That's right."

"But instead, you discovered his body."

"Yes."

A sardonic expression came over her lovely face. "It is almost like an excellent play I read last year," she said. "I declined the role because my part had too few lines, but the basic situation of it was very good. According to the police—in the play, that is—the person who found the body was the one most likely to have done the deed." Her gaze swept over him again. "Did you kill the Colonel, Mr. Ames?"

"Hardly."

"Well, someone did, didn't he? And we are all very much indebted to him, are we not?"

"Did you see anyone else when you visited Colonel Mann on Monday evening?" He could see that the question startled her, but only for a moment.

"No."

"But you do acknowledge that you went to see him?"

She pulled herself up; her expression became arrogant—prideful. If she were older, MacKenzie thought, she might be described at this moment as a grande dame, but she was still too young for that. Not more than thirty-one or -two, he thought.

"That is what the police wanted to know," she replied.

"Ah. They have questioned you?"

"They most certainly have. And as rudely as can be, I must say. What is the name of that dreadful little man—?"

"Crippen," he supplied; it was not a guess.

"Crippen, yes. Horrid person! He behaved as if he believed I was the guilty party, can you imagine?"

"Yes. I can. He is not a man of—ah—delicate manners. But then, in his position, he can hardly afford to be."

She shuddered. "It is too galling to think that we pay him to abuse us like that. Why, he practically accused me of the crime!"

Ames allowed her a moment to banish the odious Crippen from her thoughts, and then he asked, more gently than he had intended, "But you did go to see the Colonel on Monday evening?"

"Yes."

"And you didn't see anyone else?"

"I passed a man in the corridor. But in the Colonel's suite—no."

"Just the Colonel?"

"Yes."

"Without success, I take it?"

"Without success." Her voice was suddenly flat. "If you had ever had any dealings with Colonel Mann, Mr. Ames, you would know what a hard, hard man he was. He had not a drop of mercy—of simple human kindness—in him. So, no, I was not successful. He was demanding a sum of money that was far beyond my ability to pay. And in any case, since he so thoroughly destroyed my reputation some years ago, I was not about to pay him this time around."

"So why did you go to him?"

"To—to try to make him see reason, I suppose. It was foolish of me, I admit. Reason, to a man like that, was simply and only money. I knew the moment I stepped into his room that I had gone on a fool's errand."

"How long were you there?"

"Not more than ten minutes."

"And when you left, you went to the theater?"

"No. Monday is my night off. I came back here."

"Which your maid will attest to."

"Of course." She gave him a wry smile. "What do I pay her for, Mr. Ames, but to say what I tell her to say?"

"In a situation like this, I hardly think it is a matter for jest—"

"I am not jesting. I am simply telling you the truth. I was here on Monday evening, all during the time that some-one—finally—killed the Colonel, and Hilda will swear to that."

Ames shifted a little on his chair, and finally he put his hat on the floor on top of his gloves.

"Do you know a man named Richard Longworth?" he asked.

"Richard Longworth?" She hesitated; then: "Yes."

"How well?"

"That is rather impertinent, Mr. Ames."

He shrugged. "I beg your pardon."

She eyed him narrowly. "Richard Longworth? I have met him." She lifted one shoulder and let it drop; it seemed an extraordinarily sensuous gesture. "I could not tell you where, but I do recognize the name. Does that satisfy you?"

Not quite, he thought, but he let it pass.

"He had the program from your play in his room at the Hotel Brunswick."

"Many men have the program from my play in their room."

"I am sure they do. But his room is adjacent to Colonel Mann's."

She made no reaction.

Ames was aware that he was too warm. He felt awkward in the presence of this woman, and it was not a sensation to which he was accustomed.

And time was passing, and he was no nearer to finding Val's letters. He reminded himself that doing so was the object of his visit to this woman; he must not let her deflect him from it.

"Mrs. Vincent, do you own a pearl necklace?"

"A pearl necklace? Why, yes, I do."

"Could I see it? I assure you this is not idle curiosity."

She contemplated him. "I would be happy to show it to you, but unfortunately I cannot. It broke last week. It is at the jeweler's, being repaired."

"Do you—might there be some matching piece to it? A bracelet, perhaps?"

Now she was smiling at him again. "No. Not a bracelet. But earrings—yes, I have those, if you are so very interested in my jewelry."

"If you wouldn't mind."

Gracefully, she rose and left the room. Ames glanced at MacKenzie and quirked an eyebrow. He did not want to speak; undoubtedly, the maid would be listening. Unless she'd been dispatched to fetch the earrings—but no, here was Mrs. Vincent, back again, the earrings cradled in her palm.

She held them out to him. He needed only one glance to

see that they did not match the pearl he'd seen in the Colonel's suite.

"Thank you," he said. Since she did not resume her seat, he rose. "And I thank you for seeing us. My young—ah—friend is most distressed, as you can imagine, and as you see, I am putting aside all courtesy in my attempt to help her."

"Not at all, Mr. Ames." Although her face was grave, she seemed nevertheless to be secretly smiling at him.

She was moving toward the door, and Ames and MacKenzie followed.

"Mrs. Vincent—"

"Yes, Mr. Ames?" She turned to look at him. She was tall for a woman—five foot seven, at least, MacKenzie thought —and with a regal yet graceful way of moving that must serve her well onstage.

"Why did you stay in Boston?" The moment he'd spoken he was appalled at himself. It was not the way he'd intended to say it; in fact, he'd not intended to say it at all. It had just erupted from him—why, after her disgrace, after having had every door in the city shut to her, after being left destitute, friendless—why had she stayed here?

"I mean," he added, trying without success to cover his embarrassment, "would you not have done better to go to New York? Or even abroad—London, perhaps?"

She did not seem offended; she looked at him calmly, almost pityingly. "I had to stay here," she said simply.

"Had to—?"

"Yes. Of course. Can you not understand that? Even if we were never well acquainted, you know me, you know my family. You know what happened to me—thanks to the late and unlamented Colonel Mann. And so because I became a pariah here, it was important to me to stay here and make people acknowledge me once more. Even if it is the kind of acknowledgment that comes with being an actress."

"I don't—"

"And I have done that, Mr. Ames. Far more than I could

have imagined. Why, I fill the theater every time I step on-stage!" She spoke without conceit; she was, they under-stood, simply stating a fact. "Success in New York, or anyplace else, would not have meant half so much to me. Even though I am no longer received in so-called 'polite society,' Boston cannot ignore me. I am a presence here, whether people like it or not. That is my triumph, Mr. Ames. And believe me, I savor it."

He felt as if she'd slapped him across the face, and it took him a moment to regain his composure—what little he'd had, in her presence.

"I beg your pardon," he said stiffly. "I did not mean to pry—"

"I would never let you do that," she replied. They were at the door. She gave him her hand; he took it, wondering if her touch would sear his flesh.

"Would you care to come to a performance tomorrow evening?" she asked, taking in MacKenzie with her glance.

Ames had no idea what he was scheduled to do tomor-row evening, but suddenly it did not matter. "Thank you," he replied. "That is very kind of you."

"Not at all," she said, and it was the truth. "Call at the box office; they will give you chits for my private box."

And with that, they were out in the corridor once more. Ames felt as though he'd been put through some kind of wringer. MacKenzie, wisely, managed to get all the way back to Louisburg Square without once mentioning the seductive attraction of Mrs. Serena Vincent, who, having once been disgraced and destroyed by Colonel Mann, was by her own admission unhappy to learn that he'd targeted her once again.

CHAPTER 14

CAREFULLY, CAROLINE POURED STEAMING TEA INTO THE delicate china cup and handed it on its saucer to the formidable old woman sitting across from her.

Aunt Euphemia Ames, who was the elder sister of Caroline's late father, nodded her thanks and declined her niece's offer of Sally Lunn.

"None of that heavy stuff for me, Caroline," she said disapprovingly. "You know my digestion is delicate."

Caroline did not know it. Aunt Euphemia had the digestion of a goat. Nevertheless, she smiled in assent; one did not argue with Euphemia.

That lady sipped her tea, made a slight wry face—Darjeeling was not to her taste—and said sharply, "Why do you read that trash, Caroline? I should think you would want to improve your mind instead of wallowing in that silly stuff."

She meant the Diana Strangeways novel, its title clearly visible on its purple cloth spine. Caroline had, in fact, been sneaking a few pages when Euphemia arrived, and she had not had the presence of mind to slip the book under her chair. She should not have been reading it, she knew; she should have been reading Emerson's *Essays,* which was the current assignment for her Saturday Morning Reading Club. Having Euphemia spot it was her punishment, she thought.

Not that hiding it would have done any good; Euphemia had an unnerving kind of second sight. Probably she would have seen it even if Caroline had hidden it behind the aspidistra plant in the corner.

Euphemia Ames was a tiny, ancient creature, barely five feet tall, with snow-white hair and brilliant dark eyes and a face as wrinkled as a walnut shell. She always wore black (for the Union dead); she always smelled like camphor; she was notorious in Boston Society for her sharp tongue and her high moral standards (thus her dislike of popular fiction); and she adored Val.

And that, Caroline had often thought, was what saved Euphemia from being completely impossible: her love for Valentine, the child of Euphemia's younger sister who, with her husband, had died of cholera in Naples when Val, left behind in Boston, had been only a year old. Euphemia had taken Valentine in, and had done—it was widely agreed—a perfectly splendid, if somewhat too strict, job of bringing her up.

Since one did not argue with Euphemia, Caroline knew from long experience that the only possible tactic to adopt was to change the subject; with luck, Euphemia would allow it.

"Valentine was perfectly lovely last night, Aunt," she said.

"Yes, I know she was. I saw her before you and Addington came for her, remember. I called to thank him for escorting her. Of course it is no more than his duty, but still."

She did not include Caroline in her thanks, but Caroline had not expected her to.

Val's maid, she thought. Surely Euphemia knew the girl had left, but how to broach the subject?

"When does he leave?" Euphemia was saying.

"You mean his trip to Egypt? Next Wednesday."

Euphemia wrinkled her nose; she looked as though she'd smelled something bad. "Why on earth does he want to go gallivanting off to a place like that? Think of the diseases he might catch."

Caroline allowed herself a little laugh. Euphemia took some pride in the fact that she herself had never traveled outside Massachusetts.

"I don't think he's concerned about diseases, Aunt. It is a wonderful opportunity for him. Professor Harbinger is a noted authority on Egypt, and he believes that Addington has real ability—"

"At what? Taking a shovel into the desert to uncover a few relics?"

"Oh, it is much more than that. They hope to find the tomb of—I can't remember which pharaoh, but a very important one, I believe. It may be filled with all kinds of treasures."

Euphemia sniffed. "Treasures! And what will they do with them? Sell them?"

"Oh, no. Of course not. They will bring them back and study them. And then they will put them into some museum, either the museum at Harvard, or the Fine Arts in Copley Square—"

"And they will expect people to go to see them?" Euphemia said. "Who would bother?"

This was not, as Caroline had realized at the beginning, a fruitful topic of discussion. Time for another change.

"Valentine said that she will stop by with George after they've done skating on the Frog Pond," she said.

She thought she saw a faint softening of Euphemia's customary fierce expression.

"Is that Alice girl with them?" Euphemia asked.

"Alice Dane? I don't know."

"Walking over, I saw Dr. Cabot coming out of the Danes' house. Alice has been sickly since the summer. I trust it isn't anything catching. And she fainted last night at the Cotillion, Valentine told me."

"Yes. She did. I know that she's—"

"But never mind about that." Euphemia set down her cup with a disturbingly loud *chink*. She stared at Caroline accusingly and drew her mouth down into a severe line. This was the Euphemia Ames, Caroline knew, who had spent her youth working with the Abolitionists; she had had the reputation of being one of the most fierce, one of the most determined.

"Caroline, I want you to tell me the truth about Addington."

Caroline's heart sank. "The truth, Aunt? I don't—"

"Yes, you do. You know exactly what I mean. Why was he visiting that terrible man on Monday evening? It gave me a bad turn, I can tell you, when Harriet Coolidge told me about it this morning at Sewing Circle. And of course she didn't trouble to lower her voice, so everyone heard."

Euphemia's Sewing Circle was the second oldest in the city; it still had half a dozen members.

Caroline cleared her throat. If you are going to lie, someone had once told her, keep as close to the truth as you can. "It—concerned someone he knew, I believe."

"Why would any of Addington's friends be mixed up with someone like Colonel Mann?"

"I don't know, Aunt. He didn't say."

"It is most unseemly," Euphemia snapped. "What will the Putnams say? What have they said already? Did they speak to you last night?"

Caroline remembered Josephine Putnam's cold stare, her grudging words of greeting.

"Yes," she said.

"With anything more than the most minimal courtesy?"

"Yes," she lied.

"I am surprised to hear it. Josephine Putnam is very careful about her associations, even if the Putnams are practically upstarts in this city." The Putnams had come to Boston a few generations after the Ameses—something Euphemia never forgot—and Josephine was only a Matthews by birth. The Matthewses had arrived well after the Revolution.

Nevertheless, George Putnam was a splendid match for Valentine, and Euphemia was quick to light on anything that might put the marriage in jeopardy.

"Well?" she asked. "Did she speak to Addington, too? Really, Caroline," she went on without giving Caroline a chance to answer, "I do think you might have alerted him to the danger of what he was doing. Was this so-called friend so important that he needed to jeopardize Valentine's position? Who is it, anyway?"

"I don't know." Tell one lie and others come trippingly to the tongue, Caroline thought miserably. She had no idea where Addington was—it was late, past five o'clock—and she didn't know, just at this moment, if she wanted him to appear or not. Probably she did.

If Euphemia was upset because Addington found the Colonel's body, what would she say if she knew the reason he'd gone to see the Colonel in the first place? Think, she told herself sternly; think of something—and warn Addington and Val, later, of what you've said so that all our stories match.

"If he'd asked me," Euphemia went on, "which I realize he would never do, but if he had, I would have told him that on no account should he ever associate with a dreadful man like the Colonel." She held out her cup. "I never could understand how the Colonel found out about the Bradshaws," she added. "Could you?"

"I—ah—be careful, Aunt, I made your cup too full. Sorry." Change the subject—again. And quickly. "How is—how is your lumbago?"

"Not as bad as it was last winter, thank goodness."

Euphemia glanced around her niece's parlor. All seemed

to be in order—all surfaces thoroughly dusted, a good fire in the grate, antimacassars freshly washed and ironed. They were managing well on just the one servant, she thought; too bad they'd had to take in a lodger, but it was better than selling up and leaving for heaven knew where.

And speaking of servants . . . "Val's maid has gone," she said abruptly.

"Oh? Yes, I believe she said something—" Caroline had been caught off guard (had Euphemia intended that?), and her voice sounded forced, not nearly casual enough.

"And when I say 'gone,' I mean just up and left, without a word. Can you imagine? And only last month I gave the girl two of my old flannel petticoats. There is no gratitude anywhere these days," Euphemia added darkly.

"Do you—she left no word?" Caroline asked faintly.

Euphemia shot her a glance. "Are you all right, Caroline? You look pale. Have another piece of Sally Lunn. No, no word at all. She stayed up to help Valentine to bed after the Cotillion, of course, but this morning she was gone. Vanished. And to make it even more mysterious, she was owed wages! It is odd, don't you think?"

Yes, thought Caroline, I do think. But it is not something I can discuss with you, Aunt.

"I never liked her," Euphemia went on. "She was Irish, you know. Mrs. Haddock thought she was sly, but she never actually caught her out at anything underhanded." Mrs. Haddock, Euphemia's housekeeper, was a woman with an even more formidable demeanor than Euphemia herself. "Ah, well, I will send Mrs. Haddock to the Intelligence Office tomorrow and put in a request for a new girl. I want one from Nova Scotia, like your Margaret. What we shall do when we have only Irish to choose from, I cannot think."

Although Euphemia, decades ago, had been a devoted advocate for the rights of black slaves, she gave little thought, nowadays, to other oppressed groups.

Caroline felt, suddenly, quite exhausted. Euphemia would be here for another half hour, at least.

At that moment, she heard the low rumble of men's voices in the front hall, and a wave of relief swept over her.

"There is Addington," she said to Euphemia. "Now you can thank him yourself."

The pocket doors slid apart and Ames and MacKenzie stepped into the room. Greetings were exchanged; Euphemia even managed a cordial glance at the doctor.

Caroline handed cups of tea to the men, who settled themselves, and then Euphemia, in her blunt, forthright manner, said, "Thank you, Addington, for escorting Val last night."

He inclined his head. "My pleasure."

"I know you don't have much truck with those social affairs, but they are important for the young women."

"You have nothing to worry about. Val was one of the belles of the ball, wasn't she, Caroline?"

"Yes—yes, she was."

The unspoken hung in the room like a sword over all their heads: Addington's name in the newspapers in connection with Colonel Mann's death.

Ames stretched his long legs comfortably in front of the fire, put down his cup, and said, "Speaking of Val, Aunt, would you allow her to come to the theater with us tomorrow night?"

At once, Euphemia was on the alert. "The theater? What theater?"

"*Lady Musgrove's Secret,*" Ames replied easily.

What was this? thought Caroline. Addington—going to the theater? Which he never did, except for a performance of Shakespeare. And not only to the theater, but to see the notorious Serena Vincent?

So that's where he was this afternoon, she realized. Odd, the sudden pang of resentment that struck her; or perhaps it was not odd at all, considering Mrs. Vincent's reputation.

Euphemia, for once in her life, was too astonished to speak. She recovered quickly, however, and said sharply, *"Lady Musgrove's Secret!* Really, Addington, have you taken leave of your senses? If Josephine Putnam found out that Val had gone to see such a thing, she would call off the wedding at once!"

Caroline had a sudden bleak vision of the endless years stretching before them all as they minded their behavior so as not to upset the Putnams.

Ames shrugged. "Just a thought, Aunt. I don't think attending a performance of that particular play—or any play, for that matter—would destroy Val's—ah—virtue."

"Nonsense!" snapped Euphemia. "Unmarried young girls don't go to plays like that, and you know it! I am surprised at you for even making the suggestion. And in any case, why are you going to it? It's hardly your kind of thing."

"I was given a box pass this afternoon. George could come, too, if he liked."

"Don't even mention it!" Euphemia retorted. "That would be most unsuitable! And speaking of unsuitable behavior, Addington, I would like to ask you why you went to see—"

The door knocker sounded. Another timely reprieve, thought Caroline. They heard Margaret answer; they heard a voice—only one—in the front hall. Val's voice. George was supposed to come with her to tea. What had happened?

Val's face was rosy from the cold; she wore a fetching short blue skating skirt that just grazed her ankles, and a matching jacket and hat.

Had she had a pleasant afternoon with her friends, gliding around the Frog Pond, Caroline wondered; or, as seemed the case from the girl's expression, had it been a disaster?

"And where is your young man?" Euphemia said as Val settled herself beside Caroline and accepted her tea.

Val did not look up as she answered.

"He—he had to leave early."

"Leave early! But he promised—"

"He didn't skate at all," Val said. Her voice was low—defeated, thought Caroline as she felt her anger beginning to build. Those Putnams!

"Didn't skate?" Euphemia pressed on. Leave it, Aunt, thought Caroline; can't you see what happened? "But it was he who organized the afternoon—"

"I think, Aunt, that we had better not inquire too closely just now," Ames said.

Euphemia shot him a defiant glance, but to Caroline's surprise, she left off her questioning.

"He said he had something urgent to attend to at the office," Val said, still in that defeated tone that Caroline found quite frightening.

George was a junior partner in his father's firm. It was an old, staid firm, like the family itself. Nothing urgent ever happened there, Caroline thought.

They passed the next ten minutes in uncomfortable small talk, and then Euphemia decreed that she and Val were going home. Ames offered to accompany them, but Euphemia declined.

"Come see me tomorrow, Val, dear," Caroline said, kissing Val's cheek as they parted. She was longing to hear more about the faithless George; perhaps he'd had a genuine emergency after all, but she doubted it.

It has begun, she thought as she returned to the parlor, and we must acknowledge it for what it is: the delicate business of separation, of George wriggling out of his engagement to Val. The little incident this afternoon, the fabrication of "urgent business," would be followed by other fabrications, other excuses to avoid her. And in the end—

No. It was too ridiculous. Even Josephine Putnam could not be so narrow-minded, so cruel.

She sat silent, brooding by the fire. MacKenzie forbore to speak, not wanting to intrude on her thoughts.

Ames, too, was aware of her mood; he dealt with it by announcing that he was going to Cambridge to dine with Professor Harbinger and deliver the book from the Athenaeum. If he had time, he said, he would call on Professor James.

C HAPTER
1 5

THE NIGHT WAS FADING TO PALE GRAY DAWN THE NEXT
morning as Caroline made her way down the steep brick
sidewalk along Mt. Vernon Street to the busy commercial
thoroughfare below. The tall redbrick houses that lined the
way still slumbered, shades drawn; in the below-stairs
kitchen windows that faced onto the areaways she could see
lights and hear the occasional clatter of pots and pans, of
cast-iron stoves being riddled as the servants started their
long days, but otherwise all was quiet. A few delivery wagons crawled the narrow streets, but the day's heavy traffic
had not yet begun. She and Addington had given up their
carriage some time before; their slot in the stables down on
the flat of the hill had been sold, the money used to pay
their mother's last doctor bills.

She turned onto Charles Street. The first Green Trolley of
the day was just passing, the horses' breath making little clouds of steam in the raw, cold air. The few people
she passed were not people she knew; they were part of
that great mass of Bostonians whose labor served people
like her and Addington: servants, grocery clerks, delivery-
men.

But that, of course, was why she was here at this hour:

she knew that Euphemia's housekeeper, Mrs. Haddock, always did early shopping on Mondays and Thursdays.

She turned in at the brightly lighted S. S. Pierce Grocers'. Mrs. Haddock was not there, but in the next moment Caroline felt a draft of cold air as the door opened and the housekeeper came in. Caroline stepped forward.

"Mrs. Haddock, you must excuse me, but I wanted a word with you."

"Oh! Miss Ames! You gave me a start."

Caroline could read the unspoken question in the woman's eyes: What are you doing here at this hour?

"I apologize for interrupting you. I know you need to do your shopping. But I just wanted to ask you—"

She had been maneuvering Mrs. Haddock to a quiet place toward the back, where they would not be overheard.

"I've only a moment," Mrs. Haddock said firmly. "It's a busy day today, and with Miss Val's maid gone missing—"

"Yes. That is just what I wanted to ask you about. Could you tell me where I might be able to find her?"

Mrs. Haddock's eyes widened in surprise. "Find her? I doubt it."

"She didn't have any family in the city?"

"Not that I know of. She was from County Cork. Said she came over on her own."

"So you don't know if she had any connection at all here in Boston?"

"No. She was closemouthed. I never really trusted her, even though the Intelligence Office gave her good enough references. I told Miss Val to check all her valuables when we realized she'd gone for good."

"And was anything missing?"

"Not that we could tell." Mrs. Haddock seemed reluctant to admit it.

"When was her last day off?"

"Afternoon only. We get one afternoon a month off, and hers was two weeks ago today."

"And you don't know where she went on those afternoons, whom she might have seen?"

"No."

"All right, Mrs. Haddock. I'm sorry to have detained you, but I just thought—"

"May I ask why you're asking, Miss Ames?"

"I—ah—Val seemed upset about it. About the girl's leaving so suddenly. And she thought she might be in some kind of trouble, and that perhaps she—we—could help—"

"Miss Val is too kindhearted. She shouldn't waste her time worrying about that one. Good riddance, I say."

Caroline bit her lip, unwilling to admit defeat. "Did she—just one last question—did she have, perhaps, some young man?"

Mrs. Haddock, just turning away, hesitated.

Yes, thought Caroline; and if I hadn't asked, you wouldn't have told me.

"There's a boy at the hardware store two doors down," Mrs. Haddock said, disapproval oozing from her pores. "You might want to talk to him."

And with that, she strode over to the counter, where a clerk was smiling at her obligingly.

The hardware store was just opening, a boy letting down its green awning, clerks inside removing dust covers from the displays. Neither of the first two whom Caroline approached could help her, but then a tall, gangling youth emerged from the back, broom in hand, and it seemed that, yes, he did know a girl who was Miss Thorne's maid.

"Did you know that she has disappeared?"

He blinked. "Naw."

"Well, she has. Do you know where I can find her?"

"Naw."

"When did you see her last?"

This seemed to be a difficult question. "Two weeks ago," he answered finally.

"On her afternoon off?"

"Yes."

"Did you walk out with her?"

"I don't want no trouble."

"This won't cause you trouble." Caroline heard the sincerity in her voice, and silently she asked pardon for it. "Did you?"

"Just to have a meal, down at the Haymarket."

"And she didn't say anything about being unhappy, or wanting to leave her position?"

"Naw. Nothing like that."

As the youth turned away, Caroline made one last attempt. "If you should hear from her, would you let me know?" She dug in her reticule for her card case, extracted one, and thrust it at him.

It was not until she was out on the street once more that she realized he hadn't said yes.

HE SAYS HE'S ALL RIGHT, MISS, BUT HE DOESN'T WANT TO be disturbed."

"Not disturbed? But why? It is past nine o'clock!"

Having risen so early to see Mrs. Haddock, Caroline felt as though she'd been up half the day. She and MacKenzie had finished their breakfast, and, concerned that Ames had not appeared, she'd sent Margaret to inquire. He'd come home from Cambridge last night after she retired, so she hadn't seen him since late yesterday afternoon.

She rose from the table, her expression suddenly taut with some premonition of disaster. What was wrong? Was Addington ill?

"Excuse me, Doctor," she said. She hurried upstairs and knocked on Ames's door.

"Addington? Are you all right?"

No answer.

"Addington? May I come in?"

Still no reply. She put her hand on the doorknob and

turned it; carefully, as if she hesitated to make a sound, she pushed open the door.

"Addington?" she said, but she did not go in.

In the darkened bedroom she saw the outline of his tall, thin form underneath the bedcovers. It did not move.

"Addington, what is it? Why haven't you come down? Are you ill?"

"No."

"But what is wrong? You've missed breakfast—"

"Leave me be, Caroline. I'll be down directly." His voice was low, oddly subdued.

Thoroughly puzzled and no less concerned, she pulled the door shut and went back downstairs to the dining room. She met MacKenzie with a bright, unconvincing smile and murmured something inconsequential.

In ten minutes Ames joined them. He looked despondent, as though all the sorrows of the world had fallen on his shoulders. Helping himself to porridge and tea, he began, without enthusiasm, to eat. When MacKenzie offered him the newspaper, he declined it—a sure sign, Caroline thought, that something was deeply amiss.

Finally, when she could stand the suspense no longer, she said, "Addington, what is it? What is wrong?"

"The expedition is canceled," Ames said flatly.

There was a moment of astonished silence as they absorbed it.

"Canceled!" Caroline exclaimed. MacKenzie felt her shock; he was shocked himself. "But—why?" she asked.

"Professor Harbinger had a fall yesterday afternoon. He tripped stepping down from his carriage and broke his leg in two places. He won't walk again for months—if ever," Ames added gloomily.

Caroline let it sink in. "But that is terrible! Canceled! Oh, my dear, I am so sorry! What a disappointment for you!"

He began to eat again. When she saw that he was not

going to reply, she said, "I suppose there is no hope of going without him?"

He shook his head. "None. Without his direction, we would be wasting our time. And besides, I doubt that the authorities would allow us onto the site without him."

"Yes. Of course. I hadn't thought of that." She sighed. "What a shame. I must remember to send a note to Cousin Miranda. She will be disappointed—although her disappointment is nothing compared to yours," she added quickly. "Well, perhaps she can come for a visit, at any rate."

This prospect not visibly lightening Ames's mood, there seemed nothing more to say. Then, as if she were trying to divert her brother's thoughts, Caroline said: "Well, Addington, at least now you can give your full attention to Val's letters. It will give you a way to occupy yourself."

He gave her a look. "I have plenty of ways to occupy myself, Caroline."

"Yes, you do, but this is so important!"

He put down his spoon and held up a hand to forestall what she intended to say. "I know it is. But I will tell you quite frankly, the more I try to find them, the more impossible the task seems to be. I am afraid we will have to leave it to the police to discover who killed Colonel Mann and—"

"And took Val's letters?"

"And took Val's letters."

Caroline stared at him reproachfully as they heard the rumble and thump of the dumbwaiter in the back passage.

"Addington."

"Yes?"

"Will you keep on—for Val's sake?"

He looked away from her. Was he imagining the hot, bright desert of Egypt, MacKenzie wondered, and the magnificent—surely they would be magnificent—ruins that now he might never see?

"Addington?"

He came back. He met her eyes.

"Caroline, as our dear departed mother used to say, you are a caution."

She brightened. "Say yes, Addington!"

"In fact, if you were not so charming, I would go so far as to call you a strong-minded female."

MacKenzie cringed. Strong-minded female! But they were the worst—the absolute worst. He had never actually met such a one, but he thought they were the type of women who were called suffragettes—that dread Amazonian type who inspired fear and loathing in the stoutest male heart.

Caroline did not seem to mind her brother's epithets. She smiled at him. "You may call me what you please as long as you say yes."

"Yes—what?"

"Yes—that you will keep on, of course."

For a long moment he did not answer. Then, as if acknowledging that she had won, he said, "Very well, Caro. I will. For Val's sake—and yours."

CHAPTER 16

"AH! MR. AMES! THE VERY PERSON I WANTED TO SEE!"
Deputy Chief Inspector Elwood Crippen came around from
behind his overladen desk, his hand outstretched, his face
wreathed in smiles.

"Did you, Inspector? Well, here I am."

It was an hour later. In deference to MacKenzie's bad
knee, Ames had procured a herdic to take them to City Hall.
He'd wanted MacKenzie with him. He had come to value
the doctor's solid, sensible presence; he thought of MacKenzie as a kind of anchor, keeping him safe—he hoped—from
any foolish excess.

They seated themselves across the desk from Crippen,
who positioned himself behind it, peering out at them from
between towering stacks of files. "I would have called on
you—and your charming sister—if you hadn't come in,"
Crippen said. "I may do so yet," he added with what Mac-
Kenzie thought was an offputting smile.

"What has happened, Inspector? Have you discovered
your man?"

Crippen pursed his lips. He looked quite pleased with
himself; his eyes twinkled, and his nicotine-stained fingers

drummed an irritating little rhythm on a folder atop one of the stacks of files in front of him.

"Man?" he said. "What makes you think we are searching for a man?"

Ames shot a glance at MacKenzie, who seemed as surprised as himself.

"What are you saying, Inspector? You don't mean that a woman—"

Crippen wagged a finger at him. "I mean that we have a suspect. Not arrested yet, but a very good suspect indeed. A female suspect," he added.

"I don't believe it," Ames replied. "A woman? How could a woman possibly—"

"Oh, yes, Mr. Ames. A woman could. And they often do. Why, I remember a case a few years ago—in Albany, I think it was—where a woman took an ax and butchered her husband and his brother as well." Crippen shuddered slightly. "Horrible."

"Do you have sufficient evidence against—this woman—to arrest her?" Ames asked.

"Not quite. Not quite yet." Crippen smiled again. "But we will. Oh, yes. Right now we have"—and he ticked off the points on his fingers—"her mention in the galleys. Three witnesses who saw her in the hotel that night. That's motive and opportunity right there. And we have even more motive, since we discovered a threatening letter from her to the Colonel among his papers. Amazing what people will put in writing, isn't it?"

"But how could she—"

"Don't trouble yourself about it, Mr. Ames." Crippen smiled beneficently. "We have it all in hand. The—ah—lady is a well-known sort of person, and she has a past history with the Colonel. Which only makes it more likely that she's our man, so to speak. She's lived a reckless sort of life, and she's just the type of woman who would—"

An unpleasant thought had taken hold in Ames's mind as

the inspector spoke, and now he could contain his suspicions no longer.

"Just whom are you referring to, Inspector?"

Crippen contemplated him. "It's really not for me to say."

"Still. Since I have an interest in this case—"

And since my cousin sits on the Board of Police Commissioners, he thought. Standish Wainwright: a man of fastidious morals who would not welcome Ames's meddling.

Crippen threw a warning glance at MacKenzie. "It has to stay quiet between us. We are still tidying up the details, and I don't want the District Attorney coming back at me for sloppy work."

He enjoys this, MacKenzie thought—his power over us. He had disliked Crippen from the first, and he'd been right.

"It is Mrs. Serena Vincent," Crippen announced triumphantly.

Even though Ames knew whom Crippen was going to name, he was stunned to hear it.

"Impossible," he said.

"Not at all. It's very possible. It's most probable, in fact. As I said, we have a few details—"

"She couldn't have done it," Ames insisted. MacKenzie was surprised at his vehemence.

"Oh? Why?" Crippen was smiling no longer.

"Because—if she was at the hotel on Monday evening, it was well before the time the Colonel was killed."

There was a little silence. Then Crippen loudly cleared his throat.

"And how do you know that, Mr. Ames?"

"As I told you, I have some interest in this case."

"Yes. You did say that."

Ames shook his head. "I don't believe it," he said. "The Colonel ruined her once and for all five years ago. Why would she take her revenge so late? Nothing he could do to her now would make any difference—"

"That isn't the impression she gave in her letter. It is

dated a week ago, and in it she says that if he doesn't back off, she will do what she must. Those are her very words. 'I will do what I must.' What do you make of that?"

Ames made nothing of it. What could he make of it? If Serena Vincent had in fact written such a letter to the Colonel, she had implicated herself long before she or anyone else knew the damage her impulsive words—and surely they were impulsive, written at some brief moment of despair—would do to her.

"I make of it that you are mistaken, Inspector." His voice sounded hollow in his ears. What could he offer to defend Serena Vincent, when she herself had so thoroughly and convincingly damned herself?

"And there is more," Crippen said. He riffled the pages of the file before him, and they realized that it must be the file on Colonel Mann's murder. Ames itched to see it, but he did not quite dare to ask.

"Yes?" he said abruptly. "What?"

"She shot a man three years ago."

Ames felt as if Crippen had kicked him in his stomach. *Shot a man—*

MacKenzie put his hand on Ames's arm. Ames had gone quite white; MacKenzie could see a little pulse throbbing hard just above his high starched collar.

"All right?" he said softly.

Ames glanced at him and nodded.

Crippen cleared his throat again. He had an insufferable look on his ugly face, MacKenzie thought: smug, self-satisfied. Even if Crippen were correct in his suspicions of Mrs. Vincent, he had no right to proclaim them so self-righteously. I detest you, Inspector Crippen, MacKenzie thought; and you will pay court to Miss Caroline Ames over my dead body.

"Well, Mr. Ames?" Crippen said. "What about that, eh? The woman is known to be violent, and while that other case had nothing to do with this one, it nevertheless points to—"

"Where?" said Ames.

"You mean, where did she shoot him? In his left arm."

Ames only just managed to bite back a scathing reply. "Where—was she when it happened?"

"Oh. You mean *where.* In New York."

"And was she charged with it?"

A sour look wiped away Crippen's smugness. "No."

"So in the eyes of the law, she didn't do it."

"Oh, she did it, all right. But somehow—I don't have all the details—she was able to get off. No charges, nothing. Of course, they are very corrupt down there in New York. You can get away with attempted murder down there—as she did—if you have the right connections."

And here in Boston? MacKenzie wondered. Boston was the most connected place he'd ever seen, a heavily intertwined network of connections, family and otherwise.

Ames stood up with such a violent movement that his chair skidded backward. The news that Serena Vincent had shot a man—no matter what the circumstances—had badly unnerved him. He thought of her lustrous eyes, her smile, her low, thrilling voice. For a moment his heart shivered as he envisioned her arrested, imprisoned, tried, convicted— No. Impossible. He didn't believe it—wouldn't, until she admitted it to him herself.

Did she know, he wondered, that she was Crippen's chief suspect? If she didn't, someone should warn her. He would do it himself, he thought. Tonight, or perhaps even this afternoon.

"Good day to you, Inspector," he said, only just managing to keep a civil tone.

"And good day to you, too, Mr. Ames." Crippen was smiling again. "Stop by anytime—anytime! And give my best regards to your sister!"

Out on the street once more, Ames stopped while he took several deep breaths.

"This case grows nastier by the minute," he said.

"More complicated, at any rate," MacKenzie replied. His knee was hurting. The clock on its tall standard near the curb said eleven-ten. Dr. Warren was to examine him at two.

Ames had started down School Street toward Washington. "Come on, Doctor. We are finally going to see someone—I hope—who can be of real help."

Limping a little, leaning heavily on his cane, MacKenzie hurried to catch up.

CHAPTER
17

THE BLACK LETTERS ON THE PEBBLED HALF-GLASS OF THE
office door said "Longworth & Sprague, Attorneys at Law."
The reception room was deserted, the secretary's desk
filmed with dust. A dead miniature palm tree languished in
the corner; a few outdated periodicals lay scattered on a
table. The place looked as though it had not seen a client for
weeks—perhaps months.

But someone was there, and now he appeared from the
inner office.

"Yes?" he said.

"Mr. Longworth?"

"Yes."

Richard Longworth was a slender man of medium height;
he was in his late thirties, MacKenzie thought. He had a
dissipated look to him: clothing not quite spruce enough,
eyes sunk back in his head, hair not combed properly. Once,
younger, he must have been handsome, but now his features
were blurred with drink, his mouth a little loose. He stood
in the doorway to his office, his hand resting against the
doorjamb as if he needed its support.

"Mr.—Ames, isn't it?"

"And this is Dr. John MacKenzie," Ames said. He

realized that if he'd passed Richard Longworth in the street, he wouldn't have recognized him.

"What can I do for you, Mr. Ames?"

MacKenzie saw that Longworth tried to smile, but the effect was more of a grimace.

"I wanted a few words, if you have the time." Ames was remembering his interview with this man's father. The family was a good one, had been good for generations. Apparently, with this poor specimen before him, it had reached the end of its goodness and was now headed down the path of degeneration. Just as Longworth Senior had said.

"Ah. Time." Longworth grimaced again, almost as if he were in pain. "Yes, I am afraid that I have plenty of that. Come in."

He stood aside to let them pass. In his office, thick, leather-bound law books lay piled on the floor; a table by the window held a few tattered folders; the inkwell on the desk was dusty, encrusted with dry black ink.

They seated themselves on cracked leather chairs; Longworth perched himself on the corner of his desk.

"It is—a personal matter," Ames said.

Longworth waited.

"About—Colonel Mann."

Longworth's expression changed slightly; a wary look came into his eyes.

"You knew him," Ames went on.

A sudden malicious grin slashed across Longworth's face. "And you, Mr. Ames, discovered his body. That must have given you a nasty shock. What business had you with the Colonel, anyway?"

"I needed to retrieve a packet of letters for a young— friend." He hated having to say even so much; he hated having to be here in this dingy office. Then Val's tearful face rose up in his mind, only to be supplanted by the memory of Serena Vincent, and he went on. "Unfortunately, I was too late. I have it on good authority that the Colonel had the letters as late as four or five o'clock. Since they were not there when I went to him a few hours later, I have been working on the assumption that whoever killed him took them."

Longworth nodded. "I see. Well, Mr. Ames, I do not have them. I wish I did." They saw his unpleasant grin again. "My pony came in last on Saturday, and I need the money. Would you have paid for them?"

"No."

"Then how did you expect to get them, man? The Colonel was—"

"Yes? What was he?"

Longworth shrugged. "You know as well as I do what he was. Everyone knew. That is why he was so successful."

Ames contemplated him for a moment. "Did you work for him?" he asked abruptly.

Longworth was taken aback at that. "Work for him? How do you mean?"

"I mean, did you keep him free of the law? I have been told that in order to avoid being sued, he must have had someone giving him legal advice. Was that you?"

Longworth gave a short laugh; he looked away and then looked back. "If you are trying to implicate me in the Colonel's murder, Mr. Ames—"

"I am not trying to implicate you in anything. I am merely trying to recover a packet of letters that will prove very embarrassing to my young acquaintance if they are made public—or even if they are shown, privately, to the wrong person. Personally, I do not give one good damn who killed the Colonel, except insofar as finding that person may help me in my search."

Longworth's eyes gleamed as if he knew some delicious secret. "You would shield a murderer?"

"Not at all. But finding the Colonel's murderer is a police job, not mine."

"Just so. Well, Mr. Ames, I cannot help you—"

"You have the suite next to the Colonel's at the Hotel Brunswick."

This brought Longworth up short. "How do you know that?"

"I bribed the chambermaid."

"Did you, indeed? That was very underhanded of you."

Ames held his gaze. "You did work for him," he said flatly. "You were his legal counsel."

Longworth seemed to be considering something; then, after a moment, he said, "And what if I was? What does that prove?"

"Nothing. Except that you may be able to help me."

"In your search for those incriminating letters."

"Yes."

Longworth thought again. "This is a very delicate business, Mr. Ames."

"It most certainly is."

"But I will tell you frankly, if I had your packet of letters, I would say so. I could probably persuade you to part with some small sum for them, and even a small sum would be helpful to me at the moment." He spread his hands wide. "But I don't have them. Honestly."

When a man like Richard Longworth said "honestly," Ames thought, it was time to doubt every word he uttered.

Longworth eased himself off the desk. "I wish I could help you, Mr. Ames, but I fear I cannot. And I must ask you to excuse me now. I have an urgent matter to attend to."

Suddenly urgent, thought Ames; a few moments ago, you said you had time to spare.

"Will you continue the Colonel's—work?" he asked, rising also. He was reluctant to leave; this man knew much, he thought, and it would take far more than this brief interview to pry it out of him.

"Continue it?" Longworth gave a short laugh. "Perhaps. It takes a skilled hand to do such work, and I am not sure I have the Colonel's talents. But—yes. I may."

"The Colonel must have had any number of people who gave—or sold—him information," Ames said. "And if you could supply me with a name or two—"

"Why should I even admit to knowing the Colonel's informants, much less give you their names? Even if I knew them, which I do not. The Colonel was a secretive man. He had to be, given the nature of his business. And, given that, the only surprising aspect of this entire case is that he managed to stay alive as long as he did."

"The nature of his business was despicable," Ames retorted.

They stood facing each other; Mackenzie was just getting to his feet.

"Despicable?" Longworth said. "That is rather extreme. After all, the Colonel did not force people to behave badly. He merely took advantage of their behavior after the fact."

"That is the despicable part," Ames replied.

He turned to go, MacKenzie behind him. They had just reached the door when Longworth said, "I can account for my time, you know."

Ames paused and turned. "You can?"

"Yes. I was playing cards all evening at the St. Botolph."

Easily checked, Ames thought; if he needs to lie, surely he can come up with something better than that.

He nodded. "Good. Then you have no reason to worry."

They moved to the outer office, and then Ames turned back. "Are you acquainted with a Mrs. Serena Vincent?" he said.

"No."

I don't believe you, Ames thought. You had her program in your room at the Hotel Brunswick.

"The actress."

"I know the name." Longworth spoke testily, as if he were suddenly angered.

"Many people know the name. She herself had some business with the Colonel—"

"I know the name but not the lady herself," Longworth said curtly. "Good day, gentlemen."

URGENT BUSINESS, HE SAID. LET US SEE WHERE HE MIGHT lead us." Across the way, Ames stepped into the doorway of a tobacconist's shop a few doors down Washington Street. MacKenzie crowded in beside him. He would replenish his supply, he thought, while he waited.

Ames watched the doorway of Longworth's office building. Many people were going in and out, and the sidewalk in front was crowded, particularly now as the noon hour approached— Ah. There he was.

Ames was only just able to keep Longworth in sight. But almost at once, Longworth turned into a doorway. From across the street, Ames read the sign; it was a Western Union office.

Was it a telegram that Longworth had intended to send all morning? Or one that he knew he needed to send only after his interview with them?

Five minutes later, Longworth reappeared and walked back the short distance to his office. MacKenzie was just coming out of the tobacconist's.

"Since we are in the neighborhood," Ames said, "we may as well pay a call on Desmond. He may have picked up something useful."

But when they arrived at the cluttered office of the *Boston Literary Journal,* they learned that Delahanty had no news despite his considerable efforts. "Nothing," he said. "I've been talking to who knows all, and I haven't heard a thing."

Delahanty looked frazzled. He was pacing his little office, back and forth, back and forth; his mane of red hair looked as though he'd been caught in a high wind without a hat.

"What's wrong, Desmond?" Ames asked, unable to keep

from smiling a bit at his friend's rather ostentatious display of creative distemper.

"Oh, nothing at all," Delahanty said sarcastically. "Mother of God! The nerve of some people!"

He waved his hand at his desk. Aside from the usual piles of manuscripts and printers' proofs, Ames saw a dozen or so large sheets of foolscap with scribbled lines, crossed-out lines, arrows darting up and down, little diagrams with squares and rectangles and small, inked-in circles. They were silent testament to the torments of composition, not unusual in a place like this, except he knew that Delahanty, like many of his fellow Irishmen, was fluent with words both written and spoken.

"What's all that?" he said.

Delahanty groaned. "It is my miserable attempt to come up with a script—complete with stage directions and costume suggestions—for the Christmas Revels."

Ames had attended the Revels only once. He had a memory of some of his acquaintances bounding about the stage in strange getups, bells on their caps and shoes, shouting nonsense rhymes and expending, in general, a good deal of energy.

Not, as Caroline would say, his cup of tea. Nor hers, either.

"How did you get dragged into that?" he asked.

"Fool that I am, in a weak moment months ago, I told Mrs. Dane that I would write this year's script. I'd forgotten all about it. And she wants the thing finished by next week."

Ames could not help laughing. "Come now, man, it's not the end of the world if you don't turn in a completed script for the Christmas Revels!"

"Oh, isn't it? I don't count myself as a coward, but I tell you in all frankness, I don't relish having to make that particular announcement. Not to that lady. I'm glad you'll be halfway around the world by then, so you won't see the performance—if it ever occurs."

A pained look came to Ames's face.

"What's wrong, Addington? Did I say something—"

"The expedition has been canceled," Ames said shortly, and he explained about Professor Harbinger's broken leg.

Delahanty was appropriately sympathetic, his own problems, for the moment, put aside. "I tell you what. Let's go to lunch at Durgin-Park. I haven't been there since I returned, and I miss it."

The market dining rooms at Durgin-Park were on the second floor of the North Market Building in the heart of the Haymarket district, just beyond Faneuil Hall. Patrons were seated not individually, but at long, communal tables that now, at the height of the noon hour, were crowded with men from the city's business district. Fifty cents, here, bought a thick slab of good Yankee pot roast, mashed potatoes, gravy, a side dish of cranberry sauce, and a bottomless cup of coffee; fish or fowl were less expensive. This fare was delivered by surly waiters in shirtsleeves and long white butchers' aprons. They rushed back and forth from the kitchen like demons, slamming plates down on the tables with a defiant air, as if they dared anyone to challenge their arrogant attitude; they met requests for extras—a glass of water, say—with a ferocious sneer.

Noting MacKenzie's bemused expression, Ames said, "You wonder at the ungraciousness of our servers, Doctor? They are a trademark attraction of this place, and the reason that many people like to dine here."

MacKenzie accepted this without comment, but he noted it to himself as another item for his mental file labeled "Mysterious New England Behavior."

They ate quickly, conscious that others were waiting for their places, and within the hour they were outside in the Haymarket once more. All around them the busy market district swirled with activity, carts and wagons lumbering by, men shouting, small boys darting in and out. MacKenzie saw the carcasses of rabbits and half-haunches of beef hanging in the butchers' stalls that lined the ground floor of the domed Quincy Market Building opposite; on either side were farmers' wagons filled with country produce, potatoes and onions and great mounds of orange pumpkins and vari-colored squashes.

"Your appointment with Dr. Warren should take no more than an hour?" Ames asked him.

"I would think not."

"Then—" Ames produced his pocket watch, flipped it open, and thought for a moment. "When you have seen him, perhaps you could meet me afterward at the St. Botolph, at, say, between four and four-thirty?"

"Certainly." MacKenzie sighed to himself. After his consultation with Dr. Warren, he'd wanted to go to No. 16½ to spend a delicious hour before the fire with Miss Ames.

"And where are you off to, Addington?" Delahanty asked. "Something to do with the Colonel, no doubt."

"Yes."

"And you don't want to say what that might be?"

"No." Most definitely, he did not; and in any case, she might not be at home.

CHAPTER 18

THE TELEGRAM ADDRESSED TO AMES ARRIVED SHORTLY AF-
ter Caroline's solitary lunch. As she finished her coffee, Margaret came into the dining room bearing a small silver tray
upon which lay the flimsy yellow Western Union envelope.

Caroline stared at it as if it were an evil omen; in her
present state of heightened alarm, it seemed to be a portent
of some further disaster. At once she wanted to banish it—
throw it into the fire.

But of course she could not do that. It was for Addington. And aside from that, she wanted to know what it contained. Opening it in his absence was out of the question, so
she would have to suffer its presence until he came home.

She took the telegram from the tray and carried it into
the parlor, where she put it on the mantel. At once she knew
that that was the wrong place for it; she should take it into
his study, she thought.

But she left it and went to look out at the square.
Through the lavender-glass windows, the shrubbery looked
oddly colored, a kind of purplish-black. She'd seen it so all
her life and it had never bothered her, but just now it did. It
seemed eerie, and somehow threatening, as if it were the

shrubbery in a fairy tale by the Brothers Grimm, harboring goblins.

She felt terribly restless. Her petit-point bag lay by her chair, but she was in no mood to do petit point. On the side table was the Diana Strangeways novel. Yes: if she could become immersed in that—as she probably could—the time would pass.

By three o'clock, when Val came, she felt better; but one look at Val's face brought her back sharply to reality.

"You haven't heard from him today?" Caroline said.

Mournfully, Val shook her head. She looked ill, thought Caroline. Ill—and sad. A little surge of righteous anger swelled in her heart. Drat that George Putnam!

After failing to come to tea yesterday despite his promise to do so, he had failed today to communicate in any way, Val said. No appearance at Aunt Euphemia's, no flowers sent in repentance, no note for her to receive when she returned home from her Sewing Circle—nothing.

"But you will," Caroline said in a determined voice. She put her hand on Val's arm. Val did not look up. "Hear from him, I mean. I simply can't believe that he would—"

"It's not George," Val said dully. "It's his mother. You know what she's like. She's so terribly—proper. And this business with the Colonel—" She broke off in a sob, and Caroline got up from her chair and went to where Val sat on the sofa and put her arms around her.

"Don't, Val," she said softly. "Please don't cry. It doesn't do any good, and it only makes your eyes hurt and go all bloodshot."

But as Valentine sobbed against her breast, she thought, *Remember, Caroline Ames, when you yourself wept your heart out for a young man who went away and never came back. Remember that . . . and, perhaps, let Val weep as she will.*

"I k-k-keep thinking, what would she say if she knew the

truth?" Valentine got out between sobs. "What would she say if she knew that Cousin Addington's business with the Colonel was about *me*? She would immediately insist that George break off with me. And perhaps she does know. Perhaps that's why George has been so—so cold all week. I could feel it on Tuesday night at the Cotillion—that he was turning against me. And his mother was, too."

She took a long, shuddering breath; then she straightened, patting the few strands of her hair that had come loose, adjusting the bodice of her dress. She was wearing a little French number, straight from the workrooms of M. Worth in Paris, which Euphemia, in her delight at Val's match with George Putnam, had decreed Val must have. It was middling blue, with an astonishing array of tucks all down the front so that it looked as though it were molded to Val's figure. The sleeves were full at the shoulder, and the skirt, in the latest style, was mercifully free of a bustle; it flared out slightly at the bottom in a graceful, swaying effect when Val walked.

Caroline herself had never had a dress from M. Worth, but she did not envy her young cousin. In Caroline's world, Paris dresses did not exist; and besides, as she did not hesitate to admit to herself if to no one else, her figure was far too plump to look right, as Val's did, in such a creation.

"You mustn't give up hope, Val," she said gently. "I am sure this terrible mess will work itself out somehow. And I know George isn't so foolish as to—to give you up simply because Addington happened to find the Colonel's body."

"He would be right to do that, Caro. You know he would. No man wants a fiancée, never mind a wife, who is tainted by scandal." Her voice was rough with tears, but she kept them in. "And so—I have given this a good deal of thought—if he does change his mind, I can bear it." She took a deep breath and went on. "I have begun to harden my heart."

"Don't say that!"

"Yes. I will say it. I have begun to harden my heart against him. I must, don't you see? In order to survive after he—after he—" She broke off and bit her lips.

You mustn't harden your heart, Caroline thought; you mustn't grow sour and bitter, never allowing yourself to fall in love again.

Before she could speak, Val was getting up, preparing to take her leave. Just then they heard the door knocker, and then a man's voice in the front hall—not a voice that Caroline recognized. She tensed.

Margaret pushed apart the pocket doors. In an unusual gesture, she pulled them shut behind her before she spoke. Her eyes were wide with alarm, but, well trained as she was, she kept her voice low.

"It's the police, Miss."

"Did you tell them that Mr. Ames is not at home?"

"It's just the one police, Miss. And he didn't ask for Mr. Ames. He asked for you."

SHE'S NOT AT HOME," SAID SERENA VINCENT'S FORBIDDING maid.

Ames felt a stab of disappointment, and he was surprised at how strong it was. Stronger, surely, than the occasion demanded?

"Do you know when she will return?"

"No."

"Or where I might find her? It is rather important."

"She's at her dressmaker's. She'll go from there to the theater."

So that was that; he could not envision himself barging in on a fitting to impart his news.

He would pay another call, then, before he met MacKenzie: down Commonwealth Avenue to Arlington, across Arlington and through the Public Garden.

It was a brisk autumn day, the sun flirting with the

clouds. As he crossed at Charles Street and strode up the long slope of Beacon Street opposite the Common, preoccupied with his thoughts, he did not notice when an acquaintance, standing on the steps of the Somerset Club, spoke to him as he passed. The acquaintance felt no rebuff; Addington Ames was known as a longheaded fellow given to much study and cogitation, often so absorbed in his meditations that he did not recognize even his closest friends.

At the corner of Joy Street, he turned up to his destination, where he was shown to a cheerful upstairs sitting room at the front of the house. A woman stood to greet him.

"Mr. Ames." She held out her hand, and he took it.

Grace Kittredge was a small, slight woman, unostentatiously dressed, with fading blond hair and a face that once must have been attractive. What remained of her youth lay in her eyes, which were blue and had an intelligent look to them.

"How can I help you?" she added.

He reached into the breast pocket of his jacket and took out the letter he had found in the Colonel's desk, signed by "G.K." He held it out to her. "Does this belong to you?" he said.

She stared at it for a moment. She managed—just—to keep hold of her composure, but as she accepted it, he saw her face crumple into a grimace of pain.

Instantly she recovered. How he admired these women, trained up from infancy to preserve their surface calm no matter what debacle they faced! His sister Caroline had never taken to her training completely; her emotions were often plainly reflected on her face regardless of how she tried to conceal them.

Mrs. Kittredge held the letter, still staring at it; then, without unfolding it, she sank into a chair. He sat opposite her, watching her with some concern.

"It does," she said softly. "How did you—how do you come to have it?"

"I took it from the Colonel's desk on Monday evening."

"Ah." The ghost of a smile appeared for a moment on her lips. "I read in the newspapers of your—discovery. How very dreadful for you."

"Not as dreadful as for him," Ames said with an attempt at gallows humor.

"No. I suppose not." She pressed her lips together as if nerving herself up to something very difficult. "I thought of Tuesday as execution day. I didn't have the money he demanded. I went to him—"

"When?" Ames said sharply.

"Oh—last week. He was implacable. Then I wrote him this letter, begging him for mercy, and I was literally counting the hours until Tuesday morning, when his paper would be published. Instead, I learned that you had discovered him, and his paper didn't come out. Do you know if it will?"

"At this point, I doubt that it will, but—"

He broke off at the look of terror that came to her face.

"It probably will not," he hastily amended. Briefly, he told her why he'd gone to the Colonel, and why, now, he was trying to speak to anyone who had had recent dealings with him.

"I have no interest in discovering who did the deed, Mrs. Kittredge," he concluded. "My only concern is to find those letters before one more person's life is ruined by the Colonel's devilry."

She contemplated him. "Yes," she said softly, "that is what it was, isn't it? Devilry."

"Do you have any idea who might have betrayed you to him?"

"Who— No. None at all. And it wasn't I who was betrayed, Mr. Ames, it was my son."

"Ah."

"A few weeks ago, my son took what has been officially called a 'medical leave' from the College. The truth—and of course I speak to you in confidence—is that he was expelled for stealing."

Ames felt a little stab of surprise at that, but he said nothing.

"Stealing from the Porcellian Club," she went on. "He was deeply in debt from gambling. He was the treasurer of the club, you see, so he could easily doctor the books."

"How did the Colonel learn of all this?" Ames asked.

"That is what I cannot understand. No one except a few fellow Porcellians—and the Dean of the College, of course—knew what had happened, and none of them, I am sure, would have gone to the Colonel."

"But someone did."

"Yes."

"And you have no idea who that might have been?"

"None."

"Your son—?"

"No. I asked him, of course, but he had no idea either. It was the thought of that betrayal that sickened him, I think, more than anything."

"Is he here now?"

"No. He is taking the waters at Bad Nauheim. To keep up the story of his ill health, you see."

"It would be most helpful," Ames said, not wanting to press her further but feeling frustration beginning to creep over him once more, "if you could think of even the most unlikely name, someone who worked as an informant for the Colonel, perhaps—"

She shook her head. "I am sorry, Mr. Ames. I have done that over and over. I simply don't know."

There seemed to be little more to say, so he rose and took his leave. The afternoon was darkening toward evening, and a bitter wind blew up from the Common as he headed down Beacon Street once more toward the Back Bay and the St. Botolph Club where, he hoped, Dr. MacKenzie would await him.

The theater tonight, he thought—to be endured with the knowledge that Crippen suspected Serena Vincent of the Colonel's murder. Somehow he must find a moment to speak to her, to warn her—but how? Not before the curtain went up; not in her dressing room at intermission. News like that might throw her off and ruin her performance. Impossible that she had done it; no woman could have done such a deed. All his life, he had been brought up with the belief that although women, frail sex that they were, might weaken in matters of the heart (as Serena Vincent had done, succumbing to an adulterous affair), they were in no way capable of felonious acts like murder.

No. Crippen was on the wrong track altogether. And if Crippen was on the wrong track, he, Ames, must try to set him on the right one.

CHAPTER
1 9

DEPUTY CHIEF INSPECTOR ELWOOD CRIPPEN STRETCHED
his stubby legs toward the sea-coal fire and accepted an iced
lemon cookie from the plate that Caroline held out to him.
He bit into it, raised his eyebrows in approval, and chomped
down the remainder. "Well, now," he said through a mouth-
ful of crumbs, "this is very cozy, I must say. Very cozy indeed."

As his glance traveled around the room, Caroline was
acutely conscious of the telegram propped on the mantel.
Oh, why had she been so foolish as to put it there? She
should have put it where it belonged, in Addington's study.
Now here it was in full view, and Inspector Crippen surely
must see it, must wonder at it.

She stared at him with a kind of fascinated dread. Why
was he here? Was it some kind of trap? Were there other
police waiting outside around the corner, ready to spring on
Addington when he returned?

She closed her eyes for a moment, trying to calm herself.
She'd had to receive the inspector when he called; it would
have been unthinkable—tactically unwise—to refuse him.
And while she'd managed to seem calm and composed, in-
wardly she writhed with apprehension. He'd come for help,

he'd said, in deciphering the Colonel's galley; it lay now on the low table between them. But then he'd chatted on as if he were paying a purely social call, and for this endless half hour since he'd arrived, the galley had lain untouched.

Which was all for the best, Caroline thought, because the moment they began to look at it, Val's initials would spring out at them, and even Elwood Crippen would make that connection; few people in Boston had those particular initials.

"More tea, Inspector?" she asked, smiling at him. She'd been smiling at him since he came in, and her face ached from it.

"If you please," he replied. He looked at her with a kind of greedy acquisitiveness that made her shudder. She had joked with Addington often enough about Crippen's supposed fancy for her; but now, here in her own parlor, it did not seem "supposed" at all but very real. The thought of being courted by him made her flesh crawl, and so that he would not see her thoughts plain on her face, before she picked up the teapot she bent down to pick a thread from her skirt.

Oh, where was Addington—or the doctor? Why did they not come to rescue her and Val from this awful interview?

She poured Crippen's tea and glanced over at Val, who had gone white and silent the moment Crippen came in. Caroline realized that she should think of some way to get Val out of the room, but she could think of nothing that would not draw attention to the girl.

On the other hand, if she stayed . . .

Cripped swallowed several gulps of the steaming tea and set down his cup and saucer with a little crash.

"Now, then," he said, suddenly all business. "About this here—ah—paper."

He picked up the galley and began to scan it. "I don't mind telling you, Miss Ames, I'm at a loss here." He shot her a sly glance. "All these hints and initials that I can't make head nor tail of. I thought you might be able to help me a bit, deciphering. Your brother said you would. And you, Miss," he added, nodding toward Val.

Val made no reaction. She sat with her eyes downcast; Caroline had the sense that she was trying to will herself to be invisible.

" 'L.M.,' " Crippen said, reading from the printed sheet. " 'Who should know better than to fib about his supposed inheritance.' Any idea who that might be?"

"I—no," Caroline said. Her voice sounded odd, rather strained. That would not do, she thought; she must pretend to cooperate, at least.

"How about this," Crippen went on. " 'Mrs. F.D., bedecked with diamonds at Mrs. Gardner's crush—but who gave them to her?' Any idea of that?"

Caroline hesitated, and knew that he saw her do so. "It— I don't go to those big affairs, Inspector. So I really don't—"

"All right," he said. Was it her imagination, or was he becoming irritated with her? "Let's try this one. 'A certain lady with dark hair not from Nature, who frequently escapes to the pleasures of Saratoga Springs, should be more discreet at the gaming tables.' " He looked up at her, his pale eyes narrowed. "How about that, Miss Ames? Do you know any ladies with 'dark hair not from Nature'?"

"It might be—Mrs. Crawford Smyth."

Crippen had whipped out a small notebook, and now he wrote down the name. "With an i?"

"Y," she said. He crossed out and wrote again.

Val looked as though she were going to faint.

"And here we have . . ." Crippen scanned the page. Then he looked up—a sharp interrogative look that made Caroline's heart skip a beat. She reminded herself that this foolish-seeming little man must not be so foolish, or he would not have been promoted up through the ranks of the Boston Police to his present position.

" 'Miss V.T.,' " he read. " 'The amorous correspondent

who shows promise as a writer of ladies' romantic fiction. She should be more careful about whose hands her efforts fall into.' "

Caroline watched, fascinated, as he turned to Val. "Any idea about that, Miss Thorne?"

Val started as if he'd slapped her. "I—I don't know what to say, Inspector."

"You'd best say the truth, Miss," he replied, and his tone now was not sharp but almost kind. Clever man, thought Caroline.

"The truth," Val repeated.

"Always the best policy, Miss," Crippen said softly.

Val blinked. Caroline saw with relief that her eyes were dry, no sign of telltale tears.

Val gave a strangled little laugh. "The truth, Inspector, is often more complicated than it seems."

"All the same. Did you have business with Colonel Mann?"

"Yes," she said, and in that one short word Caroline heard all the misery of her young life.

"And did you go to see him on Monday last?"

"Yes."

"About what time would that have been?" He had his notebook at the ready, pencil poised like a dart.

"About four o'clock."

Be careful, dearest, Caroline thought.

"And did you see anyone else while you were there? Any other—petitioners, let us say?"

"No. No one."

"Ah." He sounded as if she had given him a significant piece of information.

"And you didn't see him again?"

"No."

"You can account for your whereabouts on Monday from—let us say—four-thirty on?"

"I can, Inspector, but—"

178 · CYNTHIA PEALE

"But—?"

"I live with my aunt." Val's voice was calm, through what effort of will Caroline could hardly imagine. "She is elderly, and rather old-fashioned. She knows nothing of—of my business with Colonel Mann. She would suffer a shock if she did know—possibly a shock that would be detrimental to her health."

Crippen waited. How predatory he looked, Caroline thought.

"And so while I say that I can account for my whereabouts after I saw Colonel Mann, I must beg you to take my word. I was with her—with my aunt. But if she were to find out that the Colonel was—" For a moment, Val's calm shattered; then she went on. "If my aunt were to discover that I was being blackmailed by the Colonel, I do not know what that discovery would do to her. It is bad enough in her view that Cousin Addington found his—found him and got into the newspapers because of it. Please, Inspector Crippen, please do not question my aunt about what I have told you. The shock might kill her, and I say that quite honestly."

Crippen, ignoring his notebook for the moment, fixed her in his sights still as if she were some kind of prey.

Which she was, Caroline thought. Oh, Val!

Suddenly Crippen smiled—a broad, comforting smile that made him look like an overgrown—and very ugly— cherub. "All right, Miss Thorne," he said. "I won't bother your aunt—or not just yet, at any rate."

AT THE ST. BOTOLPH CLUB, THE MEMBERS DOZED IN THEIR chairs before the fire. It was late afternoon: the quiet time. The only activity was in the card room at the back, where the play went on more or less uninterrupted around the clock. Here, the heavy draperies were drawn against the fading light, the air was thick with tobacco fumes, and the men's faces around the green baize table were intent—ferocious, even—as they seized their cards, played them, won or lost, and played again.

When Ames appeared in the doorway, no one looked up. He waited until the hand was finished and the players relaxed a bit—not much—and sipped their drinks while the tally was made. A balding man with dark whiskers—Enright, thought Ames—looked up and saw him and nodded.

" 'Afternoon, Ames," he said. "Care to join us?"

"No, thank you."

Ames approached the table. Enright had been shuffling the deck, but now he stopped.

"Longworth," Ames said. Was it his imagination, or, when he spoke the name, did a sudden tension enter the room—a tension greater than was there already?

"What about him?" Enright said.

"Was he here on Monday evening?"

Everyone looked blank. Then the man sitting to Enright's left said, "I can't remember."

"I can," said a man whom Ames recognized as Daniel Weld, a notorious high liver. "Yes—he was."

"No," said Enright. "I don't think so."

"He lost—what?" Weld said, as if Enright had not spoken. "Five hundred?"

"More than that," said another man. "Nearer a thousand, I'd say. But it wasn't Monday. It was Tuesday."

"Monday," said Weld. "I know it was Monday."

Enright shrugged and glanced up at Ames with a grimace. "There you are," he said. "Not very definite, is it?"

"No matter," Ames said. "Sorry to interrupt."

But already they had forgotten him. Enright was dealing, and all their concentration was fixed once more on the small slips of gaily colored pasteboard that would determine their fate.

He returned to the lobby where, impatient for MacKenzie to arrive, he began to pace under the disapproving gaze of the steward.

The outer door opened; two men came in, neither of whom was MacKenzie. It was four-thirty; he and the doctor needed to be at No. 16½ by six o'clock for early dinner if they were to arrive at the theater on time.

The outer door opened again, and MacKenzie came in.

"I hope I didn't keep you," he started to apologize as he approached. "Dr. Warren had a full house today, and an emergency case as well."

"What was his verdict on your knee?"

"Oh, very positive. I don't seem to have done myself any lasting damage."

"Good. Now. Here is what I want to do." Ames led the doctor to a quiet alcove away from the steward.

A few moments later, he had left MacKenzie at the club and was walking down Newbury Street to Berkeley, where he crossed to the Natural History Museum and turned left toward Boylston Street. It was full dark now, cold, with a stiff wind from the west. He had checked the time before he left the club: four forty-two. He walked rapidly, passing from light to darkness to light again under the streetlamps. He kept his eyes on the sidewalk, his thoughts on what he would attempt in the next few moments.

As he waited to cross at Boylston, jostled by a clutch of young men emerging from the Massachusetts Institute of Technology building to his right, he eyed the bulk of the Hotel Brunswick opposite. The entrance and the first and second floors were ablaze with light—the new electric lights, harsh and glaring. People swarmed in and out, for the Hotel Brunswick was a popular meeting place as well as one of the busiest hostelries in the city. But around on Berkeley Street, to the side and rear of the building, it was darker. Which suited Ames's purposes exactly.

He crossed and went on down Berkeley Street. At the alley at the rear of the hotel, he paused and glanced behind him. For a moment he thought he saw, silhouetted against the lights of Boylston Street, the figures of two men. But immediately they disappeared, melding into the dark bulk of the hotel building, so that he was not sure they had been there at all. Stop it, he thought; his nerves were getting the better of him.

In the alley, the noise of the traffic was less, but in its place was the chuffing and snorting of the railway cars pulling into and out of Providence Station, one block away. Glancing up at the sky, he saw clouds of white steam from the engines.

The alley was dark; like all Boston alleys, it undoubtedly harbored rats. He stepped carefully, alert for shadowy creatures slithering in the gloom. In a moment he had reached the door he sought, the rear door to the hotel. It was unlocked. Slipping in, he found himself in the well of an iron stairway. He ascended rapidly, past unmarked doors on each floor. If someone discovered him here, he would claim to be a guest, momentarily disoriented, trying to find his way back to his room.

Past the kitchen floor; past the first floor. By the time he had reached what he estimated to be the fourth floor, where the Colonel had had his suite, he was slightly winded, but only slightly. He stepped into the corridor to look at his watch. Four forty-seven. Not bad. And if the return to the St. Botolph Club could be made in equally good time . . .

He entered the stairwell again and started down. It was miraculous good luck that he had encountered no one, he thought; pray his luck held until he was outside again.

In no more than a minute he had closed the outer door behind him and was safe in the alley once more. He paused to take a breath. The air smelled of coal smoke and horse droppings faintly overlaid by the sickly smell of gas—city air, familiar to him from childhood.

If he'd made it here in quick time, Longworth could have done the same. Now get back to the St. Botolph, time the whole business, and home to dinner.

Rapidly he loped down the alley to Berkeley Street. In the

next moment, a blow caught him on the side of his head; it stunned him, but he stayed on his feet.

Someone caught his arms, pinioning them behind him while a second man hissed: "Where's the money, then, Mr. Ames?"

In the gloom of the alley, he couldn't see the fellow clearly, and in any case, he wore a kerchief tied over the lower half of his face, muffling his words.

Struggling to free himself, Ames wrenched his arms, but the fellow—a big bruiser—had him fast in a grip of iron.

The interrogator reached out and seized Ames's jaw, roughly shaking him. "Eh? Where is it?"

What money? he wondered. The Colonel's? Well, he could tell them nothing about that.

He gasped as the fellow's fist landed in his ribs. It was hardly a fair fight, but this was not Crabbe's Boxing and Fencing Club. Street toughs used brass knuckles; he'd be lucky if he escaped unscathed. A second punch landed just above the first, knocking the breath out of him, and for a moment, he thought he would lose consciousness. The fellow was asking him again, but the voice seemed faint now, and far away.

And then, even fainter, he heard footsteps, someone shouting—"Ho! You, there!"—and suddenly the iron grip on his arms loosened for a second and he tore himself free. He whirled and, catching his captor off guard, landed a blow to his throat and a second to his jaw. He heard the crack of bone: not his.

Behind him, a furious battle was taking place: the newcomer, whoever he was, flailing with his cane, beating the interrogator about the head and shoulders, beating him to his knees, beating him into submission until the fellow cried out for him to stop.

"All right! Leave off!"

The big one with the crunched jaw backed away from Ames and lumbered down the alley toward Clarendon

Street. The interrogator lay in a crumpled heap on the cob-blestones, seemingly unconscious. The rats will get him if he doesn't come to, thought Ames.

He drew an experimental breath. Not bad. His ribs ached where he'd been hit, but he didn't think they were broken.

MacKenzie's sturdy form stood beside him in the dark.

"Doctor," Ames said, "I am in your debt."

"Are you badly hurt? They looked as though they meant to do you serious harm."

"But didn't, thanks to you." Ames shook himself and glanced again at the man lying at their feet. He nudged him with his boot toe and heard a groan in reply.

"Who sent you?" he demanded.

No reply except another groan.

"Well?" he barked, nudging again, harder.

The man moved, lifted himself to one elbow, shook his head.

"Jimmy Doyle," he mumbled.

"Flash dresser, gaiters, diamond ring?"

"That's him." The man had levered himself into a sitting position, and now he peered up at Ames. His kerchief had slipped, but in the darkness, his face was only a pale smudge.

"Did you know the Colonel?" Ames asked.

"No."

"Never met him—never went to his rooms?"

"No."

"Doyle thought he had money in his hotel suite? Thought I took it?"

"Yes."

The man tried and failed to stand, falling back onto the cobblestones and groaning again, more loudly.

"You can tell Mr. Doyle for me that he sent you on a fool's errand," Ames said. "He missed getting the Colonel's money—if there was any—by a good hour or more on

Monday night. If he's wise, he'll give up trying to find it now. Come on, Doctor."

They left Ames's assailant in the alley and started back toward Boylston Street. At the front of the hotel, a herdic-phaeton drew up and they climbed in. They traveled in silence for a while, and then Ames said, "What prompted you to follow me?"

"I don't know," MacKenzie admitted. He'd had a feeling, a hunch, call it what he would; and, feeling slightly out of place at the St. Botolph on his own, he'd ventured out.

Ames grunted. "Good thing you did. In a fair fight, I could no doubt have beaten them, but as it was—I doubt it."

He fell silent, reflecting. Despite his misadventure, he was not disappointed. His trial run, from the St. Botolph Club to the Hotel Brunswick and back, had been interrupted, but still, he'd learned that an agile, limber man—a man like himself, a man like Richard Longworth—could have gone to the hotel and back, with time in between to accomplish his deadly purpose, in approximately fifteen minutes.

So Longworth could have been at cards on Monday evening, and he could have excused himself for a brief time, gone to the hotel, dispatched the Colonel, and arrived back at the card table in considerably less than half an hour. Just a little break in an evening of cards, Ames thought grimly; just a little intermission to take care of some pressing business. And he had learned something else: perhaps it was money, after all, that had provided the motive for the Colonel's murder, and not some dark secret about to be revealed.

More: they'd followed him, had perhaps been following him for some time—ever since his name first appeared in the newspapers. He'd not been mistaken when he thought he'd seen them before he turned into the alley.

MacKenzie, steadying himself as the cab jounced along, had grown thoughtful as well. He had never feared for his own safety, but now, given the incident just past, he had a thought for Ames's sister. Had they somehow put her into danger? Would the men who had attacked Ames attack her? He remembered his fear of an intruder at No. 16½, the night he'd found Ames stargazing. Perhaps he'd been right to be afraid. He wanted very much to see her, to reassure himself that in his absence, she'd come to no harm.

The cab drew up; they were home.

CAROLINE HEARD THE FRONT DOOR OPEN, AND A MOMENT later the two men came in, MacKenzie limping a little. She noted the look on his face when he saw Crippen.

"Doctor," she said, smiling at him with genuine pleasure—and relief.

"Miss Ames—Miss Thorne—Inspector."

He sat down; Ames stayed by the doorway. "I see you have accepted my sister's invitation to tea," he said to Crippen.

"How could I not, Mr. Ames?" Crippen replied with a self-satisfied smile.

"And your investigation—"

"Coming along."

There was an awkward little silence. MacKenzie eyed the inspector with a wary gaze, and Crippen seemed openly annoyed at the doctor's presence.

Why is he here? MacKenzie thought. He said he had his suspect; why, then, does he bother to harass Miss Ames and her young cousin?

In the next moment, to Caroline's surprise and relief, Crippen stood up. "I must be going," he said to Caroline, picking up the galley and folding it into his pocket. "And I thank you for your hospitality—and your help."

Was he mocking her? As she pulled the bellpull for Margaret to show him out, she hoped he would not see she was glad to be rid of him. She remembered, later, having said something inane about how pleasant it had been to see him again. She remembered the little light that appeared in his eyes as she said it. Somehow, they got through the moments of his leave-taking. When he finally departed, Ames went with him into the hall to have a word, and Caroline sank into her chair with an exclamation of relief.

"I am so glad to see you, Doctor! I mean, I am always—" No, she thought. Ladies do not speak so boldly. "I mean," she corrected herself, "it was so good of you to appear just at that moment." She looked at Val. "Are you all right, Valentine?"

"Yes." But she was still very white, and her voice was faint.

"You must go upstairs and rest—" Caroline began.

"No. No, I am all right. It is just that— Oh, Caro! What if George learns that I have been questioned by the police!"

At that, all MacKenzie's gallant instincts rose up and nearly strangled him. "He questioned you?" he said. "But surely he cannot do that unless you have counsel present, and—"

Caroline interrupted him. "It was not a formal interrogation, Val," she said. "I mean, you just happened to be here when he called on me. I was the one he wanted to question, not you!"

"But he did question me," Val replied. "He—I—oh, what shall I do if he goes to Aunt Euphemia? If she finds out—and George—"

"They will not. Inspector Crippen does not need to question Euphemia, and he knows that. Don't you agree, Addington?" she asked as he returned to them from seeing Crippen off.

"Question Euphemia?" They saw a hint of humor in his dark eyes. "In that give-and-take, Crippen wouldn't stand a chance."

"Do be serious, Addington. And do reassure Val that he wouldn't waste his time—"

Ames sat beside Valentine and took her hand. "Inspector

Crippen is hardly the most brilliant man in the world, dear girl, but even so, he is no fool. And, no, I do not believe he would waste his time interviewing Euphemia. And even if he tried, she would send him packing. Is that for me?" he added, meaning the telegram.

"Yes." Caroline handed it to him. He ripped it open, extracted the flimsy yellow sheet, and scanned it. To Caroline's intense disappointment, he did not reveal its contents, and so she turned to MacKenzie.

"Inspector Crippen came to ask me about the initials in the Colonel's galley," she said. At once she saw his outrage, and she felt a sudden little surge of pleasure because of it.

"But to subject you—and Miss Thorne—to questioning!" he began.

Abruptly, Val stood up. "I must go," she said.

"I will walk with you," Caroline offered. "It is dark—"

"No. Really, I prefer to go alone. But thank you. Good day, Doctor. Cousin Addington."

MacKenzie half rose and sank back again. While the two women had a last word at the door, he thought about Inspector Crippen. Surely, despite his bravado, he wouldn't be so bold as to actually pay suit to Miss Ames?

He gave himself a little mental shake. Let the fellow do as he would. Caroline Ames was a woman of great good sense. She would never entertain a courtship from the likes of Elwood Crippen.

And meanwhile, he, John Alexander MacKenzie, had the advantage, living as he did in her household, seeing her every day. In the spring, he thought, when his knee had fully mended, when this wretched business with Valentine Thorne was over and done with one way or another—then he would see the lay of the land, so to speak, and perhaps, with luck, he would have some encouragement from this charming and sympathetic woman who had, somewhat to his surprise, stolen his heart.

His reverie was interrupted as Caroline returned.

"Thank goodness you two came home at last!" she exclaimed. "What a time we had of it! What does the telegram say, Addington?"

"Do you know this woman?" he asked, handing it to her. She read the words pasted in narrow strips along the paper:

Will call today at 5:30 stop Important stop
Marian Trask

She nodded. "Yes. And you do, too—or you've met her, at least. She was at the Cotillion. Small, dark, rather vivacious. I don't know her well, but I see her from time to time. And she is on the committee at Agatha's. As a matter of fact—" She thought for a moment, remembering her promise to look for clean secondhand clothing as Mrs. Trask had requested. She'd forgotten all about it. "Today is her day at the Bower. She must intend to come here straight from there."

She glanced at the little Gothic clock on the mantel. It was nearly a quarter to six.

"Whatever can she want of me?" Ames muttered. He was not happy at the thought of an interview with a woman he hardly knew, probably about something of no interest to him—some new charity committee, perhaps.

On the other hand, Trask was a name he'd seen recently. In the Colonel's ledger, in fact, dated over two years before and with a hefty sum attached to it. And a check mark.

"While you wait for her, you can have your tea," Caroline said. "Did you"—and she gave him a look along with his tea—"*did* you tell Inspector Crippen that I would be happy to help him, Addington?"

"I—yes. I told him to call any afternoon. As you yourself instructed me to do, if you remember."

"Well, his visit was most poorly timed, I must say. Poor Val nearly went out of her mind worrying that he would take it into his head to pay a visit to Euphemia. Never mind that George might learn she had been questioned by the police."

Ames made a small sound of irritation. "Crippen's prize suspect is the wrong one, to begin with, and now he comes here and badgers you and Val—"

The clock struck the hour. Ames sipped his tea. It was hot and reviving, soothing to the ache in his ribs. Should he tell Caroline he'd been attacked? No.

"Marian's late," Caroline murmured. "I hope she won't stay too long," she added, her natural instincts for hospitality at war with her wish not to be late for the theater. She seldom went to the theater, except for the occasional performance of Shakespeare (she'd seen Edwin Booth's Hamlet, a life-changing experience); and of course the play itself, this evening, might not be anything much. But to be the guest of the star, to sit in a box—and, yes, to see a work that was perhaps on a par with her beloved Diana Strangeways—that was a treat indeed. Neither Diana Strangeways nor the unknown author of Mrs. Vincent's play was in the same league as Shakespeare, of course; but, she reminded herself, not everyone needed to be. There was a place in the world for lesser talents.

The little clock ticked relentlessly on. It was five past six. In the square, lamps on their tall posts glowed brightly in the darkness. Caroline lifted her head to listen for the sound of a carriage, but she heard nothing beyond the soft ticking of the clock and the faint hiss and murmur of the sea-coal fire.

She took up her petit point, part of a set of new seat covers for the dining room chairs. It was a floral arrangement in blue and yellow; she was only halfway through this first piece, and already it was beginning to bore her.

Ames shifted restlessly in his chair. "Where is the woman?" he muttered irritably. He wanted to go upstairs to wash and change in plenty of time for dinner.

Caroline thought, perhaps Agatha had had some

emergency that required Marian to stay late. Perhaps Marian's carriage had not arrived at the Bower on time to pick her up. Perhaps—

Ames stood up. "I am going up to wash," he said. "If she comes, give her some tea and tell her I will be down directly. Women have no sense of time," he added—gratuitously, Caroline thought, since she herself was always punctual to a fault.

MacKenzie said that he, too, would go upstairs, and shortly Caroline heard the whine of the little elevator. She worked the last of a purple-blue iris and stared for a moment at her basket of yarns. Should she start on the yellow rose?

No, she thought. With a secret sigh of relief, she thrust the canvas into her workbasket and closed the lid. One canvas a month if she was really faithful to it, she thought. There were twelve chairs.

She got up and went to the window. Louisburg Square lay dark and quiet, as it always did; no sign of a carriage bearing their caller. Time to go upstairs and change to her gray silk that she had worn to the Cotillion; she had no other dress that would be remotely suitable. She'd leave the gas turned up so that if Marian finally did arrive, she would not be greeted by a darkened parlor.

Odd, thought Caroline as she went up to her room. Why would Marian go to the trouble of sending a telegram if she did not intend to keep the appointment? Some people thought Marian Trask was rather flighty; apparently they were right.

CHAPTER
20

LADY MUSGROVE'S SECRET WAS ALL THAT CAROLINE HAD
hoped for and more. The setting was the drawing room of a
country estate; it was a most magnificent stage set, lavishly
done up in the latest fashion. Almost too lavishly, perhaps,
with busy, patterned wallpaper, luxurious draperies, much
overstuffed furniture, several potted palms, and a plethora
of gewgaws on every horizontal surface. And the play itself
was splendid after all, she thought happily; it had a dastardly
villain, a beautiful heroine (Serena Vincent, of course, whom
Caroline had not seen in years, not since Serena's marriage
and subsequent disgrace), a handsome (although a trifle
weak-looking) hero, and enough shouted declarations of
hate and love and betrayal to keep any audience on, so to
speak, its toes.

Caroline herself was comfortably seated in the box Mrs.
Vincent had offered to Addington. She stole a look at him.
His long, lean face was unreadable in the dim light that
came from the stage; she could not tell if he was enjoying the
production or if he were merely enduring it because Mrs.
Vincent had invited him as her guest.

And why had Mrs. Vincent done that? she wondered.
Was she, however improbably, attracted to Addington? Not

likely, she thought; he was not her type at all. Mrs. Vincent, since her disgrace, had traveled with the fast set, and whatever else Addington was, he was not that.

Caroline realized that Dr. MacKenzie was looking at her. "Good, isn't it?" she whispered to him.

He nodded. "Very," he whispered back, and she was aware of his lingering glance before he returned his attention to the stage.

Act One had set out the problem; now, in Act Two, complications, in true melodramatic fashion, were arising. As Serena Vincent's seductive voice gave depth and meaning to her essentially silly lines, the villain threatened her in stentorian tones; the hero, for the moment, was absent. In her torment, Mrs. Vincent dashed back and forth across the stage; she was dressed in a green velvet gown, cut shockingly low, that displayed her stunning figure.

Caroline sighed. Her own figure was not stunning; it never would be. She was a little too plump, a little too short to cut a dashing figure like Serena Vincent's. If she got up on that stage, people would see not a willowy, curvaceous figure of a woman, but, rather, a modestly dressed, slightly overweight female approaching middle age. It didn't matter that she hadn't a lot of money to spend on her wardrobe, Caroline thought, because no matter how much she spent, she would never look like Serena Vincent.

She returned her attention to the play. The villain was saying something about the heroine's dark secret; Mrs. Vincent was defying him and doing it splendidly, all prideful, injured womanhood, her lovely, slender white hands pressed to her lovely, swelling white bosom.

Ah! The hero had returned. He had bounded in wearing jodhpurs and high boots; he brandished a pistol.

Ames, who was sitting on Caroline's left, nearest the stage, felt the tension rise in the audience. It was due entirely, he thought, to the skill of the actors; certainly the play itself was no more than mediocre. Amazing, how a second-rate effort like this could draw audiences week after week; it had opened in early September, if he remembered correctly, and now here it was the middle of November, and the house, on this Thursday night, was nearly full.

He glanced down across the rows of faces in the orchestra below, dimly illuminated by the reflection from the stage lights. Every last person seemed enthralled; the house was deathly still.

It was, of course, primarily Mrs. Vincent's skill that carried the play, enchanting the audience night after night. Amazing, to think that if it had not been for Colonel Mann and his filthy blackmail, she might have continued quietly for the rest of her life as the proper wife of a proper Boston Brahmin, her adulterous affair a well-kept secret, and all her energy and fire, now so splendidly displayed on the stage, would never have been discovered.

"Vile dastard!" she cried, and Ames heard a few gasps from the audience at a female's use of profanity.

The villain and the hero were scuffling now, building up to some kind of climax for the second act curtain. One down and then the other, Mrs. Vincent hovering on the sidelines. Would she interfere? Or let them fight it out themselves?

How beautiful she looked, Ames thought. Of course, they used heavy makeup, those actors and actresses; but still. Amazingly beautiful—and something more. She had a quality to her that was at once mysterious and alluring. Mysterious: yes, she was that. Could all her energy and fire have prompted her to kill Colonel Mann? He could not believe it. He assumed she had a great many opportunities to get herself into trouble, given the life she led, but did that trouble include murder? No. Impossible.

He'd see her after the final curtain to warn her that Crippen meant to arrest her. And he'd try to reassure her, tell her he knew that Crippen was way off the mark. Serena Vincent hadn't murdered the Colonel any more than Ames himself had. He'd be willing to bet on it—and he was not a betting man.

He glanced down into the orchestra. The tenth row center was occupied by half a dozen or so St. Botolphers; he'd heard that some of them came back every week. Pining, no doubt, for Mrs. Vincent. Ames's mouth curled down into a grimace of contempt. They might come to admire her—to lust after her, even—but there was not one of them who had the intestinal fortitude to actually marry her. Not with her disgrace hanging over her like a black cloud. No, they would come to see her, and perhaps even offer her supper—or something more—afterward, and they would buy her photograph which was available in all the shops, and perhaps they would even, in their dreams, make love to her. But they wouldn't make an honest woman of her—not after she'd been so damaged by Colonel Mann.

His eye was caught by a movement in one of the boxes opposite. A man alone. Ames stared, wanting to make sure. Yes. It was Richard Longworth. Now what was he doing here? He'd denied knowing Mrs. Vincent. Had he been lying? Probably. And if he'd lied about that, what else had he lied about?

Things seemed to be reaching some kind of climax onstage. The struggle between the hero and the villain was, for the moment, at a standoff; the two men had sprung apart, and now the hero was aiming his pistol.

A shot rang out.

And then, a second later, the hero shot at the villain, who slumped to the floor.

With a loud *whoosh,* the heavy red plush curtain came swooping down.

But instead of the applause that might have been expected, the theater was dead silent. No one moved; no one made a sound.

Then they heard a woman's scream, and suddenly all was

pandemonium, people shouting, leaping out of their seats, a few intrepid souls even running up onto the stage, trying to find the opening in the curtain.

Caroline sat frozen with shock. As the houselights came up, MacKenzie said, "What was that? A shot—from the audience?"

"Apparently," Ames said. For one terrible moment, his heart had stopped; now he felt it starting up again.

Two shots—but only one of them supposed to happen. Someone had taken a shot at the players onstage—timed precisely, but not precisely enough, to coincide with the shot called for in the script.

And unless either of the actors, the villain or the hero, had some enemy here tonight, the bullet had undoubtedly been intended for Serena Vincent.

He looked across to the box opposite. Richard Longworth had vanished.

I⊤ WAS MEANT FOR *ME*, MR. AMES!"

Serena Vincent, ignoring the pleas of her maid, paced back and forth in her dressing room. She had changed into her costume for the last act, a pale pink confection that was, Caroline thought wistfully, extraordinary with her auburn hair. Crowded into the room with her and her maid were not only Ames and Caroline and Dr. MacKenzie, but the manager of the theater, a husky, ruddy man with a bristling gray mustache who looked, just now, as though someone had punched him in his ample paunch.

"How do you know that?" Ames replied. He agreed with her, but he wanted to hear her reasons.

"Because—because—"

"Five minutes!" came the cry of the call boy in the corridor.

"Because it *was!* I know it!"

She has some secret, he thought; many, perhaps. Who knew what entanglements she'd gotten herself into, running as she did with the fast crowd? And did those entanglements involve Richard Longworth, whom he had seen not half an hour ago sitting in a box opposite his own?

"Mrs. Vincent," the manager said, "I beg you—"

She stopped in front of him as if she had only just noticed that he was in the room.

"Can we delay for five minutes longer?" she asked.

"We can—if you tell me you'll go on."

"No!" snapped the maid. She glared at the manager.

The manager ignored her; Mrs. Vincent did not.

"I must, Hilda," she said.

"Not on my life!" the woman exclaimed. She was an odd kind of servant, Caroline thought; but obviously she was much more than a servant. She was some kind of guardian who believed her duty was to shield her mistress from— What? Death?

Caroline shuddered. Mrs. Vincent was right; the shot had been intended for her. Who else? Both the actors had been standing well away from her. There was no one else onstage, and the shot had missed her by inches.

Caroline listened with a little frisson of horror as, now, Mrs. Vincent said, "I moved, you know." She was talking to Ames, but they all heard. "Usually I stand right where— where the bullet entered the scenery. But tonight, I don't know why, I moved, just at the last instant—"

Her voice cracked a bit and she put her hand on Ames's arm to steady herself—a gesture that was not lost on Caroline.

"One minute!" the call boy shouted.

"Mrs. Vincent, I must insist—" the manager began. He started when Ames rounded on him.

"Be quiet, man! Can't you see she's had a shock? Go out and tell the audience you'll give them their money back— tonight's performance is over!"

"Now, now, just a minute—" the manager said. "I'm running this theater, if you please, Mr.—ah—"

"Never mind, Mr. Ames," Mrs. Vincent said. She gave him one long, unreadable look, and then she took her hand from his arm and turned toward the door. "Mr. Moore is correct. The show must go on!" She smiled brightly—too brightly—and said to her maid, "Am I all right, Hilda?"

Caroline thought she saw tears in the woman's eyes as she scrutinized her mistress. "Yes," she said. She reached up to refasten a rhinestone-studded hair clip in Mrs. Vincent's coiffure. "You're just fine."

As the actress turned to leave, Caroline saw the maid bite her lips as if to keep from crying. She is terribly frightened, she thought; but why? Does she know who did this?

The manager, somewhat reassured that he would not lose the night's box office receipts, followed Mrs. Vincent out. Ames glanced at his companions. "Doctor, would you see Caroline back to our box?"

"Where will you be, Addington?" she asked.

"In the wings." If the manager allows it, he thought. He wanted to be near Mrs. Vincent, even though, in the wings, he would be little help to her should the assailant attempt another shot.

But as Caroline made to leave, she felt a touch on her arm and turned to see Mrs. Vincent's maid staring at her with a beseeching look.

"Could I have a word, Miss?" she asked.

MacKenzie was waiting for her; Addington had gone on ahead.

"Just a minute of your time, Miss," the maid added.

MacKenzie would wait for her in the corridor, he said. It was not a place, he felt very strongly, suitable for a lady on her own.

The maid shut the dressing room door; then she hesitated for a moment as if she were considering very carefully what she wanted to say—and how to say it. She was a drab, spare woman of about fifty; her eyes were bright with alarm, her thin lips quivering.

Then: "You don't know me, Miss," she said abruptly.

"No."

"My name's Hilda Fay."

The surname, at least, meant something. The Ameses had once had a live-in cook named Mrs. Fay, back in the days when the house had been more fully staffed. Caroline had been in her late girlhood at the time, seventeen years ago or so.

"We had a cook—" she ventured.

"My sister. She used the Mrs. because it made her sound more experienced, like. Not that she wasn't a good cook—you can testify to that yourself, I guess."

"Yes—yes, she was a wonderful cook," Caroline said, her voice warming as she remembered. "She did a lovely blanc-mange. And her drop biscuits were the lightest I ever had."

"And when she took ill," Hilda went on, "your mother paid for her doctor bills and all." She sniffled. "I never forgot that, Miss. How good your mother was to my Ellen. If she hadn't had that morphine at the end, I don't know what we would have done, she was in that much pain."

Caroline felt slightly embarrassed. She had been just a giddy girl back then; she'd never thought once to inquire about the cook who had left the family's employment.

"So when Mr. Ames came yesterday afternoon," Hilda went on, "I knew who he was. And I never would have spoke to you now, except that I'm scairt."

She looked scared, Caroline thought—really frightened.

"And I've been trying to think, who would have done it?" the maid went on.

"You mean, who would have shot at Mrs. Vincent just now?"

"It was him." Hilda's lips clamped down on the word like a bite.

"Him? Who is that?"

"That lawyering fella. Richard Longworth." She'd suddenly acquired a sour look.

Longworth. Who might have worked for the Colonel.

"Why do you say that, Hilda?"

"Because he's crazy for her."

"That isn't a reason to shoot her, is it?"

"It is if she don't feel the same for him."

"Ah."

"He was with her on the night—the night it happened."

"The night what happened?"

"The night someone killed that scum."

"You mean Colonel Mann?"

"That's the one."

"Yes? Go on, Hilda."

"Well—Mr. Longworth came in early, a little past seven, and he started right in on her. 'Come away with me,' he said.

" 'Don't be a fool,' she said. 'Why would I go away with you?'

" 'I can't stand it any longer,' he said. 'I will kill him.' "

"Who?"

"He meant the Colonel."

"I see."

"And then he said, 'Or I will kill myself.' And then he said, 'Or I will kill you.' "

"Meaning—Mrs. Vincent?"

"Yes. He was raving. I never heard anything like it."

"But he didn't do any of those things, after all, did he?"

"I don't know."

"But if he was with Mrs. Vincent—"

"He left."

"Ah."

"But then he came back."

"Do you know what time?"

"He left around seven-thirty. Came back about an hour later. And so now—the Colonel is dead, and just now someone has taken a shot at *her.* And if he didn't get her this time, he'll get her soon enough. Don't you see, Miss Ames? I'm telling you, that shot was for her, and it won't be the last!''

THE PLAY WAS OVER. ACT THREE HAD LASTED FOR PERHAPS half an hour, but for Ames, it had seemed endless. He stood in the wings and watched as Serena Vincent, trouper that she was, played her part. The audience knew what had happened, apparently, for when the curtain opened, a wave of applause greeted her. She held her pose, and when the applause died, she acknowledged it by a single graceful nod.

From time to time, Ames looked into the darkened theater, but he was on the wrong side to see the box where Longworth had sat, and so he could not tell if he was still there.

At the end, the police—not Crippen, thank God—waited in the corridor. Serena Vincent, amazingly composed, came off the stage after the audience's ovation and greeted them calmly. She could tell them nothing, of course: no, she had no idea who would have done such a thing, no idea that she had any enemies.

Ames waited until they had finished questioning her, and when at last they were done, he was able to have a private word with her.

"Yes, Mr. Ames?" She lifted both her hands and he took them, gripping them hard. They were icy cold.

"I did not have the chance to tell you before—" he began.

In the harsh light of her dressing room, he saw the shadows under her eyes, the lines of tension around her mouth.

"Yes?" She did not pull away from him, and as he held her hands, he felt them grow warmer. "What is it, Mr. Ames?" The words were impatient, but the tone was not; she spoke softly, almost intimately, and her eyes—her lovely eyes—gazed at him with what seemed to him trust and—perhaps—admiration.

He was aware of the maid hovering in the background.

"A private word, if I may," he said.

"Of course." She turned to the maid and passed some wordless message; at once the woman left the room, closing the door behind her.

"Now," Mrs. Vincent said. She still left her hands in his, and it was not a passive thing: he felt her grip, strong and oddly reassuring. "You were about to say—?"

"Inspector Crippen has you in his sights," he said. He heard the urgency in his voice and wondered if she did.

She accepted it with no more than a lowering of her eyelids—and then a swift raising of them again, to stare at him quite boldly. Then, to his astonishment, a small smile curved her lips.

"Are you trying to tell me that Inspector Crippen believes that I killed Colonel Mann?"

"Yes."

"Perhaps this little episode tonight will change his mind."

"Possibly. But he is very stubborn, and once he gets an idea into his head—"

"I understand. You have warned me, and I am grateful to you."

"If I can be of any help at all to you—" How inadequate that sounded.

"Yes. I will let you know." She was smiling at him, but what was in that smile he could not tell.

She smiled at many men, he thought; and many men, no doubt, would offer to help her. But perhaps not now, not in this messy affair.

He tried to think of something else to say to her—something to reassure her, to comfort her—but he could not. So he left her, reluctant as he was to do so, and went outside to find Caroline and the doctor.

At once, Caroline told him her news, and as he listened to her, he felt the sharp pang of betrayal. Why hadn't Mrs. Vincent told him about Longworth's threats?

But all he said was "Interesting."

"Interesting!" Caroline replied, keeping her voice low. They were standing in the crowd under the theater marquee. "More than that, I'd say."

"It doesn't jibe with what he told us, at any rate," Ames said. "And if he absented himself from her for that particular hour, the hour when the Colonel was being killed—"

"You'll tell Inspector Crippen," Caroline said.

"I—yes. I will." And perhaps it will help to deflect Crippen's attentions from Mrs. Vincent, he thought.

The night was cold, with a strong wind from the north. A long line of carriages and hackney cabs was inching along the curb in front of the marquee. At the corner of Tremont Street, a newsboy was crying his wares.

"Extra! Extra!" he called. "Read all about it!" He was a ragged little fellow who looked undernourished and even sickly, but he was very loud. "Murder in the South End! Read all about it! Woman murdered!"

People were hurrying up to him, crowding around. Ames shouldered his way in. Tossing two pennies to the child, he took the folded newspaper—it was a late edition of the *Traveler*—but he waited until he was away from the crowd and with his companions once more before he snapped open the heavily inked sheets and read, in the harsh glare of the streetlight, that at about five-fifteen that very afternoon, on Columbus Avenue in the South End, a woman had been shot to death.

Her name was Marian Trask.

CHAPTER
21

"TEN THOUSAND DOLLARS!" CAROLINE EXCLAIMED. SHE held her brandy glass, but in her astonishment at what Ames was saying, she had neglected to take even one sip.

"Yes," Ames replied. "A nice round sum." He had told them about seeing William Trask's name in the Colonel's ledger.

"What did the check mark mean?"

"I assume it meant that the amount had been paid."

"Do you think Marian was coming here to tell you something about Colonel Mann?"

"I have no idea. But I imagine she might have been, yes."

They were at home once more, having walked up Park Street and over the top of the hill. Ames had laid more coals on the fire, poured the three of them a small brandy apiece from his precious store, and taken his place by the mantel, one booted foot resting on the brass fender.

Caroline tried to settle her thoughts. Ten thousand dollars was such an extraordinary sum—an unimaginable sum—that she could not quite grasp it.

She glanced at MacKenzie, and he smiled at her. She felt suddenly reassured. In this world gone—apparently—mad, here was one sane and sensible man. Addington was another. You are luckier than you know, Caroline Ames, she thought.

Her notice of him prompted MacKenzie to offer a thought. "They say they have no suspect." He gestured toward the newspaper, which lay, black headlines uppermost, on the low table between them.

"No," Ames said curtly; Caroline recognized his tone, even if the doctor did not, as the one he used when he was being dismissive of something—or someone—stupid. Not the doctor in this instance, she understood, but the police. "They call it a random street crime. Ridiculous."

"But if it was not—" Caroline began, and then she hesitated, grappling with the implications of the thought she was trying to express.

"Addington . . . if it was not a street crime, and if, as you say, Mr. Trask's name was in Colonel Mann's ledger—"

He gave her a look. "Yes?"

"Well—I mean—might Marian's death have some connection to the Colonel's?"

He nodded. "It might, indeed."

"And so, if it was not random—if someone hunted her down"—she shuddered a little—"that person would have known where to find her. No—wait—she was coming to see you—"

She was getting it wrong, she thought. Addington would only be further irritated if she went on.

"She didn't intend to walk here, surely?" MacKenzie put in. She caught his eye, and at once she felt better. He understood what she was trying to say, and apparently, he was ready to say it for her.

Ames looked at him. "Doubtful," he said.

"So where was her carriage?" MacKenzie asked. "Or, if she wasn't to be called for by her own carriage, why was she not in a herdic?" He thought for a moment. "And how far away is Columbus Avenue from—what did you call it?" he asked Caroline.

"Bertram's Bower." Yes, she thought; this was the point she'd been trying to make. "It is in the South End, on Rutland Square—not far from the avenue. If she intended to come here in a herdic, she would have had to go to Columbus Avenue to find one, but— Where are you going, Addington?"

He had finished his brandy and was getting up from his chair. "I am going to bed," he said. "And first thing tomorrow morning," he added, "I think I must go to the Trasks'. Doctor, will you come?"

Caroline felt a little twinge of envy. It was *not* fair, she thought, that the men always got to do the most interesting things. "May I—I would like to come with you, Addington."

"Really? It may not be pleasant. We may, in fact, not be allowed into the house."

"I don't care. I know Marian's sister, and if she will talk to me—"

"Of course. In that case, you must accompany us."

THE TRASK MANSION—FOR THAT IS WHAT IT WAS, MAC-Kenzie thought—was a large, white limestone edifice on Commonwealth Avenue near Gloucester Street. A police wagon waited at the curb, the horses' breath steaming in the cold air. The house showed no evidence of a family bereaved, no black drapery at the windows, no mourning wreath hung on the front door. But then, he thought, given the circumstances of Marian Trask's death, perhaps they did not want to draw attention to it.

Ames pulled the doorbell knob, and through the heavy wooden panels, they heard the faint sound of ringing within. After what seemed a long time, the door opened.

"Yes, sir?" On the butler's smooth, impassive face they could see no hint of what must be the turmoil inside the house.

Ames handed over his card and asked to see Mr. Trask.

"He is not at home, sir," the butler said, not bothering to look at the little scrap of pasteboard.

"I understand," Ames replied. "But this is an extremely urgent—"

"I am sorry, sir. Mr. Trask is not at home to anyone."

Caroline, peering past Ames, past the butler's stiff form, could see nothing beyond the vestibule.

Ames tucked his card back into his pocket. "Thank you," he said, and the three of them went back down the front steps to the sidewalk. The butler closed the door behind them.

Ames stood for a moment, thinking, while Caroline and MacKenzie waited. It was a raw, chilly morning, threatening snow. On the mall, the spindly trees were spaced out, black and bare, looking hardly strong enough to withstand the long, cold New England winter that lay ahead. People hurried by, oblivious of the trouble within this imposing dwelling.

"I will go to see—" Ames began, but just then the Trasks' door opened, and two men came hurrying down the steps.

". . . Medical Examiner," Caroline heard one of them say.

It was Inspector Crippen.

"Why, Miss Ames!" Crippen exclaimed. His eyes lighted up with pleasure, and his rotund body, tightly encased in a brown Chesterfield, seemed to expand a little, threatening to burst his buttons.

They exchanged greetings. Crippen looked even more self-important than usual, MacKenzie thought; his brown bowler was pushed back to expose a swath of graying hair, and as he spoke, he rocked back and forth on his tiny feet as if he were an oversized mechanical toy.

"And to what do I owe this pleasure?" Crippen asked. He directed his question to Ames, but he cast a roguish glance at Caroline. MacKenzie felt his insides twist.

"A condolence call, Inspector," Ames replied smoothly.

"But they won't see you, will they? No." Crippen thought for a moment, and then he jerked his head. "A word, Mr. Ames? Won't be a moment, Sampson," he added to his companion, who nodded and strolled in the opposite direction.

Crippen walked Ames far enough to be out of earshot before he spoke again. Then: "A nasty business, Mr. Ames. The lady was by herself—"

"A casual street crime?" Ames asked. "Do you really think, Inspector, that—"

"I don't think anything yet," Crippen said a touch testily. "But here it is, Mr. Ames. You being friendly with these people and all—"

"I hardly know them," Ames interjected.

"But you travel in their circle," Crippen replied. "And you know them well enough to—ah—come to offer your condolences." Despite the cold, his brow was filmed with a sheen of sweat. "Now hear this, Mr. Ames. Something very odd. The deceased's husband says she sent them a telegram yesterday afternoon. Asked that her carriage not call for her as it customarily did when she had an afternoon over at the Bower."

Apparently, Mrs. Trask had had a busy day at the Western Union office, Ames thought.

"And what do you make of that?" he asked.

"Nothing, at the moment. But it would seem that perhaps the man who perpetrated the crime was someone who knew her, after all. Knew her well enough to know where she'd be yesterday afternoon. And knew that she always had her carriage call for her there."

"And knew that she'd canceled it?" Ames asked.

"Ah," Crippen replied, nodding. "That's a question, isn't it?"

"Have you spoken to the people at the Bower?" Ames asked. What with Crippen's touchy vanity, it was a delicate business to suggest a line of inquiry to him.

"Not yet. We will, of course. But—"

"Inspector, I think you should know that Marian Trask sent me a telegram yesterday afternoon, as well."

"Did she, indeed?" Crippen's eyes narrowed.

"Yes. She said she wanted to see me, and would call about five-thirty. Which leads me to believe—"

Crippen wagged an ungloved finger at him. "Don't leap, Mr. Ames. That's one thing I've learned. Never make that leap without you have a very good reason to do so."

Ames ignored the little man's patronizing tone. "Which leads me to believe," he repeated, "that Mrs. Trask was, in fact, expecting her carriage. She would have wanted to get from the Bower to Louisburg Square on time."

"Now, that's not necessarily so, Mr. Ames, not at all," Crippen said, still rather patronizing. "What if she didn't want her coachman to know she was coming to see you, eh? What about that? You know how servants gossip. So she would have canceled him and gone over to Columbus Avenue to find herself a herdic."

"Yes. Perhaps." It was true, Ames thought; it made sense.

"What did she want to see you about, anyway?" Crippen asked.

"I have no idea."

"You're sure? Some little tempest in the social teapot, eh?"

"I didn't know the woman at all well, Inspector. I cannot imagine why she wanted to see me."

"But she did, didn't she? Enough to set it up beforehand rather than just make a casual call in the hope of finding you at home?"

"Yes, but—" He caught himself. It was bad enough that he had been the one to find Colonel Mann's body; it was downright dangerous to let Crippen know he'd rifled the Colonel's files as well.

He leaned in, as if he were confiding a secret. Which, in

fact, he was. "I heard, a while ago, that Mrs. Trask's husband paid a large sum to Colonel Mann."

Crippen shot him a wary look. "Did you now?"

"Yes."

"When did he pay it?"

"Oh—two or three years ago, I believe. Just idle gossip, you understand. But if it was true, it might have some bearing on the death of Colonel Mann."

Crippen digested it. "So you're trying to tell me that this case has some connection to the Colonel's?"

"Yes."

Crippen pursed his lips. "I don't think so, Mr. Ames. With all due respect—and I remember how helpful you were in that affair last year at the Somerset—but I don't think so."

"Have you compared the bullets?"

Crippen stared at him. "You mean the one that did in the Colonel and this one here, with Mrs. Trask?"

"Yes." Ames realized that until he'd said it, the idea had not occurred to Crippen.

"No," the little inspector admitted. "No, we haven't done that yet, Mr. Ames. The M.E. had a hard time, I don't mind telling you, but he found it eventually. But listen, Mr. Ames, if Mr. William Trask was being leaned on by the Colonel, why would he have paid up—when did you say this was? two or three years ago?—and then waited until now to kill him? And waited to kill his own wife, too, *if* it was him who done it *and* if she was the one who caused the trouble? Why not take the action at the time?"

He laid a hand on Ames's coat sleeve. "Listen here," he said, and suddenly his voice was soothing and gentle— a policeman's trick, Ames thought. "I know you want to get back those letters you told me about, but the letters are one thing, and this business here is something else again. And it's not a job for civilians, Mr. Ames, really it isn't. Why don't you just take that sister of yours back home and leave it to us. We'll sort it out on our own, see if we don't."

Ames choked back the retort that sprang to his lips. He realized that Crippen was eager to leave. "About the incident last night at the Park Theater—"

"Incident?" Crippen frowned.

"Someone shot at Mrs. Vincent."

Crippen's face cleared. "Yes, I had the report on my desk this morning. As far as my men could tell, it never happened."

"What do you mean, it never happened? I was there, I heard it—"

Crippen shook his head. A condescending, almost pitying expression came over his ugly little face. "If someone took a shot at Mrs. Vincent, where is the bullet?"

"In the scenery, of course."

"Ah, but they looked for it in the scenery and they couldn't find it."

Ames remembered the stage set: a country drawing room, overdecorated, plush draperies and garishly patterned wallpaper. An easy thing, to overlook a bullet in a place like that.

Crippen was smiling at him now, still unbearably smug. "Those actresses will do anything for publicity. Anything. And I wouldn't put it past her—"

"Don't be ridiculous," Ames snapped. "The woman was nearly killed right there on the stage. If she hadn't moved—"

"D'you know what I think, Mr. Ames? I think—if someone did take a shot at her, and I'm not saying they did—but *if* they did, it was a put-up job, and we don't need to worry ourselves about it." He nodded in the direction of the Trask mansion. "Now, I've got to get me on the warpath, so to speak. My detective looks nervous, pacing back and forth, and I've got to keep him busy. So I'll see you soon, Mr. Ames, and I wish you a very good day."

And with that, he betook himself down the sidewalk. As he passed Caroline, he swept off his hat to her and gave her a cheery farewell; then he and his detective climbed into the police wagon that waited at the curb, and they were gone.

Ames strolled back to Caroline and the doctor.

"Well?" said Caroline. Her pretty face was pink-cheeked with the cold, and her eyes were alive with interest. "What did he say?"

"Nothing much," Ames replied. "I tried to alert him to the fact that there was some connection between Mrs. Trask's death and the Colonel's, but he didn't seem to take to the idea."

"Pshaw." Caroline shook her head. "Of course there is a connection, Addington! Isn't it obvious?" She lowered her voice, although there was no one about to overhear. "After what you discovered in the Colonel's ledger about Mr. Trask making that enormous payment—" She thought about it. "What on earth could have happened that the Colonel could extort such an amount from them?"

"From him," Ames corrected her. "It was his name written down, not hers. Still," he added, "I suppose it could have been an indiscretion of anyone in his family, and he would have been the one the Colonel blackmailed. Do they have children?"

She blinked, trying to remember. "A daughter, I think. Not quite of an age to come out."

"So if this happened two years ago—"

"She would have been far too young to have done anything that warranted such a large demand."

"And payment," he reminded her. "The man paid. That is evidence enough, I should think, of some kind of—shall we say, misbehavior."

"Yes." Suddenly she brightened. "Addington, I wonder if Marian's sister is here this morning."

"You said you know her?"

"A little. More than I know—knew—Marian. She lives

around the corner in Gloucester Street. She is best friends with Frances Adams," she added as if that explained her connection to the woman.

Without waiting for his permission, she turned and hurried up the Trask steps once more, but after a brief exchange with the butler, she rejoined them.

"Not there," she said, puzzled. "I wonder why. She lives so close by, why didn't she come at once?"

"Perhaps she did, last night," MacKenzie offered.

"Yes. But she should be here this morning, as well. If ever there was a time for family to gather, it is a time like this." She made up her mind. "I will go to her, Addington. Surely she will be at home. And perhaps she can tell me something."

And before Ames could protest, she had set off, a small, determined figure in her dark gray walking suit.

The two men watched her for a moment, Ames with something that was not quite exasperation—she might turn up something, after all—and MacKenzie with a kind of wistful admiration.

Then Ames collected himself. "Come on, Doctor. I see a vacant herdic over there. Let us catch him before someone else does. I want to go downtown."

CHAPTER
22

"EXCUSE ME, MADAM. AH! MRS. DANE! I BEG YOUR
pardon."

Ames had nearly collided with her in the corridor as she
rushed out of Richard Longworth's office.

He was astonished to see that she was in tears.

"Are you all right?" he asked.

She brushed at her face with her gloved fingertips.

"Yes—yes, of course I am." She took a breath and forced
a smile. She was not a good-looking woman, but she had a
certain imperiousness to her, a certain sense of her own not
inconsiderable status in the city's social hierarchy—a status
she had achieved by her own determined efforts. And for
that, one had to admire her. Not *like* her—he knew that
Caroline did not particularly like Isabel Dane, and with
good reason—but admire her, yes. And if she were a trifle
too obviously ambitious for her rather plain, rather shy
daughter, Val's friend Alice, well, there were worse sins than
that.

But why was she at Longworth's? Was he, in fact, continuing the Colonel's dirty business, and had he settled on
Isabel Dane as a victim? What could a clever, canny woman
like Isabel Dane have done to merit a threat of blackmail?

Ames felt the beginnings of righteous anger stirring in his bosom—not at Isabel Dane, but at Richard Longworth and his late employer. He put his hand on her elbow to lead her a little way down the dingy hall, away from MacKenzie.

"Mrs. Dane," he said softly. "Are you—have you had an encounter with Mr. Longworth?" As he gripped her elbow, he could feel her tremble, even under the good stout fabric of her woolen walking jacket.

"I—it is nothing," she said.

He cast about for the right words. "If you will permit me—my cousin Valentine and your Alice are dear friends, and therefore, even though you and I are not well acquainted—"

She was pulling away from him, and he released her.

"Yes, Mr. Ames, but I am late for an appointment—"

Of course, if Longworth was blackmailing her—but for what?—she wouldn't want to confess it to him, a virtual stranger.

The blackguard! To persecute helpless females—!

"Don't pay him," he said firmly.

"I beg your pardon?" She looked genuinely confused. Good, he thought; she can dissemble with the best of them.

"I said, don't pay him. No matter what he threatens, don't give him a penny. It is the only way he can be stopped—from continuing the Colonel's business, I mean. Did you know he worked for Colonel Mann?"

"No," she said rather faintly.

"Yes. He has told me as much. And he has threatened to carry on the Colonel's filthy work. If he tries it, he must be stopped now, at the beginning. Once let him get a foothold, let people start paying up to him as they did to the Colonel, and it will be too late."

She stared at him; he could not make out her expression. Astonishment? Dread? Then she seemed to stifle a laugh. Hysterical, he thought. What had happened between her and Longworth?

THE DEATH OF COLONEL MANN • 215

"You are very—very kind, Mr. Ames," she said a little breathlessly. "I—I am quite all right, I assure you. Mr. Longworth has made no threats against me."

Then why are you here, he thought but did not say.

"You are sure?" he asked. "Because if I could be of help to you—if you would like me to speak to him for you—"

"No!" she said a little too quickly. "No—it is quite all right. If you will excuse me—"

She turned away from him and, nodding to MacKenzie, went down the stairs to the street.

Ames stared after her, his eyes narrowed in thought. Then, remembering his own business with Longworth, he went to the door with its black lettering, "Longworth & Sprague."

As before, the outer office was deserted. Presumably, however, Longworth was inside. Ames crossed to the closed inner door, knocked, and without waiting for a reply, opened it.

Longworth sat at his desk, his head in his hands. At the sound of the door opening, he did not look up. "I can tell you nothing more, Mrs. Dane," he said.

When Ames did not reply, he glanced up. "Oh," he said. "I thought—"

He looked terrible. His hair was in wild disarray; his eyes were sunk back into his head, and they had a haunted look, as if they had seen—what? His own ruin? His face was unshaven, his cravat loosened, his shirt collar dingy and awry. Before him on the desk was an ashtray filled with cigarette stubs; the air in the office was stale with smoke. As he reached for the cigarette box to take out another, Ames noticed that his hands were trembling.

Longworth tapped down the cigarette, put it between his lips, and struck a match against the side of its box. He needed to strike it several times before it caught, and when it did, his hand was shaking so badly that he had trouble touching the flame to the cigarette's tip. After he succeeded, he inhaled deeply and blew out a stream of smoke. Turkish, thought Ames, and rather cheap. "What do you want?" Longworth said.

"I want what I wanted yesterday," Ames replied. He was amazed that a woman like Serena Vincent would ever have had anything to do with this man. And he, poor devil, was infatuated with her. Was that the reason for his desperation? Neither Ames nor MacKenzie sat down, and Longworth, after that first glance up, kept his eyes on the desk in front of him.

Longworth shook his head. "I can't help you, Mr. Ames. I thought I made that clear."

"But I believe you can." Ames put his hands on the desk and leaned in close. "In fact, I believe you can tell me who killed the Colonel."

"No."

"And Mrs. Trask, as well."

Longworth looked up at that. "No," he repeated; his voice was hoarse, and his hand, holding the cigarette between two slim fingers, still trembled visibly.

"No? Why did her husband pay ten thousand dollars to the Colonel two years ago?"

"He— I don't know."

"Yes, you do!" Ames slammed his hand on the desk, causing Longworth to jump.

Go easy, friend, thought MacKenzie. He had been standing slightly behind Ames, but now he stepped forward. "Perhaps Mr. Longworth can—"

"Go away, both of you!" Longworth exclaimed. "I can't help you! I can't even help myself, so how can I help you?"

"Come on, man," Ames persisted. "I don't care who did what, I have my own interests to pursue, and I need to know."

Longworth stared at Ames, but he said nothing. He looked like a whipped dog—like a man who had lost all hope. The sight of him gave MacKenzie the willies, and he looked away.

"Make a bargain with me, then," Ames said, straightening. "Perhaps, if I can help you, you will help me."

A slight sneer curled the corner of Longworth's mouth. "There is no way you can help me, Mr. Ames."

"Perhaps I can. What do you—"

"For God's sake!" Longworth shouted. "You barge in here, you make demands, you hound me and hound me— I tell you, I don't know who killed the Colonel! I don't know what business the Trasks had with him! And I don't know who has your damned letters!"

"Mrs. Trask's death is not what the police think it is," Ames said. "I believe that whoever killed the Colonel probably killed her. I don't care who that is—I am interested only in finding a packet of six letters. You are one of the few people who can give me information—if you will. A young woman's future depends upon it. Can you really deny her whatever help you might give her?"

"I deny her nothing," Longworth said through clenched teeth, "but I repeat—why won't you listen to me?—I cannot tell you anything!"

You are lying, thought MacKenzie.

Ames seemed to think the same. "Yes," he said, "you can. Why were you at the theater last night?"

"The—" Longworth was caught off guard at that. "I went to see the play," he muttered.

"You've seen it before, surely."

"No."

"You are a poor liar, Richard Longworth."

The insult had no effect; Longworth remained slumped in his chair, his face slack with fatigue and despair.

"You saw what happened," Ames went on. "Someone shot at Mrs. Vincent. Was it you?"

"No! Why would I do such a thing?"

"Because you and she are—"

He found that he couldn't say the word: lovers. Longworth was infatuated with her, Caroline had said, recounting the maid's story. And he made threats against her—and against the Colonel as well.

"I believe you had reason—in your own mind, at least," Ames concluded.

Longworth stared at him. "You are wrong, Mr. Ames. I would never—"

"You threatened her."

"Who told you that? Never mind—I can guess. Her maid doesn't like me, and I must admit, the feeling is mutual. No, Mr. Ames, I did not shoot at Mrs. Vincent last night. I would like to know who did."

Ames took a step back; he held Longworth in his gaze for a moment, and then he lifted his shoulders in a dismissive shrug and said, "Very well. As you wish."

He turned to go, and MacKenzie followed. They had crossed the outer office and reached the hall door when they heard Longworth cry, "Ames! One word more, if you please!"

Longworth had come to the connecting door; Ames turned to face him.

"Would you—I would ask a favor of you."

Ames waited.

"If anything should happen to me—"

"Yes?"

"Would you look after Mrs. Vincent?"

And you denied even knowing her, Ames thought.

"Yes," he said. "I will."

CHAPTER
23

"It is so kind of you to come with us this afternoon, Doctor," Caroline said as she dodged a small boy rolling his hoop down the Long Path across Boston Common. The branches of the tall, leafless elms that lined the path thrashed in the cold north wind, causing men and women both to hold on to their hats. Caroline's was gray, trimmed with purple plumes; she grasped its brim tightly as she half turned to speak to MacKenzie.

"My pleasure," he said, and he meant it.

"It's Beethoven and Mozart today, so you're in luck. No Brahms. He is so very *heavy,*" she added.

Since he didn't know one from the other, he merely nodded and clutched his own hat.

Caroline glanced around to Val, who followed them. They were on their way to Friday afternoon Symphony at the Music Hall on Tremont Street. Euphemia, who attended with Caroline and Val ordinarily, had stayed home today, saying she felt the onset of *la grippe.*

Val had been deeply upset at the news of Marian Trask's death; all during lunch, which she'd taken with the Ameses, she had kept coming back to it in a horrified way, until finally Caroline had had to tell her ever so gently to let it go.

But Val hadn't been able to do that. "She was in the Christmas Revels a few years ago. In the chorus. And I believe she was a jester, too. I remember she wore slippers with bells on them."

Now, as they crossed the Common, she was aware of Val's silence, her lagging pace. Somehow, Caroline thought, we must prevent her going into a decline. Declines were fearsome things; some people went into them and never came out. It would have been helpful if I could have seen Marian's sister this morning, she thought, but the sister—grieving? away from town?—had not been in.

At Tremont Street, Caroline saw several people she knew, and inside the Music Hall, after settling herself between Val and MacKenzie, she saw more: Mrs. Sears, and the Misses Curtis; old Dr. Leverett and his daughter, and a young girl whom Caroline recognized as a Leverett cousin. Mrs. Lee and her sister, Miss Abbott; Mr. and Mrs. Loring; Mr. Parker Wigglesworth, solitary as always.

Despite her several layers of warm clothing, including her best flannel petticoat, and despite the warmth of the hall, she felt a sudden chill. It was the same chill she'd felt three evenings before at the Cotillion: who, among all these familiar faces, had been a victim of the Colonel's? And, more to the point, who had been his informants?

Val touched her arm. "Alice isn't here," she said.

Caroline looked to their right, to the two vacant seats three rows down, usually occupied by Isabel and Alice Dane.

"She must still be unwell."

"Yes," Val whispered. "I just don't—I don't know, Caro. If only I could see her, talk to her—"

"Perhaps tomorrow," Caroline murmured soothingly. "Would you like me to call around and see? I could take her some jellied beef, or something like."

Val threw her a grateful smile. "Yes, would you? And

perhaps Mrs. Dane would give you some news of Alice's condition—"

She broke off as a little murmur swept the hall and the conductor, a stern, forbidding German, strode purposefully onto the stage. He waited, his back to them, until the murmur subsided; then he brought down his baton and the first strains of the "Pastoral" Symphony floated out.

Caroline put aside all her forebodings as she gave herself up to the music. She loved these Symphony afternoons; she was sorry that Addington never wanted to come. After a few moments, she glanced at MacKenzie. His face bore an expression of polite interest, nothing more. He looked steadily at the platform, at the musicians laboring away under the conductor's baton; then, aware of her glance, he turned to her and gave her a smile of extraordinary sweetness.

Her heart thudded for a beat or two and then settled back. It had been a long time since a man smiled at her like that; it had, in fact, happened only a few times, and then—

And then he went away, the voice in her mind said. But she had promised herself, long ago, not to think about him. He was gone; he would never come back. And even if he did, now, after all this time, would she welcome him?

Probably not, she thought. No: definitely not. For a moment, aware of the doctor's solid, comforting presence beside her, she ceased to hear the music. Over the past few weeks, she had come to rely on him—to think of him as a friend in a way that she'd never thought of Addington. Addington was her older brother, her protector; as she'd grown up, he'd been almost a father to her (their own father being always so busy with his practice, and he'd died years ago). And women needed men to guide them, to protect them; everyone knew that.

It was just that sometimes Addington's guiding hand grew rather heavy. Truth to tell (but she never would have told it, never would have confessed it to anyone), she'd been looking forward to his absence this winter. So there had been a small bit of regret for herself, as well as her larger regret for him, when the expedition had been canceled. Poor Professor Harbinger. . . .

The first movement ended. To her horror, she saw Mac-Kenzie lift his hands as if to clap, and before she could stop herself, she reached over and put her hand on his. She shook her head, smiling to take the sting from any reproof.

He was not offended. He smiled back at her, and shrugged as if to say, I am an uncouth westerner, unschooled in classical music.

The second movement began. She took back her hand. She could still feel the sensation of it—ungloved, naked—touching his. She didn't mind that he didn't know when to applaud. She didn't, she realized, mind at all.

It was dark outside when the concert ended, and colder than ever. Caroline asked Val, "Will you come to tea, dear?"

Val started as though her thoughts had been miles away. "Didn't I tell you? George promised to meet us for tea at Bailey's."

This was a Boston institution, a fabulous ice cream parlor and tea shoppe a few doors down Tremont Street.

"He did? Oh, but that will be lovely," Caroline exclaimed. Bailey's had a kind of enchantment to it, dark wood and tiny, polished marble tables and stained glass lamps; surely there, in that warm, bright place, over a cup of tea and a plate of ice cream and tiny, sweet iced cakes, George would begin to behave well once more.

The sidewalk was crowded, people jostling by, and Caroline found that somehow her hand had been tucked into the crook of Dr. MacKenzie's elbow. This felt odd at first—Addington never let her take his arm—but after a moment, she found that it felt quite pleasant as well, so she let it stay.

At Bailey's, they managed to find a table in a far corner. "He said he'd be here," Val said, anxiously scanning the crowd. "He especially promised, because he knew I was upset about the other day."

"Perhaps he has been held up—" Caroline began, but Val cut her off.

"He *promised,*" she said. Caroline heard a note of coldness in the girl's voice that she had not heard before.

They waited. George did not come. At last, when the waitress had appeared for the second time, they asked for three ice cream teas.

Valentine sat mute and stricken, but there was a stubborn set to her mouth. As Caroline looked at her young cousin's pale, still face, she thought: just as Val said, her heart is beginning to harden. And that, in the end, may be what saves her when her letters, as surely they will, turn up at last.

CHAPTER 24

"MR. AMES—HOW KIND OF YOU TO COME SO PROMPTLY."

Serena Vincent rose to greet him, holding out her hand with a look of genuine relief. She was as lovely as ever, but with an air of tension that for all her actress's skill, she could not conceal. Hardly surprising, he thought as he took her hand and felt, like a small shock to his system, the pressure of her grasp.

He had not thought of his coming to her as kind; after receiving her telegram, he'd hardly been able to get through lunch, so eager was he to see her. To learn what she had to tell him: apparently something urgent. Or, at least, that was what he told himself: that he wanted to see her only to hear what she had to say, and for no other reason. Almost, he believed it.

"You wanted to see me," he said unnecessarily.

"Yes," she breathed. He caught her scent—some heavy, sensuous perfume. It was not the scent of a proper Boston lady. "If you don't mind—could we go out? I will just fetch my hat and coat."

Left alone in her pretty sitting room, he looked around. All was as it had been when he'd visited her before—tasteful, expensive, and the Yorkie eyeing him from its pillow.

Except— Ah. There on the mantel. He went to look at it more closely. It was the diamond bracelet that he'd seen in Longworth's room at the Hotel Brunswick. It lay half out of its box, as if she'd left it there carelessly.

Or perhaps Longworth himself had left it there?

He remembered what Caroline had told him of the maid's confession the evening before: Longworth besotted with Mrs. Vincent, threatening her, threatening himself— and the Colonel. Longworth had denied any connection with her, and she with him; it was hardly surprising they both had lied. Their motive for lying was something else, however. If she—

She was back, wearing a green velvet coat and matching hat; the color suited her marvelously well, he thought. He wondered if she'd ever had her portrait painted. John Singer Sargent was making a name for himself in society portraiture; he'd do Serena Vincent justice and then some.

The maid let them out—the same who had attended Mrs. Vincent last evening at the theater. A devoted servant, Ames thought. So why had Mrs. Vincent wanted to leave her apartment just now? Because she didn't want the maid to overhear what she had to say, obviously. So what did that mean?

They walked along Berkeley Street toward Boylston. The only woman with whom he was accustomed to walk was Caroline, and not that often with her. Serena Vincent was much taller than his sister, and he realized he liked it, that height.

"They have questioned me again." Her lovely profile was taut, almost grim.

"The police, you mean."

"Yes."

"And—?"

The sun had come out, but the day was cold, the wind brutally whipping her skirts, his Inverness cape. As they waited to cross at Boylston Street, she slipped her hand into the crook of his arm. "Shall we go to Bailey's?" she said. There were a number of Bailey's; this one was across the street.

"Wherever you like."

They found a quiet table by the window with no other patrons nearby. The waitress took their order and vanished.

He looked at Mrs. Vincent across the table. The cold air had reddened her cheeks a little—or was it face paint? He hoped not. To the casual observer, she would have looked perfectly calm. But he saw the little line of tension between her brows and the slight trembling of her full, exquisite mouth.

"Well?" he said. "What happened? Was it Crippen who spoke to you?"

She gave a short, bitter laugh. "Spoke to me? Hardly that, Mr. Ames. Cross-examined me was more like it."

"You should not have submitted to it without a lawyer present."

"Next time—if there is a next time—I won't. But that isn't the most important thing I have to say to you, Mr. Ames."

She fell silent as the waitress brought their order—coffee for him, a bowl of clam chowder and a chicken sandwich for her. This was, she said, her supper; she would go to the theater directly from here.

She took a few spoonfuls of soup, and then she said, "You know, of course, about Mrs. Trask."

"Yes."

She looked away from him for a moment as if she were trying to come to some difficult decision; then she went on.

"She was blackmailing Richard Longworth."

He felt it reverberate all through him. "Why?"

"Because—obviously—she knew something about him. Something damaging enough to demand money for her silence."

"How much money?"

She waved her hand. "Thousands."

"And do you know why?"

"No. But I do know that he was terribly upset about it, so whatever it was, it was true."

He remembered Longworth's haunted eyes, his desperate manner.

"She is—was—such a *silly* little woman," Mrs. Vincent went on. Her voice was calm, but her eyes flashed with anger. "Such a little busybody. I wouldn't be surprised if she were one of the Colonel's spies. Do you know, it was she who discovered that poor boy, Harry Morgan, in flagrante?"

"Who?"

"Harry Morgan. I believe you met him when he ran into you the day before yesterday, at my front door."

"Ah." He nodded. He'd forgotten about Harry Morgan, but now he recalled a tall, fresh-faced, handsome youth. "In flagrante with whom?"

"I have no idea. Harry never told me, but she was obviously a girl of good family."

"Why obviously?"

"Because otherwise he wouldn't have felt the need to seek refuge with me on the Vandergrifts' yacht. As it was, if he'd tried to show his face again in polite society, Mrs. Trask would have made him persona non grata, and well he knew it."

Yes, she was right. If Harry Morgan had been discovered with, say, some servant girl, no disgrace would have attached to him.

"And on the strength of my rescuing him," she went on, "he has been staying at the American House Hotel all the autumn, laying siege to me."

"You are not suggesting that it was Harry Morgan who killed Mrs. Trask, are you? Possibly in revenge for—ah— uncovering him, so to speak?"

She laughed. She was spooning up her chowder again, seemingly with good appetite. "Hardly," she said. "Harry isn't the killing type."

"How do you know that?"

She lifted one elegantly clad shoulder and gave him a wry smile. "A woman in my position, Mr. Ames, has to be a fairly quick study of men's natures."

"Yes." He felt himself flush. "I see."

"I doubt that you do, but take my word for it."

"And what—or who—would you say is the killing type, Mrs. Vincent?"

She thought about it. "The one with the most to lose," she said finally. And, seeing his expression, "Why do you look surprised at that?"

"Because it is exactly the answer a very learned man—a Harvard professor, in fact—gave to me not three days ago."

She smiled at him. What depths of mysterious femininity were in that smile—and what traps for the unwary, he reminded himself.

"You understand that you have given me, just now, the name of someone with an even stronger reason than Harry Morgan's to have killed Mrs. Trask."

"Yes." She watched him steadily. Her smile vanished, replaced by an expression of the utmost gravity. In it, he saw no compassion, no sorrow, no sympathy for the man she had implicated—the man who had been, despite her denials, her lover. Ames was sure of it.

He reminded himself that according to her maid, she'd rebuffed that man. So apparently he had become a nuisance to her—or worse.

And what better way to get rid of a nuisance than to implicate him in murder?

Was she capable of such a thing?

She was, he realized, a complete mystery to him. As were all women, but this woman more than most.

"Have you told the police about Mrs. Trask's blackmail threat to Mr. Longworth?"

She gave him a look that was equal to any of Caroline's. "Of course not."

"Why not?"

"He has trouble enough, wouldn't you say?" Her lovely eyes hardened for a moment. "Let the police do their job. It is no affair of mine."

Oh, but it is, he thought. Because—as I have warned you—Crippen has you in his sights.

"Do you think Longworth killed Mrs. Trask?"

"No."

"Why not?"

"Because he was with me."

So that may have been the telegram Longworth sent yesterday, Ames thought, asking for a meeting with her. Either they were going to cover for each other again, or she was lying. But why give Longworth the motive for Marian Trask's death if she intended to show that he couldn't have killed her?

"Why did you send a threatening letter to Colonel Mann?" he said abruptly.

He'd intended to catch her off guard, and for a moment—no more—he succeeded.

"Because—oh, I don't know!" She'd finished her soup; her sandwich lay untouched. "Because I was angry, I suppose. Because he'd ruined me once, and I wanted him to know that he couldn't do it again."

"It was, wouldn't you agree in retrospect, a foolish thing to do?"

"Perhaps. Yes—obviously. But how could I know there was someone even more desperate than I was to—to get rid of him?"

"You admit you were desperate?"

She gave her head an angry little shake.

"I wanted to—to prevent any gossip that linked me to Mr. Longworth."

"Because?"

"Because, as I have already told you, I want to stay here. I am determined to stay here. And if I continued any association with him, that would have become impossible. I survived one scandal in Boston, Mr. Ames, but I doubt I could survive two."

He thought of the maid's tale: Longworth's threats, his pleas, his desperation.

"How did you meet him?"

"It was . . . in New York."

"Where you shot a man three years ago."

Her gaze was steady—almost too unnervingly steady—as she reached for her sandwich. He reminded himself that she was a skilled actress. "Yes."

"Why?"

"It seems I have no secrets from you, Mr. Ames." She bit into her sandwich, chewed, and swallowed. He waited.

"He was a pest," she said. "He—threatened me."

"And Longworth came to your rescue."

"Yes. He was very kind—very helpful. He—he managed to get any charges against me dismissed."

"How convenient."

"You may call it that. At the time, I called it providential. It was . . . a bad time for me."

"Why were you in New York when you have said you want to pursue your career in Boston?"

For a moment, he thought she would not answer, but then, very quietly, she said, "I went to New York on a personal matter, Mr. Ames. I can say no more about it than that."

"I see." He didn't—or not entirely—but he let it go. They were silent while she took a few more bites of her sandwich; then she pushed the plate away.

"I must be going," she said. "They want a run-through of

the third act. My co-star is, shall we say, a little shaky in his lines."

Something that will never be said of you, Ames thought. He signaled for the check, and while they waited, he said, "Have you given any further thought to who might have fired that shot at you last night?"

"Yes. And I can't imagine—"

"Inspector Crippen does not believe that it was intended to harm you. He thinks it was some kind of publicity stunt, and in any case, they cannot find the bullet."

She raised a skeptical eyebrow at that.

"Have you considered that it might have been Richard Longworth?" he asked.

"No!" Her vehemence surprised him. "It was not he."

"How can you be sure?"

"Because—it was a reckless act."

"Entirely in character, from what I know of the man." And, when she did not answer: "He has threatened you, has he not?"

"Yes." Her eyes were downcast, her voice almost a whisper.

"He wants you to go away with him?"

"Yes."

"Which you refuse to do."

"Yes." She lifted her chin a little as she stared at him. "A happy relationship between a man and a woman, Mr. Ames, may be the greatest gift life can give. But as I do not have to tell you, it happens very rarely. Most relationships are less than ideal, and many are less than happy. So I cling not to a relationship with a man, not even to the hope of a relation-ship, but to the security—and the independence—of my work. It is a state of existence I would wish for many women, trapped as they are."

She was speaking from a perspective that he found alien in the extreme; he wanted to bring the conversation back to specifics.

"And so—?"

She shook her head. "When they find that bullet, Mr. Ames—if they do—and if they compare it to Mr. Longworth's gun, I am positive it will not match. If, indeed, he even owns a gun." And then she surprised him by saying with a rueful little smile, "I suppose you are no closer to finding the letters you told me about?"

"No. I am not."

"I am sorry. They must be causing your young friend a good deal of anguish."

"Yes."

"Is she pretty?"

"I beg your pardon?"

"Is she pretty, your friend?"

"Why—I suppose she is, yes."

Her lips twisted in a bitter grimace. "Tell her, in the event that she is disgraced, if she loses her place in society as I did—tell her to come to me. She can make another life for herself on the stage. As I did."

But she has not your courage, he thought, nor, perhaps, your strength.

As they left, the sun was low in the west, long, thin orange-red clouds above it. A crescent moon hung in the pale sky above the Arlington Street Church steeple. It would be another cold night, Ames thought, but clear; perhaps he'd take out his telescope.

He offered to walk with her to the theater, which lay a few blocks away, past the Public Garden and the Common. She accepted with what he thought was a grateful smile, and they set off. Near the corner of Arlington, however, she halted for a moment—no more—to speak to someone.

Or, rather, to accept someone's greeting.

"Good afternoon, Mrs. Vincent." The speaker was a tall, imperious-looking woman who was, Ames realized with a little shock of surprise, a woman he knew. She was, in fact, a woman of his own and Caroline's circle; the last time he'd seen her she had been in some distress.

Isabel Dane.

Serena Vincent met and held Mrs. Dane's gaze. "Good afternoon, Mrs. Dane," she replied. Her smile was proud and haughty and, just a bit, maliciously pleased. And with good reason, Ames thought: women in his circle, women like Mrs. Dane—especially Mrs. Dane—did not ordinarily speak to women like Serena Vincent.

He touched his gloved fingers to the brim of his hat as Mrs. Dane acknowledged him with a nod, and the moment passed.

They moved on, across Arlington Street and down Boylston toward the theater. Mrs. Vincent spoke, but not of the incident just past; she chatted easily, lightly, of nothing consequential, and Ames, remembering his manners, spoke easily in return.

But all the way to the theater, and even after he left her, he felt the question nagging at him, and he could think of no reasonable answer: why, in broad daylight, in the midst of one of the busiest streets in the city, had Serena Vincent been greeted by Isabel Dane?

They parted at the stage door. She gave him her hand in its black kid glove; even as she smiled at him he reminded himself of the many men who must have been captivated by that smile.

"Thank you," she said.

"You are very welcome."

"Will you stay in touch with me?"

"Of course."

"And you will let me know if you find the letters?"

"Yes."

She turned away from him, and for a moment, after the elderly attendant had closed the door behind her, he felt bereft. It was nearly twilight now; the Symphony crowd would just be getting out. He might, if he wished, go along to the Music Hall to join Caroline and Val and the doctor for the walk home.

He did not wish. He wished to see someone—anyone—who might help him untangle this twisted chain of events and lead him to—he needed always to remind himself—what he had sought four days ago, and what he sought still: Val's letters.

At this point, he still had no idea who that might be.

He pulled his cape more closely around himself as he braced against the bitter wind blowing down across the Common. The lights were just coming on, Tremont Street clogged with traffic from one end of the Common to the other, and well beyond. One could walk more quickly along the top of all those conveyances, Ames thought, than seek to be transported inside them. An underground railway like London's was in the works for Boston, he knew; they had better get on with it.

After a time, as he proceeded past the stylish shops and restaurants, he realized he was not walking aimlessly. There was someone he could see—someone who might, in fact, be able to tell him something useful.

But when he inquired at the desk of the American House in Bowdoin Square, he was told that the gentleman had checked out early that morning and had left no forwarding address.

Harry Morgan, it seemed, upon learning of the death of Mrs. Trask—as surely he had—had left town in a hurry.

CHAPTER
25

"HE'S THREE SHEETS TO THE WIND," SAID DELAHANTY, "but still, he's not so far gone that he can't talk. Talk! My God, I can't shut him up. When I suggested sending for you, he agreed at once. 'Evening, Doctor."

The three men—Ames, Delahanty, and MacKenzie—were in the lobby of the St. Botolph Club. It was Friday evening, shortly before eight. After Ames's disturbing interview with Serena Vincent, and his failure to see Harry Morgan, he had looked forward to his dinner and a quiet evening in his study meditating on the day's events. But then Delahanty's urgent telegram had come, summoning him to the club, and so he had foregone his dinner to answer his friend's summons. Caroline had volunteered the doctor's services, and, to please her, MacKenzie had been glad to go along.

"Where is he?" Ames asked Delahanty now.

"In the private members' room, alone."

From the rear of the building, they heard voices raised in anger.

"Trouble back there?" Ames asked.

"There's some quarrel about where to put the Sargent portrait, apparently."

The club's annual Art Show, scheduled to open tomorrow. Ames had forgotten it.

"All right," he said. "Let's see him."

"Wait." Delahanty put a warning hand on his friend's arm. "Do you know who he is?"

"No more than that he is Godfrey Orcutt, noted journalist and world traveler. He's scheduled for a talk here next week, is he not?"

"That's right. But I should tell you also that he is Mrs. Trask's brother."

Ames's mind raced as he heard MacKenzie's exclamation of surprise. "I didn't know she had a brother."

"Since he's hardly ever in the city, there is no reason why you should know it. There was some family disagreement, I believe, so he hasn't been back in years. This visit, so he says, was an attempt to reconcile."

They followed Delahanty to the members' room. Sitting alone by the fire, slumped in a wing-backed chair, was a man whose red-rimmed eyes and disheveled appearance announced a soul if not in torment, then at least in severe pain.

"Mr. Orcutt?" said Delahanty as they approached. "Here is Mr. Ames, as I promised. And his friend, Dr. MacKenzie."

Godfrey Orcutt made a futile attempt to rise; failing that, he slumped back into his chair and raised bleary eyes to his visitors. "Good of you to come," he mumbled. "Help yourself." He waved a hand toward the table next to him, on which were a half-empty bottle of whiskey and one empty glass.

Delahanty had fetched wooden Windsor chairs from a row along the wall, and he and Ames and MacKenzie seated themselves in a little semicircle around the wheezing, perspiring Orcutt.

"Mr. Orcutt," Delahanty began, "tell Mr. Ames what you have told me."

Orcutt blinked, trying to focus on Ames. "My sister," he said hoarsely. "My poor sister is dead."

"I know she is, sir, and you have my deepest sympathy," Ames said.

Orcutt blinked; a tear dribbled down his unshaven cheek. "Dead," he repeated. "My dear girl. And in such a dreadful way—" He broke off in a sob; after a moment he put his fists to his eyes like a crying child.

Delahanty said in a low voice, "Give him time, Ames. He's really cut up, poor fellow."

Ames pressed his lips together in annoyance. To be cut up was one thing; to show it, quite another. Particularly, to show it in public. After a moment, Delahanty produced his own clean, white cotton handkerchief to replace Orcutt's sodden ball of silk. Orcutt took it, wiped his eyes, blew his nose loudly, and took a deep breath.

"Such a dreadful way, Mr. Ames," he said again. "Can you imagine—shot dead on the street? Who would do such a terrible thing? She was the sweetest, kindest person in the world, everyone loved her—"

That was not what Ames had heard. He had heard that Mrs. Trask was a voyeur—and a blackmailer. More, he had seen her husband's name in Colonel Mann's ledger next to a staggering sum of money.

"It was not a random killing," Orcutt went on, and suddenly he sounded quite sober.

"The police think—" Ames began.

Orcutt waved his hand in annoyance. "Don't talk to me about the police," he said. "I have lived and worked in some of the most backward, corrupt places in the world, and I can tell you that the police are the same everywhere. They need to preserve public order, and to do that, whenever they are confronted with a murder that might outrage the public's sensibilities, they claim to solve it as quickly as possible, whether or not that solution is the correct one. The police are saying that Marian's death was a random street crime. What nonsense!"

"Why do you say that?" Ames leaned forward and rested his elbows on his knees.

"Because I believe it. For one thing, I went to Bertram's Bower today. The police had not even been there yet, can you imagine?"

"And what did you learn there?" Ames asked.

"That Marian was puzzled when her carriage did not come for her. Someone sent a telegram to her house yesterday afternoon, canceling it. But that someone was not Marian. According to the people at the Bower, she expected her carriage to call for her at five o'clock, just as it always did."

Ames nodded. "I should probably tell you, Mr. Orcutt, that while your sister may not have sent the telegram canceling her carriage, she did send one to me, asking to call on me at around five-thirty yesterday afternoon. Or at least it purported to come from her; whether in fact she actually sent it, we may never know."

Orcutt struggled with it. "All the more reason why she would not have canceled her carriage."

"There is the thought that perhaps she would not have wanted her coachman to know—because servants do gossip—that she was coming to me. But if, as you say, she wondered why her carriage did not come, we may assume that she did not send the telegram canceling it."

"After I went to the Bower today, I visited every Western Union office in the South End," Orcutt said. "They all had their signed receipt books, but I found none with Marian's signature."

"The telegram will have its point of origin noted," MacKenzie put in. "So you need not have troubled—"

Orcutt, who had been fixed on Ames, now swung around heavily to stare at the doctor. "Who are you?" he demanded.

MacKenzie cleared his throat, thrown a little off balance by Orcutt's hostile tone. "I am—"

"Dr. MacKenzie is my close friend," Ames cut in. "You may speak freely in front of him, and be assured of his discretion."

Orcutt made a gasping sound that was, they saw, an attempt at a laugh.

"Discretion," he repeated. "Yes, that is what we must have, is it not? Here in this tight little world of Boston Society. Let us have discretion by all means. We may have nothing else, by God, but we do have our discretion!" With his last words, he slammed his hand down on the table next to his chair, making the whiskey bottle and empty glass jump. He seized the bottle and lifted the glass to pour. His hand was so unsteady, however, that he missed, and whiskey went spilling all around their feet, making Ames exclaim in annoyance.

"We can do no good here," he said to Delahanty, rising to step back from the alcohol-drenched carpet. "You should get him to bed upstairs and hope that he awakens relatively sober tomorrow morning, and with not too bad a hangover."

Orcutt seemed not to have heard; he had managed to get a little whiskey into the glass, and now he was gulping it down, his eyes closed.

"Don't go yet, Ames," Delahanty begged.

As they settled down again in front of Orcutt, Delahanty reached out and none too gently prised the glass from his hand. "Mr. Orcutt," he said, "we have summoned Mr. Ames away from his dinner so that you could tell him what you have told me. And you haven't told it all yet."

Orcutt peered at him. "It's no use," he said after a moment. "What can he"—and here he waved his hand at Ames in a dismissive gesture—"do for me, after all? What can he do for Marian? She's gone—my poor little sister—" He broke off, threatening to dissolve into tears again.

"You must tell him," Delahanty said firmly. "He may be of help."

Orcutt blinked. Visibly, he was trying to make his brain work, and it seemed a painful process. "Yes," he said at last. "You are right. Summoned from his dinner. My apologies to you, Mr. Ames. And to you, too, sir," he added, nodding at MacKenzie.

"What you told me, Mr. Orcutt," Delahanty prompted.

"What I told you. Yes." Orcutt shifted his heavy body in his chair; then, as if his head had suddenly cleared, he leaned forward, his small, bleary eyes fastened on Ames.

"I have just returned from the Argentine, Mr. Ames. A most interesting country. Revolution, massacre, assassination—everything. I traveled a good deal. I met people from all walks of life. They would often approach me with their stories, which they felt might be of interest to my readers back here in the United States."

He paused, as if remembering.

"You were saying that people approached you," Ames said.

"Yes. Approached me. Well, one day a few months ago, a gentleman came to call. I was in a provincial capital in the interior. A pleasant place, with some rather wealthy landowners. This man was one of them. He had heard that I was not only from the United States, but from Boston. He asked me to do him a service. It seemed that he had a daughter— and a grandchild, as well. This young woman had married an American man some years ago. An American man from Boston, in fact."

Ames waited.

"For a while," Orcutt went on, "they were a happy couple, at least to all appearances. But then things began to go wrong. I got a sense of money embezzled, the girl's father— the man who came to see me—realizing that his son-in-law was less than honest, gambling debts, and so forth. And then, one day, the American disappeared. Vanished. Gone without a trace. They tried to find him, but without success. The odd thing is—" And here Orcutt broke off as if he was considering it. "The odd thing is, this American never bothered to assume an alias. Apparently, he kept his own name the entire time he was in Argentina."

He paused. Then: "Can you guess what that name is, Mr. Ames?"

"I can."

"Then you tell me."

"No." Ames saw in his mind's eye the anguished face of an old man speaking with evident pain of his wayward son—a son who had failed in Argentina as he had in Boston. Mrs. Vincent had told him that Longworth was being blackmailed. She hadn't known why, but Ames, now, did. "I would rather hear it from you."

"Very well." Orcutt hiccupped; then he leaned forward so far that MacKenzie, fearing he would topple to the floor, put out a hand to steady him.

"His name, Mr. Ames, is Richard Longworth."

For a moment, no one said anything. Delahanty shot a glance at Ames, but Ames did not return it; he stared intently at their informant as if he were trying to read that whiskey-soaked mind. Then: "You told this to Mrs. Trask." It was not a question.

Orcutt blinked. "How did you—"

"But to no one else, I take it."

"Correct. I told only Marian."

"Why?"

"I beg your pardon?"

"I said, why? Why did you tell her at all? If it was none of her business—"

"A little harmless gossip—"

"Did you know that Mr. Longworth is married? Here in Boston, I mean."

Orcutt shook his head. "No."

"Your sister did not tell you that?"

"No." Again, Orcutt seemed to be painfully exercising his brain. "Married? Here in Boston?"

"Yes."

"But—" It was too much for him; he couldn't work it out. Ames helped him.

"It occurs to me, Mr. Orcutt, that if your sister let it be known to Longworth that she had this information about him, that would have made her a marked woman, would it not?"

"What are you saying?" Orcutt was breathing heavily, with an audible wheeze.

"I am not saying anything. I am merely hypothesizing that if—I repeat, *if*—your sister was so unwise as to approach Longworth with this extremely interesting bit of information, it might have put her in danger. Since Mr. Longworth has married—for a second time, apparently—since returning to Boston, and married a fortune at that, I cannot imagine he would be happy to have it known that he has in fact a previous wife, alive and well in Argentina."

As the implications of what Ames said began to sink in, Orcutt uttered a low moan; he brought up his hands to splay them over his face, as if to hide himself from all the world.

"No," he moaned. "No. No. You are saying that I was instrumental in my sister's death. Oh, no."

"Mr. Orcutt—" Delahanty began.

Ames silenced him with a quick motion. "Wait," he said softly. Then he turned back to Orcutt. "Mr. Orcutt, have you told this to the police?"

Orcutt slid his hands down from his face and dropped them into his lap. "I told you my opinion of the police, Mr. Ames. What good would it do for me to go to them with this information?"

"I don't know. It might do some."

Orcutt shook his head. "No. I do not believe that. I believe—I believe that we must find this man—this cur—this

cad—Longworth!" He shouted the name, and simultaneously he heaved himself up out of his chair, nearly pitching
forward onto his trio of visitors.

Hastily they moved out of his way. Propelled by inertia,
Orcutt kept going until he came up sharp against a massive
ebony table near the center of the room. Jolted by the impact, he stood panting, his head hanging, his hands spread
flat on the table's surface.

"Time to get him upstairs," Ames murmured to Delahanty. "And while you do that—MacKenzie will help you—
I will just go and see if our friend Longworth is staying here
tonight."

As Delahanty and MacKenzie each took an elbow to steer
Orcutt out of the room and into the lobby, the journalist
had one last thought for Ames.

"That fellow," he said, speaking once more in the too-
careful enunciation of the inebriate, "is bound to be trouble,
Mr. Ames. Have a care if you speak to him. And tell him I
will call on him tomorrow."

No, thought Ames. I will not tell him that. And you, Mr.
Orcutt, do not even know the worst of him. You do not
know that he betrayed his second—albeit illegal—wife by
having a liaison with Serena Vincent. You do not know that
he fattened his purse by working for Colonel Mann.

As MacKenzie and Delahanty coaxed the sodden journalist up the stairs, Ames went to the desk. Was Mr. Longworth staying here tonight? he asked.

He was not, the desk man said.

"Could he have gone upstairs to one of the rooms reserved for members' use without checking in?"

No, the desk man said frostily. Surely Mr. Ames must
know that every member who took an overnight had to
sign in.

Ames could think of two or three occasions when that
particular rule had been honored in the breach, but he did
not argue. "Cards in the back?" he asked.

The desk man nodded. "Yes, sir. The usual."

Ames made his way along the corridor to the small, smoke-filled room. He looked in, nodded to the one man who looked up to see who had come, and ascertained that Longworth was not present.

So where are you, desperate man? he wondered as he went back to the lobby to wait for his companions. *The one with the most to lose.* Was it Serena Vincent's voice he heard, or Professor James's?

From the rear of the building, people were still arguing loudly. There would be bad feelings, no doubt, long after the Art Show had opened and closed; the members of the St. Botolph Club could hold a grudge as well as anyone.

Delahanty and MacKenzie were coming down the stairs.

"Safely tucked in?" Ames asked as they joined him.

"Dead to the world," Delahanty replied. "If you'll pardon the expression."

"He'll be miserable in the morning, no doubt," MacKenzie added.

Delahanty, looking weary from his evening's ordeal, said, "How about a bite to eat? We can still get something from the kitchen."

"No, thank you," Ames replied. Unease nagged at him, driving away what little appetite he had. "I must go. Stay if you wish, Doctor, although I would be glad of your company."

MacKenzie thought longingly of the boiled beef and scalloped potatoes waiting for them at Louisburg Square. Then he put that thought aside and said, "Of course. Where are we headed?"

"To the Park Theater," said Ames.

They found a herdic at the door. The nighttime city was quiet, the horse's hooves making what seemed an unusually loud clatter. Ames sat quiet, gnawing his lip. *The one with the most to lose*—and who had more to lose than Richard Longworth?

And if Longworth had in fact killed Mrs. Trask, and the Colonel as well, what would stop him from killing again? He had given Serena Vincent ample evidence of his desperation. He had threatened her, had let her see in no uncertain terms his willingness to perform desperate deeds.

Because he loved her so much?

Or because now, at last, he saw the end of his own reckless life looming before him?

"Hurry, man!" Ames called to the cabbie.

But the cabbie was already hurrying, the horse trotting along at a fast clip. It was only Ames's growing sense of disaster that made the journey seem so long. He would go to Mrs. Vincent, yes, and he would tell her what he had learned about Longworth, and—yes—he would see her home safely, warn her to lock her door, warn her not to admit Longworth under any circumstances, warn her to hire a guard for herself, never to let herself be alone for a moment until this affair was at its end.

At the corner of Boylston and Tremont streets, they alighted and Ames thrust coins at the driver. The theater district was quiet, the evening's entertainments not yet over. They hurried around into the alley, to the stage door. Ames pounded on it. After a moment it opened a crack, and the elderly attendant peered out.

"I need to see Mrs. Vincent," Ames said. "It is an emergency. I will wait for her in her dressing room."

"She's not here."

"What do you mean, she's not here? The play is still going on, is it not?"

"It is not." The old man opened the door a little wider, and now they could see that the backstage corridor, ordinarily well lighted and filled with people, was dim and deserted.

"What's wrong?" Ames said. He stepped forward and pushed the door open. "Where is she?"

The attendant shook his head. "No performance tonight, sir. She's gone."

"Gone? What do you mean?"

"With the police, sir. They came tonight and took her away. She's been arrested for Colonel Mann's murder."

CHAPTER
26

"AT LEAST SHE IS SAFE," SAID AMES.

"Safe!" Caroline exclaimed. "How can she be safe when she is arrested for murder?"

"Arrested she may be, but at least, in the Tombs underneath City Hall, she is protected from Longworth."

They were in the dining room at No. 16½. Ames and the doctor had returned from their fruitless visit to the Park Theater, and now, past ten o'clock, they were having their supper at last.

"That poor girl," Caroline said after a moment.

Ames looked up at her from his plate. "What poor girl?"

"Lydia Longworth."

"The second Mrs. Longworth, you mean."

"Yes. She is such a lovely person, and I know how dearly she loves him."

"More fool she."

"Yes." She thought for a moment, trying to concentrate on all that Ames had told her so she wouldn't have to think of Lydia Longworth. "Addington, what does all this mean?"

"Why—" He paused, wanting to get it right. "I suppose it means that Richard Longworth, who worked for Colonel Mann, who was deeply in debt, who had a wife living in

Argentina when he married here, who was being black-mailed by Mrs. Trask—I suppose it means that Longworth is the man I have sought ever since I discovered the Colonel's body on Monday night. Mrs. Trask, by the way, was not only a blackmailer but a snoop. She discovered some young couple in flagrante at Newport last summer, according to Mrs. Vincent. So she may well have worked for the Colonel, but she didn't kill him. No: I suspected Longworth all along, and now, it seems, I was right."

"And the letters?" MacKenzie asked.

"Oh, he has them, I am sure. I will go to him again tomorrow—after I speak to Inspector Crippen."

"You haven't seen him?" Caroline asked.

"No. We went to police headquarters, but he wasn't there."

"And I suppose there was no chance to see Mrs. Vincent?"

"Not tonight. I will try tomorrow. But first I must see Crippen. Damn the man! I don't know whether to congratulate him for keeping Mrs. Vincent safe, or excoriate him for being so pigheaded. He's had her in mind for the Colonel's murder from the start, and now that he's actually got her in hand, so to speak, it will be all the more difficult to show him his error."

Caroline tried and failed to muster some small feeling of sympathy for the glamorous, the notorious, Mrs. Vincent. They finished their meal in silence. When Margaret brought up their coffee, Ames refused it. He wanted to sleep soundly, he said. Soon he left them, and Caroline and the doctor were alone.

"More coffee, Doctor?" she asked.

He shook his head. "Thank you, no."

"Smoke if you like."

He nodded his thanks as he filled his pipe. The grand-mother clock in the hall chimed ten-thirty.

"Doctor—"

"Yes?"

I have to ask him, she thought. I hardly know him, and yet I feel as though he is an old friend. He was smiling at her, waiting to hear what she had to say. So, somehow, she had to find the courage to say it.

"I—there was something I wanted to ask you."

"Yes?" He inhaled heavily to get his pipe going.

"Something—personal." He was a doctor, after all; he must be accustomed to dealing with people's troubles.

"It is about Addington," she said. She heard her voice, stiff and strained, not her normal voice at all.

"What about him?"

"It is just—well, I was wondering—about Mrs. Vincent."

"Yes?"

"It—she—" Really, Caroline, she thought, you sound like a ninny. Get on with it. "I wondered if you have any idea of what Addington's feelings for her are."

"His feelings—?"

"I mean—" And now, suddenly, everything came out in a rush, and she heard herself chattering as if she could never stop. "You see, he has never—I mean, he has always been a—everyone says he is a confirmed bachelor. And he is, I believe, just as I am a—well, I am a spinster, neither of us has ever— There was one time, years ago, when he was attracted to a—a young woman, a very silly girl, flighty, not his type at all. I wonder why it is that serious, intelligent men like Addington are so often attracted to flighty females. Have you any idea?"

"I don't—" He was embarrassed; he felt himself flush, and he reached for his handkerchief to dab at his moistening brow.

"No, of course you don't. Men don't, in general. But do you understand what I am trying to say? I mean, Mrs. Vincent may be very beautiful—indeed, she is—but she is also an actress, a woman who was disgraced. So you see—"

At last he understood. "You mean, Miss Ames, that you

are concerned that your brother might have developed an unsuitable attraction to Mrs. Vincent?"

"Yes," she breathed. She felt as though an enormous weight had been lifted from her shoulders. "That is exactly what I mean. Oh, how good of you to understand."

He felt as though he had performed some kind of heroic deed for her, when all he had done was listen to her confide her worries to him. She was sitting across the table from him, so he could not reach her hand; he pushed back his chair, stood up, and went around to where she sat. Feeling as though he did some rash deed, he rested his hand on her shoulder. He could feel her slight tremor as he did so.

"My dear Miss Ames," he said softly. He heard the thump of the dumbwaiter in the back passage; he had only a moment to speak before Margaret appeared to collect the remains of the meal. "Your brother is a sound man—a very sound man." It was high praise, and she understood that. "I doubt very much that at this point in his life he will do anything rash. Mrs. Vincent, attractive though she may be, is hardly his type of woman."

For an instant—no more—she wanted to put her hand over his. But no, she had been foolish enough; she didn't need to compound her foolishness.

Margaret, looking run off her feet, knocked and came in. MacKenzie moved away; Caroline stood up.

"Thank you, Margaret," she said; and, turning to Mac-Kenzie, "And thank you, Doctor."

THE NEXT MORNING, THEY HAD HARDLY BEGUN THEIR breakfast—Saturday bacon and eggs—when they heard the door knocker. The next moment, Valentine appeared. She must not have slept at all, Caroline thought, scrutinizing the girl's pale face, the dark circles under her eyes.

"Good morning, dearest," she said. "Come have some coffee—or would you prefer tea?"

"Nothing, thanks." Val accepted the men's greetings and sat down next to Caroline. The day had turned mild and misty, and she had brought with her a breath of salt air and smoke, overlaid by her own eau de cologne. She sat perched on the edge of her chair, her gloved hands clasped tightly around the little reticule resting in her lap.

The morning paper (which Ames had examined, criticized—"Can't they ever get it right?"—and put to one side) lay on the corner of the table. Val glanced at its bold black headline announcing Serena Vincent's arrest and then immediately glanced away.

She opened her reticule and produced a folded letter. "This came in the early mail," she said, handing it to Caroline.

Caroline scanned the few lines, came to the signature, and uttered an exclamation of dismay.

"Why, this is from George!" she said to Val. "And with not a word about his rudeness yesterday afternoon—"

Wrong to bring that up, she thought as she saw Val's expression.

In his note, George asked to see Val at five o'clock that afternoon.

"No," said Val. "Not a word about that." She had taken off her dark blue kid gloves, and now she sat nervously working her hands, twisting her engagement ring around and around on her finger until Caroline wanted to put her hand on Val's to make her stop.

Ames looked at Val from beneath his dark brows and said gently, "Valentine, can you think of any way Mrs. Trask might have known about your letters?"

Val's face seemed frozen, and her lips hardly seemed to move as she said, "No. She couldn't have."

"Why not?"

"Because—"

She is in pain, Caroline thought; real physical pain. But of course one feels pain when one's heart is broken. Val would hardly be human if she didn't feel it.

"Addington—" she began.

"No, Caro, it is all right." Val suddenly stopped twisting her ring. "She couldn't have," she said to Ames, "because she was not in Newport that summer—the summer before last. The talk was that her husband forbade her to come. Such nasty gossip—and, really, she wasn't such a bad person. I rather liked her the few times I met her."

Do we tell Val the truth about Mrs. Trask? Ames thought. Is there more to that truth than we know? Had Mrs. Trask known about Val's letters? Had she given—or sold—them to the Colonel? Impossible to say, now; and in any case, the letters had already done their damage even though, presumably, the Putnams knew nothing about them.

Suddenly, Val said: "George is going to break our engagement."

"Oh, Val, dear, don't say that!" Caroline exclaimed; but even as she spoke, she chided herself. Why shouldn't Val say that, when it seemed to be the truth? People lived all their lives denying the truth, but sometimes the truth had to be acknowledged.

And dealt with.

It was fortunate, she thought, that Euphemia was laid up with *la grippe.* The interview with George was bound to be excruciating; Euphemia's presence would only make it worse.

Val managed a little smile. "I may come around afterward."

"Of course, dear. Do!"

After Val left, Caroline and the men finished their breakfast. Then Ames announced that he was going out; where, he did not say. MacKenzie, whose knee was aching somewhat, agreed to meet him that afternoon at the St. Botolph for the opening reception of the Art Show.

"They always have something worth seeing at those get-ups," Ames remarked. "You may even meet a real live artist, Doctor."

After MacKenzie had retired to his room, Caroline went into the parlor. A fog was moving in; through the lavender glass, the evergreen shrubs and black wrought-iron fence around the little oval looked faintly blurred.

It was just past nine o'clock. At ten, she was expected at her Saturday Morning Reading Club. She felt she ought to go, even though she had not finished the week's assigned reading in Mr. Emerson's *Essays.* Mr. Emerson had been, no doubt, a wonderful man, but . . .

She sighed. She was in no mood for either the Saturday Morning Club or Ralph Waldo Emerson. She was far too keyed up and tense to sit placidly for two hours while one or another of her friends discoursed on transcendentalism.

In her mind's eye, she saw a thin, dark-haired woman flitting from group to group at the Cotillion: Marian Trask.

Who had, apparently, committed some indiscretion that caused her husband to pay ten thousand dollars to Colonel Mann.

And who, if Serena Vincent were to be believed, had tried to blackmail Richard Longworth.

Who was, apparently, a bigamist.

Until the past few days, Caroline had viewed the world as a more or less kindly place, well disposed toward people like herself. Now she knew differently. Now she knew that she and Addington—and Valentine; especially Valentine—were as vulnerable as anyone else to scandal's hot, foul breath. It had scorched Valentine; she herself had been singed a little, too. Forever afterward, she would carry the scar on her heart—her soul.

Why had Mrs. Trask wanted to talk to Addington?

As she turned from the window, she made up her mind. The Saturday Morning Club, today, would have to do without her.

CHAPTER
27

HALF AN HOUR LATER, THE MIST HAD THICKENED BUT THE air was still mild, and so Caroline was too warm as she hurried past the brick and brownstone town houses that lined Beacon Street. It would not do to remove her gloves, but as she waited to cross at the corner of Berkeley, she surreptitiously undid the top button of her woolen jacket.

Her destination was five blocks distant. It seemed, suddenly, a very long way yet to go. She was not very tightly corseted today, but still, her body was constricted; she would not have been able to wear this outfit or any other, if it were not. Not for the first time, she thought of the Sensible Dress League and its somewhat eccentric devotees who urged women to give up lacing. People laughed at them, mocked them for being unladylike, but perhaps they were right, all the same. Surely it could not be what nature intended, to bind oneself up so tightly that one could hardly breathe?

Ten minutes later, a little breathless, she was climbing the brownstone steps of a house on Gloucester Street. There was a small mourning wreath on the door, and all the blinds were down. Still, that was the custom for houses in mourning; it didn't mean the occupant was not there.

"Yes?" said the black-clad maid who opened the door.

"Is Miss Henshaw at home?" Caroline offered her card, but the maid did not take it.

"No, Miss. Not today."

"I understand. But this is most urgent—"

"Who is it, Betty?" came a voice from within.

As the maid turned to answer, Caroline thrust her card at her again and said, "Here—please show her this."

As she waited, she thought, a month ago—a week, even—I never would have been so pushy—so rude. But a week ago seemed an eternity; she was a different person now, and she could never again be the Caroline Ames she'd been then.

After a moment, the maid came back and admitted her. A woman who might have been Marian Trask stood in the drawing room doorway, and for a moment the sight made Caroline's heart jump. Then she reminded herself that Marian Trask was dead, and she went forward.

"My dear Susan. I am so very sorry."

"Yes." Miss Henshaw took Caroline's outstretched hand. Her black dress seemed to have drained all color from her face; Caroline had never seen anyone so pale, not even Valentine, this morning. "Please come in."

The drawing room was shuttered and dim; one gas jet burned beside the mantel. "I apologize for intruding," Caroline went on, "but I must—I have an urgent reason for asking to speak to you."

Miss Henshaw sat on a slippery-looking horsehair sofa; Caroline sat opposite her on a tufted, fringed, armless chair.

"You don't need to apologize, Caroline. What is it?"

"I don't know if you know this," Caroline began, "but on the day she—on the day of Marian's death, she had sent a telegram to my brother, saying she would call on him at five-thirty in the afternoon. That was her day at the Bower—"

"I know. She went there regularly."

"Yes. As I do myself. Well, in any case—she never came, of course, because she—"

Miss Henshaw nodded.

"And I was wondering if you could tell me why she wanted to see him," Caroline finished.

Her words lingered in the air and seemed to echo loudly in her ears. I was wrong to come here on what must seem to her a flimsy excuse, she thought; I make impossible demands on this poor woman, I am being thoughtless and inexcusably rude—

"I saw your brother's name in the newspaper," Miss Henshaw said abruptly.

Caroline nodded. "Yes. He—"

"Found the Colonel's body." Miss Henshaw sat very straight, her hands folded in her lap; she might have been discussing the weather, Caroline thought, so cool was she, so oddly dispassionate.

"Unfortunately—yes." Caroline leaned forward as far as her corset would allow. "I regret more than I can say, having to disturb you at this sad moment. But, you see—well, Addington went to the Colonel to retrieve some letters written by a—by a young friend of ours. I tell you this in confidence, and I know I can trust you to keep it. The letters were very indiscreet, and the Colonel had threatened to reveal them—and her—in *Town Topics.* I needn't say how embarrassed she would have been if the Colonel had carried out his threat."

She could not tell for sure in the dim light, but she thought she saw tears glisten in Miss Henshaw's eyes.

"And so you see—"

"Did Mr. Ames get them?" Miss Henshaw interrupted.

"The letters? No. Unfortunately—no. He did not. But we know the Colonel had them late that afternoon, so Addington thought that probably the person who—who killed the Colonel took them."

Miss Henshaw thought about that for a moment; then: "And what does all this have to do with Marian?"

Caroline had in these few moments gone so far beyond the

bounds of proper female decorum that she felt like someone else entirely, someone who had no feeling for another's sorrow, someone hard and cold, ruthless in her pursuit.

Val, she thought; I am doing this for Val. She had a brief vision of George Putnam breaking his engagement, and the sight stiffened her resolve.

"It has to do with—Marian's death," she said. "I mean—Addington believes it is somehow connected to the Colonel's. He believes she had something important to tell him, something that might have helped him in his search."

"For the letters? Or for the man who killed the Colonel?" Suddenly Miss Henshaw lost her chilly demeanor; she put her hand on Caroline's and pressed hard.

"Does your brother believe that the man who killed the Colonel also killed my sister?"

"He believes—that it is possible."

"I see." Miss Henshaw sat back, pressed her lips together, and stared at her caller with unblinking eyes.

I have failed, Caroline thought. She knows something, but she will never tell it—or not to me, at any rate.

And what, exactly, might it be? Has she seen Godfrey Orcutt (a nom de plume, obviously) since his return, ostensibly to mend family relations? He is her brother as well as Marian's. Does she know—surely not—that he told Marian about Richard Longworth's being a bigamist? Does she know Marian tried to blackmail Longworth on the strength of that information?

And how can I tell her that, she thought. I should never have come here. She will never—

"We speak in the strictest confidence, Caroline."

"Yes, of course."

"What I am about to tell you must not reach the police."

I can't promise that, Caroline thought, but "Yes, I understand," she said.

"You know the Colonel was a wicked, wicked man."

"Indeed he was."

"I firmly believe that even as we speak, he roasts in hell."
Caroline nodded.

"About two years ago, he demanded money from Marian. And of course she couldn't pay him. She never had money of her own. Everything belonged to her husband. And so, in the end, for the sake of their daughter—my niece—William paid. He is not a kindly man, my brother-in-law." Miss Henshaw's face hardened into lines of anger. "He was always—very harsh with Marian. I believe that it was because of that—because of his treatment of her—that Marian, very foolishly, I admit, succumbed to the advances of someone else."

Don't move a muscle, Caroline thought, or you will distract her and she will break off.

"Somehow, Colonel Mann found out about it," Miss Henshaw went on.

"Did she ever learn who it was who told him?"

"No. She had her suspicions, but she didn't know for sure. It was one of two people, she said."

"But she didn't tell you their names?"

"No."

"And the man she—the man who—"

"You mean, who was her lover?" Miss Henshaw shook her head. "That name will not help you, I fear. He is dead now, in any case." She paused, thinking about it. "Well, they are both dead now, aren't they? So perhaps it doesn't matter if I tell you. His name was Winston Sprague."

That name meant nothing to Caroline beyond the fact that the Spragues were an old Boston family like her own; there had been a Sprague girl in the debutante circle a year ahead of Caroline's who had—Caroline searched her memory—married a man from Philadelphia and vanished from the Boston scene.

"And he is dead, you say?"

"Yes. He died last year in London, of pneumonia."

"I see."

"I wonder if you do. Can you imagine what Marian's life was like these past few years?"

"Well, I—"

But Miss Henshaw, having begun, was not now to be stopped until she had unburdened herself completely.

"Her husband paid off Colonel Mann, to be sure, but he took his revenge on Marian all the same. Oh, yes. Her life was a living hell ever since. There is no other way to describe it. William wouldn't speak to her, you know. And he cut her allowance to nothing, so that she had to come to me to beg money just to pay her seamstress to alter what clothing she had. New ones were out of the question. He wouldn't allow her to entertain, he wouldn't allow her to see her friends, he even forbade her to go to Newport the summer after he paid the Colonel's blackmail. But last summer—this past summer—we outwitted him, Marian and I. I have a friend whose sister is married to William's uncle. The uncle has a place at Newport. He was persuaded to invite Marian for the summer season. Since the invitation came from family, William could not refuse. So Marian had her time at Newport, after all."

During this recitation, Miss Henshaw's face had become suffused with an emotion that could only be called fury. Yes, Caroline thought: fury—and hatred. For William Trask, who had discovered his wife's adultery, who had paid dearly to cover it up, and who had, afterward, exacted his revenge on her.

Had Marian gone to work, so to speak, for the Colonel—who had ruined her—to get the money her husband would no longer supply? Or had she simply taken a leaf from the Colonel's book and tried a little blackmail of her own?

It was possible. Caroline didn't know how it would help them to retrieve Val's letters, but she would tell Addington all the same. Perhaps he would see something in it that she herself did not.

Miss Henshaw had begun to cry. "I will miss her so," she

said. "We were always very close, and ever since that awful business with Colonel Mann and his blackmail, we grew closer still. And now she is gone, and it is all his fault!"

Whose fault? Caroline wondered. Her husband's? The Colonel's? Or this Winston Sprague's, whoever he was?

Miss Henshaw put her face into her hands and sobbed and sobbed. Caroline felt tears come to her own eyes as she stood up; she hesitated for a moment, and then, just as Dr. MacKenzie had done for her last night, she put her hand on Miss Henshaw's shoulder.

"I am so sorry," she said softly. "Please believe me when I say that I apologize for disturbing you this morning. And I thank you for seeing me—for confiding in me."

Miss Henshaw turned up her tear-stained face. "I am glad you came, Caroline. And if there is anything more I can do—anything at all—do not hesitate to call on me. If Marian's death was not a random street crime—if it was somehow connected to Colonel Mann's—why, then, I will do whatever is in my power to help you and your brother."

CHAPTER 28

"WINSTON SPRAGUE," AMES REPEATED. HE STARED AT Caroline, his dark eyes alight with interest. "You're sure?"

"That was the name she gave me, Addington. He died last year in London, of pneumonia. Who was he? Did you know him?"

He'd been pacing the parlor; now he moved to the lavender-glass windows. He stared out at the fog-shrouded square; the houses opposite were obscured, and the evergreen shrubbery inside the high iron fence was a blur of misty, purplish gray-green.

"He was Richard Longworth's law partner." The photograph in Longworth's room, he thought, with its dates: 1843–1890.

"Oh." Caroline absorbed it. "Addington, Susan Henshaw said that Marian thought that only one of two people could have betrayed her to the Colonel. And if Winston Sprague was Mr. Longworth's partner, then—"

"Yes. Longworth probably knew of the affair, and so he was undoubtedly one of the people she suspected. Hence her eagerness to get her revenge by blackmailing him after she heard Orcutt's story. In fact, Longworth may well have betrayed her to the Colonel. On the other hand," he went on, "I find it difficult to believe that after her nasty experience with the Colonel, she would have gone to work for him. But if she did, she might have told him Longworth's secret after Longworth refused to pay her the blackmail she demanded. In which case, Longworth was being pressed from two sides—thus making his situation all the more desperate."

He turned to face his sister, but it was MacKenzie who caught his eye.

"And how did your morning go?" the doctor asked.

"Badly," Ames replied.

"You did not see Mrs. Vincent?"

"No. Nor Inspector Crippen, either. The man is out chasing his tail somewhere," he added gloomily, "while she sits in that miserable dungeon." He did not know for certain that the Tombs was a dungeon, but he imagined that it was. Yes, she was safe there—from Longworth, at least—but to think of that lovely woman immured in such a place disturbed him more than he'd thought possible.

He'd gone to Longworth's office, then, but he'd failed there, as well. The door was locked, the room beyond it dark and silent. In the end, to work off the nervous energy that was building up strongly enough to choke him, he'd gone to Crabbe's for an hour of fencing. He'd come out of it drenched with sweat and hurting from a pulled muscle in his thigh, but no less anxious.

But now—yes, now he must see Longworth, must hunt him down no matter what the difficulty. Longworth held the key to his search, he was sure of it.

Margaret announced lunch just then, but as they sat down at the table, the door knocker sounded. In a moment, Margaret appeared with a telegram—for Caroline.

"Oh, dear," she murmured, gingerly accepting it. "Whatever can this be?"

Feeling as though the thing would explode under her

fingers, she slipped out the folded yellow sheet and opened it.

"Oh," she said, and they heard the relief in her voice. "It is nothing. I mean, nothing connected with— It is from Dr. Hannah. She wants me to come to her this afternoon to help out."

She glanced up to see MacKenzie's face, and she laughed. "Don't look like that, Doctor! Yes, Dr. Hannah—Dr. Hannah Bigelow—is a woman, a female physician. She runs a free clinic over on Columbus Avenue, and Saturday afternoon is her walk-in time."

Ames allowed himself a smile. "You do not approve of female physicians, Doctor?"

"Well, I—" MacKenzie reminded himself to go carefully. He was, in fact, offended mightily by the notion of a female physician. He had heard that such creatures existed, but he had never met one and never wanted to. The knowledge that the delightful Miss Caroline Ames not only knew such a one but intended to go to assist her (and what form that assistance might take, he did not allow himself to consider) upset him profoundly.

He coughed and took a sip of water to buy himself a few seconds. "It is not a matter for my approval or disapproval," he said when he could speak again.

"No," Caroline said gently. "It is not. I will go immediately after lunch, Addington. Dr. Hannah's receptionist has undoubtedly been taken ill or called away for some reason, and she needs someone to direct traffic, as it were. People come to her by the dozens on Saturday afternoons, since aside from the City Hospital it is the only place they can get care free of charge."

MacKenzie waged a little struggle with himself. Then: "Miss Ames, if you will permit me—has it not occurred to you that you might catch some disease in such a place? I would be happy to substitute for you, if I might be so bold as to offer my services, and perhaps I could even—ah—assist the lady in her work."

"Why, thank you, Doctor." She smiled at him, and he was relieved to see it, glad that his obvious distress at the idea of a female physician had not turned her against him. "That is very kind of you. Very kind indeed. But I think—well, I will tell Dr. Hannah of your offer, of course. But I think today I should go on my own. Most of her patients are female, and they go to her rather than to the City Hospital because they do not want to be treated by a man. No offense," she added quickly, "but they are poor people, and they are not used to doctors in any case. They wouldn't see one at all if they couldn't see Dr. Hannah."

So it was settled that MacKenzie would join Ames, as arranged, at the St. Botolph Club at four o'clock for the opening reception of the art exhibition, and he went upstairs to rest while Ames took himself off once more.

Caroline had meant to spend the afternoon finishing Diana Strangeways' new novel. She'd felt guilty about it, particularly since she'd missed the discussion of more uplifting work at the Saturday Morning Reading Club, but she was longing to see how the story came out.

Now, however, she mustn't even think of opening it, because once she did, it would be too painful to stop before the end. No, she must leave at once for Dr. Hannah's. If she left the clinic by five o'clock, she could be home in time for Val, should Val need to see her after the interview with George Putnam.

George Putnam. Caroline's heart had briefly lifted at the thought of spending a few hours at Dr. Hannah's clinic, for she was fond of her, and more than that, she admired her very much. Dr. Hannah had had a bad time of it in medical school, faced as she had been by the prejudices of the men in her class; since passing her qualifying examinations, she had devoted her life to the poor. Caroline knew herself well enough to admit that she had none of the iron determination that had enabled Dr. Hannah to persevere, but she was grateful for the opportunity, now and then, to help her.

But now George Putnam had intruded once more into her mind, and her thoughts turned dark. George Putnam was going to break Val's heart, if he had not done so already. Caroline's supply of improper words was pitifully slim, but as she cast about for a name bad enough to call him, one came to mind.

He is a dastard, she thought. Really he is!

She went into the parlor. Beyond the windows she saw the lavender-tinted fog, thicker now than ever. She would walk to Dr. Hannah's, she decided, since to take a herdic or a hack cab in heavy fog was always dangerous. Sound was muffled, horses ran into each other, people were injured. Far safer to take one's chances by walking, dangerous though it was at the crossings. Even this morning, coming back from Susan Henshaw's, she'd narrowly missed—

Susan Henshaw.

Who was Marian Trask's sister.

Caroline's thoughts raced, stumbling over themselves.

In that tempting Diana Strangeways novel that she was not to finish this afternoon, there was a moment when the heroine, desperate to disentangle herself from the twisting coil of Miss Strangeways' truly enthralling plot, came upon a photograph.

And in that photograph—a group sitting, a dozen people at least—she found the answer to the question upon which her life depended.

A photograph.

It was odd, Caroline thought, how the mind worked. Professor William James had spent his entire professional life studying the mind. One day soon, she thought, she must find—or make—the opportunity to talk to him about it. Assuming that such a learned man would take the time to talk to her, a mere woman, about anything other than the most trivial subjects.

A photograph. A photograph. Where, in the past few days, had she come across a photograph that might tell her—what?

Yes. She remembered now. On Tuesday afternoon, searching for her ivory fan on the closet shelf in the guest room, she'd come across an entire album of photographs. She'd been so intent on finding her fan that she had hardly noticed the album, had just pushed it aside.

She heard the grandmother clock strike the half hour. It was one-thirty. She needed to hurry if she was to reach Dr. Hannah's clinic in time.

But now that she had had the memory of that photograph album—a memory jarred by the inestimable, the incomparable Diana Strangeways—she could not leave the house without seeing the particular photograph she remembered. Or thought she did, at any rate. She hadn't opened that album in at least a year, and the photograph in question dated to well before that, if her memory served.

She hurried up the curving staircase, her hand skimming the carved mahogany balustrade, her heart pounding hard. She closed the guest room door softly behind her and fetched the footstool from before the fireplace. The closet smelled of lavender; it was filled with her summer dresses, all neatly wrapped in muslin bags. She pushed them aside and stepped onto the stool. A box of summer gloves, another of lightweight summer underthings, petticoats and chemises— Yes. There it was.

For a moment she was afraid, because now she knew what she would see when she opened that album; her memory was clear now, and complete.

From overhead, she heard the muffled thump of Dr. MacKenzie's footsteps as he made his way across his room. He was supposed to be resting; she hoped he wasn't going to come downstairs looking for her. Just now, she did not want to see Dr. MacKenzie.

Get on with it, she thought.

She stepped down from the stool and carried the album to a small writing desk by the back window. The white light reflected from the fog was more than enough to see by; she didn't need to turn up the gas.

The album's thick pages were stiff with glue and the heavy rectangles of photographic paper pasted onto them. Her hands were cold, her fingers reluctant to do her mind's bidding. She knew what she would find; how could she have forgotten it? Here were page after page of photographs, some going back to her girlhood, of parties and picnics and all the happy occasions of her life, pictures of the charity galas she'd had a part in, and the Fourth of July celebrations, and a costume party one New Year's Eve.

Her hands were still; she stopped turning the pages. Here it was: the photograph she'd sought. And for a moment, she thought perhaps she'd been wrong; perhaps this fading sepia-toned image would tell her nothing.

She bent to look more closely.

Yes. It was what she'd remembered—exactly.

For a long moment she scrutinized it; then, gently, she closed the album. She was trembling. She stood up, carried it to the closet, and replaced it on the shelf. Then she returned the stool to its place and paused for a moment, resting her hand on the white-painted mantelpiece. The clock in the hall was chiming the quarter hour. It was late. She needed to hurry if she was to get to Dr. Hannah's in time.

CHAPTER
29

AMES STRODE DOWN WINTER STREET, PAST LOCK-OBER'S, half hidden down its little alley; past jewelers' windows, and haberdashers'. The narrow sidewalk was thronged with Saturday afternoon shoppers, people jostling him, now and then someone polite enough to say "Beg your pardon, sir."

He jostled back. His errand was infinitely more important than any of theirs. His errand was life-and-death, literally.

At Washington Street he crossed and pressed on toward the doorway he sought. He went in, climbed the long, narrow flight of stairs, and walked down the dimly lighted corridor. His footsteps were loud, echoing in the silence. The building was empty. But one person, perhaps, had come in: to tend to some crucial final business before locking up and leaving forever.

The office was dark, seemingly deserted as it had been earlier. Ames put his hand on the knob and turned it. He hadn't expected the door to open, but to his surprise, it did.

The little reception room was gloomy, the only light coming from the one dim gas jet in the corridor and, faintly, from the office beyond.

"Hello?"

No answer. But still, he told himself, the door had been unlocked just now; this morning, it had not been.

The door of the inner office was slightly ajar. He pushed it open.

Richard Longworth sat at his desk as if he'd been waiting—for whom?

"Mr. Ames," he said.

"Mrs. Vincent has been arrested," Ames said.

"I know."

"Well, for God's sake, man, you must give yourself up now! You cannot allow her to be taken for a crime she did not commit!"

Longworth looked ill, Ames thought; ill—and haunted, as if his mind harbored secrets that soon would drive him mad.

"Which crime would that be, Mr. Ames?"

"Why—the murder of Colonel Mann, of course."

Longworth shook his head. "No," he said. "She did not do that."

"The police believe she did."

"She was with me that night."

"You said you were at the St. Botolph."

Longworth shrugged. "I lied."

Ames bit back the angry words that sprang to his lips. This man before him was a man in crisis; he needed to go carefully lest Longworth freeze up and refuse to tell him anything.

"How long had you been working for the Colonel?" he asked in what he hoped was a less accusatory tone.

"Why do you want to know that?"

"Because I cannot understand why Mrs. Vincent would have taken up with you if you worked for the very man who ruined her."

"I didn't work for him when she and I first met."

"Where was that?"

"In New York."

"When?"

"About three years ago. She was—" He broke off, as if a sudden memory had distracted him.

"She was the most beautiful woman I had ever seen," he said softly. "She still is. I fell in love with her instantly, I don't mind telling you. You think something like that can happen only in books, but believe me, it can happen in life as well."

He fell silent, lost in his memories. After a moment, Ames said, "Was that when she shot a man?"

Longworth looked up sharply. "Who told you that?"

"It doesn't matter. She did, didn't she?"

"Yes."

"Why?"

"Because he was a rotter. A thoroughgoing rotter. He—"

"Yes?"

Longworth shook his head, refusing to continue.

"Why was she in New York?" Ames persisted. "Had she been offered a part there? She told me she wanted to stay in Boston."

"It was—a personal affair."

"What?"

"Nothing to do with this case, Mr. Ames."

"I am beginning to think that everything has to do with this case."

To his horror, he saw that Longworth had begun to weep. He was quiet about it: no harsh sobs, no panting breath, just a silent stream of tears dropping down his cheeks. For a moment, he put his hands up to his face as if to shield himself from Ames's gaze; then, wiping his eyes, he said very low: "If you must know, Mr. Ames, she went to New York to have an illegal operation."

Ames felt the shock of it rocket through him. He realized that such things happened, of course, but not to anyone he knew. Such things belonged to some other world—the world of reckless, amoral men and loose women, women who lived in the demimonde. Women like Serena Vincent.

"And the man she shot—?" he said.

"Was—yes—the man responsible for her condition. She told me he tried to stop her from—from going ahead with it. Of course he had no right to do that. None. He followed her to New York, managed to find her, became violent. She had acquired a gun—a little pearl-handled shooter—some time before that, when she'd had trouble with a particularly persistent admirer. Women in her position often have to put up with such hazards."

"Like the shot taken at her the other night in the theater."

"Yes."

"Where you were. I saw you there."

Longworth's face twisted into a grimace. "I don't even own a gun. Search if you like."

"But I have it on the word of Mrs. Vincent's maid that you threatened to kill her—and yourself."

"Bluff, Mr. Ames. Pure bluff." And now again, Longworth began to weep, loudly this time, harsh sobs tearing at him.

Ames felt he must ask his questions quickly, before the man collapsed completely and was no longer able to speak. "And so, when you met Mrs. Vincent in New York, you helped her in her difficulty. I imagine there was some to-do with the authorities."

"Some. She was lucky—she only gave the fellow a flesh wound in the arm. And, yes, I helped her. The District Attorney was my mother's second cousin. He was—cooperative."

"Hmmm." Ames forbore to comment on this. "What did she think when you began to work for the Colonel?"

"I didn't tell her."

"Did she ever find out?"

"No. But she would have understood—I know she would have. She knew that I needed money. Needed!" He laughed—a harsh, ugly sound. "I was desperate for cash, I don't mind telling you. She offered me money herself, but I wouldn't take it. Even a man as hard up as I am has some standards."

"Even in the face of Mrs. Trask's blackmail?"

Longworth stared at him, the shock plain on his ravaged face. "How did you know about that?"

"I can't say. But I see from your reaction that it is true. She was blackmailing you, was she not?"

Longworth reached for the cigarette box on his desk, opened it, and without offering one to Ames, took one and fumbled to light it.

"All right, Mr. Ames. Yes, Mrs. Trask—that bitch—did try to get money from me. From me!" Again, the harsh, bitter laugh. "Better to try to get blood from a turnip. I have no money, and I told her so."

"Did you kill her?"

"No."

"You had an excellent motive for doing so."

Longworth inhaled furiously, blew out clouds of smoke. "No. I mean—yes, that may appear to be so. But I didn't do it. I was with Mrs. Vincent."

"Her maid told me she would be at her dressmaker's that afternoon."

"Then her maid lied. And besides, why would I take such a risk—to kill that stupid woman? I could never understand why Winston—"

Ah, thought Ames. Now we come to it. "Why Winston what?"

"Since you seem to know so much, Mr. Ames, you probably know about him, as well. Yes. My partner—carrying on an affair with Marian Trask. Poor fellow, he is dead now." He paused, remembering.

Then he went on: "I could never understand what he saw in her. She was nothing but a bag of bones and a hank of hair. As much charm as a lamppost, a shrill little shrew, always poking into everyone's business— Well. There's no accounting for taste, is there?"

No, thought Ames, there is not.

"And the way they had to conduct themselves!" Longworth said. "Sneaking around, always on the verge of being found out! One would hardly think she was worth it. At least I can go to Serena when I please, more or less. But Winston had to depend on—"

"On what?"

"On whom, you should say. Mrs. Trask needed help to conduct the affair—a friend to cover for her when she and Winston had an assignation. So it was a difficult business from beginning to end. They say the French do these things more skillfully, but this isn't France, is it? Poor old Winston was a nervous wreck, hiding in corners as if he were some kind of criminal. At the last, just before they were exposed to Colonel Mann, Winston told me he regretted the day he ever met her."

"Where was that?"

"At the Christmas Revels. Winston played one of the jugglers, if I recall correctly. Had to dress up in a damned stupid costume."

"Who was the friend who covered for her?"

"I don't know."

"Did you betray her to Colonel Mann?"

"No."

"Who did?"

"I don't know that, either. But he had very good information, whoever he was. Old Trask paid up on the spot."

Longworth took a final drag on what was now merely the stub of his cigarette and then smashed it out, violently, in the metal ashtray. Long after it was extinguished, he continued to pound it until it was a mush of tobacco shreds and torn paper. Then, very quietly, he said, "Why did you come here today, Mr. Ames?"

"To try to help Mrs. Vincent."

"Did you ever find those letters you were looking for?"

"No."

"Any idea, more than you had when you first asked me about them, where they might be?"

"No."

Longworth began to laugh. It was a horrible sound, almost like a dog's bark. And, having begun, he couldn't seem to stop. "That will teach you a lesson, Mr. Ames," he gasped. "Don't involve yourself in other people's problems! You started out searching for a packet of letters, and look where you find yourself! Trying to find a murderer!"

"Perhaps I have succeeded," Ames said quietly.

Suddenly, startlingly, Longworth stopped laughing.

"No," he said. "You have not."

"Prove it."

"Prove that I did not kill the Colonel? Or Mrs. Trask, either? I've told you where I was, both times. One gentleman to another—isn't that enough?"

Hardly, thought Ames. If you are a gentleman, Richard Longworth, I am Marie Antoinette.

"I see," Longworth said. "It isn't. Look—" He shook his head. "I don't know how many times I have to tell you this, but I *did not kill Colonel Mann.*"

Ames watched him. "Or Mrs. Trask, either?"

"No! Especially not her, the stupid bitch. Stupid, troublemaking bitch—to come to me with such a story, to try to get money out of me—me!" He was trembling so violently that his teeth chattered.

"But the story was true," Ames said quietly.

Longworth was silent. Then: "Yes." He made a strangled sound that was nearer a sob than a laugh. "You are looking at a ruined man, Mr. Ames. But ruined though I am, I had

nothing to do with either of those deaths, I swear it! Here—
I will swear it on the Good Book if you like!" He whirled
around and without needing to search for it took a Bible
from the shelf behind him. Holding it in his left hand, he
placed his right hand on it. "I *swear*—by this Book, by my
mother's grave, by my own damaged soul—by anything you
like, Mr. Ames. I did not kill them!"

He kept his eyes steadily on Ames's. They were of some
indeterminate color, and, just now, wide and staring. Ames
met them steadily with his own dark gaze, and he thought,
beyond all reason, beyond all that I know of him, I believe
him.

"And you did not betray Mrs. Trask to the Colonel?" he
asked.

"No. I did not."

"And you know nothing of the letters I seek?"

"No. Nothing."

Longworth laid the Bible on the desk in front of him.
Ames stood up. The man before him was a bad debtor, an
addicted gambler, an adulterer, a bigamist. Until this moment, Ames had believed he was a murderer as well.

But he had seen something, just now, in Longworth's
eyes—some inkling of truth, some faint trace of honesty, of
decency, perhaps—decency, in spite of everything.

"Mr. Longworth, I told you that I came here to try to
help Mrs. Vincent. On the other hand, I will tell you quite
frankly that last night, when I heard she had been arrested, I
could not repress the thought that at least in jail, no matter
how uncomfortable she might be, she would be safe. Safe
from you, I thought."

Longworth seemed, suddenly, exhausted. "She has nothing to fear from me, Mr. Ames."

"There walks in this city a man who has killed two people in the past week—yes, I believe the murders are connected—and has made an attempt on Mrs. Vincent as well.
If that man is not you . . ."

"It is not, Mr. Ames. I have sworn it."

"Then the man who did is very dangerous."

"More dangerous than you thought I was?"

"Yes." Ames considered it. That man, whoever he was, was the man who had the most to lose. But who could possibly have more to lose than Richard Longworth? "Far more dangerous. Who is Mrs. Vincent's lawyer?"

Longworth gave him a name.

"Will you go to see him?" Ames asked. "And tell him not to request bail for her?"

"I imagine he's already requested it and been refused. They don't bail first-degree murder suspects who may flee."

"Still. Make sure he understands her situation. Can you do that?"

"Of course. If you think it necessary."

"I do." Ames held out his hand. "I must go now. Will you be all right?"

Longworth did not rise, but he did take Ames's hand. He gave it a brief shake and let it go. "Yes," he said. "I will— now. Oddly enough, Mr. Ames, I am glad you came, although I would not have said so when you walked in. I feel—relieved, in some odd way, for having spoken to you."

Relieved, Ames thought as he went out. It was a notion completely foreign to him—to blurt out one's dark secrets to a virtual stranger, to admit one's horrendous blunders and failings— No. It was not his way, never would be.

The fog had thickened; it was only three-thirty and already growing dark. The crowded street had something of the look of a new French painting he'd seen at the Vose Gallery—blurred, indistinct, not a clean, clear line on the canvas.

No day for a herdic, he thought. He'd take the omnibus and hope to get to the club within the hour.

CHAPTER
30

THE ANNUAL AUTUMN ART SHOW AT THE ST. BOTOLPH
Club was an event much anticipated, not only for the small
cachet it gave to its members, marking them as men of cul-
ture and good taste, but also for the chance to buy, every so
often, a painting that might, in time, turn a handsome profit.
Promptly at four o'clock, the doors to the spacious exhibition room at the rear of the building were thrown open, and
members and their guests streamed in.

Ames found Delahanty and MacKenzie waiting for him
in the lobby. "What is it, Ames?" Delahanty exclaimed.
"You look as though you've seen the banshee herself."

Ames smiled to cover his discomfiture—did his feelings
show so plainly?—and handed his hat and his Inverness
cape to the porter.

"Traffic," he said. "The fog's thickening up badly."

They joined the steady stream of people thronging in and
began their perambulations, starting with the wall to their
right. There were perhaps fifty paintings spaced out around
the room; in the center, at the back, was a large canvas that
had been given the place of honor.

But what with the crowd, and the need to consult the
program, and the need to speak to people as he made his

way, Ames had become impatient with the whole business by the time he'd seen less than half the exhibition.

"Lots of effort went into this one, wouldn't you say?" Delahanty asked. It was a middling-sized canvas, a still life of fruit and cheese and a bottle of wine.

Ames grunted. He was not interested in still lifes. He moved on. The next painting was a portrait of two children, a boy and a girl. They stared mournfully out from the canvas as if they had been reluctant to pose; they were dressed in their best, ruffles and satin sash for the girl, an uncomfort-able-looking Little Lord Fauntleroy suit for the boy, and they looked very unchildlike. They have an ambitious mama, he thought, who makes them suffer this even when they are so young. To what lengths would she go, he wondered, when they were older?

People pressed in; he moved on. He spoke to several members, and to their wives or daughters; he acknowledged the wave of someone from across the room.

He should not have come here, he realized. After seeing Richard Longworth, he should have taken the opportunity to be alone with his thoughts. The St. Botolph Club, on the afternoon of a crowded opening, was not the place to do it.

But as he turned to tell MacKenzie that he was going to leave, the doctor touched his arm.

"Look at that," he said.

Ames followed his gaze to the large painting that had been given the best place at the back of the room; they were near it now, with, for the moment, hardly anyone ob-structing their view.

He stared at it, all thought of leaving suddenly vanished. It was, he saw, a most magnificent painting. He recognized the artist as John Singer Sargent, a man well known to Bos-tonians, for, young as he was, he had painted many of the city's wealthiest, most prominent citizens—and their wives.

This painting was of a woman—some wealthy man's wife.

The man had commissioned it, Ames knew, not only to have the painting itself but also to make an announcement to the world: I am a rich man, and this richly bedecked woman is proof of it. See her, and envy me.

The woman in the portrait stood in a pose that was becoming known as the Sargent stance. Corseted body half turned from the viewer, hands splayed, head oddly tilted— she looked as though, at any moment, she would scream out her nervous tension for all the world to hear. Her eyes were averted, and yet you could see in the way she stood, almost as if she were poised for flight, that this was a woman in mental turmoil.

Why did Sargent do that, Ames wondered—pose them like that? Did he see something in them, did he look into their souls and see some hidden torment there that he wanted to reveal to the world?

And why, moreover, did people allow themselves to be portrayed so? By now, Sargent was well known, almost notorious. These nervous, agonized women had become his signature trademark. People knew what they would get when they commissioned a portrait from him: they would get something like this, which was, admittedly, a most magnificent portrait, but one that showed far too much of its subject's interior life. He might as well have painted her naked, Ames thought, so deeply has he violated her privacy.

Someone came up at his side: Professor James.

"Amazing," he said.

"Do you think so?"

"Yes, absolutely. Look at the tension in the line from her neck down through her right arm. I don't mind telling you, Ames, the man who painted that portrait may know more about the human psyche than I do."

Ames looked. And now, at last, he realized that he knew this woman. She wore a gown of what was called Nile green (the Nile is not green, he thought, but brown) and held a half-open fan. Sargent had painted her, as was his wont, to be far more handsome than she was in fact, which was why he'd not recognized her at once.

"I'd like to speak with her," James went on. "She looks like a fascinating subject."

"Better you speak with Mr. Sargent," Delahanty offered, "since it is he who made that fact obvious."

James smiled. "I have spoken with him. He may be a brilliant artist—I believe he is, in fact—but he either cannot or will not elaborate on how he comes to understand so well the people—particularly the women—whom he portrays."

Delahanty chuckled. "Trade secrets, no doubt. What do you think, Doctor?"

MacKenzie studied the portrait. "I think it's rather bold," he said. "If I had a wife—which I do not, alas—I would not want her presented to the world in this way. What secrets that woman has—what mental anguish! But look, Ames." He spoke more quietly now, turning aside. "Look at the necklace."

"Yes," Ames muttered. He stared at the portrait—at one particular part of it, which was the woman's slim, swanlike neck (and surely, in life, her neck was nothing like that?). Around that neck she wore a necklace—a handsome piece, probably some kind of heirloom, or perhaps it had been a wedding gift from that same husband who had commissioned the picture.

"Addington?" It was Delahanty speaking to him; he did not answer. Keeping his eyes on the portrait, he reached into his breast pocket and touched his small leather-bound notebook. He had carried the image of this thing with him from the moment he'd found it on the floor of Colonel Mann's suite and hurriedly sketched it so that he would remember it correctly. He had looked at it repeatedly since Monday night; he did not need to look at it again to be sure. He would recognize instantly the pearls that matched it.

The pearls that matched it were before him now, in this

magnificent portrait, in this study of a woman tortured by demons she'd revealed to no one except—surely inadvertently—this gifted artist, this genius with paint and canvas who laid bare people's souls for all the world to see.

For the moment, Ames did not care about this woman's soul. He cared about her pearls. In the portrait, the necklace was whole—not one pearl missing. But of course, even if one had been missing, the artist would have painted it in.

But she would not have worn it if it had not been whole. He did not know her well, but he knew her well enough— her pride, her blazing ambition—to believe that.

So the necklace had been undamaged when this picture was painted—sometime in the past year, without doubt. The pictures at the St. Botolph exhibition were always new ones, straight off the artist's easel.

"Addington?" Professor James had moved on; it was Delahanty speaking to him again.

He felt a sudden surge of something that was not panic but was very close to it.

"Are you all right, Addington?" Delahanty asked.

He needed to get away—out of this room with its chattering mob and its rising temperature, its smell of too many highly perfumed bodies too close together. He needed to have a little time to sort out the facts that were racketing around in his brain—isolated facts that until an hour ago had made, he'd thought, a logical path to the door of the man he sought.

But he'd been wrong about that. He'd known it when he'd left Longworth; and now he knew it all over again, much more forcefully.

Wrong.

Someone besides Longworth had worked for Colonel Mann—for a long time, perhaps years. Someone who knew many people in Boston Society, and who had the running of the Christmas Revels, with all its attendant opportunities for matchmaking.

And someone, two years ago, had told Colonel Mann about Marian Trask's affair with Winston Sprague. Perhaps had even abetted the affair, as Longworth said.

Had that person been at the Colonel's rooms on Monday night? Yes—almost surely. And she had dropped a pearl from her necklace.

Had the Colonel told her the necklace wasn't payment enough? Not enough for the secret—what could it have been?—that someone had told him about her. And so had she—desperate—killed him?

So she herself had been betrayed to the Colonel. By whom? By Marian Trask, whose affair with Sprague had been revealed to the Colonel?

Mrs. Trask had sought revenge—bitter revenge that must have been deeply pleasurable to her, sweet and soul-satisfying.

But she had paid for it with her life.

One of two people, Mrs. Trask had believed, had betrayed her to Colonel Mann—she hadn't known which. She'd blackmailed one: Richard Longworth.

Who was the other? Was it this woman—*this* woman? Knowing of Marian Trask's affair with Winston Sprague, had this woman told the Colonel about it?

On Monday night, had she argued with him? And in the end, had it been she—in panic, in despair—who killed him? Why? Had he known something about her that was so terrible that it caused her to kill him?

Valentine, he thought. Did she know something, too, that might put her in danger?

"Dr. MacKenzie, I need you to do me a service."

"Yes?" MacKenzie, startled, met Ames's blazing dark eyes.

"I must ask you to go to Val. You know the address? Tell her that I ordered you to take her to Louisburg Square and to stay with her until I come. Your weapon is there? Have it with you, then. She will be expecting her young man shortly, but that cannot be helped. If necessary, she must postpone her interview with him. She must leave Euphemia's house, and she cannot be left alone. You must make her understand that. Can you do that?"

"Of course."

Delahanty was listening, openmouthed. "What is it, Ames?" he asked. "Have you had some revelation?"

But already Ames was turning away. "Yes, and pray it didn't come too late," he flung over his shoulder.

"Ames!"

But he was gone, heedless of Delahanty's cry. He pushed his way through the crowd, ignoring the startled exclamations as he went, muttering an excuse here and there, nearly knocking one old gentleman off his pins as he careened into him, escaping into the hall, the lobby, demanding his hat and cloak from the startled porter. Then at last he stood on the front steps and paused, drawing in deep breaths of the cold, foggy air—much colder now, a raw, bitter night—trying to order his thoughts as he waited for MacKenzie to follow him outside. They said a parting word, and then he watched as the doctor hurried away, limping across Arlington Street and into the Public Garden, lost in the fog.

The pearls, he thought. He had seen them at last: the pearls that matched the one he'd seen in Colonel Mann's suite on the night the Colonel was murdered.

And the woman who owned them, the woman who wore them so proudly in her portrait by John Singer Sargent, was the mother of Alice, Val's dearest friend, the woman whose ambition for her daughter knew no bounds, the woman—not the man—with the most to lose.

AT DR. HANNAH BIGELOW'S CLINIC, THE AFTERNOON WAS winding itself down as darkness fell. From her station behind the reception desk, Caroline scanned the half dozen patients still waiting to see Dr. Hannah. If no one else came in, they'd finish in good time for her to be on hand for poor Val after her interview with George Putnam.

She smiled at a woman who had looked up and met her eyes. A humble, impoverished woman, like all of them here, she wore a faded scarf around her head, and her clothing was patched and shabby and none too clean. Many of these women lived in tenements without running water, Caroline knew, and soap, even the cheapest soap, was perhaps, for them, a luxury.

The woman sniffled and then coughed—a deep, wrenching cough that must have hurt her, Caroline thought. Pleurisy, perhaps. Or—far worse—tuberculosis, consumption, the White Plague, as it was known. The women here suffered everything: consumption, broken bones, cancers, female disorders of all kinds, complications of pregnancy, complications of self-mutilation, botched attempts to rid themselves of a pregnancy—another mouth to feed—that they could not afford.

And not for the first time, Caroline thought, how can I say "poor Val," when here before me are women who are truly poor? Who will never know the life Val has had—and, for that matter, I have had as well? Yes, we've had to watch our pennies, Addington and I, but we have never known the hardship these women face, and probably we never will.

Nevertheless. Poor Val. Who had said that she met the young man of the letters—the young man who had, indirectly, caused all this trouble—at the Christmas Revels.

A photograph of which—jolly, laughing faces—Caroline had unearthed earlier that afternoon.

The outer door opened, letting in a draft of cold, damp air. The women sitting on benches around the room looked up briefly, expecting to see someone like themselves. When they did not—when they saw that the person coming in was as different from them as if she had come from another world, as indeed she had—they stared at her. They could not help it.

She was a slight, delicate young woman dressed in the height of fashion in a brown tweed walking skirt and matching jacket. Peeping beneath the hem of her skirt were dark-brown morocco shoes; perched on her pale blond hair was a pert little brown hat decorated with a pair of barred bronze-and-black feathers. Above the high, lace-trimmed collar of her white shirtwaist, her face was as pale as the fabric itself. She stood in the doorway as if she could not quite believe where she was. Slowly she gazed around the room, taking in its bleakness, its barrenness, the benches occupied by the impoverished women come to seek Dr. Hannah's charity. It was painfully obvious that she had never been in such a place before, and for a moment she seemed tensed to flee, as if she could not bear to seek the help that she must desperately need, or she would not have come here at all.

And then at last her frightened eyes met Caroline's.

"Why, hello," Caroline said after a moment, knowing her shock must be plain to see. She forced a smile as she thought, but did not say, Does your mother know you're here?

CHAPTER
31

DARKNESS NOW, AND FOG SO THICK HE COULD NOT SEE across Arlington Street. He searched for a herdic, but he could not distinguish one in the dark mass of slowly moving shapes. In the traffic's near standstill, drivers were shouting in frustration, and here and there a horse reared up, panicked at being so tightly hemmed in.

On foot, then. Safer in any case, in this blinding miasma of the elements.

He could see no way clear, but he thrust himself in, ducking under the flailing hooves, ignoring a driver's angry imprecations, darting out of the way of a brougham trying to back up.

Safe across, he plunged into the Public Garden. It was dangerous at night, footpads and thugs awaiting their prey, but he had no time to take the longer way around.

He went swiftly, and soon he was at a half-run. Danger here, too, of colliding with another pedestrian, but he had no choice; he could not walk at a normal pace, not now, not when he carried in his mind's eye the image of that woman in her pearls, her ostentatious, probably heirloom pearls. Did she even know that on Monday evening last, in the Colonel's suite, she had dropped one of them on his garish carpet?

Or had she been too frantic to escape, too appalled at what had happened there in that overheated room, the Colonel dead on the floor and by her hand? Almost certainly by her hand.

Had she given the necklace to the Colonel earlier—days or weeks before, and had she gone there that night to reclaim it?

Or had she taken it to him that night—in lieu of payment, perhaps, an offering to deflect his malice, his greed, his threats to expose her?

For what? What had she done to put her so fatally into the Colonel's power?

He—or she—who has the most to lose.

What did she have to lose? Not her own position, surely, but her daughter's. Yes—Alice was her Achilles heel, her vulnerability. It was—it must have been—for Alice that she had paid the Colonel what he demanded, if not a sum of money, then a priceless pearl necklace.

Across the miniature suspension bridge, its globe lamps blurred and dim; across Charles Street and into the Common, darker even than the Garden, its long, straight paths obscured in the fog, danger lurking here, too, but no matter. He strode on, his long legs eating up the distance. Agonizing moments before he could cross Tremont Street, but then he was on his way down to Washington, past Eben Jordan's store, people making way for him, a tall figure of a man in a trilby and flowing cape, coming at them from out of the fog and quickly vanishing again like some phantom from their dreams, their nightmares.

By the time he came to Longworth's building, his heart was pounding in his ears, and despite the raw cold, he was drenched in perspiration. He paused, one hand on the wall of signboards, to catch his breath before he went in and climbed the stairs.

The place was dim and deserted as it had been before, no one about, the offices empty until Monday morning. He strode down the long, echoing corridor and came to the door he sought. Dark here, too, no one inside—and yet the door opened when he tried it.

He went in. The reception room was in shadow, the inner office beyond its partly opened door more shadowed still.

"Longworth?" He spoke in a low tone, but still, his voice sounded alarmingly loud in the silence.

No answer.

Go in, he thought, and speak to him. Despite the silence, his every instinct told him that Longworth was in that inner room, waiting for him, perhaps, and now at last prepared to tell him what he needed to know.

"Longworth? Are you there?"

Silence.

He did not want to open wider that inner door. He wanted to hear Longworth—miserable chap, sitting alone in darkness, contemplating the ruin of his life—to hear Longworth reply before he did so.

He stood motionless in the little reception room of what had been the firm of Longworth & Sprague, poor Sprague, dead in London after a most unsatisfactory affair with Marian Trask. . . .

Who had been betrayed to Colonel Mann . . .

Whose husband, as a consequence, had paid the Colonel ten thousand dollars . . .

Who had found Harry Morgan in flagrante . . . with whom? Who was that girl of good family whom Mrs. Trask had seen with him?

And Mrs. Trask had learned of Longworth's bigamy and had tried to blackmail him for it. . . .

And, like the Colonel, had been silenced forever. . . .

How did it all fit together?

Longworth knew. Longworth could tell him, he was sure. He tried one last time. "Longworth?"

He put his hand on the wooden panel and pushed.

The door opened.

From what he could see, the room was empty of any human presence. Desk, chairs, bookcases—but no Longworth.

But it was dark, hard to be sure. He felt very strongly that he did not want to go in, but he did so all the same.

In the darkness, he knocked into a chair, stumbled, and caught himself. "Longworth? Are you here?"

Silence. And yet—someone was here. He knew it, he could feel it even as his flesh began to crawl, even as his heart, which had momentarily quieted, began again to beat in a fast, frightening thump-thump that nearly suffocated him.

Something caught at the corner of his vision.

Something—some dark thing, a solid blot of darkness in the dark, shadowy room.

It swayed a little, and it was that movement that his peripheral vision had registered.

He stood quite still. He did not want to turn to see it fully, and yet he knew that he must, for he felt—he knew— that it waited for him.

There was a human presence in the room, just as he'd feared; or, at least, a presence that had been human not long before. It was human no longer now, and he knew that, knew it even as at last, reluctantly, his heart in his throat, his sight piercing the gloom, he turned to face it.

Dangling from a rope attached to an overhead heating pipe was Richard Longworth's lifeless body.

In Euphemia's parlor, Valentine sat on a small velvet chair before the crackling fire and went over again in her mind the speech she planned to make to George when he arrived.

She'd had all day to compose it, and now, in the late afternoon, she felt that she knew it perfectly. It was a good speech: not too long, not too bitter, with just the right amount of condescension to let George know that she considered him to be the loser in this affair. He was going to lose her, wasn't he? That was the way she wanted to think of it: not that she would lose him, but that he would lose her— and, she hoped, spend the rest of his life regretting that loss. Regretting that he had been so weak—there was no other word for it—as to mind his mother's objections to her, now that she was connected, however peripherally, to Addington's scandal.

But really it is my scandal, she thought. Mrs. Putnam, you don't know the half of it.

She lifted her chin in an unconscious gesture of defiance. All week, ever since Tuesday morning when Addington's name had appeared in the newspapers, she had known in her heart that this moment would come—the moment when George, to pacify his mama, would break their engagement. Until today, she had not been able to fully face that fact, but now, at last, she had. George was lost to her. He was coming to tell her that—would be here, in fact, at any moment. But she was going to tell him first; for the rest of her life, she would have that small satisfaction—that she had spoken before he did. It would be she who broke off with him and not the other, more humiliating, way around. And when she did—

The door knocker sounded. Through the closed parlor doors, she heard the butler going to answer. She took a deep breath—as deep as her corset would allow, at any rate, which was not very.

The doors slid open; the butler held out to her a silver tray bearing George's card. She told him to show George in. She stood very straight, pulling herself up to her full height, her shoulders well back, as she waited before the fireplace.

George came in pink-faced but solemn, and he was hardly in the room with the doors pulled shut behind him before he began to stammer out what it was he had to say.

"Valentine, I—"

She stopped him with a grave look that matched his own; she did not hold out her hands to him as she usually did, but stayed quite still.

"I know why you've come, George. But I want to say it first."

"But, Valentine, I want you to—I mean, it is important that you understand. That is to say, I don't want—"

"Please, George. Don't try to explain." Ordinarily, having greeted him, she would have offered him her cheek for a chaste kiss, but she did not do so now.

"Valentine, I *must* explain—"

"No. It is not necessary." Strange, she thought, how cool she felt, how absolutely in control, and oddly outside of herself, too, so that she seemed to be watching herself as she spoke, watching as the two of them stood awkwardly together and yet so far apart, separated now by a chasm of ancient, iron-clad social custom.

"You have come to break our engagement," she said. So cool, chilly almost—and that was good, she thought. I mustn't let him see what I feel.

His mouth dropped open, making him look foolish. Valentine was seized by a sudden desire to laugh, but she repressed it.

"Very well," she went on. "Let us break it." She slid his ring from her finger and held it out to him.

"Oh, no," he said quickly. "You keep it, Valentine. It was meant for you—"

"No," she said. "I don't want it." When he did not move to accept it, she reached out and took his hand and pressed the ring into it, closing his fingers tightly around it.

"As you wish." His face, pink at first from the cold, was pink still, and she realized that he was blushing. With, she hoped, embarrassment.

"Be sure to tell your mother that I gave it back," she said as lightly, as pleasantly, as she could.

"I say, Valentine, this is very decent—"

She silenced him with a look that she prayed was proud and haughty, a look that George's mother herself—even Isabel Dane, that most proud and haughty matron—would have given in like circumstances. "And tell her, too, that this is your loss."

He started at the insult. "Well, now, I don't know about that—"

"Yes," she said; she heard the coldness in her voice, and it gave her courage. "Your loss, George. You know as well as I do it is not my fault" (here she mentally crossed her fingers) "that Cousin Addington was in the newspapers. And that's what this is all about, isn't it? Your mother doesn't want you to marry me because she is afraid of scandal. She doesn't want the Putnams associated with someone like me, someone who has a notorious relative who gets involved in a messy business like murder. From the way you're behaving, you'd think Addington killed the Colonel, for heaven's sake!"

George had grown sullen under this assault, and now he glared at her. "You have to admit, it was a nasty thing for poor dear Mama to see," he muttered.

"Oh, George, grow up! You have to get free from your mother's apron strings eventually, you know." Not that Mrs. Putnam had ever worn apron strings in her life, but that was neither here nor there. As Val spoke the words, she realized they were true. George was—probably irrevocably—a slave to his mother's bidding. His wife, whoever she was, would be a slave to it as well.

Suddenly, surprisingly, she felt a tremendous sense of having freed herself from some overwhelming burden. She turned and tugged the bellpull hanging by the mantel. Instantly (had he been listening outside the door?) the butler appeared.

"Mr. Putnam is leaving," she said.

Without a word of farewell, and still clutching what had

been her ring and was now once again his, George turned and went out.

Alone in the parlor, Val sank onto a small brocade sofa. She realized she was trembling. It was over: that splendid match, the engagement to a young man everyone had said was so perfect for her. But she saw now that he was not, had never been perfect. How could people have been so blind? How could she?

Aunt Euphemia, thank heaven, had not been witness to the scene just past. Aunt Euphemia, thank heaven, was still in bed with *la grippe*. She would have to be told, of course, but not just yet. Telling her could wait—until tomorrow, or the day after that. When Euphemia had her strength back, and when she, Val, did as well.

Despite the blazing fire, she was cold. Tea, she thought; and soon, perhaps, she would go to Caroline. She would tell Caroline all about it, and Caroline would understand, just as she always did.

Val wondered if Caroline would understand the most astonishing thing, the most appalling thing: that she, Valentine Thorne, was not devastated by what she had just done. Far from it, she felt nothing but relief. Liberating, almost joyous relief. She was no longer engaged to George Putnam. It was as if an enormous weight had been lifted from her shoulders.

Would Caroline understand that?

Val stood and tugged the bellpull again. She wanted her tea. More, she wanted to think about what to do with her life. Addington had not found her letters, true, but perhaps that wasn't so important now.

She could go abroad, she thought. Mary Leicester was leaving soon to spend the winter in Rome. Perhaps, Val thought, I could go with her. Yes, winter in Rome, spring on the Riviera—why not?

As the maid came to answer her summons, she heard the

door knocker once more. Surely it was not George come back for some final parting shot? She'd nerved herself up just now and had carried it off, she knew, remarkably well; she didn't know if she could do it again.

But it was not George's card on the butler's tray this time, but Dr. John Alexander MacKenzie's.

"Yes, of course," she said. She smiled. She didn't know Dr. MacKenzie very well yet, but Caroline seemed fond of him, so he must be a worthwhile person.

"Dr. MacKenzie!" she said, going to greet him. But then, in the next moment, "What is it? What's wrong?"

"Nothing, I hope." He stood before her, solid and four-square, his broad, honest face a study in worry and concern. He hadn't given his hat to the butler but held it, along with his cane, and didn't shake the hand she offered to him.

"What do you mean?" she said. "Is Caro—has anything happened to her?"

"Not that I know of," he replied. "She went to help out at that female physician's clinic, said she'd be back in time to see you." His expression had soured when he'd mentioned Dr. Hannah, Val noted.

"Miss Thorne, I'm here because your Cousin Addington told me to come. He wants me to take you to Louisburg Square. I'm to keep you safe, he said, until he gets back."

Val stared at him. "What do you mean, keep me safe? From what?"

"I don't know. I'm just telling you what he told me. Could you get your things? We'd better be off."

He did know, of course—or he had a notion, at any rate. He'd seen the portrait, seen the pearls that matched the one in the Colonel's suite.

But what that meant—the full implications of it—he had no idea.

Val's thoughts whirled as she did his bidding, but she made no further protest. She instructed the butler to tell Caroline to follow them to No. 16½, in case Caroline came here straight from Dr. Hannah's clinic. Then she took her cloak and hat from the hall tree and, with MacKenzie behind her, went outside.

Fog shrouded the familiar street so that it was a wilderness of white, and she hesitated for a moment on the little flight of granite steps as she realized she could hardly see. But Dr. MacKenzie's reassuring presence was beside her, and so after a moment she ratcheted up her courage and went down the steps to the narrow, uneven brick sidewalk. Carefully they made their way along. The slimy damp on the bricks made walking even more treacherous than usual, and so, throwing propriety to the winds (and not for the first time this afternoon, she thought), Val offered her arm to the doctor in deference to his knee.

"Should be the other way around," he observed, "but I thank you for it, Miss Thorne. I don't want to be laid up all over again."

Beyond that, they did not speak. Val's thoughts were in turmoil. What had happened? Why did Addington believe she needed to be kept safe? He had learned something, that was obvious—was it something about her letters, the cause of all the trouble? Those stupid, foolish letters that her younger self had written in the first bloom of false love.

They turned into Louisburg Square and came at last to No. 16½. In the vestibule they saw the empty hall tree and knew they were the first to arrive. As they divested themselves of their hats and outerwear, Margaret appeared from the back of the hall and Val asked her to bring tea—which, now, she wanted very much. Her face and hair and skirts were damp and chilled; at this moment, the thought of a cup of hot, reviving tea was the most alluring thing in the world.

They went into the parlor, where Margaret had already turned up the gas. A low sea-coal fire burned in the grate. Beyond the lavender-glass windows, whose shutters had not been closed nor the curtains drawn, Val saw not the familiar streetlamps strung out around the square but only blank darkness, a lavender-colored darkness pressing in. She should ask Margaret to close the shutters, she thought; and then she thought, no, leave them open. It will light the way home for Caro and Addington on this bad night. She had not yet begun to worry unduly about either of them, but she soon would, she knew.

Margaret entered with a laden tea tray, and Val sat down to pour. "This will do us good," she said to MacKenzie, smiling up at him, and he managed a smile in return and said that, yes, it would. He would rejoin her in a moment, he said; he needed to fetch something from his room, and—

The sound of the door knocker, very loud, startled her so that she jumped and spilled a little tea into the saucer. She heard Margaret's voice and another—a woman's voice also. Not Caroline; she would not have needed to knock, not unless she'd lost her key—

The pocket doors slid open, but before Margaret could say a word, the woman behind her pushed past her and came into the room.

It was Isabel Dane—but not the woman Val had known all her life as the mother of her dearest friend. This woman was as different as could be from that dignified, rather chilly, rather intimidating figure. This woman was someone else altogether: someone desperate, someone close to panic, someone who had abandoned all pretense of normal civility and decorum.

"Why, Mrs. Dane—" Val began, but before she could say anything more, Isabel Dane interrupted her.

"I am looking for Alice," she said abruptly. "Have you seen her?"

CHAPTER
32

THE DRIVER CURSED LOUD ENOUGH FOR CAROLINE TO HEAR and with an audible *crack!* brought his whip down on his horse. Seated on one of the small sideways seats in the back of the stalled herdic-phaeton, Caroline uttered a little cry of her own. Dreadful, cruel man, to vent his frustrations on the poor dumb beast!

She must get out, she thought, even though they were only at Boylston Street. She'd been wrong to take a herdic. Repeatedly during the journey from Dr. Hannah's clinic the driver had pulled the horse up short, narrowly avoiding a collision with vehicles coming at him out of the fog; once, Caroline had been jolted so hard that she had nearly been thrown off her seat.

Now she could bear it no more—being stuck in traffic, waiting, powerless to act, when all the while she had a desperate need to see Val, to speak to her, reassure her that all would be well.

And more: to warn her.

She raised her clenched, gloved hand and rapped hard on the little window that separated her from the driver. He slid it open and peered in at her.

"I will get out here," she said. She thrust a half-dollar

coin at him through the opening and turned away from his angry glare.

"What about me, lady? I'm stuck here," he growled.

"I'm sorry," she said; already she was opening the door and climbing down. "This is an emergency!" She slammed shut the door and immediately needed to dodge out of the way of a pair of grays lashed by their driver, trying to get through the narrow opening.

Somehow, she managed to reach the sidewalk. Traffic was at a standstill, the sound of the drivers' cries muffled by the fog, nothing to be seen beyond the length of a few paces.

There. She had made her way across Clarendon Street. Now get down to Berkeley, down to Arlington, the tall brownstone spire of the Arlington Street Church lost in the darkness and swirling fog. Yes, she could manage well enough for that, and she could traverse the distance much more quickly on foot.

The raw, bitter air seared her lungs as she crossed Arlington Street and entered the Public Garden. The streetlamps strung out along the walkways were dim, pale, misty moons that gave no light to see by. Still, she knew the pattern of the paths; she could navigate here well enough. Crossing Beacon Street at Charles would be another matter.

Does your mother know you're here, she'd thought when she saw that pale, trembling girl in Dr. Hannah's waiting room. But what a ridiculous idea. The girl was Alice Dane, and of course her mother hadn't known.

She'd collected herself and made Alice welcome. Alice had recognized her as well, of course, and for that one bad moment, Caroline had thought Alice would panic and run away. She was in pain, that much was obvious. She'd stood stock-still for a long moment, and then, with an agonized little cry, she'd sunk down on the nearest empty bench and moaned softly, bending over, clutching herself around her middle.

Caroline, as she knew she must, had put her into one of

the examining rooms and sent for Dr. Hannah. The doctor would come in a moment, the harried assistant had said. The assistant was a female medical student from Boston University, and not for the first time, Caroline had thought that the experience of working for Dr. Hannah might put the young woman off doctoring for good. Alice had collapsed onto the examining table, sobbing as if her heart would break.

"It hurts," Alice had moaned, pressing her hands over her abdomen. "And I'm bleeding a lot. A *lot.*"

Caroline had put her arms around the girl and tried to soothe her. "Dr. Hannah will be here in a moment," she'd said. "Hush now, you'll only make it worse."

"How could it be worse?" Alice had sobbed. "Miss Ames—you don't know what has happened."

I can guess, Caroline had thought.

"Mama was so intent on my making this match," Alice went on. She spoke rapidly, as if she feared she would faint and not be able to tell it all. "She said I had to go to New York for a—an operation. She—someone gave her a name," she added as if Caroline must not think that a proper Boston lady like Alice's mother would know where to procure such a service.

"I was desperate," Alice continued. "I didn't know what to do. We had to keep it a secret or I would have been disgraced for life, I would have had to go away, I never could have married anyone. And it hurt so much, Miss Ames—that dreadful woman there cut me up inside so that I thought I would die of the pain. She said I would heal, but I never did. I've been bleeding ever since, and hurting—*ah!*"

She writhed away from Caroline's embrace and wept, shuddering; then she turned back, her face streaked with tears. "No one would ever have known," she said, "if it hadn't been for Mrs. Trask. But she—saw me."

"Saw you," Caroline said. "What do you mean?"

"In the woods. At Newport. With . . . Harry Morgan."

Ada Morgan's youngest: a charming youth, but wild.

"And . . ." Caroline saw once again the scene at the Cotillion: Marian Trask's bright, malicious eyes raking over Alice. That moment of seemingly innocuous social pleasantry had been, in fact, as good as a spoken threat: not only do I know your secret, Alice Dane, but I am prepared to reveal it.

"You told your mother that fact, told her the night of the Cotillion, after you fainted—?"

"Yes." It was no more than a whisper from Alice's pale lips.

"She hadn't known it till then?"

Alice shook her head.

And yesterday, thought Caroline, you saw the news of Marian Trask's murder. And you suspected—

A rap on the door; the assistant looked in. "Doctor's coming now," she said, and pulled the door shut again.

Alice looked up. "Will you stay with me, Miss Ames?" she said piteously.

"Yes, of course."

"I'm frightened."

"You don't need to be frightened, dear. Dr. Hannah is very gentle—very kind."

But all the kindness and gentleness in the world could not help damage like this. Caroline had seen women here before, injured in this way, butchered and infected; even if they lived, they could never have children. Not to have children seemed, to Caroline, the worst of fates, probably since it was, she thought, her own.

What had Isabel been thinking of, to subject Alice to such a procedure?

But even as the thought came to her, she knew the answer: Isabel had been thinking of Alice's prospects. To have the girl spirited away to bear her fatherless child in some foreign place would have put an unacceptable crimp in Isabel's ambitions. And even worse, perhaps, would have been the prospect of Alice's marrying Harry Morgan—the cause of her trouble, a feckless ne'er-do-well, not at all the kind of son-in-law Isabel had planned to acquire.

Another knock at the door, and Dr. Hannah Bigelow came in. She was a small, thin woman with graying hair and wide, luminous eyes; her face was worn and lined, and yet, Caroline thought, it was a face far more beautiful than that of many society beauties. She gave no greeting to Caroline—none was needed—but went directly to Alice and took her hands.

"Well, my dear," she said softly. "And what is your trouble today?"

Caroline stepped aside but made no move to leave the room. Dr. Hannah glanced at her inquiringly; this was not standard procedure.

"She asked me to stay," Caroline murmured in explanation.

"I think that won't be necessary," Dr. Hannah said. And to Alice: "Will you let me see you alone?"

Alice gazed into those shining, all-seeing eyes, and suddenly it seemed as if the girl's burden had been lifted. She visibly relaxed; she nodded. "Yes," she whispered.

But then, as Caroline turned to go, she said, "Miss Ames! Wait!" She removed her hands from Dr. Hannah's grasp and fished in her reticule. She paused for a moment; then she seemed to come to some decision, and she withdrew something she had carried there.

"Take these, Miss Ames. They belong to Val. I—I found them in Mama's room. I don't know how Mama came to have them."

Excuse me." In the fog, a large, fat gentleman had almost knocked her down. She was at the corner of Charles and Beacon. The street was jammed solid with horses and vehicles. From out of the fog she could hear the cries of frustrated drivers—"Make way there! Out of the way! Coming through!"

But no one moved. Impossible for her to get across. For a woman alone to try to make her way through that solid mass of horseflesh and carriage wheels was an invitation to disaster. Three or four other pedestrians—all men—stood at the curb beside her, all looking as desperate as she must look herself.

"Link arms!" The voice came from one of the men. As he spoke, he seized the arm of the man next to him, and that man, muttering an apology, seized Caroline's. She understood: they were going to form a human wedge and try to batter their way across.

And somehow they did. Breathless, her hat knocked askew, she found herself safe on the other side. She gasped her thanks to the men who had helped her and stood for a moment safe on the sidewalk in front of the S. S. Pierce grocery store. There were a few late customers within, but already the boys were drawing heavy canvas covers over the display cases preparatory to going home.

"I don't know how Mama came to have them."

Caroline's hands clutched her bulging reticule; she felt the clasp to make sure it still held.

She had been so surprised when Alice had given the packet to her that she'd not been able to speak. She'd taken it reflexively, and then Dr. Hannah had begun her interview with Alice and Caroline had gone out, carrying the packet with her.

Val's letters.

Which the Colonel had had on Monday afternoon, but which had not been in the hotel suite when Addington found the Colonel's body some hours later.

"I don't know how Mama came to have them."

Ah, but perhaps I do, thought Caroline; and for a moment, standing on the sidewalk in front of the grocery, she felt ill.

Mama—Isabel—had them because she had taken them from the Colonel's suite. She had gone there on Monday evening—she must have. Had she searched his rooms for some random thing she might take away with her? Or had she known the letters were there and looked for them specifically?

And if she'd known that, it could have been only because she herself gave them to him. Because she had worked for him.

Had she also killed him?

Either he'd been dead when she went to him, or—yes—she had killed him.

Why? If she had worked for him, why would she have killed him?

Because he was blackmailing her, too. Someone must have told him about Alice.

And who had known about Alice? Who had discovered Alice with Harry Morgan?

Marian Trask.

But Isabel hadn't learned that until late Tuesday night, after the Cotillion. And on Thursday, seizing her opportunity, knowing Marian would be at the Bower . . .

Isabel and Marian had once been good friends. She'd seen the evidence of that earlier this afternoon, when she'd hunted out the photograph: a happy group at the Christmas Revels, two smiling women at the center, arms linked: Isabel Dane and Marian Trask. But then someone had betrayed Marian to the Colonel—one of two people, Susan Henshaw had said, and what better suspect than Marian's so-called friend, Isabel Dane?

Well, Marian had gotten her revenge, hadn't she? Had gone to the Colonel—must have done, right after the Newport season—and told him about Alice, thus putting Isabel in the Colonel's power.

Revenge.

But had Marian known the worst of it—that Isabel had taken Alice to New York, not for a funeral, but for an illegal operation?

Probably not. But who had known?

The person who, as Alice had said, had given Isabel a name.

The third person whom Isabel had tried to silence. But she hadn't succeeded; the shot had missed. The police couldn't find the bullet, Addington said.

Who else knew about Alice?

Did Val? No. Almost surely not. But did Isabel realize that? Would Isabel try to eliminate Val, too, from the list of people who knew—or might know—Alice's secret?

And Val's letters . . . Isabel had probably known about them since the summer before last, when Val, at Newport, had had them returned to her. Val had stayed with Isabel and Alice that summer . . . and Isabel, knowing about her letters, could have bribed Val's maid to take them . . . could then have given them to the Colonel in lieu of a payment she couldn't make when he started to blackmail her about Alice sometime in the past two months.

She set off again, hurrying toward Chestnut Street. Rather than wait for Val to come to her, she would go to Val. She hoped Euphemia was still laid up. And George— please let him be gone. She would give Val her letters immediately, of course, to relieve her from the burden of her worry. But more important—much more—she must warn her about Isabel.

She turned the corner. Not far to go now. As she paused to catch her breath, she felt cold fear pluck at her heart, at the edges of her mind. Then she hurried on through the fog.

THE WARDRESS SHUT THE DOOR WITH A LOUD CLANG, AND Ames faced Serena Vincent across the battered metal table.

They were in a room adjacent to the cells, but even with the door closed they could hear the cries of the women locked up. As she had been—with the dregs of the city, prostitutes, felons, petty thieves. And yet the experience seemed not to have soiled her. She sat quietly, beautiful even in her drab prison garb. But she looked unwontedly fragile, too, he thought—stunned. Not surprising, given that she'd been incarcerated here for the better part of twenty-four hours.

Most irregular, Crippen had grumbled. Well, he was right about that, at least. They'd sent for her lawyer, but he hadn't arrived yet. On this late Saturday afternoon, Ames thought, he was undoubtedly at home, preparing for his evening's engagements.

"What has happened?" she said.

"Bad news, I'm afraid—but good news, as well. You'll be out of here within the hour."

"They said they wouldn't give me bail."

"Bail is beside the point now. I have managed to convince Inspector Crippen that he arrested the wrong person."

"For the murder of Colonel Mann?"

"Yes—and for Mrs. Trask's, also. They succeeded—at last—in matching the bullets. And if they ever find the bullet that was aimed at you at the theater, I believe it will match also. They searched your apartment for a weapon, Crippen said, but they couldn't find one."

"They tore the place apart, I have no doubt."

"They may have, yes. It is their job."

"Do they think I disposed of it after murdering the Colonel and Mrs. Trask?"

"Not now they don't."

"Is that your good news?"

"Yes."

Her hands were clasped on the table. He reached over and covered them with his own as she held his gaze steadily. "And the bad?" she said.

Not just yet, he thought. "Mrs. Vincent, yesterday afternoon on Boylston Street, a woman spoke to you."

"Yes?"

"You know to whom I refer. Mrs. Dane."

Her face took on an expression of—what? He couldn't put a name to it. Pride, pity, an awareness of some harsh truth beyond anything he knew.

"What of it, Mr. Ames?"

"Well—it is just that—women like Mrs. Dane—ambitious women, who believe that they need to be—ah—careful in their associations, would not ordinarily—"

He was botching it. She finished it for him.

"Would not ordinarily speak to a woman like me?" She managed to smile, but he heard the stinging bitterness in her voice.

"Yes."

She arched an eyebrow. "I cannot say what Mrs. Dane might do in any particular situation." She withdrew her hands from his. "What is your bad news, Mr. Ames?"

"Richard Longworth is dead."

She stared at him for a moment in stunned silence. "How?"

"By his own hand."

And now her last vestige of strength seemed to desert her, and she sagged in her chair as if she would faint.

In an instant, he was on his feet and at her side to catch her as she slipped sideways. He seized her shoulders, feeling her warmth through the flimsy prison cloth, and eased her straight as he shouted for the wardress.

"Poor man," Mrs. Vincent said softly. "He was always so very—"

So very what? Ames thought. So very in love with you? So desperate to keep you that he was driven half mad, driven to threaten you, and, in the end, to take his life rather than live without you?

She moved, and he thought at first that she was pushing

him away, but then he realized that she'd put her hands over his, pressing them to her shoulders as if his touch kept her conscious. Her head was bowed, as if the weight of her glorious hair was suddenly too heavy. He saw the line of her cheek, her throat, and for an instant—no more—he wondered how it would be to touch that luscious, creamy skin, to brush it with his fingertips, to bend and touch it with his lips. . . .

The door opened. The wardress entered, followed by a man Ames did not know.

"She's fainting—get water—smelling salts—"

"No. I don't need anything."

"My dear Serena!" the stranger exclaimed. In two steps he was at her side, staring at Ames with a hostile look across the top of her drooping head.

She pressed Ames's hands to her shoulders one last time, and then, quite deliberately, she removed them.

"Mr. Coolidge—Mr. Ames," she said. Then she looked up to smile at Ames. "Thank you. I am all right now."

He stepped back. The wardress had disappeared. Coolidge—her lawyer—was a man of about sixty, with graying hair, a canny, narrow face, and gold-rimmed spectacles. Ames knew his brother but not him.

Mrs. Vincent turned to Coolidge and said, "I am to be released, Mr. Ames tells me."

"And about time, too, my dear. I have told Crippen, I will bring charges against him—"

"No. No charges. I just want to leave. What time is it?"

"A little past six," Ames replied.

"Time to get to the theater, then," she said.

"Impossible!" Ames addressed himself to Coolidge. "The woman who committed the crime for which Mrs. Vincent was arrested—yes, it is a woman—is still at large. And very dangerous, I believe. Mrs. Vincent must go directly home, and she must not leave her apartment under any circumstances. You must instruct the concierge not to admit anyone. I would even suggest that you hire a guard for her—"

"Oh, surely that is not necessary," Mrs. Vincent interrupted.

"In any case, you must not think of performing tonight—not at all, in fact, until this business is settled once and for all."

She glanced up at Coolidge. "Perhaps we should listen to him, Frederick. He is very knowledgable."

Coolidge frowned. "How do you know that she is in danger?" he asked Ames.

"Because—" Impossible to speak of such things, Ames thought, but he had no choice. "Mrs. Vincent, I would ask you—I gave you a name just now, someone who spoke to you yesterday. But I must be sure—did she also speak to you this past summer in Newport? Ask your help, perhaps?"

She stood up, seemingly recovered from her shock at the news of Longworth's death, and she lifted her chin a little as she replied. "I cannot tell you that."

"You must."

"No. I cannot."

"But I must make absolutely sure—"

She had stepped away from the table, and now her lawyer moved protectively to her side.

"Frederick, will you take me home?" she said to him.

"Yes, of course."

Ames felt a sharp pang of envy. He'd pressed too hard, and now he'd lost whatever gratitude she'd had toward him.

Then Coolidge said firmly, "No more questions, Mr. Ames," and the wardress came back, bringing neither water nor smelling salts, and it was time to go.

As Ames left the room, he glanced back. Mrs. Vincent had moved into Coolidge's arms and was resting her head on his shoulder.

Damnation!

He took the stairs to the first floor two at a time. Should he speak to Crippen again? No. Undoubtedly Crippen was gone in any case, to deal with Longworth's suicide. Ames couldn't wait; he had to see to Val.

He emerged from City Hall and stood on the broad granite steps. He was a fastidious man, very clean about his habits, but just now, having visited the Tombs in the basement, he felt dirty, soiled in a way that would not be washed clean with soap and water.

He took a deep breath, inhaling the sour salt smell of the sea, the smothering fog. He could not see as far as the curb, and across the way, at the Parker House Hotel, the big globe lights at the entrance were nearly obscured.

Go to Val, he thought. Even with MacKenzie's protection, she needed to be told, to be warned.

And still he hesitated, reluctant to plunge into that white, fog-drenched wilderness. He needed time to think, and yet he had no time, he needed to get to Val.

A man, hurrying up, bumped into him, muttered an apology, and continued on through the great heavy doors. The little incident spurred Ames into action. With what seemed an enormous effort, he set off. He'd go to Euphemia's house first, to make sure that Val and MacKenzie had left for Louisburg Square.

With a mounting sense of dread, he forced himself to walk quickly. Then he began—tried—to run. His legs felt like lead; they would not obey him, they hardly seemed to move. His breath came hard and painfully sharp, and he heard it tearing at his lungs, gasping, never enough, he could not get enough of that sour salt foggy air. Beacon Street lay before him, up the hill to the State House. Up and up—this little hill had never seemed so steep, so endless. He could see nothing beyond himself. As if from a great distance, he heard the muffled cries of frustrated drivers, the neigh of a panicked horse, the murmur of people walking past, ghostly figures haunting this weird white landscape, appearing suddenly out of the fog to startle him and then, as swiftly, disappearing again.

He came to the top of Beacon Street. The redbrick State House loomed dimly before him, its gilded dome invisible. He clung to a lamppost to catch his breath. He must get hold of himself. There was work to be done yet, tonight, and he must be ready for it.

A spectre came toward him out of the fog. He heard his own cry of terror die in his throat.

A man, passing, stopped to stare at him.

"All right, sir?" the man said.

"Yes—yes, thank you." He did not recognize his voice; it was a stranger's voice, harsh and ragged.

He pushed himself away from the lamppost. "Quite all right," he said.

The man walked on, down Park Street; Ames went on down Beacon and turned up Walnut. In his mind's eye was not the body of Richard Longworth, not the frowning annoyance and blank confusion of Deputy Chief Inspector Elwood Crippen, not even the pale, anguished face of Serena Vincent, but something else entirely: a magnificent portrait by John Singer Sargent of a woman in her pride, her torment, wearing her heirloom pearls.

CAROLINE STUMBLED A BIT AS SHE HURRIED ALONG THE last of the sidewalk leading to Euphemia's house. A bad night, a terrible night, but she had good news for Val, and that thought cheered her. Yes—concentrate on the good news: Val's letters had been returned. It would be an enormous relief for Val, never mind what had happened with George. Val would find someone else, some splendid new young man, and one day there would be a wedding, after all.

At Euphemia's, lights gleamed through the cracks in the shutters. Please let George be gone, Caroline prayed again as she mounted the steps and brought the door knocker down sharply. And if Val—

"Good evening, Miss Ames."

"Good evening, Saunders. I wonder if—is Mr. Putnam here?"

"Mr. Putnam? No, Miss. He left a little while ago."

Thank heaven. She wanted to enter, but the butler did not step aside. "Miss Val isn't here, Miss Ames. She left with—ah—Dr. MacKenzie, I believe the gentleman's name is. She said to tell you that they went to Louisburg Square."

Dr. MacKenzie. Now why had he come here and taken Val away?

Because Addington had told him to, of course. There could be no other reason.

"Thank you, Saunders." Even as she tried to sort it out, she remembered Euphemia. "How is Miss Euphemia?"

"Still laid up, Miss, but on the mend."

"Good. You don't need to tell her that I called."

"Yes, Miss."

Home, she thought. I must get home. What has happened?

Before the butler could say anything more, she had started off again, slipping on the uneven, fog-coated bricks but determinedly pushing on. She thought she heard him calling after her, but she couldn't make out what he said and she didn't want to turn back. Something about Euphemia? She wasn't sure. Well, she'd see Euphemia tomorrow in any case. When she came to Louisburg Square she almost sobbed with relief. Only a moment more—and, yes, there was Val now, standing in the window. They hadn't closed the shutters, probably to allow the parlor lights to stream out, as much as possible, into the darkness and gloom of this dreadful night, to light Caroline's way home. The thought warmed her, and the sight of her young cousin spurred her on.

She hurried up the steps, her key in her hand. Inside, she did not stop to shed her damp jacket and hat but went at once into the parlor, throwing open the pocket doors, a glad cry on her lips.

"Val! Wonderful news! You won't believe—"

But Val's startled gaze, which had briefly met her own, suddenly veered to one side, and Caroline's words died on her lips as she followed it.

A woman stood by the fireplace. Her face was tortured, her eyes wild. And there was a fourth person in the room, as well: Dr. MacKenzie.

Caroline opened her mouth to say something to the woman. Later, in fact, she thought she did say it, and perhaps she did. Everything happened so quickly that, searching her memory afterward, she could never be quite sure.

"Why, Isabel"—yes, that was who it was, this frantic woman with the blazing eyes and the oddly twisted mouth— "whatever are you doing with that gun?"

CHAPTER
33

A TREMENDOUS EXPLOSION SHATTERED THE SILENCE, AND Caroline felt a blow—a painful, agonizing blow—that knocked her to the floor. She was conscious of MacKenzie's horrified expression as he leaped forward. He and Isabel wrestled for a moment; then MacKenzie fell. Through a haze of pain from the searing wound in her shoulder, she heard Val screaming and MacKenzie shouting, and she smelled gunpowder, a sharp, acrid smell that made her want to retch, or perhaps it was the pain that did that.

In the next moment, as she thought she must be dying, she saw the others from what seemed a far distance; their voices echoed oddly in her ears as she realized she was losing consciousness, and she fought to keep it.

Isabel had seized Val by the arm, and now she was herding her toward the door as Dr. MacKenzie painfully raised himself from where he had fallen.

"Don't try to follow, Doctor," Isabel said—and how strange her voice sounded, choked and dry as if it hurt her to speak. "If you do, I will kill her—I swear it."

She meant Val, Caroline realized, and she tried to protest, tried to make some motion, however fruitless, to stop Isabel. But she could not; she lay on the floor just inside the pocket doors and saw the room revolve, fade in and out, fade to black.

When she came to, MacKenzie was leaning over her, his face a rictus of worry, or perhaps it was the pain from his damaged knee that made him look so. He was opening her bodice, searching with skilled, amazingly gentle hands to see where she had suffered her wound, and now Margaret's face appeared as well, and she uttered a shriek before she clapped her hand over her mouth.

"Miss Ames, can you hear me?" MacKenzie was saying to her.

She must have said yes, because his expression eased a little and he looked up at Margaret, dear Margaret, so faithful all these years, and said to her, "Fetch a cloth and hot water. Hurry, woman—and bring sal volatile, too, if you have any!"

And then Margaret's face disappeared and Caroline was aware that MacKenzie had awkwardly lowered himself to sit on the floor and was cradling her head in his lap. He was speaking to her, but she could not understand what he said. The next thing she remembered was Margaret coming back.

Carefully, with a touch as gentle as a woman's, MacKenzie eased her shirtwaist off and cleansed her wound and bound it. A clean wound, he told her, and it would heal well. She was conscious of the pain, but as she kept falling in and out of consciousness, the pain came and went as well.

Sometime later she realized that someone had put a pillow under her head and a blanket over her supine body. Margaret was bending over her, administering the horrible sal volatile that was meant to bring her out of her faint.

Feebly, she pushed Margaret's hand away. She hated sal volatile. She would come to on her own. She looked around the room. Dr. MacKenzie was gone. But someone else had been here as well, she remembered. A woman—two. Val—and Isabel Dane.

With a movement that sent a white-hot stab of agony through her body, Caroline sat up.

"Where is Val?" she asked.

"Gone, Miss," Margaret replied.

"With—?"

"Mrs. Dane."

With Isabel. And Isabel, she remembered now, had had a gun. Had shot her—and had threatened to kill Val.

She fainted again.

In the fog, MacKenzie willed himself to ignore the agony in his knee as he hobbled to the end of the square, to Pinckney Street, and stood motionless, listening.

Where had they gone—that madwoman (for surely she was mad) and Valentine? Valentine, whom he had been told to protect, whom he had failed to protect, and who was now, without doubt, in danger of her life.

He listened. The fog pressed in at him from all sides, smothering sight, smothering sound— Nothing.

But then—yes—he heard a sound and he turned, cupping his ear. Impossible to tell from which direction it had come, and yet he had heard it, he was sure.

"Mrs. Dane!" he called. "Are you there?" Immediately, he cursed himself. If it were Isabel Dane, she would not answer him.

But something was there—something, or someone, coming at him from out of the fog from the other end of the square. He started toward it, limping badly now, in no condition to go after anyone, let alone a madwoman carrying a gun.

He tried to hurry, but his knee was on fire. He gritted his teeth as he put his weight on it, his cane slipping on the treacherous wet bricks, and then he was falling, crashing to the ground once again, and this time, he knew, for good—

right in front of No. 16½, he realized as he saw the face of Addington Ames loom over him.

"Where is Val?" Ames demanded, crouching beside him.

"Gone," gasped MacKenzie. In a few words, he told Ames what had happened. "But Miss Ames will be all right," he added. "The bullet went clean through her shoulder. It is Miss Thorne who is in danger." He broke off with a groan. "I failed you."

With a muttered oath, Ames helped the doctor to his feet and into the house, into Margaret's care. Then, with a word to his sister, he was gone, out into the night once more.

Find Val, he thought. Find her before Isabel Dane can kill her, too. She has killed twice in this affair, and she tried to kill Caroline and Mrs. Vincent. Another death will make no difference to her.

He loped along the square to Mt. Vernon Street. He stopped at the corner to listen. Nothing: the fog swallowed all sound. He might have been alone in this silent white world.

Carefully, he inched his way down the steep slope to West Cedar Street. He held his breath, straining to hear. At the corner, he paused again.

"Val?"

No answer. No sound of women's boot heels tap-tapping along the brick sidewalks, no cry for help from Val, no warning shout from Isabel Dane.

Cautiously he moved along West Cedar Street, but after a moment he turned back. Where would Isabel go? Not this way.

At Mt. Vernon Street again, he turned down to Charles. Suddenly, clattering down the hill behind him, he heard the sound of carriage wheels, the thudding impact of horses' hooves on the slippery cobblestones. A runaway carriage— and in this fog, hurtling at such speed, it would surely collide with the mass of stalled traffic at the foot of the hill.

He leaped forward, but even as he reached the curb and

stumbled over it into the street, the carriage tore past him, a dark, speeding shape in the fog-drenched night, come and gone all in an instant. He'd had a glimpse of the driver—a woman. Not Val, he thought. Mrs. Dane? And is Val inside with Isabel Dane at the reins, trying to escape, so that even in this blinding, killing fog she risks their lives—?

"Addington!" She appeared out of the darkness like a wraith, and she ran to him and clung to him for her life. He was surprised at how small she seemed, small and delicate and yet very much alive, her beautiful face wet with tears, her corseted body shuddering, shivering, without jacket or cape.

He started to murmur reassurance, but before he could say more than a few words, she gasped, "Mrs. Dane is trying to escape! She—"

A woman's shriek tore through Val's words, followed by the sound of a crash. And then, even in the fog, even over the sound of splintering wood and grinding, snapping metal, he heard another, even more anguished cry. A death shriek it was, and no mistake: someone mortally wounded.

Val froze in his arms. She turned her head toward Charles Street, which lay below, a tangled mass of traffic, and if that runaway carriage had hurtled into it—

Heedless now of the danger, and with Val clinging to him, he slipped and slid down the last steep slope. In the swirling fog, illuminated by the blurred, haloed streetlights and the even feebler sidelights of the massed vehicles, he could make out the figures of men running. The breakaway carriage, its horses down, was directly before him. It lay on its side, its wheels spinning, the crowd pressing in around it.

"Stay back!" he ordered Val, but she would not.

"It is Mrs. Dane," she cried, although she could not see for the throng.

Ames pushed his way through the circle of men. Someone held a torch, and by its ruddy, flickering light he saw a woman lying in the street, trapped under a front wheel. Men were trying to lift the vehicle, to move it and free her, but the downed horses were thrashing, terrified, impeding the rescue. One of them had a compound fracture; in the light of the torch, he could see the broken leg bone protruding through bloody flesh. It would need to be put down, he thought.

Heedless of the remonstrances of the bystanders, Ames crouched so that his face was close to Isabel Dane's. Her eyes were wide; blood flowed from the corner of her mouth, choking her as she tried to speak.

And now, as the men heaved the carriage one last time to free her, Val knelt and cradled Mrs. Dane's head in her lap. All around them, people were crying for a doctor to come, but Val saw that it was too late for a doctor, no matter how great his skill.

Mrs. Dane stared up at her, straining to speak, and Val bent her head to hear.

"I did not mean to hurt you," Mrs. Dane whispered. "He —the Colonel—forced me to it. He insisted . . ." She paused, choking. "He insisted on having information. About you . . . about anyone. I had to give your letters to him, or he would have ruined Alice."

"There, there," Val crooned. Scalding tears blinded her for a moment, and she dashed them away. "We will get you to the hospital, Mrs. Dane, and—"

"No." Isabel Dane, with a great effort, shook her head. She stared up at the circle of faces above her, and her eyes fell on Ames. She whispered something, but he could not hear what she said and so he bent low, putting his ear to her bloody mouth.

"I did it . . . for Alice . . ." she said. "Marian . . . and Colonel Mann."

"And Mrs. Vincent?" he said urgently. "Was it you who shot at her at the theater?" For Longworth's sake, he needed to know.

"Yes. For Alice. And I . . . almost succeeded. . . ."

CHAPTER
34

TWO DAYS LATER, AT DUSK ON A COLD AND BLUSTERY AF-
ternoon, they sat in the parlor at No. 16½ and watched
Valentine as she fed her letters, one by one, into the simmering sea-coal fire. For a moment, before she let go of the last
one, she hesitated; she held it, staring at it, and yet, Caroline
thought, perhaps she did not see it. Perhaps she saw the
menacing face of Colonel Mann; or Isabel Dane's, mad-
dened with fear; or perhaps she saw her lifelong friend, Alice Dane, fainting at the Cotillion because a woman named
Marian Trask had spoken to her and, in speaking, had
signed her own death warrant.

With a sudden, almost violent movement, Val thrust the
last letter into the fire. It caught at once; its edges blackened
and curled, smoking, and then it burst into a blossom of
bright flame before being consumed into ashes. They all
watched it; no one spoke.

Then Val turned to Caroline. "Will Alice recover, Caro?"

Caroline lay half reclining on the old fainting couch
brought down from the attic for her convalescence. She felt
better today, not so weak, but it would be a good long time,
she knew, before she recovered completely. The pain in her

shoulder had lessened somewhat, but she still could not move without agony.

"I think she will," she said, but in truth she did not know. She had had a telegram from Dr. Hannah: "She is in hospital stop Fair prognosis stop." Dr. Hannah had referred, she understood, to Alice's physical condition; her mental state was something else again. "But when she comes home she will need you, Val."

"Yes," Valentine said softly. She stayed sitting on the low stool before the fire, her exquisite profile clear and clean against the cast-iron fireback. "Yes, she will need me—and I will need her, as well." She smiled: a sight that gladdened Caroline's heart. "Mary Leicester plans to go to Rome next month," she said. "I thought I would go with her. Alice could come, too. We could winter there, and in the spring we can go to the South of France. You could join us then, Caro. Could you do that? Would you?"

"Oh—" Caroline was momentarily flustered. Visiting the South of France had never been something she'd even remotely considered. "I don't know, dearest. We'll see."

Val managed a laugh. "I know what *that* means. All during my childhood, 'We'll see' meant 'Probably not.' But think about it—do!"

MacKenzie shifted in his chair, his bad leg with its damaged knee stretched out on an ottoman before him. A setback, Dr. Warren had said; let us hope it won't be permanent. He lifted a copy of that morning's newspaper from where it lay on the floor beside him. Serena Vincent's name appeared there in a headline in large black type.

"And Mrs. Vincent?" he said. "Can she survive involvement in this second scandal?"

Ames, who had been far away in his thoughts, came back. "I have no doubt," he said, "that in this instance, the publicity will help her career. And if it does not—"

What then, for that beautiful woman with her "past," her

dubious lifestyle? She could go to New York, he thought; or, if that were not far enough, to London, to Paris, Vienna—

The thought of Serena Vincent in any of those places made him feel surprisingly unhappy. Here in Boston, he might never see her again, but all the same he liked to think she would be here; he did not want her to go away.

The door knocker sounded. They waited tensely while Margaret answered. We will never be truly tranquil again, Caroline thought, not after this. Always, when we hear that knocking, we will have a moment when we dread to learn who has come, and with what bad news.

They heard a man's voice. Let it not be Inspector Crippen, Caroline prayed. But when Margaret slid open the pocket doors and showed in their visitor, it was Desmond Delahanty, red-faced from the cold and holding a sheaf of foolscap.

He greeted them all with something less than his usual good cheer, settled himself among them, and accepted the cup of tea that Valentine put into his red, chapped hands.

"Glad to see you looking so well, Miss Ames," he said, nodding at Caroline. "Mind you don't exert yourself too much these next few weeks."

"I couldn't exert myself if I wanted to, Mr. Delahanty, and in any case, I don't. What is it you have there—a new composition?"

Delahanty shook his head. "No. Well, yes, in a way. I thought you might be able to tell me whom to give it to—or whether to give it to anyone at all—now that—ah—"

"Your script for the Christmas Revels," Ames said. He put out his hand, and Delahanty gave him the scribbled papers. "Caroline, do you think there will be a production of the Revels this year?"

"I doubt it. Now that Isabel is—"

"Yes. So perhaps, Desmond, you'll want to keep this."

And then, at the look on Delahanty's face: "Or perhaps you won't. I beg your pardon."

Delahanty sipped his tea. "I had a bad feeling about it all along, you know. About the script, I mean. I felt it was a waste of effort, that it would never be used. At the time, I thought that was because Mrs. Dane would not be satisfied with whatever I wrote, no matter how good I thought it was. But now I see . . ."

"Yes," Caroline interjected. "You were right in what you felt, but for the wrong reason."

"Poor woman," Delahanty murmured. "She had—"

The door knocker sounded once more, and he broke off as they waited for Margaret. She entered bearing the silver card tray and presented it to Ames.

"Splendid!" he exclaimed as he took the card and read the name of the caller. "Show him in!"

In the next moment, a slight, gray-haired, bearded man appeared. Caroline did not know him, but her brother obviously did; he rose from his chair, seized the man's hand, and gave it a hearty shake.

"Professor James! Delighted to see you!"

"I hope I am not intruding," James said. "But I was in the neighborhood, and I wanted to see how you were getting on."

He greeted the other two men, and Ames introduced him to the women and settled him near Caroline. She could not help staring at him, although she did it as discreetly as possible. He was famous, she knew, and for something she found rather intimidating: studying people's minds, their thoughts both conscious and unconscious (although what "unconscious" meant she could hardly imagine). She was somewhat reassured when James turned to her and said gently, "And how are you, Miss Ames?"

"Well enough, thank you."

News of her injury at Isabel's hands had not appeared in the papers, thank heaven, and how Addington had managed that she had no idea. But word of it had obviously gotten out, as she'd known it inevitably would.

She smiled at him. Really, she thought, he was not intimidating at all.

Over his shoulder, she saw the small hole in the door-jamb. She couldn't seem to stop looking at it these past two days. Addington had found the bullet, had given it to the police. No word yet on whether it matched the others, but she knew it would. And then at last, perhaps, her name would appear in the newspapers. Well, she'd deal with it when it happened, would hold her head high and simply ignore the gossip.

James's gaze shifted to the novel on the table beside her. She'd finished it last night and had begun to read it all over again; she did that often with books she particularly liked.

"I see we share a fondness for the work of Miss Strangeways," he said, smiling back at her.

And then, because her surprise must have shown on her face, he added, "I find her stories to be very entertaining. And quite good in her characters' motivations. Motivation is everything, isn't it, in fiction as in life?"

"Well—yes—I—" Caroline could think of nothing to say that would not sound foolish. The august, the world-renowned Professor William James—an admirer of Diana Strangeways!

"In fact," he said, leaning toward her as if to impart a confidence, "I will confess to you that I find her stories much more readable—and enjoyable—than my brother Henry's efforts." In a theatrical gesture, he put his finger to his lips. "But you must never tell anyone that I said so! Bad for family relationships, you know."

And then he laughed, and Caroline laughed with him, and the tension in the room dissolved as they all relaxed.

They chatted easily for a while, and then the professor said it was time for him to go. Ames saw him out, and he stood by the bow window to watch him as he made his way along the square. It had begun to snow, the lavender-colored flakes shimmering down through the light of the streetlamps.

Motivation, James had said. The one who had the most to lose.

And that had been not Serena Vincent, not even Richard Longworth, but Isabel Dane. Or so she had thought, in that frenzy of social striving and ambition and greed that was her world.

It was a fierce world, he thought. Harsh and unforgiving, as much a battlefield as in any war.

The snow was falling more heavily now, shrouding the streetlamps in lavender-tinted clouds, covering the cobblestone street and the steps of the houses, the autumn-dead greenery in the oval.

A fierce world, in which the women fought more bitterly than the men. To the very death, they fought.

He reached up to close the shutters against the night.

AUTHOR'S NOTE

IT SOMETIMES HAPPENS THAT WRITERS GET LUCKY: WE SER-
endipitously discover a character more intriguing, or more
outlandish, than many of those who come to us through our
imaginations.

Such a character was Colonel William d'Alton Mann.
The moment I found him, I recognized him for what he was:
a perfect murder victim. And so, changing his middle name
to one I liked better, I appropriated him and moved him to
Boston from his Gilded Age bailiwick, Manhattan. There,
for an amazing number of years, the real Colonel Mann
published his scurrilous newspaper, *Town Topics,* and ex-
torted money from the city's wealthiest and most socially
prominent citizens to keep their names—and their scandal—out of it.

The Colonel had spies everywhere, it seemed: not only in
New York, but also in fashionable watering holes like Saratoga Springs, Newport, and Bar Harbor. The spies might be
anyone: a servant, a Western Union telegraph operator, a
socialite with gambling debts who needed the money the
Colonel paid for information. He held court every Monday
night at Delmonico's, where he would receive his supplicants with proof sheets in hand. Pay up, he would say, or

this item about you will appear in *Town Topics.* And they did pay—lavishly—year after year.

As far as I know (and to my astonishment), Colonel Mann lived a long and healthy life and died a natural death. But the delicious possibilities he presented were too seductive to ignore, and so I have given him, in *The Death of Colonel Mann,* the fate he never met. Such are the satisfactions of writing mystery fiction, and, I trust, of reading it as well.

—Cynthia Peale

CYNTHIA PEALE IS THE PSEUDONYM OF NANCY Zaroulis, author of *Call the Darkness Light* and *The Last Waltz*, among other successful novels. She lives outside Boston, where she is at work on the second in her Beacon Hill mystery series, *Murder at Bertram's Bower*.

Please turn the page for an exclusive advance preview of

MURDER AT
BERTRAM'S BOWER

A BEACON HILL MYSTERY
BY CYNTHIA PEALE

CHAPTER 1

BOSTON: THE JANUARY THAW, 1892. A WATERY GLOOM
hung over the city like a shroud.

Day after day of heavy, relentless rain had threatened to
submerge the new-filled Back Bay, and the miniature lagoon
in the Public Garden had overflowed its banks. On Beacon
Hill, streams of water pounded the brick sidewalks and cas-
caded down the narrow streets, splashing women's voluminous skirts, splattering horses with mud up to their blinkers.
People clung to their firesides, waiting for winter to return.

In the South End, Officer Joseph Flynn of the Boston
police was making his rounds. He had been on the force for
less than a year, and he was eager to do well in this job
which until recently would not have been given to an Irishman like himself. When he saw the shape on the ground
halfway down the alley behind West Brookline Street, he
paused. Because it was night, and very dark in that district,
he could not immediately tell what the shape was. A heap of
refuse, he thought, or a pile of rags. Or, at worst, some
drunken tramp from the nearby railroad yards.

Still. Best to be sure. On the lookout for rats, his bull's-
eye lantern sputtering in the rain, he stepped carefully along.

When he came to it—to her—he could hardly believe

what he saw. He had witnessed some serious mayhem during his brief time with the force, but he had never seen anything like this. Half crouching, holding his lantern close, he stared at her for a long moment.

Dear Mother of God. What monster had been at work here? He felt his stomach heave, and he heard the anguished cry torn from his throat. His lantern clattered to the ground. Suddenly overcome, he fell retching to his knees. Then he vomited onto the dirty, rain-soaked snow.

CHAPTER 2

"I WILL PUT MATTHEW HALE NEXT TO HARRIET MASON," said Caroline Ames. Her pencil hovered over the sheet of paper on which she had written names around a diagram of her dining-room table. "He is so terribly shy with women, and Harriet can get conversation out of a lamppost."

Dr. John Alexander MacKenzie had been struggling through a life of Lincoln highly recommended by the clerk at the Athenaeum. Now he laid aside the heavy volume and rose to knock the ashes of his pipe into the grate where simmering sea coal warmed the parlor at No. 16½, Louisburg Square.

"Might she not frighten him?" he said, smiling down at her. She'd given him permission to smoke when he'd come to live here several months before, and he'd been grateful to her—for that, and for much else.

She was a pretty woman of some thirty-five years, a little plump, with fair, curly hair caught up in a fashionable Psyche knot and frizzy bangs partially covering her wide, smooth forehead. Her eyes were brown, her mouth a vivid rose, and although her cheeks were tinged with pink, he was almost certain that she did not use face paint. She wore a high-necked long-sleeved dress of soft gray, plainly made and slightly out of fashion because of its bustle. Her only ornament was a mourning brooch for her mother.

She had been fussing over this dinner party for weeks, and now it was nearly upon them. Although MacKenzie had been invited to it, he hardly cared about it—only to the extent that it was a worry for her. When she had first announced her intention to have it—"For Nigel Chadwick, who is coming from London, and every hostess in Boston is maneuvering to get him to her table!"—he had thought the effort would be too much for her. She had been wounded by a bullet in the shoulder the previous November, and while she had healed well, her normal strength and vitality had been slow to return.

And, too, he thought darkly, she was not an ideal patient, too quick to take up her multitudinous activities, many of which were good works. Only that morning she had been summoned on an errand of mercy for the Ladies' Committee at her church, and to his chagrin, she had gone.

"It is my turn to go, Doctor," she'd said.

He had protested as much as he thought he dared, for he was only a boarder, after all. "In this weather?" he'd said.

"They wouldn't ask me unless it was important. I know this family. The committee has been working with them for months—since last year, in fact. The woman is an excellent person who is trying very hard to keep the family together. I must go—but to ease your mind, I will take a herdic."

He'd offered to go with her himself, or even in her place, but she'd refused, allowing him only to go down to Charles Street at the foot of the hill to find a herdic-phaeton for her and bring it to the door. These were small, fast cabs unique to Boston, whose strong, agile horses darted about the city at all hours.

Now, safely home once more, she'd been struggling for the past half hour with the seating for her party.

"I don't think so," she said in answer to his question.

"Harriet isn't a frightening kind of person, just very chatty."

"Then by all means," he said, "you must seat her next to him."

She looked up at him, returning his smile. He was stockily built, not much taller than herself, and a few years older (she'd turn thirty-six in May). He had graying hair, a broad, honest face adorned by a not too brushy mustache, and kind, wise eyes. She'd liked him from the moment he had presented himself the previous September, bearing a note from Boston's most famous surgeon, Dr. Joseph Warren. MacKenzie, a surgeon himself with the army on the western plains, had taken a Sioux bullet in his knee; after the army doctors in Chicago had informed him that he must lose his leg, he had come to Boston, to Dr. Warren, to see if he could save it.

Warren had done so, and had recommended his neighbors across Louisburg Square, Addington Ames and his sister, Caroline, as a place for Mackenzie to board at not too great an expense while he recuperated.

The Ameses' elevator, installed for their late mother's convenience, had been a great help, particularly in the first days after his operation, when he was confined to his room on the third floor at the back of the house. Margaret, the all-purpose girl, had brought him his meals, and Caroline herself had come up once or twice a day to see how he did. Eventually, when he could hobble about, he sat by the window and enjoyed the view: down over the crowded rooftops of the western slope of Beacon Hill to the river, and to Cambridge beyond. On fine days, all the autumn, he enjoyed the sunsets, and as he recovered further and could go downstairs in the elevator, he had enjoyed the Ameses' company as well. He had become, he thought, not so much a paying boarder as a friend. Now, in the winter, he could not imagine a life apart from them. From her.

He moved to the bow window that overlooked the

square. Its lavender glass was old, original with the house. Caroline had told him it had been imported from Europe; imperfect, it had turned color when the sun first struck it. Her grandfather, a China trader and one of the first proprietors of the square, had been too thrifty to replace it. It gave the trees and shrubbery in the central oval an eerie, purplish cast; MacKenzie still wasn't used to it. This day, rain lashed against the panes, making him glad to be indoors. He'd heard about the vagaries of the New England weather before he'd come, but rain in January seemed very odd indeed.

A tall, cloaked figure was striding through the downpour. In a moment more, he had passed beneath the window and they heard him coming in.

Caroline brightened. "There! That will be Addington. He is probably soaked to the skin—I can't imagine why he felt he needed to go to Crabbe's in this weather."

Her brother was a devotee of Crabbe's Boxing and Fencing Club down in Avery Street, beyond the Common. He went there nearly every day, sometimes very early in the morning after a night of stargazing. He kept a telescope on the roof of the house, but for the past several nights, the thaw, with its clouds and rain, had made stargazing impossible.

They heard him stamping in the vestibule, and after a moment he slid open the pocket doors to the parlor. He was a tall man, whippet thin, with dark hair combed straight back from his high forehead, dark, deep-set eyes in a long, clean-shaven face, and a pronounced nose. Ordinarily, he was self-contained, not given to displays of feeling; just now, however, they saw from his expression that something was obviously amiss.

"What is it, Addington?" Caroline asked.

"Bad news, I am afraid." He carried a folded newspaper, which he gave to her. "Look at this."

As she opened it, MacKenzie saw that it was an "Extra,"

and he caught sight of the bold black headline: MURDER AT BERTRAM'S BOWER!!! And in slightly smaller type: VICIOUS CRIME!!! WOMAN'S BODY FOUND IN ALLEY!!!

Caroline quickly scanned the page. They saw her amazement—then shock, then horror. Deathly pale, she looked up at them, while the newspaper dropped to her lap.

"May I?" said MacKenzie, taking the paper and reading: Last night a young woman, Mary Flaherty, a resident of the well-known home for fallen women, Bertram's Bower, had been murdered in a South End alley not far from the Bower. A brutal crime; robbery not a motive; Deputy Chief Inspector Elwood Crippen of the city police stated that "the crime was probably the work of a deranged person."

"I am sorry, my dear," Ames said to his sister. He advanced to the fire and took up his customary position, one slim, booted foot resting on the brass fender. "I know that Agatha is your friend."

Agatha Montgomery was the proprietress of the Bower.

"I must go to her at once, Addington."

"In this downpour? Surely she will be distraught, distracted—"

Just then Margaret knocked and announced lunch, putting a brief end to Ames's protest. But as they spooned up their leek and potato soup, and ate their minced beef patties and boiled beets, Caroline explained to Dr. MacKenzie about Bertram's Bower.

"It is a most worthy establishment, Doctor. And, unfortunately, a necessary one. Agatha takes in girls who—well, they are girls of the street, if you follow."

He did.

"If Miss Montgomery felt the need to speak to you," Ames said, "she would have sent you a telegram." He frowned at his plate. He did not like beets.

"Not necessarily. She was never one to ask for help, even when she most desperately needs it. It is her brother, remember, who does all the fund-raising."

She turned to MacKenzie. "Agatha has been a friend of mine since we were children, although she is a few years older than I. The Montgomerys grew up around the corner on Pinckney Street. When Agatha was seventeen, her father went bankrupt. She never had a coming-out. She started Bertram's Bower about ten years ago, when an uncle left her a small inheritance. Now she and her brother, the Reverend Randolph Montgomery, support the place from donations."

"You go there regularly," MacKenzie said. Caroline had recently resumed most of her schedule: church meetings, Sewing Circle, Saturday Morning Reading Club, and, of course, the Bower.

"Yes. To teach the girls to read and write, and to sew and do fancy embroidery. They come to the city in search of work, and if they cannot find it, or if they find it and are then dismissed, they end up on the streets." She shuddered, and her brother frowned at her.

"Not a suitable place for you, Caroline," he said. "You know I have never approved of your going there."

"If Agatha Montgomery can devote her life to those poor creatures," she replied with some spirit, "surely I can give them one afternoon every other week."

She turned to MacKenzie again. "She is very strict with them, of course—and of course she must be. She must maintain the highest moral standards. The girls violate the rules at their peril, and well they know it. But they know, too, they are fortunate to be there, because a girl from the Bower can almost always find decent employment when she leaves. Agatha's reputation for high standards guarantees that. At first, when she had just opened the place, she used to go out at night, searching for girls on the streets. Can you imagine? She would talk to them, persuade them to go with her. She keeps them for three months, usually. Feeds them, gets medical attention for them at Dr. Hannah Bigelow's clinic. And she recruited all her friends—her former friends, that is—to teach them."

"Did you know this girl—the one who was—ah—"

"Mary Flaherty? Yes. Not well, for she already knew how to read and write when she came to Agatha, and she could sew a pretty seam. She was a lovely girl, bright and hardworking. You could see she wanted to advance herself in the world. And in fact Agatha kept her on when her three months were up, employing her as her secretary."

Her eyes held MacKenzie's in a steady gaze. "Sometimes I think the work that Agatha Montgomery does over there in the South End is more important than all our charity fairs and sewing for the poor and Thanksgiving baskets of food that the church gives out. We play at good works, but when our hour or two of service is done, we return to our comfortable homes. Agatha lives her charity, she works at it twenty-four hours a day. It is her life. Oh, dear, she must be devastated!" She turned to her brother. "And think of the harm such a scandal will do to the Bower's reputation, Addington. No one will want to volunteer, donations will fall off—they might be ruined because of this!"

"The Reverend Montgomery is a skilled fund-raiser," Ames replied. "I don't imagine this incident, unfortunate as it is, will crimp his style."

"Unfortunate!" she exclaimed. "Is that what you call it?"

"Unfortunate—yes. Hardly a scandal. It is not Agatha Montgomery's fault if some deranged person—as your friend Inspector Crippen put it—has murdered one of her girls."

"Do not call him my friend, Addington." She shook her head. "If Inspector Crippen has charge of this case, they might never find the man who killed Mary."

"True. But a random killing in the night—if it was random—is a difficult thing to solve."

"All the more reason for me to go to Agatha and see what I can do to help." Her face, ordinarily so gentle and sweet, hardened into lines of determination as she added, "So, yes, Addington, I am going to go to her. And I am going to try to bring her back here with me. She must be in a terrible state. It will do her good to get away, even just for overnight. We can put her in the front room on the fourth floor."

"You are not forgetting Wednesday evening," he cautioned, referring to her dinner party.

For a moment it was obvious that she had done exactly that.

"Oh—no, of course not. I have things fairly well in hand, and even if Agatha does stay until tomorrow, that is only Tuesday. Will you come to the Bower with me, Addington?"

"I would prefer not to."

She accepted the rebuff with only a slight tightening of her lips. "Doctor?"

"Well, I— Yes, of course."

MacKenzie sighed to himself. He'd become accustomed to a nap after lunch. But now Caroline Ames, for whom he had come to have feelings that went far beyond casual friendship, was asking him for help. He could not possibly refuse her.

"Good," she replied. "We will go at once."

Since it was obvious that nothing would deter her, Ames threw up his hands and set off in the rain once more to find them a cab. Shortly they heard the horses' hooves on the cobblestones outside, and Caroline and the doctor, stoutly protected against the weather with waterproofs, galoshes, and her capacious umbrella, bade Ames good-bye.

He stood at the parlor window and watched through the lavender glass as the narrow black cab wobbled its way to the end of the square and turned down Pinckney Street. It was early afternoon, but already growing dark. What state Agatha Montgomery would be in—or what tale of horror Caroline would bring back to him—he could only imagine.

It was a bad business, this murder. Nothing for a lady like Caroline Ames to be involved in.